ALSO BY RICHARD WILEY

Soldiers in Hiding

FOOLS'
GOLD

FOOLS' GOLD

Richard Wiley

ALFRED A. KNOPF   NEW YORK   1988

THIS IS A BORZOI BOOK
PUBLISHED BY ALFRED A. KNOPF, INC.

Copyright © 1988 by Richard Wiley
All rights reserved under International and
Pan-American Copyright Conventions.
Published in the United States by
Alfred A. Knopf, Inc., New York, and
simultaneously in Canada by Random House
of Canada Limited, Toronto. Distributed by
Random House, Inc., New York.

Library of Congress Cataloging-in-Publication Data
Wiley, Richard.
Fools' gold.
I. Title.
PS3573.I433F6   1988   813'.54   88-45207
ISBN 0-394-56865-6

Manufactured in the United States of America

First Edition

For Gigi with love

FOOLS' GOLD

1

August 1, 1899.

64° 30′ north latitude. 165° 24′ west longitude.

Nome blisters the lower lip of Seward Peninsula.

A shallow land shelf extends into the Bering Sea.

Breakers wash the flat beach.

The coastline is razor straight from West Point to Cape Nome, perhaps twenty-five miles east southeast. North, across the low mountains, is Kotzebue Sound, and then farther north, one hundred and twenty nautical miles, the Arctic Circle.

Here two rivers notch the clean coastline: the Nome and the Snake. They move into the breakers sluggishly, forming back eddies, swirling over the gutted silt beds. At the tip of the peninsula, past Port Clarence, past the village of York, lies Cape Prince of Wales, its cold nose nudging Asia; the ancestral footpath.

There is a lifeboat, loose from the freighter *Portland* and pitching toward shore. Beneath it the sockeye salmon, up from the mid-Pacific, find their way to the spawning place. At the farthest reaches they lie in the shallows of the ancient streams, inedible, silver bellies turned red, eggs planted in the silt like bean sprouts. There is a prospector's superstition that for every salmon egg a nugget of equal size, gold and round, is born of the earth itself.

Above Nome the mountains slope quickly into tundra, frozen in the winter, covered with a soggy green-gray moss during the summer months. There is a striking lack of vegetation. The tundra is covered with hummocks, bursting like cold sores through the earth, but generally the land is barren, yielding to scrub timber at best. In the uplands ptarmigan and grouse nest by the thousands. On the coastal marshes duck and geese are as thick as the winter ice.

————

Finn, an Irishman, stands down the beach watching the lifeboat nearing shore. He's a new arrival himself, as can be judged by the position of his tent in the expanding city. For an hour his was farthest south of any in Nome, then second farthest, then one among fifty. He came on this very *Portland,* voyage before last, and is meeting her now by way of fulfilling a promise. There's an Irishwoman aboard and he's had a letter saying he is to see her safely settled in.

The pilot stands in the stern of the lifeboat; the passengers sit between their hands, knuckles wrapping the wooden seats beneath them. Starboard there are larger skiffs carrying lumber and provisions to lines of men who stand in the water then string up the beach like pilings. The breakers swell, an occasional wave crashing, coasting up the beach. Seagulls call to the lifeboat, braiding the air behind it. The pilot cuts the burping engine, moves to the bow, and jumps out to turn the boat seaward again. The passengers step over the side and feel the cold salt water wrap their legs. In a moment they look to see the pilot poling himself away from them. The women step gingerly, the hems of their dresses turning dark. The men shout to the pilot, waving. A coin purse is thrown and arcs, causing the seagulls to dip toward it for an instant. The pilot catches the coin

purse and holds it aloft briefly, before everything, the boat and
the pilot too, disappears into a wave trough and is gone.

They have arrived. Finn steps forward, extending his arms to
them. The rhythm of the line of men passing provisions up the
beach does not break; heads turn toward the newcomers but
hands are steady. The two women place their bags on the sand
and lift their skirts, kicking their feet. Henriette, in sealskin
jacket, frowns at her wet ankles and sand-covered shoes. Ellen
steadies her while she empties them.

Two of the passengers are Japanese and one of them cannot
speak English at all. They are dressed in white shirts and collars
and are carrying their jackets across their arms. The younger
one is the spokesman and speaks to the others and then to his
companion. They have traveled six months and have arrived in
Nome on schedule. The younger is called Fujino, the older,
Kaneda.

When Henriette finishes drying her feet she helps Ellen, who
turns away from the men and balances on one foot. Ellen is the
Irishwoman, it's clear to Finn, and though they are strangers
they are from the same part of Ireland and share the same
family name. Finn walks boldly up to them.

"Well then . . ." he says.

———

In August of 1899 Nome was a village of tents. Wood was piled
up, lumber for the building of the real town, but as yet there
were only tents, then up past them, way up toward the tundra,
a single three-story wooden house. The village wound from its
center like a galaxy. There were paths between many of the
tents, but there were no real streets yet, and toward the beach
the tents looked to have grown directly out of the earth, the
way loose sand banked against them so. Their flaps were pulled

back, forming triangles, or were laced like shoes against the wind, and in front of them men sat on stiff-backed chairs, strangely postured. Many small craft were on the water and many more were pulled up the dark beach, their tiny keel marks crisscrossing the sand like distant highways. Circles of men stood about. There were mules tied to rear tent pegs, and dogs were everywhere.

The five of them walked up the slow incline, pushing their heels into the sand. Finn led, the women followed, then the Japanese. Ellen, her arms pressed tightly to her sides, wanted to suggest that they all join hands. She clutched her carpet bag. It was surprising to her that there were so many who were idle here, so few working. The loose friendship formed aboard ship tightened for her as they entered the town. Names had been stenciled on the sides of some of the tents, and on others shingles hung from small tears in the canvas, messages burnt like warnings on their visible sides. It was like walking into a maze.

"There's no fit place for a cup of coffee," said Finn, turning and smiling at them. "There is the New York Kitchen but it's dirty, no table for a private party."

Ellen said, "If we could just sit awhile. Get our bearings," but the two Japanese turned abruptly and began saying good-bye. Fujino announced that they would be going to look for the supplies they'd need, for a place to stay the night. He stepped back and bowed deeply, thanking the two women for the pleasure of their company on the voyage. He suggested that they meet occasionally and the others agreed, hesitant to see them leave so quickly, before they had a sense of direction, a feeling for the town. Nevertheless, the two Japanese moved away. They backed down the small path, smiling, they stepped around a tent and were gone.

A lack of movement by those nearby gave the feeling that it was warmer than it actually was. Large mosquitoes floated slowly past them. Ellen and Henriette looked at the empty space where the Japanese had been. They were standing in front of the New York Kitchen, its flap bent back and held by a knife stabbed through it. Inside the Kitchen men sat bent over bowls on long benches. They brought pieces of beef or long thin fish to their mouths. Their food was all in hunks, nothing that would crumble against the uneven pressure of their large hands, but still they ate greedily, their knees pressed together to prevent loose bits from falling to the floor.

"A spot of tea then, if you don't mind the benches?" Finn said softly.

They leaned toward the low entrance, but before they could enter a briskly walking man stepped in front of them, looking inside. "Let's go now," the man shouted. "We need you all." He was speaking to no one in particular, but moved everyone. Henriette and Ellen listened to the dull sound of benches pushing through the sand, the commotion of men standing. The Kitchen emptied of its eaters, who followed the man back around a corner, quickening their pace, swatting at the mosquitoes who buzzed now, matching with their tone the gossipy chatter that had arisen from the men and from the bystanders.

Finn and Ellen and Henriette stayed a moment but then they too followed the crowd. People had come out of nearby tents and stood waiting. The men from the Kitchen paced themselves like soldiers, heading toward the beach. A path had been formed by the bystanders, by the people standing along its sides, and led from the beach all the way up to the wooden house that stood toward the foothills, slightly above the town. There was the sense of a parade, but since the crowd could not see far they were quiet and listened. They could hear the grunts of the men from the Kitchen and in a moment an unsteady wagon was pushed along the winding path and among them. The wheels of the wagon moved slowly in the brutal sand. A crystal chandelier hung from a crossboard at the top of the wagon, the tears of it touching each other, ringing softly in the warm air.

"It has the look of winter to it," someone whispered, "the way it gleams like ice."

The owner of the chandelier rode the wagon too, his feet braced, his sleeves rolled up, his arms, like those of a dishwasher, pushed among the chandelier's tears. Easy. Steady. His name was Dr. Kingman and his eyes were deep and worried.

As the wagon moved along, the path behind it closed and the people followed. Finn was reminded of the long struggle to Calvary, the chandelier, like a man with an aura, shining toward the sky. He wondered what these two women were thinking of, coming to a place like this. All these sandy men trudging. This other young girl appeared to be an American. She was frail-looking, but prettier than the hard-boned Irish one. He could see in her face the story of her leaving: family up in arms, father wishing his sons had the sense to get out and that his daughter'd stay. Finn had sisters of his own plugging about somewhere. Looking at Ellen he couldn't remember their faces being any different. They'd be farmers' wives by now, no doubt, with their hair pulled back in buns, a wisp or two of it straying about their eyes.

It took nearly an hour to move the wagon over the soft earth and up to the big house. The house was painted brown and had been furnished with tables and chairs brought from Seattle and from San Francisco. Three women stood in its doorway but quickly stepped back to allow the chandelier room to pass. In the main room on the first floor a brass hook had been embedded into the central ceiling beam. The owner and two others carried the chandelier down off the wagon and into the house. They stood on ladders in order to lift the chandelier up to the brass hook and let it settle. They heard the slight creaking of the beam as it took the weight, and they stepped back to watch it slowly stop moving. The room was quiet. No part of the chandelier had been broken. The sun through the window showed pink and clear at the edges of the chandelier. Dr. Kingman stood in its liquid light, rubbing his hands briskly on the front of his trousers. Everyone in town had seen it. The house was carpeted and clean. The workmen stood quietly on the porch looking in, their food cooling quickly in the New York Kitchen.

———

Before the two Japanese left Nome they purchased a territorial map and learned how to stake a claim. They exchanged their suits and collars for miners' clothes, bought a pack mule and a tent, and moved through the verdure and the wildflowers carrying back packs. When it rained they tucked their trousers into their boots, or took out paper umbrellas and kept moving. They hiked all the first afternoon, camped, then hiked all the next day, reaching Topcock Creek at five o'clock in the evening, two o'clock the next afternoon in Tokyo. Kaneda liked to keep track of the time so that he could stop during the day and think of his wife and his children at home. He was a carpenter by trade, but had read everything in the Japanese language on gold mining. His one regret was that he could not speak English at all. He'd tried learning it once but had failed. He needed a tutor for his children and had met Fujino by placing an advertisement to that effect in the newspaper. English was the language of the future and Fujino had lived in America and had been to England itself. When Kaneda decided to leave for Alaska he asked Fujino to go with him. Still, even with a translator it was frustrating for Kaneda not to be able to speak to anyone. He felt foolish, was afraid of offending someone, of not being able to explain.

Kaneda and Fujino pitched their tent in the waning light. They were counting on being able to mine where others could not. They'd use a water wheel and let the power of the creek move the mounds of stone and gold across the floor of their sluice boxes. They built a fireplace between their tent and the edge of the stream, catching trout and letting them cook in the oil of their frypan until the tails turned up and the eyes turned white. They had bottles of soy sauce and slender wooden chopsticks. From the back of their pack mule they unloaded sacks of short-grained rice, washed it in the stream and boiled it over the coals. They used the rice water for tea.

During their first week on the creek Kaneda built the water wheel. He made the axle shaft from a lean wooden pole, giving that portion of the pole that would go through the wheel a copper jacket. There was a perfect sandbar in the middle of the stream, a few meters from where they had camped. Fujino built a scaffolding on the bar and another on the solid tundra at the far side of the stream. Together they built a dam. They were able to channel all or none of the water toward their water wheel. When the wheel was in use the stream flowed its normal course, and when they channeled all of the water toward them the wheel stopped and the stream bed widened to within ten meters of their camp. They built a bulkhead along that shore, setting wood and stone into the earth and then flooding the area, giving them fresh water for drinking and bathing.

After the water wheel was completed, Fujino set up a hose that drew water from the stream and poured it over the axle for lubrication. The purpose of the wheel was to lift the water up, dumping it into a long wooden sluice. The sluice would have gates that could be pulled open to allow water to run through, or pushed down to stop it. When the sluice box was dammed the water wheel had to be stopped and the stream diverted over to the near channel. The sluice box ran downhill, so that even without the power of the water wheel the prospectors could empty it, simply by lifting the gate.

"If we find gold you must go back to Nome to register the land," Kaneda said, the day after completing the work. "I will stay here."

Fujino nodded. They had been working hard for a long time and were tired. He reached into a pack that was lying on the moss behind him and pulled out a large bottle of sake.

Kaneda said, "We will find gold enough to buy a better brand of sake." He waited anxiously as Fujino heated the liquor in a tin pot.

"We are seventy li from the town," Fujino said, staring into his cup. "How many thousands of li are we from Tokyo?"

Kaneda looked at the man and remembered how young he was. He knew that Fujino was interested in his oldest daughter. He had seen them talking together at the entrance to his home in Tokyo. Fujino had almost mentioned the girl twice during the long sea voyage. If he asks for her hand I will refuse, thought Kaneda. If he gets rich and asks again I will allow it.

Fujino was looking straight at him. "I will use the money I make to buy land in the center of Tokyo," he said. *"Tokyo-no-mannaka."* He stood up and wandered down to the stream. He cupped his hands and yelled, listening to his echo. *"Moshi moshi? Dareka iru no? Nihonjin iru no ka?"* He could hear only the short laugh of Kaneda now standing behind him.

"Loneliness," said the old man. "You are so proud of your loneliness that you yell at the mountains. You are a modern man but our water wheel could have been built in the same manner five hundred years ago." The sake spun lightly on his lips and the old man laughed.

"Only the voice of the modern man ..." he said. "Ha ha. I've got it.

> Only the voice of
> the modern man disturbs the
> peace of the river.

"That's you. The modern man. Five-seven-five, too. Try to top it."

Kaneda stepped back to the tent and to his blanket, laughing and muttering his haiku. After Fujino drank the rest of the sake he poured the water over the fire, listening to it hiss and die. And soon he too went to sleep, counting on his fingers, trying to think of a retort.

———

In a few days Finn was free of the women, though he didn't much like what they'd decided to do. They had taken jobs, both of them, as day laborers in the New York Kitchen. Ellen was a scrapper, pushing dried eggs and beef bones into the waste pits, and Henriette moved among prospectors taking food orders. Finn was with them when they saw the notice, but he'd not said anything against it. It was his job to see them safely off the ship, nothing more. Though he'd enjoyed once again hearing the soft strains of an Irishwoman's voice, he knew he'd be smartest not to get involved. They had cots to sleep on, those two, and that wasn't bad. There were few enough women in Nome with their own beds.

Finn was not a prospector. He'd heard what had happened half a century before in California, and he knew that the same thing would happen here. Oh, the wild fortunes would be made by the prospectors all right, but the moderate ones would be made by the others: the store owners, the builders, the publicans. Finn was good with his hands, and thought that, when the opportunity presented itself, he'd go into construction. He considered himself lucky, though at forty-five he hadn't yet much to show for it. In the nineteen years he'd been out of Ireland he'd worked on the railroad and been a salesman. And though he'd been more than a little successful as a salesman—women thought of him as handsome—he was here now with the idea of building a town.

For a month, ever since his arrival, Finn had drifted with the milling crowd, waiting for his opportunity. He listened to the accents and the different languages. There were other Irish, there were Asians, Indians, Frenchmen, there were Jews. He floated through the restaurants and bars, careful about the spending of his money. He watched men, hundreds of them, fanning over the tundra to work the mines during the day and closing in on the town in the evenings or on weekends. There was a sense of generosity, one toward the other, each man knowing he would strike. Finn adjusted himself to the mood easily. He discovered one night that the owner of the Gold Belt saloon was Irish, and from then on that was where he spent his time.

This evening Finn pulled on his heavy boots and waded into the low surf for loose bark and driftwood. He leaned it against his tent to dry then stoked his stove with the previous day's collection and sat alone in front of the fire's red glow. At ten o'clock Finn changed his shirt and stepped out into the bright night. The Gold Belt would be full now and it would be proper for him to make his entrance. This pub had a wonderful game, a contest really, and though Finn had been signed up for days, tonight was the first time that he'd actually be allowed to play. There could be only one contestant at a time, and tonight, after the long wait, it would be Finn. He worked his way along the soft sand paths, two gold coins heavy in his pockets. He felt the heft of them, one to each side, like the weight and balance of his father's gold watch.

The Gold Belt stood opposite the New York Kitchen, and as Finn passed he saw Ellen and she saw him. She leaned against the handle of a long broom just at the entrance, her hair a shambles, her eyes gone tired. Finn slowed some and, looking in her direction, turned and stopped.

"Top of the evening," he said.

"It's a different world here, I'd say," said Ellen. "At home the pubs'd be closed by now."

"Oh yes," said Finn. "But the longer hours take away the tendency to gulp."

The weight of Finn's two coins stood him evenly in front of

her. It takes an Irishwoman to criticize the drinking habits of strangers, he thought. Finn asked after Henriette and inquired as to the difficulty of the work. He spoke politely, but he had the contest on his mind and in a moment excused himself and stepped toward the bar.

From the cool path Ellen watched him go and watched the movement of the miners through the smoky tent flaps. Mouths were wide, heads were thrown back, but somehow no sound reached her. Strange that pubs were so open here. One could walk by and see directly in. At home they were always closed, political. At home men drank and talked darkly, their heads just off their pints. Ellen could remember her father coming in, always at ten after the closing hour, the gist of an argument still with him. He would stand in their narrow hallway looking down into the kitchen, but he'd not see her until his thoughts caught up with him. And then he'd throw back his head, his features turning fatherly once again and he'd laugh. . . . But not here, she thought. No serious talk here. She could see faces that she knew from the New York Kitchen, and she could see Finn, standing at the bar, holding a fistful of it. The first joke she could remember was her uncle quoting from the Bible: "As it says in the book of Guinnesses . . ." he'd said, and it had taken her years to understand.

Ellen stood transfixed in the shadows. Now, after such a short time, she was beginning to say "prospectors" just as she used to say "farmers." She laid slabs of beef or fish before them; she carried dozens of brimming mugs of coffee, placing one in front of each dull face. Ellen sighed and stepped back into the kitchen and began clearing the dirty plates away. She had to bend to get into the corners where the ceiling sloped to the wall. She guessed among her traveling companions it would be those two Asians who'd make it. The Japanese. They'd left for the unclaimed lands on the very first day. A people like that, shifty-eyed and small.

When Ellen finished for the night she walked once more past the Gold Belt and saw Finn again, holding his black mug up timelessly. It would be a shame to go directly to bed but she'd not be going into one of these saloons. Saloons indeed. Pubs was what they were no matter what fancy name you gave them. She walked between several of the tents, her black shoes twisting on the soft ground. Here, as everywhere, there was a mixture of sand and moss. She left the path, popping from between two tents to walk on the beach for a while. The tents behind and beside her glowed pale and ghostly in the night, and she could hear voices from within them. Men were making plans, women laughing. Was it the same everywhere then, Ireland, America, Alaska? If it was, then what was there to gain anywhere in the world? Ellen looked at the water. She looked at herself standing there in her black dress, the waves stepping loudly toward her. She raised her arm and spun around in the wet sand until her hair pushed against her forehead, the ends of it flowing into the gray night. She pointed east and then south a little. Follow your finger to Ireland, she thought. Hullo, daddy, what time is it there? Are you home from the pub yet? She spun a little more and danced a little. The tents, the sea, the tents. Oh how she'd spun in the fields of Ireland: the house, the fields, the house. She slowed a little, tired. She came back along the rim of the horizon, pointing at each dim star, looking, trying to find a familiar constellation.

––––––

Inside the Gold Belt Finn drained his pint and took another from the owner, a man who was praising the beauty of his own bar.

" . . . and with so little good hardwood around," he said. "It comes from the Philippines and there's not a scratch on it. It's used to the dainty drinking habits of the Spanish, I suppose."

The owner pushed a large cloth about as he spoke, polishing one place or another, not getting far from his conversation with Finn. The bar too had come on the *Portland,* a few voyages ago, but though the tent was large, the bar, with its dark red grains, would not quite fit. It pushed against the end of the tent and against the flaps. Before winter there would be a building big enough to make the bar look small, but now it was grotesque.

Finn looked at his long reflection in the warped mirror behind the bar. It made him look thinner than he was, made him think less of himself. The mirror was attached to the canvas wall and was never still, so that in its reflection a calm man looked nervous.

"I'm heavier than I appear to be," Finn told the owner. "I'll not be fooled into thinking I'm not."

"Only another half hour until midnight, then we'll see."

The owner was referring to his contest. "Worth your weight in gold," he called it, a game he'd invented and one that had filled his saloon with hopefuls each night of its running.

Finn looked from the mirror to his body. He checked his pockets for extra weight and then slipped his boots from around his thick feet.

At exactly midnight four women dressed in the costumes of ballerinas walked to the front of the tent and began unlacing the canvas, untying it from the wooden pegs in the corners. They rolled the tent sides up, exposing the twilight. A breeze lifted papers off the tables and moved the dust around the floor.

One of the girls came close to Finn. "The trick is in the sacks," she said. "Only the ones near the bottom are correctly marked."

The customers moved their chairs around so that they were facing a small platform. Several more of the bar women came forward carrying chains and lengths of hollow pipe and began assembling a huge balance scale on the platform, one which in every detail except size matched the scale in the assayer's office. When the scale was complete, the plates on either side of it sat firmly upon the wooden stage; one was empty and on the other was a straight-backed chair. The scale had a crank in the back of it, and at its side someone had placed a wheelbarrow full of sacks, sand representing different amounts of gold dust, the weights clearly marked on the outside.

"I'm on then," said Finn, walking around the beer stains in the earth to the place where the scale was constructed. The owner was there waiting for him.

"Here's our candidate," he told the calming crowd. "Finn Wallace from Ireland, who should have it down for he saw it done here last week and then the week before. But for those of you who have come by ships still weighed in the harbor I'll explain that all the man needs to do is place these sacks on the scale to the one side, and then place himself upon the chair over here. After he is ready I'll crank him, and the sacks too, high up off the ground, and we'll all watch the central needle just as we do when we are weighing our own week's work. If he is within a pound, or within two, he'll receive a pack mule and sundry equipment and goods, enough to allow him to strike out on his own. Also, and perhaps he'll feel it's more important, he'll win an entire night's drinking, compliments of the house."

The owner stood down and looked toward a girl, who brought Finn forward. From the open side of the tent dim stars could be seen. The crowd was quiet; the wind blew in without notice. Finn walked over to the wheelbarrow and began placing twenty-pound sacks on the scale. He chose only those sacks near the bottom, setting the others aside.

"I know my own weight," he said. "I've weighed the same for fifteen years."

As he neared the end of the weight placing, many of the

customers stood, trying to see how much he'd put on. Finn lifted two hundred and five pounds onto the scale, then looking at his clothes and the chair he placed another ten-pound sack on top of it.

"If I'm wrong it's the lifting of these sacks that's caused it," he said.

A ballerina offered Finn another pint glass but he waved it away and sat back easily.

"Lift away then," he said. "When you're ready."

When the owner moved to the back of the scale the silence broke, the crowd began yelling instructions.

"You're heavier than that, bud. . . ."

"You're lighter by ten."

Finn stared calmly down off the chair at them. And, though the customers argued hotly, they stepped back and pulled their chairs and tables with them, making room. Outside people stepped onto the paths to watch. Though it was past midnight the streets were still busy. Finn saw the forms of dozens of people in the gray night.

The owner turned the crank at the back of the scale, slowly lifting the two sides of it off the ground. Everyone watched the space between the scale and the platform increase. The sides of the scale lifted unevenly and the needle swayed, first toward Finn, next toward the sacks of sand. The scale was lifted high and when it stopped moving the needle settled on the center, or perhaps half a pound in the direction of Finn.

"He's a winner!" bellowed the owner, coming out from behind the scale and pointing at the needle. "It's almost exact!"

The ballerinas and the customers cheered. Finn watched them jumping about below him. Even outside the tent he could see some of the ghost figures leaping into the night. The owner took hold of the chain that supported the sacks of sand and pulled it toward the back of the stage so that the scale became a swing, sending Finn out over the people in the bar and out through the rolled-up canvas wall and into the street. Finn glided above the sandy paths, then back into the Gold Belt and over the customers once again. Round and round, the owner kept him moving, faster and faster.

Finn could see the shadows of people standing in front of their tents far off toward the beach. He could see Ellen, standing back by the New York Kitchen, and from one place he could see the sea itself. Finn heard the shouts of the people and the slight crash of the waves from the beach. In a moment one of the sacks of sand slipped off the other side of the swing, and Finn dipped slightly down. The audience got louder. Four or five of the costumed ballerinas kicked their legs in unison, leading the customers in their applause. Finn spun on, outside and in, the scale a replica of the one down through the town, heavy on the counter of the assayer's office.

———

Ellen woke Henriette with the news that it was time they got going, that Finn would accompany them, that the Eskimo village was a good two hours away. They were traveling out of Nome to buy fish for the New York Kitchen, and Ellen saw the strong back of Finn's new mule as the help they needed. Also, Finn knew the Eskimo village and could make introductions, help them with the bargaining.

Ellen stepped into a dress then out of it again and into her first pair of trousers. They hung from her in wrinkles but were warm and followed the action of her legs, surrounded them at whatever pace she chose. If her father could see her now he'd hold his breath, she thought, or scowl and call her his son. It made her laugh. Here was Henriette in trousers too, happy to be leaving the city for a day.

The two women left the Kitchen loosely clothed, tucking in

the corners of their shirts and looking about for strangers. Finn's mule stood blank-eyed near their tent and the man himself was ready, the blear of the previous night's drinking washed from his eyes, his mood expanding for them like the fellow country-man that he was, like an older brother taking charge. When they started up the beach the waves were high and it was over-cast and gray and raining. The mule pushed his stub legs into the sand and in a while the tents sank behind them, only the tops visible, even the largest blending with the landscape. They walked past the outskirts of town to the mouth of the Snake, where the water touched the powerful sea. There was a raft on their side of the river and a rope stretched across it and was tied in the secure mist of the far bank. The mule sat back eying the situation.

"This is the site they've chosen for the Army post," said Finn, putting his arms around the mule's neck and tugging. "There'll be American soldiers here before winter." He strapped a piece of canvas around the mule's eyes and rode him onto the raft. Ellen and Henriette stood beside the animal, holding its head. It was easy crossing the river, the current taking them from one side and tossing them toward the other. The river washed the sand from their feet and matted the hair around the mule's hard hooves. Finn held on to the thick rope, pulling. The only danger was in letting go, or in letting his feet slip from the slick wet planks. All three imagined the raft bobbing out to sea. Finn saw himself hanging from the cross rope, watching it go. He imagined the women waving their hands and the confi-dent mule staring peacefully into the dark folds of its blindfold.

When they bumped on the far bank of the river the mule bolted, running off the raft and down the beach a ways. Ellen saw its sightless head turning to her out of the grayness, so she walked over and held it, waiting while her companions secured the wet raft to a tree. The mule, nostrils deep, dipped its head toward her and she covered its ears as she'd seen her father do.

"Whoa," she said, "calm yourself, donkey." She waited until Finn took hold of the loose reins before she stepped forward and led them along the narrow beach. She walked just ahead of the animal, letting it see her wide back and lose itself in the plaid pattern of her jacket.

In two hours they came out of the gray morning and saw the Eskimo village, circles of wooden lean-tos pushed into the melting ground. Around the village poles were placed in the earth with rows of drying fish stretched on lines between them. Eskimo children ran toward them on the sand and Finn reached down and hoisted them, one and then the others, high up over his head. There were open bags of salt, kayaks and canoes pulled high up the beach.

A man approached them extending his hand. He was Finn's age, but looked to Ellen like Kaneda, the older of the two Japanese. The man's name was Phil and he was the head of the fishermen's group, the one that did all of the dealings with the people from Nome. He said, "You've come just ahead of a storm." He pointed up the beach to a large lean-to and told them that there was another group, visiting Eskimos from Port Clarence, and that there would be plenty of fish to buy. He asked them to follow him and they turned and threaded their way up to the lean-to, walking between the sacks of salt, followed by the children.

When they entered the lean-to they found the group of visitors sitting in a circle talking to a white man, Reverend Raymond, a teacher and the pastor of the village mission. The group from Port Clarence stuck their fingers into bowls of meal, spoke softly, and munched on dried fish.

"You should plan on spending the night," said Phil, once the Port Clarence group had spread out, making room for them all to sit down. "Soon it will be too dark and stormy for you to make your way back."

The Reverend Raymond sat forward smiling and trying to

shake their hands. "There are plenty of places to sleep," he said, his mouth still half full of food.

Few of the Eskimos in the group spoke English, but one of them, sitting next to Ellen, asked her questions and got answers, which were translated by the reverend.

"Have you come for the beginning of Nanoon's womanhood?" the man asked. The reverend answered without waiting for a response.

"They have come to buy fish," he said.

"We have come for Nanoon's womanhood," the man told the reverend to tell Ellen. "Everyone is excited about it."

"Today is the day that one of Phil's sisters begins her passage into womanhood," said the reverend. "Everyone is feeling rather festive. We'd be happy if you'd join in the celebration."

Ellen looked from one to the other of her traveling companions. She could see a lengthy row of lean-tos opposite her and a smaller, newly built hut in the exact center of the village. There were no tents here and all of the buildings had one open side facing away from the sea, away from most of the wind and the rain. On each lean-to a heavy skin tarp covered the entire front and could be rolled up or down depending on the weather. The inside walls of the lean-to where they sat were covered with insulating furs. The reverend told Ellen that each of the structures had to be rebuilt each summer. He said that as soon as the support poles were placed in the ground they began to sink down toward the permafrost causing the entire village to slowly sag.

At a suggestion from the reverend, Ellen got up and left with him to take a tour of the village. The reverend was a tall man, and seemed a happy one. He was a Protestant and told her that he'd been in the village for four years and had built his own home and taken over the duties at the school from his predecessor, who'd given the villagers their Christian names. He was from Wisconsin and had gone to seminary in Minneapolis. He had a brother in Alaska someplace, panning for gold.

"This is one of the few villages on the peninsula," he told Ellen. "Most Eskimo families simply travel about looking for good fishing ground and a place to sleep. I mean during the winter, of course."

Ellen walked next to the man, feeling quickly as if she were being courted. The reverend didn't take her arm, but that was the feeling she had, nevertheless. They walked all along the clean village paths and down to where the canoes were kept and back toward the tundra, where there were several trees standing tall and surrounding the reverend's closed and lonely house.

"I've worked hard on this place," he said. "May I show you where you and Miss Henriette will be sleeping?"

Ellen smiled slightly and followed the man up onto the small wooden porch, where a hide swing hung from ropes. The door to the house opened wide and as she entered Ellen saw that the woodwork inside was darkly stained and polished, that the two rooms were divided only by hanging pelt curtains, and that one contained a porcelain washbasin with wildflowers in a stone jar. There was a ladder leading to a loft, where the reverend had a large desk and where there was a real glass window looking out over the village and out to sea. There were two slim leather chairs. Ellen sat in one while the reverend ran down the ladder again to make some tea.

Ellen could see that it was raining now and she could hear the reverend whistling with his tea kettle below. She felt at ease here, and looked forward to spending the night in this house, away from the oppression of Nome. The reverend moved like a man half his size. He was back up the ladder with teacups, then quickly down again, and back with the steaming pot and a bowl of sugar.

"It's English tea," he said proudly. "I've been thinking of brewing a cup for weeks now."

"This is the first place in Alaska that has given me the feeling of a home," she told him. "You have a beautiful view."

"I can really go home if I request it, you know," he said,

sitting down across from her. "But if I don't I might be here forever. It's a nice place after you get used to it."

Ellen nodded and blew across the surface of her tea. She pictured herself sitting straight, having tea with a stranger. Her grandmother had taught her how to have tea with gentlemen. Ellen could feel the fire from the kitchen below, and when she looked up she noticed the reverend holding his teacup high and looking at her over the top of it.

"Well then, here's to a happy stay for you and all your friends. I hope it will be profitable, both spiritually and in other ways." He winked at her so she inclined her head and took a sip. The reverend had more tea ready and poured for her before she had quite finished what was in her cup. When he spoke to her she looked him directly in the eyes but when she spoke she looked at his forehead. It was one of her grandmother's tricks and she was sure he hadn't noticed. The reverend made it easy for her by taking whatever subject she did and making it his own. She mentioned the fish that they had come to buy and he talked for five minutes on what a thrill it was to catch a salmon from a canoe. He invited her to try it the next morning if the storm was gone, and she accepted. They were getting on well. Below them through the window they could see the open end of the lean-to where the party was taking place. Ellen saw Finn sitting cross-legged on the floor. She saw Henriette, crouched on a low stool, slightly above the others, leaning into the conversation.

———

Finn, lifting his head from the circle of Eskimos, could see the two still figures framed in the window. First he noticed the trees, then the house, then the two figures in the window. They seemed pasted on the glass. He was talking to Phil and watching the

Eskimos from Port Clarence, who sat across the circle. It was nearly time to begin the ceremony for Phil's sister Nanoon, so they all looked about, hoping to get a glimpse of her walking toward them. Phil looked at Finn. "Today's my sister's day," he said. "She begins her weeks alone. You couldn't have come at a better time."

Finn's legs ached from sitting in one position for so long and he stood and stretched. He'd been watching the preparations but hadn't known whether to ask Phil about them or not. Phil's sister was reaching puberty and Finn knew it was an important time. He imagined Phil needed to be alone for a while, so he borrowed a sealskin jacket and stood in the increasing rain looking for a place to relieve himself. He'd already had several bowls of the food, several glasses of wine. Phil directed him toward a creek bed from where he could still see the house of the reverend, but not the window. Rain struck his face and neck so he struggled to pull up the tough hood of the jacket and was immediately too warm inside it. He wondered where the boy had taken his mule, and at that same moment decided to keep the mule, not to try to sell it as previously he'd thought he would. Finn watched the rain hitting the quiet water of the stream. It was odd that the Eskimos had chosen this little stream as the village toilet. If he hadn't known he'd have thought it as clean as any, for it was as clear.

Finn turned and started back along the path that Phil had shown him. He was away from the main village, but in the first lean-to he came to he heard voices and saw through the side of it the perfect face of Nanoon, that sister, the one whose day it was and who would be entombed for the winter in the feathered hut at the center of the village. Her head was already wreathed with white feathers, circling it like petals, and Phil's wife and sisters moved about her. Finn felt he could see the change from girl to woman right there before his eyes; he felt he could see the innocence leaving. When Nanoon saw him her lips parted as if to speak, but Finn stepped away quickly. And as he looked back toward the main village he saw Henriette watching him too, from inside the party lean-to and low down on her three-legged stool. Henriette waved so Finn tipped his hat to her, dancing once around like a circus bear.

At dusk the population of the village swelled and people strolled between the lean-tos under pink parasols. In one lean-to there was a barrel of rum and in another were long salted strips of jerky. Ellen and the reverend were back, and soon, in a lean-to hidden from them all, someone began playing a piano. The rain dampened the thin parasols of the strollers and the music forced them to walk and step in straight lines and circles, all heads turned toward the small round hut at the center of the village. Finn found the reverend and Ellen and stayed with them.

And Phil was right about the storm. Though it was still early the long day was cut to darkness by clouds moving shoulder to shoulder across the sky. Finn and the reverend and Ellen watched the clear spaces disappear. They had walked to the mule house, where Finn's mule stood, nostrils rigidly taking in the storm, and now they were walking back. This was the public section of the village, where the storage houses were and the animals were kept. It was the section of the village farthest from the beach, and some of the buildings were built like the reverend's, closed on all four sides. There was lightning, quick as the raising of an eyebrow, then thunder, rolling in low over the waves.

In the main village the paths were less crowded now. The rain slowed movement, keeping the people inside, engaging them in the act of eating. And there was the beginning of activity around the special hut. People looked toward it or peered in the direction from which Nanoon would eventually come.

"She is so beautiful," said the reverend. "It's a pity you won't be able to see her face."

Phil stood at the entrance to his own lean-to now, and signaled with a lantern that Nanoon was ready. All the children of the village formed a line from his lean-to to the special hut, getting down on their hands and knees and waiting. When she came out Nanoon was dressed entirely in feathers, and all of them were white and all were from the Snowy Owl, who even now, some thought, perched on the trees around the village in order to see that the ceremony went well. When the people saw her the piano stopped and everyone turned their heads to watch her pass. She walked with one leg on either side of the kneeling children. She walked over them, dropping each onto the earth behind her like the children she would bear.

Nanoon was alone, and though her face was completely covered Finn was sure that she was looking directly at him, that her round owl's eyes sought him above all the others. When she got to the hut Phil went over and, without looking at her, pulled back the feathered doorway, allowing his sister to crawl on through. He closed it again immediately and called his other sisters forward to sew the flap shut. That was all. Phil and the members of his family shook hands, the kneeling children stood and ran away, and the piano started up again. The reverend looked from Ellen to Finn and sighed. "Is there anything more beautiful than ritual?" he asked.

———

Inside the lean-to where the party had begun the visitors from Port Clarence were congratulating Phil on the smoothness of a ceremony well done. People sat in a circle again, but at its center this time there was dancing. Two men and two women stepped toward and away from each other, then tapped whoever would be next and sat down. Visitors were always chosen first, but when Finn and Ellen and the reverend walked in they were, nevertheless, surprised to see Henriette dancing opposite Phil's wife and with two of the men from the Port Clarence group. The piano could still be heard but the dancers were not taking their rhythm from it. Rather, the audience clapped out the rhythm and the tempo for them.

Henriette danced with a loose grin on her face. While the others moved in and out to the constant clapping, she did a kind of hop, coming down on both feet and then turning all the way around and hopping back. Seeing her embarrassed Ellen, but before she could react Henriette sat down and Ellen herself was pushed into the circle and was joined by Finn, the reverend, and by another of Phil's many sisters. Ellen stood stiff-backed for a moment but found that made her more self-conscious than dancing. She hopped as briefly as she could, trying to follow the woman across from her. She looked sideways, hoping to glare at Finn, if she could catch his eye, but he wasn't looking at her. Rather he leapt high into the air and came down shouting. And the reverend danced lightly and with skill. No one noticed Ellen's discomfort.

They danced until there was a break in the clapping, then chose others to take their places. Ellen chose the person nearest her and quickly sat down where that person had been. She was deeply embarrassed and watched everyone to see if they perceived it. She sat with her back to the wall, thank God not over where Finn was with his back to the howling wind. It was the first time she had ever danced, the very first. Ellen watched the others but after a while began to relax and saw herself up there dancing as well as they did. She pictured her entire Irish family watching her dance and frowning. She saw them sitting in the circle, clapping for her, and she saw herself moving her body in front of them, sometimes holding up the hem of her skirt, sometimes swishing it back and forth. She imagined her father looking at her ankles and getting angry, so she tapped him on the head and sat in his place while he jerked around up there, his hips and knees working like those of a puppet. Oh, he would frown. Ellen clapped for her father and smiled as he danced grotesquely around. She'd make him dance in his pub; if he weren't careful she'd make him dance in the street!

Ellen opened her eyes to the Eskimo dancers and watched as another and another group began. Everyone had to dance. Everyone would. Ellen saw Henriette across from her clapping and grinning. She saw Finn and the reverend, and she saw herself again. It was easy. She closed her eyes and there was her father, still bounding about, sweating from the exertion of it all. He pumped his legs and moved about the room and jumped and turned and twisted. How long would he hold up? she wondered. He tried several times to tap his way out of it but the people around him pulled back, moving their heads just out of his reach.

Ellen was shocked that she'd let her own father work himself so. She knew he wasn't in the best of health. Still she watched. Heel toe, heel toe, his black boots kicked and shuffled. Ellen clapped on steadily, now thinking of home, now watching the Eskimos. Across from her Finn had fallen away into the night. She could see him standing dimly back there, next to that feathered hut. He put his ear to it, then shouted, then listened. He was trying to make himself understood, trying hard to hear the voice of the virgin through the howls of the storm and over the general cacophony of the night.

The storm made it seem late, and darkness made everyone cold and reminded them of winter. Soon the fronts of the lean-tos began blinking shut like eyes, the candles and kerosene lamps folding under pelt doors. Ellen and Henriette walked quickly through the storm following the reverend. Finn slept at Phil's place, at the far end of a long line of Phil's relatives, in a smallish space formerly occupied by Nanoon. The moment before Phil rolled down the hide front of his lean-to they all stood together, peering through the darkness at the shining hut and at the storm.

"Soon she will be a woman," said Phil. "Those Port Clarence men will be falling all over themselves."

———

The reverend had hot water ready for washing quickly. He gave Henriette his bed and had prepared a special cot for Ellen up in the loft. He himself would sleep on the floor at the bottom of the ladder. The reverend provided each of the women with a stiff nightshirt and stood out on the cold porch while they changed into them. When he came back inside his house he turned down the light and fumbled with the buttons of his clothing in the dark. He wore a long white nightshirt like the one he had given Ellen. He also wore a nightcap and held a candle in a small tray and went about the house checking.

The reverend gave the women some time to get to sleep and then stood at the bottom of the ladder, quietly, listening to the regular rhythm of Ellen's breathing above him. Tomorrow he would take her fishing if it wasn't raining. Then he'd help her load the fish she wanted to buy on the mule and he'd walk with her to the edge of the village. The reverend reached down and quickly pinched the wick of his candle. Gray smoke disappeared into the closing darkness. He heard the rustling of bedclothes. He heard Henriette cough and turn and he thought of her occupying his bed, her head on his pillow.

When the reverend thought enough time had passed he let his weight come down softly on the bottom rung of the ladder and brought his other foot up to it. He looked straight forward into the darkness, his hands tightly gripping the ladder's sides.

He took another step with his right foot and pulled his left foot up after it. He could hear nothing of Ellen though he could still hear Henriette turning fitfully below him. His stomach was knotted tight and he thought of how freely he'd be able to stand here tomorrow, when the women were gone. The reverend stepped up again, tipping his head back and raising his eyes over the edge of the floor of the loft. He took one more step, inching his whole head above the plank and resting his chin on the worn surface of the floor. The white bedding was a pale cocoon on the boards in front of him. He held his breath, would move no closer. He could have reached out and touched her. The reverend fell into a deeper quiet than he would have thought possible. His hands were locked on the railing and his eyes grew used to the darkness, bringing her more and more toward him. The rain, like a branch, tapped loudly on the picture window as if in warning.

Ellen, in the warm bedding, had still not slept and was looking toward the ceiling of the loft, imagining she could hear the reverend sleeping below. She thought she could see the rough ceiling beams outlined in the air. She was tired but could not sleep. It seemed to her the whole loft was pitching back and forth, rocking her like the tight bed of the ship she'd come in. She tried to empty her mind of thoughts, to rest. Tomorrow they would need to get the fish and start back early. It would be hard work and they'd be nearly a day late. She imagined herself unhappy in the New York Kitchen again. It would be very busy, that's one consolation. And the muscles in her legs would be sore from dancing.

———

The Eskimo village, Nome, and the camp of Kaneda and Fujino on Topcock Creek form a triangle, each point hidden in the slick topography of the mossy peninsula. They are outposts at the edges of the gold fields and men sit in each, looking out to sea or at the gray-soaked mountains. If it is stormy, as it is this night, the entire peninsula is covered with blackness, with the sounds of coming winter. In the estuary birds will sink in their moss beds, only their tulip necks extending darkly. Everywhere everyone sleeps. In Nome the bars have closed early, tent flaps have been bound with rope as the storm pushes the sea into a froth. Some of the tents, pegged too close to the water's edge, are awash as the tide scoots under the canvas walls and across the hard-packed floors. In Finn's tent the legs of his stove sink four inches into the freshly wetted sand.

At their camp on Topcock Creek, Fujino and Kaneda have completed another day's work and have eaten and talked and bathed. The frypans and dishes of their evening meal are submerged in water at the edge of the pond. Already their supply of sake is diminished, but they are beginning to find gold in the water-washed sand of their sluice box. Soon Fujino will go back to town to file the claim they have staked but Kaneda is disappointed. Though it is a good strike, it is not what he had hoped for. Like carpentry this job requires many hours of work each day for the gold they find. And here the gold has been washed to a fine powder by the forces of the stream, the largest nugget found being just the size of a child's fingernail. Most of the gold can barely be seen. It must be processed, clearly separated from the black and red sand that is everywhere.

Inside the tent, next to the sleeping men, sits a box filled with the gold they have found thus far. This gold is free of the sand it rose with and is shining. It has taken the form of flat cakes, honeycombed and porous. For days they have been using the same process. After the gold and sands have been washed and are drying in the bottom of the sluice, Fujino passes a powerful horseshoe magnet over it, pulling much of the black sand away. Kaneda then mixes a flask of mercury with small parts of what remains and waits for the gold and red sand to form an amalgam. After that all that is left to do is to heat the volatile mercury, letting it evaporate away and leaving the gold alone, hot and drying, taking each time a different shape, like snowflakes.

The two men have collected several dozen such snowflakes, each stacked upon the one before it. They work full days, each with his own job, both men digging, both loading the long sluice box with sand and moss and gravel. During the first few days Fujino and Kaneda spoke more than they do now. Kaneda is the boss and the cook, Fujino the one who does most of the lifting. They speak of home rarely, neither of them mentioning Kaneda's daughter. They see only tundra wolves and beaver, and once, only once, they saw a huge brown bear fishing near their camp in the morning.

In the evening, after they have eaten and after Fujino plunges the tin plates and frying pan into the water, Kaneda often leans back and tells a story. He was a student of Japanese history and remembers all the interesting stories he has read. He tells Fujino about the warring years of the fifteenth century and of the unification of the country under Hideyoshi. He talks about very ancient history, when a woman was the ruler, and he talks about the introduction of various religions to the islands. Fujino had studied history too, in school, but it is nice to hear the rambling voice of the old man here in this lonely country. He has become a listener though he was hired as a translator.

Fujino had thought, on the ship, that they would be among men here, not by themselves far away and hiding, and he often wonders what life is like in Nome. He saw it and was not impressed on that first day, but he would like to see it again. He looks forward to going in to file the claim. He will take a day or two and will drink in the bars and find those who came on the ship with him. They are too self-sufficient out here. If he could he would think of a reason for having to go to Nome once a month. If for nothing else he would go because he needed a break, some time to himself among people. Fujino has respect for Kaneda but Kaneda is an old man and can afford to be by himself all the time. He no longer thinks of women and has passion left only for gold.

Sometimes after working there is nothing to do but sleep and Fujino is not yet ready for it. On these occasions, though his body is tired, he walks quickly out along the creek bed and up into the hills. There is nothing else, no different land, no people, but at least there is movement. He can stretch his legs, extending his stride into long leaps along the bending course of the river. He makes up games for himself, rules for walking. Sometimes Fujino is gone for hours, returning to the camp well after Kaneda is asleep. It is a hard life for a young man. He often tells himself so. Still, he is a good worker and he knows Kaneda likes him, even respects his ability. Things are going according to plan. He will make enough money to buy some land, if not in the center of Tokyo, at least somewhere nearby. He will ask for the hand of Kaneda's daughter and Kaneda will not be able to refuse. If they are here a year, even two, what does it matter? Life will be the same at home, only he will be different. He will have money and a wife and a rich father-in-law. And he will know a good deal more about Japanese history.

As the two men sleep the storm moves north out of sight and across the low mountains toward the Arctic Circle. The darkness is replaced by summer gray and the sky becomes clear. Sleepers turn in their beds at all three points of the triangle: in the Eskimo village, in Nome, and on Topcock Creek. The sun is almost risen and another day has come.

———

The reverend started up the ladder at five, quiet, trying not to wake Henriette. Ellen was already dressed and waiting, the bedding she had used rolled upright, leaning against the loft railing.

"I would have come earlier," he said.

Through the loft window they could see that the village was still closed and sleeping, though the rain had stopped and puddles were spaced about the ground, reflecting silver and blue. Here and there dogs lay on their sides, gray fur moving slightly in the wind. One dog trotted up the main path and out along the beach. Ellen and the reverend stepped quietly down the ladder and once outside walked quickly through the village to the boathouse. The reverend pulled a short, wide canoe out and down a slick ramp to the water's edge. He'd brought along poles and lines, and a small bucket of herring to be used as bait.

"If we're lucky we'll have a strike soon," he said. "Early morning is feeding time and they're usually swimming high."

"I don't swim so well," said Ellen, looking at the canoe. "I've never been fishing before."

The reverend placed Ellen in the middle of the canoe and waded out a few feet before stepping in himself. There was only one paddle so the reverend used it, paddling from the stern, sometimes changing sides, lifting the paddle over his head or swinging it around behind him so that the water would not drip into the canoe. They glided, the bow turning now slightly port, now slightly starboard. The rippling of the water against the sides of the canoe was the only sound. In five minutes they were well off the beach and somewhat down toward Nome. The reverend threw a makeshift anchor over the side and let the rope slide through his hands until it went slack and the stone settled in the soft mud of the shallow bottom. The canoe swung around and drifted until the rope was taut again and stretching.

Ellen turned slowly, bringing her feet close to her body and over the seat so that she was facing the reverend. He quickly baited the two barbed hooks and, handing Ellen one of the poles, told her to let the line out by hand, counting twenty times as she did so.

"If you feel a strike," he said, "wait just a moment before you start reeling it in. Let the fish set the hook. He'll do that by himself. Then he's all yours."

Looking back at the village, Ellen could already see a few people walking back and forth across the beach. She could see the feather-topped roof of Nanoon's coming-of-age hut. She was about to speak when a silver salmon leapt from the water a few feet from them and toward shore. The belly of the fish flashed in the sun then slapped the clean surface of the sea again and was gone. Soon concentric circles rocked the canoe.

"My God," said Ellen.

The reverend was pleased and proud.

"That was a big one," he said. "Maybe he's yours. He's heading for your hook right now."

As he said it the tip of Ellen's rod dug deeply into the water and she jerked it back and stood up, almost capsizing the canoe.

"Hold it!" shouted the reverend. "Sit down. Let him set the hook!"

The pole had gone slack again and for a moment Ellen thought the fish was free. But just as she was about to say so the pole bent double again and she froze, holding up the tip of it but doing nothing else.

"All right, you've got him," whispered the reverend. "Now turn the handle, bring him in."

Ellen fumbled with the crank on the side of the pole and quickly the tension was gone again and once more she thought that the fish had escaped.

"Just keep it coming," said the reverend. "He's still there. Keep the line taut."

"It's a heavy thing," she said.

The fish leapt again, slicing the water with the line it was dragging, shaking its head like a dog. Ellen kept cranking, taking in the line. The fish was deep and then shallow, there was tension and then there was none. In a moment, looking over the side, Ellen saw the slender brown back of the fish floating, then touching the canoe and gone in a flash.

"He's tiring now," said the reverend. "You've got him."

And indeed it did seem easier as she again pulled the fish into view and watched it treading water just below the surface, facing the canoe and waiting.

The reverend lowered a long gaff over the side and brought it up, skillfully lifting the fish, its tail swinging, out of the tranquil sea. The fish flopped once or twice on the bottom of the canoe and the reverend removed the hook and then hit the fish several times with the blunt end of the gaff. It lay long and silver in the bottom of the boat, its gills quivering, its jaw working open and shut.

"He's a beauty," said the reverend. "Fifteen pounds is my guess. Maybe more. You did well."

"I've never seen anything like it," said Ellen. "Is it dead?"

"Oh yes, I've taken care of that. We'll salt it when we get to shore and you can take it back and have your own special supper."

He looked at Ellen. He had taken the hook from the fish's mouth and was rebaiting it. He threw it over the side and picked up his own pole. He pointed at her line and gestured so Ellen let the line slowly out, counting it back into the water once again.

By the time Ellen had her fish the whole village was awake and smoke was rising. Henriette awoke to the empty house and reheated the still lukewarm coffee that the reverend had left on the stove. It was a comfortable house. She climbed to the loft with the coffee and two thick slices of bread and jam, settling into a chair in front of the window. She could see the canoe on the water and all of the lean-tos of the village below. Here and there dogs stood, waiting for scraps of food to be thrown out to them. Most of the lean-tos were opened now, their hide fronts rolled up exposing their insides. Strange way to live, she thought, every day opening up the front of your house so that others can see in.

Henriette was feeling better about being in Alaska. She saw Finn through the window, walking by himself around the front of one of the lean-tos. She was relaxed, daydreaming. It seemed to Henriette that she could feel herself coming into focus for the others. It always took people a long time to get to know her and she could feel that happening now. She saw Phil come out of his lean-to to throw a piece of food high into the air over the dogs. He went back in and quickly rolled the front up and began to sweep hard until dust ballooned around him. She saw the canoe come ashore and recognized its occupants and saw the fish that the reverend was carrying. Henriette knew they would be leaving soon, so when she finished her bread and coffee she went back down the ladder and thought once again how pleasant it would be to live here, in this house, in this village. She took the cup she had been using into the kitchen and dropped it into the sink. The cup split easily in two, the handle half of it taking the shape of a sugar scoop. There were only two pieces and Henriette picked them both up, frowning. She looked around the kitchen for a few minutes and then slipped the broken pieces into a small sack and put the sack in the bag she had brought with her from Nome. And then, after straightening up the bed she'd slept in, she slipped into her sealskin jacket and left the house.

Henriette went directly to Phil's lean-to and said good morning, waiting until Phil and his family turned around and noticed her. Soon Ellen and the reverend came in carrying the fish and telling the story of the catch, and Finn came back and remained quiet at the entrance, standing behind them all. It was time for them to leave, so Ellen handed Phil a list written the morning before by the owner of the New York Kitchen and Phil checked off the items with a soft lead pencil. Everything was there and he would have it loaded on the mule and ready in fifteen minutes. They bargained. Ellen felt like paying Phil's price, but held out for two cents less per pound. Had she purchased the fish when they'd first arrived she might have gotten a better price, but as it was she felt happy and felt that she was among friends.

The reverend cleaned and salted Ellen's salmon and placed it in her arms. It was the only strike they'd had, he reminded her, and she had done well. While they stood and talked, three young men brought the pack mule to them and stood back to examine the steadiness of the load. The young men pushed the load at each other, leaned into it, making the mule brace his feet. Ellen waited until they were through and then placed her own fish in a canvas sack and hung it around the mule's neck.

"Like the pendulum in a grandfather's clock," she said.

The reverend laughed and put his arms out as if to encircle the entire group. He put them down again. "Good-bye," he said. "I've so enjoyed our visit."

Everyone shook hands. Phil with Finn, the reverend with Ellen. Henriette shook hands with the three young men who'd loaded the fish. They were all standing near Nanoon's small feathered hut.

"Everyone is anticipating how beautiful she will be," said Phil. "No one can imagine it."

They walked together to the outskirts of the village and then stood and shook hands again.

"Good-bye!" they all shouted. When Ellen and Finn and Henriette walked away from the Eskimos the warm wind carried their voices toward the sea. The three young men still waved at them. The mule stopped and Finn hit him once on the flank. The sky, of course, was clear, the storm gone. They would be back in Nome by noon, back to work, back among civilized men.

2

Modeling it after one she'd seen in the Eskimo village, Ellen opened up a public bath. Nome seemed dirty to her after her return and she knew of only one way to clean it up. She gave notice at the New York Kitchen, bought a double-sized tent and two huge copper tubs, and hired Henriette to come help. Ellen had regained a sense of industry from her visit to the village. The tent she bought had two rooms and in the back, next to the copper tubs, she placed an iron stove that had burners for the heating of two buckets of water at the same time. Henriette would be responsible for keeping the fires going and for keeping the water hot.

It was amazing how Ellen's opinion of Henriette had changed since the trip. Now she seemed a quiet, warm-hearted girl, where before she'd seemed only slow. Ellen had been quick to judge again and she was sorry for it. It was one of her faults. Henriette had told her that she might quit the New York Kitchen, might possibly take the next ship south, before Ellen offered her the job. She told Henriette she'd give her eight dollars a day, and at night, after the last of the bathers had gone, there'd be spaces where they could sleep, collapsible cots that fit between the tubs, in the back room, where everything was still hot.

Ellen had to buy the space where the bath was to sit, but she wasn't unhappy about that. Her space was sufficiently up from the beach for her not to have to worry about high water, and soon she'd have her own building on it. She'd not wait for the general construction crews to get started. She decided that if she'd misjudged Henriette it was also possible that she'd misjudged Finn and she asked him to put up the building for her. He agreed and as a beginning fashioned a dozen strong chicken coops for stacking along the far canvas wall of the front room of her bath. There would be baths and there would be eggs. Ellen bought a dozen dull chickens from a ship in port.

The grand opening of Ellen's bath was on a Tuesday. Her hours would be from noon to midnight, but today they began at nine. The night before, those who had worked on the bath used the tubs for the first time, telling each other how clean they felt and how sure they were that the business would be a success. Ellen bathed first, then Henriette, then Finn. Ellen decided that she'd charge two dollars a bath and that eggs would be fifty cents each. The first real customer was a man named John Hummel, who had scurvy and had not been out of Nome since his arrival six months earlier. Hummel pursed his lips and smiled, letting the red scurvy line show itself around the gold caps of his teeth.

"You ought to have a slogan," he said. "Something to bring people in from long distances." He entered the back room and Ellen listened to the sound the water made as it slid across his shoulders and back down into the tub.

To help with the bath's advertising, Finn had gone about the town handing out leaflets made by Henriette. Ellen and Henriette kept every inch of the bath clean and ready for use and Ellen had a sprinkling can full of water near the front room counter so that she could wet down the dirt floor occasionally, keeping the dust away. Here at least there would be cleanliness. Here it was easy for Ellen to imagine herself not in Nome at all, but still in the Eskimo village. And so she rarely went out.

If she had an errand she sent Henriette, or, indeed, would ask Finn to go. She spent her spare minutes thinking of the village and the reverend, or thinking of home. She daydreamed, wondering what the reaction would be to an Irish stone house around here, the kind she'd lived in as a child. Stone houses ... From hers it had been a forty-minute walk to the little school where she'd studied with the others, maybe six of them. There was a pub in her village and a post office and a small store. That was all. Though it was a tiny neighborhood her father never tired of talking to the same men each night. He'd go to his pub or feel guilty if he didn't. And they'd wait, the women, all sitting in the quiet living room, the same subjects returning like the hours of the day.

Ellen remembered the grandfather's clock in the narrow front hallway of that house. As a small girl she'd once hidden within it, ducking behind the sharp pendulum and staring past it and through the dusty glass as the members of her family searched for her. She must have stayed in that clock for more than an hour, for she remembered the lonely sound of its striking. It echoed through the wood and into her body. The pendulum sliced the air in front of her nose, making soft cutting sounds. Several times her mother or her sisters had stared directly at her, but they saw only themselves in the flat surface of the glass, never the girl hiding behind the sockets of their own eyes.

It was Ellen's grandmother who finally found her. Her father's mother. The small door had opened and the old woman bent down, peering past the pendulum.

"Ellen?" she had shrieked, her voice darting past the sharp seconds. She pulled the child out and stood her on the clean floor and closed the clock door without starting the pendulum again. It had moved silently, and in little circles.

John Hummel, the forgotten first customer, finished his bath quickly and startled Ellen when he stepped in front of her.

"Oh," she said.

"If you'd like me to pay?"

Ellen sat forward and looked at him. "I'll tell you," she said. "Since you are the actual first customer let's call it fair that you should have a free one."

Hummel had his money ready but stopped counting and smiled, his hand covering his diseased mouth.

"That's very kind. If there's ever anything ..." But Ellen silenced him with a short wave and Hummel nodded, spitting into his handkerchief before moving toward the door. When he was gone Ellen took the towel he'd used, quickly throwing it into a tub of waiting water. She looked around the room for something out of place and then sat back down to wait for the next customer. Henriette needed twenty minutes to ready the tubs, but before Ellen could lose herself in Ireland again the flap of the tent was pushed aside and Finn entered. He'd stopped somewhere during his rounds to purchase Ellen a grand opening gift.

"What is it?" she asked.

" 'What is it' is a question that can be answered by its opening," said Finn. He had two boxes and stretched one toward Henriette when she came through the curtain.

"To get the business off on the right foot is all."

Ellen opened her package first and held up a heavy cream-white marble egg.

"It's for giving those chickens the idea," Finn told her. "You put that marble egg in under them and they get to thinking it's real and then they get the urge to duplicate it. It truly works. It will double your yield."

With thumb and forefinger, Ellen held the egg up to the light. "I've never seen such a thing," she said slowly, one eye closed and peering at it like a jeweler. "So small and smooth yet heavy as a bantam."

In Henriette's package there was a hairbrush with a handle of marble the same color as Ellen's egg. She quickly ran it through her hair then held it up as if proving that it too worked.

"Well then," said Finn. "I'll grant there are still a few out there who don't know of the bath's existence." He lifted the remaining stack of leaflets and left again before the women could say anything about the egg and the brush.

About many of the nearby tents lumber had been stacked in anticipation of the construction crews that were even now being formed by those men who had not staked claims. Finn was confident, for he had his tools and had posted his own name. He was a man looking for a crew. There was something about a place like this. Here a man could start again. All he had to do was post a list upon the canvas side of a tent, saying that he was a boss looking for men, and some men, many of them, would sign below. Finn supposed it was because many men thought there was some secret to being boss, some obscure knowledge of procedure. But, as for him, he had his tools and just enough money to buy building materials. He only needed a helper or two, and he'd be on his way. He already had a job contracted. He told Ellen that he'd put up the bath building for two thousand dollars and said he'd have it done in a month. And he'd pay whoever worked with him fairly. Now was a time to be fair with other men, for he'd be paid back in the end, he knew.

Finn, thinking and handing out leaflets, imagined the things he would do with the money he made. The crowd flowed in the direction of the beach, and he let himself be taken with it. He tried pushing leaflets into the hands of those near him, but they were excited, so Finn put the leaflets neatly inside his coat and looked where the others were looking. Out in the bay, anchored or anchoring, stood three gray American troop ships. He could see skiffs dotting the water, men and equipment being lowered from the high decks by mechanical hoists.

"Down by the mouth of the Snake," said a voice, "they're going to build a fort."

Finn knew the site of the fort to be just where he and Henriette and Ellen had crossed the Snake a few days before, but he hadn't thought about what the coming of the army might mean. He'd seen soldiers before so turned to leave but found that a whole group of townspeople had come up behind him and that his way was blocked. He moved sideways along the edge of the beach trying again to distribute his leaflets, but the crowd had a heavy face and was moving with the soldiered skiffs, northwesterly, toward the Snake.

By the time they reached the raft landing at the edge of the river, five of the gun-gray boats had already notched the soft sandbar on the far side. Many of the men and women in Nome had come out of the tent city and walked to the bank of the Snake to watch the army arrive. They stood now close together, quiet at the water's edge. There were already a dozen soldiers on the far sand, directing the landing barges and helping to stack the shored supplies. They were organized, these soldiers. Finn liked the stiff brown shirts that they wore and the precision with which they marched, seaward and back.

"We have our own laws," said a man near Finn, shorter and calmer than the others in the crowd. As he spoke the body of men and women standing around him tightened, moved in behind him to form a V, like a reflection of the southbound birds that even now blackened the sky above Nome. "We have our own laws." Like people singing in rounds the crowd began a murmur. Finn found himself in the middle, unable to turn or to slip away with his leaflets undamaged. The soldiers on the far side of the river were at ease or were standing boot deep in the water. The man who had first spoken was quiet again, and soon the others were too.

The third ship was unloaded and more troops stood along the opposite sandbar. The officer in charge was one of the last to come ashore but the first to give an order. "Axemen ready," he said.

They would build their camp beyond the bar on which they stood and away from the river, on the flat moss of the semi-tundra. At another order from the officer the axemen turned and swung their way into the scrub, walking six feet apart and clearing everything in their path. Finn looked at the soldiers, then at their own leader, the little calm-looking man in front. Everyone was quietly watching. Finn was in the center of the group, a head above most of the others, so he put his hands to his mouth and shouted, "Hello . . . Why have you come?" He looked quickly about him, but no one took up his call. The commanding officer walked down to the edge of the water, raised his hands, and spoke back.

"By order of the President of the United States. We have come to survey the land."

Finn didn't know what to say next. It had been an experiment, his yelling. He'd wanted to see if he could get the same reaction that the short man had gotten, an echo from the crowd, a group following. The prospectors looked at him now, waiting for him to respond. On the far bank all of the soldiers stood still.

"You are not here as a police force then?" asked the short man. "You are not here as lawmen?"

Immediately the group around Finn took up the call. There was movement among them, side-stepping. The entire group turned like a divining rod, the short man its pivot. Even Finn thought the question so to the point that he heard himself saying so under his breath. They shifted a little, closed upon each other, their many feet moving.

"We have no plans to make one of our tents a jail," said the officer, smiling. "Our main job is to survey the gold region. If anyone hinders us from that duty we have the power to arrest. If not, you haven't anything to fear from us."

He turned then and marched back among the soldiers before anyone could say anything more. The little man broke the tip of the V and quickly worked his way back toward the town. Finn was next, first among the followers. The others, soon seeing that the officer had dismissed them, turned and shuffled, talking among themselves now, mumbling their way back into the dusty labyrinth from which they had come.

Finn stood beside the short man and handed him one of the leaflets advertising the bath.

"This will be a boon to the community," he said. "First we clean our bodies then we build a fine strong town."

The man read the leaflet more carefully than anyone had thus far. "You'll need a map," he said. "Nome is just a shanty town now. How would you expect anyone to find the place?"

He stuffed the paper back into Finn's hands then turned and walked away. And he was right. Finn had assumed that people would know of the bath's location from others who knew of it. But to have a map would be better. In truth it was very hard to find. There wasn't even a sign.

Finn walked back along the paths of the town, distributed a few more leaflets, and returned to Ellen's bath. He peered in through the wire mesh on the front of the chicken coops. The first chicken he saw was sitting high on an egg of her own and on the marble one Finn had given Ellen. He reached in and took both eggs in his hand and the chicken settled down once more. The real egg was warm and slightly larger than the marble one. Finn slipped it into the box on top of the coop, then slid the marble egg through the door and under the next bird. He took Ellen's watering can and was sprinkling the dirt floor of the room when Ellen came in from the outside.

"I've been about the town," she said lightly. "I saw your name but there's still no one signed up with you."

"The army has arrived. Did you notice?"

"I noticed the crowd about," she said. "I noticed the ships in the harbor."

Finn pointed to the new egg and told her about the mistake he'd made on the handouts.

"A map?" said Ellen. "And do you think in a week there'll

be a man who doesn't know the place?" She cupped the cooling egg in her hands and laughed. "Just a little time," she said, peeking in at it. "That's all we need."

Finn thought of the short man again. When that man had said a map was needed Finn had known he was right. And now Ellen made it seem not necessary at all. He was relieved that he'd not made a stupid mistake yet displeased that he'd been so easily convinced that he had. He'd thrown the last two or three dozen leaflets in a barrel and could not now retrieve them.

"I've got to find a crew for the building of this bath," he said. "If they won't sign up I'll snatch one or two from the saloon."

Finn left again quickly so Ellen walked to the tent flap and watched him go. Directly outside was the dirty back of another tent. To the left the path ran toward the beach, and to the right it wove itself further into the fabric of the town. Since it was warm outside and warmer in, Ellen decided to leave the flap open and pinned it back with a peg. In the back room both baths were ready, had been for an hour. Ellen sighed. She could clean the place again or check the long-drawn water or sit low behind the high counter and wait. The sight of foolish Finn made her remember Ireland again, the silly strengths and weaknesses of its people. With Finn as a reminder would she ever forget? It was strange but when she thought of Ireland she almost never thought of her mother or her sisters. It was always her father or grandmother who bothered her peace of mind.

Ellen sighed again and stepped across the room and sat a moment behind the counter. She took her cleaning rags and dusted more vigorously than she had that morning. She checked the chicken coops then smiled and moved the marble egg in under another barren bird. It was such a simple trick. She slid another warm egg into the box. Still, it was impossible to believe that she might double her yield.

———

Finn found Phil standing in front of the notices, looking over the lists of construction jobs. He walked up behind him and pointed, over Phil's shoulder, at the lonely name of Finn Wallace at the top of one of the lists.

"Sign here and you'll not regret it," he said.

Phil turned around slowly.

"I'll work just a few weeks. Until winter comes."

"Work with me," said Finn.

"How are the women?" asked Phil. "I have messages for them from the reverend."

"What we'll be doing is building Ellen's bath. She got the idea from the one she saw in your village."

Phil nodded and Finn smiled. "Will you have a drink then? To liquefy the working relationship, so to speak."

Finn pulled the tent flap back at the entrance to the Gold Belt but Phil hesitated before bending through. "I'm not sure they want me here," he said quietly.

The owner called out in a friendly way, waving Finn over, but indeed giving Phil a long and hollow look. He moved like a janitor, pushing an old undershirt along the counter top of his bar. The only other customer in the place was the short man from the river bank.

"You've been making yourself scarce, have you not, Finn? What'll it be?"

Finn introduced Phil. He ordered beer and watched the owner watching Phil's face as the foam from the drink clung to his lips and ran down his olive chin. The short man stood near them drinking whiskey from a shot glass. He briefly looked in their direction but it was obvious to Finn that the man had forgotten him, had forgotten entirely their conversation at the beach. The man was dressed neatly, in clean clothes, and the hands that came out of his plaid jacket sleeves were hairless and delicate compared to his thick body. Finn wanted to tell the man they had met before and ask him to join them, but he was sure the man would refuse. There was something in the way

he stood that made him unapproachable. Just the presence of
the man made Finn want to watch himself, to be careful of the
way he spoke to Phil and to the owner. He was aware of a desire
to make a good impression on this man, a feeling that was rare
in Finn's experience. He felt inferior.

The owner, rags moving, told Finn how unusual it was to
have an Indian standing against the Spanish bar. "They come
from far and wide," he said, "but rarely do we get them from
so near. Does your friend speak English? If he does I'll say he's
the first I've met who's able." The owner turned slightly and
faced Phil. "Go ahead," he said, "say something, Bub. I'm
always looking for good conversation."

The owner was smiling, but Phil felt angry and Finn's attention was split, half of it on the small man, who seemed not to
notice them at all. "He speaks English," Finn said, finally focusing. "You don't ask the Swedes and the Frenchmen for a
sample of what they can say, do you? Why ask him?"

The small man still faced forward, but spoke, catching Finn's
eye in the moving mirror. "Europeans are famous for their
facility with language," he said. "Alaskan Indians don't share
that ability, so your man becomes a curiosity. Like a parrot
among birds."

"Right," said the owner. "If the man speaks English, let's
hear it. We could ask him questions about his people. Clear up
some of the misconceptions."

The man from the beach turned half-circle and faced them
now, so Phil pushed his hands deep into his coat pockets and
came up with some cash to lay on the lovely bar. He turned
and stepped across the sawdust and out into the street without
looking back.

"What a way to treat a man," Finn said, looking hard at the
happy owner. He wanted to run after Phil, but he had a full
beer in his hand. The small man drank the remainder of his
whiskey and left before Finn did, and Finn thought maybe he

would say something to Phil, maybe apologize, maybe pat Phil on the back as he passed. When Finn left, the owner was dusting again. He found Phil standing sideways along one of the paths. They could both see the small man walking between two of the tents, heading back toward the beach.

————

Finn and Phil sat up to their necks in hot water, in the back room of Ellen's bath. Henriette brought towels and walked through the room carefully, not looking at either of the men. As soon as Ellen saw Phil she included him on her list of those who'd be allowed free baths, but he was absolutely the last. He and Finn would begin construction in the morning. They spoke over the cloth walls between the tubs of just how they would go about their work. Already they had enough lumber for the frame and knew where they could get more, but the price was high. Ellen would have to pay right now for the wood, though the payment due the two laborers could be made any time. They spoke between the baths, in and out of the two rooms of the establishment: "And upstairs will be the sleeping quarters," Ellen told them. "Four rooms. One for Henriette and one for myself and two that we could let or that either of you could use."

"I'll be building a house up around my own tent when this is finished," Finn said, splashing.

Ellen lit a large fire in the front-room stove and they cooked fish, a salmon brought by Phil and given to Ellen and Henriette as a gift from the reverend. The two men dried themselves briskly in the hot bathroom, then dressed in warm clean clothing. The smell of salt salmon reached them. They'd bought a cot earlier and taken it to Finn's tent for Phil to sleep on. They would be roommates until the project was finished and Phil returned to the village. It was nearly midnight by the time they began the meal, by the time the sun finally finished disappearing over the rim of the earth. All four of them caught the festive mood that they remembered sharing at the village. They wanted it to continue. Ellen relinquished the last remnants of her first impressions of Finn, felt them slipping away like fishing line into the water. Henriette felt herself opening, blooming into full membership in the group. And Phil thought the three the most likable of the outsiders he'd met, excluding the reverend, and he was willing to live for a while as they did, to accept them as they were and to take what the city brought him. They laughed and stripped the salmon, eating everything. They held up the fine-boned skeleton and looked at each other through it. Finn called it a comb and pretended to run it through his hair.

"Don't laugh," said Phil. "That is how such things are discovered."

"Invented," said Finn. "The comb was invented, not discovered."

Phil leaned forward. "That is a good example of the extravagance of your language," he told him. "You attach two words to the same concept thus making understanding difficult. Invention. Discovery. What's the difference?"

Finn, full of the warmth of the front-room fire, held the salmon bones in front of him, playing them like a harmonica. He followed the line that connected the words "invention" and "discovery" in his mind but could make nothing of them. He thought about the short man again, thought of him as inventing gold, then knew, suddenly, where he had seen the man before. He pictured those delicate hands stuck like flesh bumpers among the tears of that chandelier. He was Dr. Kingman, the man who, indeed, had invented gold in Alaska, had made the first big discovery. He had charted the course of the lives of all these men and of Finn and Ellen and Henriette. Only Phil was his equal, though Finn hadn't known it that afternoon in the bar. Finn saw the future tying him, tying his life, irreversibly to that of Dr. Kingman. Like invention and discovery they were on opposite ends of the same thread, not one without the other but both, like the two sides of the same gold coin.

———

Fujino couldn't sleep and was too excited to walk the hills. He had packed and repacked the finely webbed snowflakes, laying fine Japanese paper between them, trying not to let them crack or to let sections chip away from the patterns that had been formed. He was going to town, leaving in the morning. He would stake their claim and would see the varied faces of other human beings. He was hired as a translator, he often told himself, but hadn't spoken a word of English since his arrival. Fujino felt himself growing strong from the work, and as the weeks passed he realized that his body had adjusted itself, that he was equal to it. At the end of the day he was ready for rest and at the end of the night he was rested for work. Not like Kaneda. The old man needed him and there had been a subtle shift in the kinds of work they did. Fujino was working more, the old man less. Still the old man had a better eye for gold and better patience for scanning the muddy bottom of the sluice. Without him, Fujino knew, he would not have made a strike at all.

Often in the evening after dinner and directly after relating to Fujino some new aspect of Japanese history, the old man succumbed to such heavy sleep that nothing would wake him. Fujino sometimes sang then, from deep in his lungs, but the ashen face of Kaneda, his future father-in-law, would not move; his muscles were in total repose, skin hanging from his facial bones like chicken fat.

This night, though, even the old man stayed awake in speculation as to what the changes might be in the new city of Nome. When they arrived Nome was only tents, and lumber piled like collapsed houses. What would have happened in all this time? They could imagine streets that ran smooth and parallel. It was something, Kaneda had said, to be in on the building of a city. They talked and what they imagined constructed on the brutal shore was a small Tokyo. Each in his imagination had raked the tents and the milling men from the beach just as one might rake an area in preparation for the landscaping of a garden.

The two men talked to each other as if sharing the same vision. They got great satisfaction from what they thought had become of the city. Kaneda showed no sign of going to bed, and though the sake had been gone for weeks they allowed themselves the drunkenness of reflection.

Fujino would leave in the morning, carrying the golden snowflakes and the claim papers. He would take the mule and try to make the journey quickly. While he was gone, it was decided, Kaneda would also rest. He would keep the mine in operation, but would be satisfied, not with half, but with only a third of the gold per day that they had been accustomed to. Fujino was not to hurry, and was not to brag about the claim or show his purse unnecessarily around the new buildings of the town. It was very exciting. Kaneda really wished he could be going too, or that he might be the one to go since only one could.

At the height of their excitement, when conjecture had grown and they were happy, Fujino mentioned Kaneda's daughter. It was a mistake, he knew, but he did not run after his words with apologies or quick changes of subject. "More than anyone else I miss your daughter," he said, and they both remained quiet. It was not for Fujino to speak now. He would wait. Such a thing was unheard of, but surely Kaneda had recognized the unexpectedness of it, the way it escaped as from a locked cell. Fujino would not look at the old man. They sat like two Buddhas, teacher and student. He could expect nearly anything: a burst of anger, a laugh. The old man pushed another piece of bark onto the fire and began to speak.

"Our nation of Japan is in reality one family," he said. "Perhaps I am involved with its history for the same reason that another man might be interested in retracing his family tree."

Fujino listened sitting up, head bowed deeply toward the fire.

"I wish my branch of the family tree to grow well and I wish my grandchildren to bear my name and understand life precisely as I do."

The old man stopped again but Fujino did not look up. What was he saying? What did it mean? There was nothing but silence again. Ah history! Kaneda had been thinking of Japan as a family and had remembered several events in the family history that Fujino still had not been told. Tonight he would tell about events he himself could half remember. As a young man, for example, he saw with his own eyes the black ships of the American fleet as they entered the port of Shimoda. He would not speak of his daughter again so Fujino relaxed and began to remember his upcoming journey. He still sat stiffly before the fire, but he thought of Nome. He listened to the old man's melody, a slow introduction, then a detailed description of the large-boned face of Commodore Perry.

———

Finn and Phil bought heavy canvas aprons and filled their pockets with long nails. They dug a square trench and worked for twenty hours mixing concrete and pouring the bath's foundation. Finn insisted that it all had to be done at once, and that if they watched their starting time they'd be able to do the entire job during daylight hours. They had enough wood for the frame and had a promise of more wood, a promise that they would not have to stop for lack of supplies. Above the swirl of tents, here and there, other such frames were rising. Occasionally they saw an entire finished building side, blond boards reflected in the sun.

Phil knew the ground and said that poles should be hammered into it, the tops of them surfacing and sticking like earth fingers, just into the hardening cement. That was what they had done with the reverend's house. It would keep the structure in place for several seasons, perhaps longer. They were going to put the building up around Ellen's tent; there was no other way. Later they would unfold the canvas, tuck it out through the door and then complete the interior. The ground floor of the building would have a high ceiling, but the upstairs would be small, enough space for a man to stand up, but no more. The idea of a bath had caught on, it seemed. Ellen told them that they were getting twenty customers a day, enough to pay for supplies and to pay Henriette and give Finn and Phil some of what they were owed as well, as a show of good faith.

"We know your good faith without having it displayed in coin," Finn said, but he took the money anyway, and used it to buy wool shirts. Winter was sliding down off the top of the world, creeping up to the edges of the farthest gold fields, and they were cold at night.

The frame of Ellen's bath went up in a day. The two men worked with nails in their mouths, occasionally shouting at each other unintelligibly. Others worked in other parts of the city, and when Phil or Finn looked away for a moment they would sometimes wave at the others, nails falling from their lips and sticking in the ground like icicles. This was industry: the city of Nome inching upward, the men working long days without complaint. And Ellen's bath, empty most of the day, was crowded at night. Lines of men stood with towels over their arms. Business was booming. Ellen and Henriette often worked well past midnight, then took baths themselves, splashing and talking over the curtain at two or three in the morning.

Finn and Phil had been working for three days when John Hummel, the man with scurvy, the first man to bathe in Ellen's bath, invented beach gold. He had been a loner all his time in

Nome, a man who stooped when he spoke to others and covered his bloody smile with his hands. He spit constantly, rubbing his small mouth along the long sleeve of his shirt to dry his disease away. He used a walking stick and when he stood in one place he dug it into the ground. Hummel often roamed the beach, where the stick moved more easily, where the liquid that ran from his mouth was quickly absorbed by the easy sand. This day he noticed five gold nuggets standing like little sentries around the end of his stick, so he picked them up and then sat down on the ground for an hour of hard thought. This was not fool's gold and he was no fool.

Hummel cupped his hands and scooped the sand and dug deep. He found a nugget here and there and setting them with the others formed the letter H on the ground next to him. When he looked back toward the city he could see Finn and Phil and other builders high on their perches like birds with hammers. He scooted along the ground, digging, making a trough that moved him toward the water line. Hummel found most of his nuggets within twelve inches of the surface and discovered that the vein was perhaps three feet wide and moved up from the water in an almost perfectly straight line. When he moved his digging position, he took with him the nuggets he'd found and re-formed the H shape until it became too large and began to worry him. He changed his strategy, spelling his entire name in smaller letters four inches high. And by the end of the day he had spelled not only his full name but the names of his mother and two of his sisters, and in capitals, the name of the new state of Idaho, where he was born. He plunged the nuggets deep into his pockets and hunched over them when he walked. What was he to do? He walked like a crab past the assayer's office a dozen times that evening, knowing that to sell the nuggets would mean revealing his find and sending the whole town to the beach, like swimmers. He was no fool. This was not fool's gold.

John Hummel waited until the line diminished before paying

his two dollars and entering Ellen's bath. He usually came at the end of the evening, and Henriette hated the sight of him, for it meant that she would have to spend extra time scrubbing at the heavy sides of whichever tub he used. She imagined that spittle of his everywhere, and would not let the slightest part of her skin touch the tub. Here was a man who leaked and she could not abide him.

Tonight Hummel slipped into the back room quickly and took off his sandy clothes. He had purchased a canvas sack, so, naked and shivering, he quickly transferred all the nuggets to it and took them into the tub with him. His white chest heaved at the sight of the sack of gold. He climbed into the hot water and lowered himself, holding the sack before him like a fig leaf. He felt the weight of it against his crotch and leaned his head back and let the red spittle stain his chin. What did he care? He was rich. He opened the sack under the water and looked through the steam at it and plunged his hands into it, moving the nuggets about with his fingers. He washed his gold with soap. He washed his body, extending long fingers into his mouth and scrubbing up and around his peach-colored gums.

Hummel had only his sandy clothes, so he slapped them against the side of the tub before he could bring himself to crawl back into them again. He was a rich man and these were the clothes of a beggar. Already he felt it. He let the sack of gold lose the water through its seams and then looked again and was content that the color was now purer than it had been on the beach. He was a rich man but would have to tell some-one if he wanted to exchange the gold for money. He would have to ask someone to exchange it for him if he expected to keep his secret, and he decided that he would ask Ellen. She had always been kind to him, had never avoided his eyes while staring at his drooling mouth like the others always did. He waited until he heard Henriette leave the tent, until he thought that Ellen would be alone, then dressed and clean he took his sack of gold through the curtains and laid it on the counter before her.

————

Fujino arrived in the dim town at midnight, the mule walking beside him like an equal. For the last six hours it had been necessary to save the mule's energy so it would not tire and fall. He did not recognize any of the tents or half-buildings and didn't know where he would sleep. He thought of Kaneda at their camp, telling himself stories. Now, though he was in the city, the place he'd thought of each day since his arrival at the creek, he was exhausted and wanted only to sleep. It would be better to examine what had happened to the place in the freshness of morning. Presently he came upon the iron beds of a new hotel piled high in the street. A tent stood beside them and at its flap was a man with a cigar box in his hands.

"Welcome, weary traveler," said the man.

"Is this a hotel?"

"It is a place to sleep."

Fujino handed the man large coins and, taking the pack from his mule, entered the dark tent. There were many sleepers lying about on the ground, on the mattresses that would soon be used on the gleaming beds. The man dropped the coins into his box and tied the tired mule to a post outside. He pointed toward a stack of brown blankets on the table.

"Checkout time is eight-thirty," he said.

————

Ellen looked at John Hummel's gold and told him to go to the assayer's office. "I've no proper place to keep it," she said. "Many men would come in here for that."

Hummel shuffled for a moment and then, like a bat, folded his body around the gold and went directly out. He stood on the bent path before he entered the assayer's office. Once inside he watched as the assayer added weight to the side of the scale opposite his sack. The man was tired and not aware that Hummel wasn't just in from the mines. A guard sat, propped against the wall, on a stool next to him.

"That's good clean gold. Twelve hundred," said the assayer.

"Beg your pardon?"

"Twelve hundred dollars. Do you want it on account or in cash?"

"Cash. Twelve hundred dollars . . . ?"

The assayer opened a heavy safe and placed the gold on the bottom shelf. He took bank notes and coins and placed the correct amount on the counter before Hummel. "There you are, sir. Looks like you're on your way."

Hummel scooped and shoved the money into the sack that had contained his gold. He turned to leave but turned again.

"I found it on the beach," he said, standing straight. "I want to stake a claim."

The assayer looked up from his books and the guard sat down on all four legs of his stool.

"The beach?"

"I want to stake a claim. Right now."

The assayer took a handful of claim maps from under the table and showed Hummel what he had to do to register his claim.

"This brown space is Nome," he said, "and you'll be able to recognize all the rivers and streams and the coastline here. You mark in red the site of your claim and give me a dollar and then we both sign here at the bottom."

Hummel turned the map around on the table, looking until the rivers and the coastline came clear to him. He took up a pencil and drew heavy lines all along the beach directly in front of the city. He would claim from the Snake to the Nome, the

entire beach; that was safe. He turned the paper back and let
the assayer see what he had done. His dollar rang slightly on
the hardwood counter.

"That's our beach," the man informed him.

"That's my claim."

"But it's not possible to make a claim inside the boundaries
of the town."

The guard stood and walked in small circles. He had a shot-
gun slung across his arm and he swung his toe back and forth
like a schoolboy.

"That's my claim," Hummel said again, hoping.

"I'm sorry . . . You found this gold on our beach?"

Hummel pulled the dollar back toward him, letting it fall into
the open mouth of his canvas bag. He looked at the assayer and
at the guard.

"It's mine gold," he said, turning. "This is really mine gold."
He hung the money bag around his neck and went directly to
the beach again. It was still gray midnight and he was able to
find the spot where he'd found the nuggets earlier. The tide
was considerably lower now so he dug twenty feet farther, turning the handle of his walking stick in the drying sand, looking
again for the gold in the full darkness of the early night.

By daybreak the news had spread. The story of Hummel's find
had closed the entire town. Twelve hundred dollars, some said
more, and he'd tried to claim the entire beach as his own. Those
who didn't know Hummel remembered him when others mentioned the man with the stooped walk and the bleeding mouth,
and they laughed.

Fujino heard about the strike in the New York Kitchen and
again at the assayer's office. He'd exchanged his gold for much

more than twelve hundred dollars and left it in the assayer's safe. He asked around town for Ellen and Henriette and was told about the bath and by mid-morning had made his way there and pushed open the canvas flap, his arms loaded with gifts.

"Hello," he said. "I am Fujino."

The flap that led to the back bathroom was pinned open. Ellen alone remained; the rest had gone to the beach, following the news and the people, and she was pouring cold water into the blackened pots on the fire.

"Come in," she yelled, not hearing who it was.

When she emerged from the back room Fujino bowed and extended the gifts toward her.

"My lord, Mr. Fujino. Does news spread that fast then?"

"I am so glad to see you."

Ellen shook his hand in both of hers. Though the young man had been on the trail and had slept in a public tent, he was fresh-looking and smiling broadly. He'd changed into clean clothing and had wet his hair, combing it down flat across his head.

Ellen said, "Are you changing claims then? Do you know about the beach?"

"I have turned in our profits. We are doing very well. Mr. Kaneda sends his warmest regards."

"He is not with you?"

"He will work the claim slowly until my return. Where is Miss Henriette?"

"You've *not* heard about the beach gold, have you? They all went down to Finn's tent to dig. It seems he's located very near the main lode."

While they were talking Phil came in, so Ellen introduced them. The two men looked at each other for a long moment, bowing rather than shaking hands.

Phil told Ellen that the numbers of people on the beach were growing and that Finn was having a hard time protecting even that portion of sand that his tent sat upon.

"Most of the town is there with shovels," he said. "All construction has stopped."

"What about the bath?" she asked.

"Finn thinks we can make money. He thinks we all can but he wants us to work together. Equal shares."

"But the bath."

"What is important is to complete the building before winter. We have decided that I will remain here working alone and that you and Finn and Henriette will work the ground of the beach. We have found gold under his tent already."

Ellen looked at Phil and at Fujino, who was still smiling.

"I'm supposed to close the bath?" she asked.

"There will be few customers while this strike is on."

Ellen turned to Fujino and asked him if he'd like to join her in a walk to the beach, then she put on old clothes in the back, leaving Phil and Fujino alone in the front room. Phil was older than the young Japanese, and thinner. He thought Fujino looked like an Eskimo, even like particular Eskimos he had known. Ellen had told him about the Japanese friends they'd made on the ship and he tried now to think just exactly where Japan was. He thought of maps he had seen in books and he remembered hearing someone say "the islands of Japan," so this must be an islander.

Fujino said, "Excuse me, but I am surprised that you look like my partner, Mr. Kaneda. I believe you have Japanese blood."

"Japan is a long way from Alaska?"

Fujino nodded. "It takes weeks by boat."

Ellen came out of the back wearing trousers. "I'll find them at Finn's tent?" she asked Phil, and when he told her yes she and Fujino went outside and took the left path, walking slowly on moss and sand. At the beach the tide was high, the ocean slapped the wounded land, and hundreds of people were digging. Trenches were already so deep that only the heads and shoulders of the diggers showed above ground. Men dug and

women carried buckets of water from the sea, pouring it over
the red and the black sand and shaking loose the gold. Fights
broke out. People poked sticks into the earth at four corners of
the lot they were staking, then patrolled the edges of their land
with clubs. Even from the top of the beach it was difficult reaching Finn's tent. People watched them suspiciously until they
had passed.

One man walked out chest deep into the churning sea and
was attempting to set stakes down through the water. He leaned
on the thin poles he carried and pushed hard, but though they
would stick for an instant, the sea quickly turned them sideways
and floated them away, erasing his weak boundaries, and he
was frantic. Soon the tide would turn, would creep out, and he
wanted the land ready for shoveling when it did. Fujino watched
with fascination. The man will surely drown, he thought. He
remembered Kaneda and the peaceful proficiency of the job
they were doing. This man's mouth and eyes filled with salt-
water and his partner threw him a hammer, screaming at him
from the beach when the hammer dropped, slid under the blanket of the sea and was gone.

Fujino looked at Ellen. Finn's tent had never seemed so far
to her. People she knew, customers from the bath, stared blankly.
Occasionally, from the beach, the dim sun caught the sand at a
proper angle, and the metal yellow flashed in their eyes. It
hadn't the delicacy of the snowflakes Fujino and Kaneda had
found, but it had the color, and when the finders washed the
gold it glowed like the sun itself, but darkly. People here were
as sharks, had taken some portion of the beach in their mouths
and were shaking it violently, ripping it from the earth like
flesh. It was not yet noon but the beach was churning. And the
beginning of winter was only days away.

Finn's tent was in a lucky position and, like the others, Finn
and Henriette had used the four corners of it as the four mark-
ers of their claim. They were digging inside the tent. The stove

was turned over and pushed aside and the cots had been ripped apart, the wood used for stakes, for extending the claim as far as they could toward the water. The canvas walls were rolled up on all sides. So far they had found only three sizable nuggets but they'd seen streaks of gold in the sand and were building a sluice. They looked up and saw Ellen, and when they saw Fujino they stopped and came over. All around them others bent their backs, pushing the sand around. The town had emptied, the beach was full. Out along the horizon the ocean moved into a slight froth. The water was getting colder each week and there were no ships or visible smoke stacks.

———

"Quicksilver is the only proper way to get at the gold." Fujino spoke and the others listened. He told them how he and Kaneda had used mercury to extract even the finest powder, losing nothing. A rivulet six inches wide wedged through the sand at the edge of the tract they'd staked. Fujino took off his coat and after digging for a moment announced that he could increase the flow, that the rivulet might indeed be a perfect enough natural sluice to suit their needs. He told them they should buy a magnet, a large jar of quicksilver, copper for the bottom of the rocker, and that they could use Finn's old stove for the fire. He could see that Finn hadn't mined before and that if they were going to make the project work they would need to do things right from the beginning. All around them frenzied townsmen dug. Fujino spoke quietly, but the three of them knew that what he said was what they had to do. Even Ellen was convinced without a word that the proper thing was to close the bath and work here, and before an hour had passed she and Henriette had started back toward the eye of the city to buy the supplies. It was decided that each of them would get an equal share and that Fujino, if he stayed, would become a full partner. They assured him that a week of his time was all they would need. He told them about Kaneda and said he had to return with supplies, that the old man believed the entire trip would take only a few days, but Finn asked him to imagine Kaneda's reaction if he returned with twice the amount of money expected. "Twelve hundred dollars," said Finn. "In an afternoon and using a stick."

Fujino knew that if he went back with more than Kaneda expected the old man would be surprised and happy. He'd be able to make up for having mentioned the old man's daughter the evening before he left and Kaneda would surely praise his industry, would realize finally and forever that Fujino was no ordinary Japanese, that he was one of a few, not afraid to reach for a chance but still embodying those qualities that all Japanese cherish. And it really did seem to be a good strike. A chance to practice his English as well. He turned back toward Finn and said that he would stay until they were set up but that he must return well before winter. It was really too good to be true. Work one mine and get the profits from two. He said yes and smiled and bowed and said yes, yes, until they were both grinning and shaking hands.

By the time things were settled Ellen and Henriette had returned with the supplies. There was no more copper plating, however, in the whole town. They brought food and extra clothing and they brought a chicken, squawking and turning its head around. They had seen Phil and told him everything and Ellen had pegged the front of the bath shut and left a note that said only, "Gone for gold." Fujino told them stories while they dug of how the gold when it was extracted from the sand would form a fine comb, how, like a snowflake, it would appear different each time. Ellen had remembered him when she was back at the bath and had also brought blankets, taking the walls from between the baths. They carried everything across two boards,

Henriette at the front, Ellen behind. When they arrived Henriette said, "This is the life."

It was decided that Fujino and Finn and Phil would sleep here, that the women would go back to the bath. They could hear shouts from claims along the beach and occasionally someone would leave, holding a sack to his belly and looking about. They boxed a portion of the rivulet, loaded it with sand and gold, and watched as the water pushed the lighter materials away. Henriette was in charge of the magnet, a horseshoe, which she held in both hands and moved over the mixture, laughing. The black sand jumped to her magnet like magic, and she flung it away happily. Ellen started the round stove, first trying to scrape off some of the fish and beef that was burnt to its top. She took Finn's old frypan and gave it to Fujino, who showed them what to do. He put bits of the red sand in the pan then poured a portion of the quicksilver over it. He rocked the pan gently, letting the gold dust settle in the heavy silver. He took the top of the frypan, the lid, punched a hole in it, then took a piece of rubber hosing, attached it to the hole in the lid, and poked the other end into an old whiskey bottle, ready to be sealed. He set the pan on the hot stove and they all stood close to watch. Presently, through the clear glass of the bottle, they saw the volatile mercury settle, falling out of the invisible air and re-forming, the same silver glob they had placed in the frypan. Fujino removed the frypan lid and showed them the gold sitting in a bowl of burnt sand, connected thinly like the perfect web of a spider.

"A golden snowflake!" cried Henriette. "It's marvelous."

Fujino stood like a proud father. He held his palm open and pointed with his entire hand. He smiled.

"We had dozens and dozens of these," he said. "They fit together, one on top of the others."

Ellen asked if it was all right to pick it up so Fujino hooked it with a small stick and handed it to her.

"Hold it over paper. Don't let parts of it fall."

Ellen held the webbing gingerly. She cradled it. She crouched on the sand and held her knees together so that any falling particles would land in her lap. It was pure gold. She looked up at Finn, beaming. Pure gold and the shape of a snowflake! Finn stepped forward with a clean box and offered it. "We'd best get started," he said softly, "if we want to make this venture worthwhile."

They worked the rest of the day, until evening, until the sun no longer kept the region gray. Now there was real night, the first any of them had seen since arriving in Nome. Other people struck lanterns and swung them over the holes in which they worked. All along the beach it was so. Lights and voices, cries spinning through the dark like bats. There were more than a thousand people now, working and calling themselves prospectors. Those on one claim did not speak to those on another. The bars of Nome, the Gold Belt and the others, were closed and pegged like Ellen's bath. The lights of the city moved to the beach, some of them liquid and seeming to come from the depths of the sea itself. Down toward the Snake, toward the tight tents of the army camp, more voices could be heard. The soldiers patrolling the area had been forced to ride their mules and horses knee deep in the water to bypass the busy prospectors. The soldiers made Finn remember Dr. Kingman and smile. Miners working close to the city had heard of the beach strike and were coming down, abandoning the mines. Work was stopping everywhere.

At the top of the beach, above Finn's tent, a group of men sat drinking from bottles, talking of beach gold. They were near Finn and Fujino so the two sat back, eating the food that Ellen had brought, and listened, waiting. Phil would be there soon as well.

One of the drinkers said, "It is replenished. We need only to rest at high tide then dig again at low. The gold is replenished by the sea. We'll be rich men. We can work here forever and not worry about others getting the best spots."

Fujino looked toward Finn and remembered the talks on mining that Kaneda had given him when he wasn't talking history. Surely these men didn't believe what they said. In truth there must be a very limited supply. The sea doesn't carry gold to the shore. Quite the opposite. He thought of the beach prospectors as fools then and knew quickly that he had made a mistake, that he should be getting supplies and riding back toward the real claim, the one he and Kaneda had worked so hard. The old man would be sleeping now, resting so that he could get at least a small amount of gold out of the earth while Fujino was gone. This was supposed to be a time of rest for both of them, yet Fujino was more tired than he had ever been at their claim. And he had promised a week of his time to these others. They were his shipmates, but did he owe them a week? He had seen the beach strike and knew now that it was no better than theirs. Twelve hundred dollars a day is what had convinced him. But that would not be equaled again. The ocean battered the gold into a powder finer even than that of their creek. To get a thousand snowflakes here would take longer than fifteen hundred there and his share would be only one-fifth of that. And now he was obligated, for he had promised Finn. But what about the old man? Hadn't he promised him also, that he would be back, that he would bring supplies and whiskey and be back soon? He wondered if Kaneda would be worried and he knew he had placed the future of the old man's daughter in great jeopardy.

When Phil finally arrived at the site the other two were asleep. He brought a bottle of whiskey and several more blankets. It was cold and cloudless. He draped Finn and the young Japanese with extra covers then sat by himself looking at the sky. Ellen and Henriette had brought several snowflakes back to show him and to hide in the bath for safekeeping. The gold had been heavier than it looked. It was the first pure gold he had ever seen. It wouldn't look bad, he thought, hanging from the necks of his wife and sisters. He would take his share as it was; it would be much more interesting that way. There was beauty in the way it formed and in its weight and color. Earlier, when he was a boy, he had found nuggets in the streams and had valued them too, for their heft and shine. But this, what he had seen today, was far superior. It was man-made and yet it was not. It was made by man and by nature. Made by man but not controlled by him.

Phil was content. He would build the bath during the day and would not only be paid for his labor but would receive gold as well. How could he do better? He would return to the village with gifts more unusual than anyone in his family could imagine and he would return to a village where the lean-tos had already been lowered, the preparations for winter already done. Phil looked at the lights of the beach. Men were peering into the dark sand, holding their long-wicked lanterns high. How foolish when they could wait until daylight. The tide was coming in again. For a while it would be in at night, then out during the better part of the day. Phil closed his eyes and listened to the waves. He could feel the blood rushing through his veins and hear it in his ears. The tide and his blood pounded rhythmically for a while inside and out. Five hours' sleep would be enough, he thought. The bath will be finished; everything will work out well.

———

For eight more days the beach was turned and gnarled, its corpse, goldless and not to be touched again, piled ten feet high. There had been a run on quicksilver; Finn and Fujino had only the large flask purchased by Ellen on that first day. They had to make it last, to use it again and again and again. They learned to seal the bottle carefully, to taste even a little of it in the unnatural air.

Fujino was still with them but was leaving in the morning. He'd stayed too long and would have trouble getting back. Three days before he'd gotten the money from the assayer, and kept it with him now always. He had readied the mule and had two dozen bottles of whiskey in boxes, ready to be loaded on the mule's back. They'd taken one hundred and nineteen golden snowflakes from the beach in the time they'd been working. Just over two thousand dollars. They'd already divided it among them so that Fujino would have the extra gold to give to Kaneda, but he was unhappy with himself and felt a growing dislike for the others. They had talked him into staying and now they took it for granted that he was in no hurry to get back. None of them mentioned Kaneda by name. Even Ellen had taken to calling him the old man. "Won't the old man be proud," she'd said a dozen times.

The old man working at one-third his normal speed would realize that it would have been better if Fujino had come directly back. Four hundred extra dollars was not enough to make up for the lost time. He had made a serious mistake. Anyway, at last, tomorrow it would be over and he would make up for it by working extra hard even though he'd had no rest during his time in Nome. Fujino checked his supplies again. He could no longer feel Kaneda's daughter close to him.

During the week Phil had taken to bringing lunch from the bath and spreading it before the prospectors at exactly midday. There were always eggs, and he usually had a smoked or roasted salmon as well. The outside of the bath was finished, each room had a window, and now he was working on the interior, building permanent shelves for the chickens and for the rows of canned goods that Ellen would sell. Phil too would go home soon, but he had no uneasy feelings. They would be glad to see him and he would be glad. Winter, he knew, could come at any moment.

Finn and Fujino had finished their lunch and were waiting

for the two women to return from the bath when they noticed for the first time the reappearance of John Hummel on the beach. He was carrying his walking stick, but he bore it over his shoulder, like a rifle, like the rifles of the army sentries that faced the beach from the other side of the Snake. The soldiers had become familiar in Nome. Many of them dug at the beach furiously during their off hours, and some sneaked across the river using night lanterns and got back tired and sandy before reveille. Hummel took his way of walking from them. He marched up and down the water line, holding his stooped shoulders back and not talking to anyone. His gums bled through his pursed lips, occasionally forcing them open, forcing him to spit.

By the time Ellen and Henriette arrived Hummel had tied his bag of money around his neck tightly and had written "$1200.00" on the outside of the canvas and was always careful to have the writing pointing out. He marched that way most of the afternoon and then at exactly five o'clock he stopped and turned toward the town. In front of him the beach looked ruined. He held his head high and pointed to the numbers on the sack around his neck.

He said, "The way I see it I've been robbed."

Even before he started to speak, many of those near him stopped work and turned to listen. Finn and Fujino and Ellen took a few steps down toward the water. There was no breeze at all, but the waves pounded behind him and it was difficult to hear. Hummel swayed, the bag a ludicrous necktie. He seemed to hang out of the air as if from an invisible gallows, his neck bent up toward the listeners, his face down.

"The way I see it I've been robbed." He raised a stiff arm pointing at everyone, swinging his hand across the horizon. "Claim jumpers is all I see here." He bent the arm at the elbow and pointed with his finger at the numbers on the canvas bag again.

"Twelve hundred dollars. There ought to be at least two more zeros. The way I see it, everyone here owes me."

Henriette thought it was like listening to a country preacher. She remembered the reverend and wondered how he would deliver a sermon. She could see him clearly but couldn't get the voice right. She had him speaking with the lilting vengeance of Hummel, but softly.

The prospectors were not able to get back to work while the man stood there. Everyone was quiet and Hummel, too, was silent for a long while before lowering the walking stick off his shoulder and pointing it at the group. He sighted down the rough wood at all the small targets. He swept across his horizon, raising his rifle up and down, trying to pass over everyone. Those who are left standing can go free, he thought.

In another moment Hummel shouldered his stick and marched off toward the Snake. One of the prospectors cheered, but none of the others did. Just one lone cheer. Afterwards there was silence everywhere. Even Phil, who had seen none of it, was bothered by the excessive loudness of his own hammer as he tapped away at the inside of Ellen's bath.

———

John Hummel was no fool. He knew mining and he knew the properties of quicksilver. Only the scurvy had kept him from making his name known in Alaska as one of the big strikers. Never mind, now his name was known. They all knew him as the man whose claim was jumped and who'd done nothing about it. He would show them, and he'd begin with Ellen, the woman who sent him to the assayer's office in the first place.

Hummel stood outside Finn's tent and waited until all he could hear was the sounds of sleep. Maybe she wouldn't be there, but these were her men and she'd feel the injury as much as they. Hummel turned back the flap and peered into the darkness. He crouched and waited for his eyes to adjust. The lantern was out, but there was a rim of orange coming from the round stove in the corner. He waited and in a few minutes could see the sleeping figure next to the stove. He could see the frypan used for making those golden snowflakes he had heard so much about, and he could see the jar of quicksilver.

Hummel moved, silent and sideways, across the room. He took long moments to get to the stove, longer to move the frypan up onto the hot top and to remove its lid. The piece of tubing was still attached to the top of the frypan and to the bottle of mercury. Slowly he undid the stopper from the bottle. It was heavy and half full of the shimmering silver substance. He held the bottle up and tipped it until it became light and empty. The quicksilver was in the pan, the pan was on the fire. He reached inside his shirt and removed a second bottle equal to the first and heavy as his heart. He poured it all in and then quickly replaced the frypan lid. The hose extended from the top of the frypan and twisted off the stove. The end of it was in Hummel's hand. He put it to his mouth until he tasted metal, and then he slid like a snake across the ground and pushed it through the bedclothes and up toward the head of the sleeper.

Hummel left the tent more quickly than he'd entered, and finding his stick in the sand, walked with it down to the edge of the water. The night was cold, it was the first time he had noticed that, and the money sack around his neck seemed lighter than usual. He turned west, toward the Snake, then left the beach near the top of the town. He too had a tent, but he had not been there in nearly a week. He expected it had been rummaged; people would be looking for his money. But when he turned back the flap and entered the tent it was cold and neat. Things were in order, just as he had left them. He'd often wanted people to see his tent; he knew they'd be surprised by it. They expected him to live like a pig because he bled like

one. Men were not so simple as some people believed them to
be.

When Hummel closed himself inside his tent he quickly located the can that he used as a spittoon. He never spit on the
floor here. He nearly always had to get up in the middle of
the night to empty the can, but he did it because he wanted the
room to be dry and clean. He sat on the bed and spit into
the can now and listened to the metallic sound of it hitting the
bottom. It reminded him of the taste in his mouth, the taste
he'd received from the end of that hose, the mercury that was
even now covering the head of that sleeping stranger. He spit
again and took a swallow of whiskey. He swung the sack around
his neck in order to rest his head upon it. It was not comfortable
having the cord always pressing into his neck but he was afraid
of thieves. He hooked his fingers on the cord and pulled until
it was loose enough for him to sleep. He woke dozens of times
to lean off his bed and spit into the can, and once to stumble
to the edge of the tent, open the flap and fling the red liquid
out onto the floor of the city. The sand, hardening every night,
didn't seem to absorb the spit like it used to. Rather it stayed
on top as if rejected, frozen into little red lakes.

———

Everyone spoke freely in Ellen's bath. They made plans to stop
work on the beach strike soon. Winter would arrive momentarily
and Phil told them what to expect: snow and wind and nearly
total darkness all the time. It was a season for waiting. It was
not like winter in other countries, he told them. He said,
"Though I have not been to other countries I am sure it is not
the same."

When Finn and Phil left the bath for the night they hurried
along the circular paths, for it was cold and they had no heavy

jackets. The bath building, finished and towering above the tents around it, shadowed them. It was the first building completed, the only one to have progressed during the rush on the beach. There were few stars and only a slice of moon, but they knew the way and once on the beach the work lanterns lit their path and they were able to see each other. Phil had a half-dozen golden snowflakes wrapped in a cloth and tucked under his shirt. They were to be gifts for his people. He even had one for the reverend from Ellen and Henriette.

Finn and Phil entered the tent and quickly wrapped themselves in their bedrolls before they noticed the metallic air. Its presence was overpowering. They smacked their lips and waited very still and quiet as if expecting to hear something. They had been gone more than three hours. Finn struck a match and lit a lantern. Phil was already standing.

"It's the quicksilver," said Finn. He lifted the lid off his frypan like a man expecting burnt breakfast.

When they pulled the blanket back off Fujino, he woke up and said something in Japanese. "*Sore wa nan da! Wakaranai! Wakaranai!*" His black eyebrows were silver now, with small drops of the re-formed mercury. His hair also had a beaded cap, and when he tried to speak again he began to cough and silver fell from his mouth. He did not try to rise.

"My God, he's tried to do himself in," said Finn. "Let's get him up to the bath."

Phil had already rolled up the side canvas of the tent to let the night wind sweep the place. It came in immediate and cold, taking what was loose and blowing it out the other side. Fujino's hands and feet were round with swelling, but when they raised him he was able to stand by himself. Phil held the lantern and Finn carried the man around the twisted paths of Nome and back toward the bath. Absurdly, though they had made the trip a hundred times, they got lost, once even entering a strange tent. Gamblers looked up at them, cards held close to their chests, stacks of gold coin leaning against dim lanterns. Fujino, his face sagging, pointed a finger at the men.

When finally they got to the bath the new doors were locked and sturdy. Phil shook the handle proudly for a second before banging on the door with both fists.

"Open," he yelled, and Finn added, "Ellen. In God's name. It's an emergency. Hurry!"

Through the crack in the door they could see a lantern dimly moving. Ellen turned the big key and swung the door open and stared at them. She wore a long white robe tied in the middle. Fujino, still wrapped in the brown blankets of the tent, fell toward her, Finn holding on to him in back.

"Is he drunk?" she asked.

"What's going on?" said Henriette, coming down the stairs from the bedroom.

"He's swallowed a gallon of quick. It's a wonder he's breath left to cough with."

Ellen's face dropped, her voice clouding. "Henriette, fill the bath then go look for a doctor. Make the water as hot as you can."

She turned back to the men. "You, Finn, get the man out of those clothes and throw them away. Hurry now."

The blanket dropped from around Fujino's shoulders. He stood nearly by himself, his eyes open and focusing on whoever stood in front of him. His mouth filled, saliva dripping from his lips. Finn took a knife and cut the shirt and undershirt off the man. He handed them to Phil, who carried them outside. Finn took Fujino's pants and wrapped him in a clean blanket.

Henriette told them when the water was ready and ran into the night, not knowing where she was going. Phil went with her. There was a doctor in Nome, they had heard, but they didn't know his name or where his tent might be. She would look, she said. She would not return until she found him.

Ellen and Finn took Fujino into the back bathroom. The walls had been freshly done and the whole room had the smell of newly-cut wood. They had not yet painted, and in places the new boards bled, the sap running down the walls. It was a pleasant smell.

The bath water was getting hot. Finn put his hand in, pulled it back quickly, then put it in again. It was hot but it would not burn, he decided. Ellen took the blanket and Finn lifted Fujino up and lowered him into the tub. It was difficult to bend Fujino's legs, but once inside he sat without making a sound, staring through the steam. Some of the quicksilver on his head and eyebrows slid lazily off him, disappearing when it entered the water.

Ellen got a bucket from the fire and, after testing it with her hand, poured it little by little down over Fujino's head. All the visible mercury washed away with it.

Finn said, "He's got a lot of the bloody stuff in his body. We needn't worry about what is on the outside."

Fujino's mouth was open and a black line appeared on his lower gum, running all the way along, just below his teeth. It made the gum look hard and bloodless. His lips too were darker than before and his hands, gripping the sides of the tub, were swollen and weakened.

They left Fujino in the tub for nearly an hour, then took him out and wrapped him in warm blankets and put him in one of the rooms upstairs. The walls up here bled like the ones below. The room had a cot in it, and a window and a door. They put a lit lantern on the floor beside the cot and left the door open so that they could hear any sounds he might make. It was such a pleasant new building that even going up and down the stairs gave them a feeling of clear satisfaction. They sat quietly and drank tea and looked up when Phil and Henriette came back alone, no doctor to be found. The weather had turned and Phil and Henriette warmed their hands on teacups. The four of them stood around the stove, then moved a few feet and stood in front of the new windows. Had it been daylight they might have been able to see the mounds of gnarled beach between the tents. But it was night and through the clean glass they could see only darkness.

"It's snowing," said Henriette. "It's begun to snow."

As she spoke smallish white flakes darted through the darkness, one or two of them landing on the outside ledge or melting against the window. A larger flake pressed its intricate design against the glass and then began to fade away. Darkness with flecks of white. Winter moved like a hand over the city, the flakes lacing together to form a blanket. On the beach the rivulet that they'd used turned slowly to ice and was covered with snow. The mountains of sand grew solid and immovable. No one would be going back to the beach again. The snow began to mount on the window, building from the bottom, its whiteness rising. From the sky the lights of the city disappeared, one by one, like dying fireflies. None of them thought of sleep. They moved from the window to the fire to the window. The snow sealed the eyes of the city, leaving it dark. Even after the sun had risen no one noticed. They might have stayed this way forever, the house quiet, winter falling. It was peaceful. They had no thoughts. The four of them turned toward each other when Fujino first began to scream. It was abrupt, an irritation. He screamed twice more before the first of them ran toward the stairs.

3

Glass windows, one to a wall; four figures, each with a face pressed to glass. The world outside swirled in white funnels, the ground rose. Winter had arrived, in one day, as fully as it would. The sand on the beach was immovable, the tools of the miners frozen to it, as much a part of the earth now as the gold. The tents puffed smoke into the air but the smoke lacked movement, seemed to freeze in its upward curve. And Finn's mule was dead. It stood stiff-legged and staring at the bath from the post where it had been tied. Finn had forgotten the mule, who would stand there now, perhaps collapsing only with the spring thaw, or, like a variation of the groundhog myth, awakening to its shadow and moving on.

Fujino survived to scream. He was cared for by the others in rotation. Finn, Phil, Henriette, one at a time climbed the stairs to see him. They looked in at the new door with its sap still running and listened to his complaints of itching and watched as he drew sharp fingernails across his thighs. His gums still held the dead color of lead in them and he talked. He screamed for Kaneda and for Kaneda's daughter. *"Kimie! Kimie!"* he said, using her given name bravely and for the first time.

Snow fell for three days and then stopped and turned concrete, a wave across the city. Doors would not open. The only way to leave the bath was through a window. The four stood in still positions until their muscles ached or they thought of Fujino. They stoked the fire or ate eggs and listened to the clucking chickens with equal disinterest, equally lost in thought. Phil imagined himself in heavy clothes, heading out the window and off toward his village. The storm had stopped so there was no reason for him to stay. He thought about offering to go to Kaneda to explain, but he did not. He pictured himself arriving at his winter village with hide strings around his neck, the golden snowflakes dangling. He would place one around the neck of each of his women, one atop the cool hut of his little sister, Nanoon. There would be movement in the village, and by now the ice of the bay would have holes in it for fishing. Phil had prepared everything for his return. He'd readied the supplies and the gifts and the money. By the time he got there the winter homes would be dug and warm and he would be able to speak as many hours as he liked each day with his children. He imagined the golden snowflakes as the talk of the town.

Phil turned from the window and picked up his pack. He visited each of the others where they stood, saying good-bye. He told them that he was long overdue at home, that they would meet again in the spring. He said, "Things look bad for the Japanese," then backed out of the window, pack first, feeling the snow break under his feet. The three watched Phil walking away. He turned once, swatting the flank of the dead mule and grinning. They all heard the dull thud of the slap and saw the snow falling from the frozen body.

After Phil left, the rotation fell apart. Henriette alone sat in a chair at the side of Fujino's bed watching and noting each of his movements, everything he said, on pieces of paper. She had it in mind that she was his nurse, and nurses kept records. She liked it better upstairs, for her mind was more directly connected to what she saw. Unlike Finn and Ellen she was not given to living in her imagination. In her the past and the future met as they were supposed to. She relied on her senses as the others relied on their memories, as the others tried to understand their lives by thinking.

Henriette kept Fujino's room warm and marked everything she saw or heard or smelled on her pieces of paper. She told Fujino that there was no doctor but that time healed all wounds, and when he screamed for Mr. Kaneda she patiently informed him that Mr. Kaneda was not there. And when Fujino was quiet she entertained him by telling him stories, or by describing the world around them, standing at the window and telling him what she saw.

"It's all ice and snow, really," she would cheerfully say. "There are no people and the ground is so pretty. The strangest thing I see is a dead mule who won't fall down but who stands in his frozen tracks staring right into the house. The poor thing. It's Finn's mule. Sometimes from this window I feel as if he is looking directly up at me, looking right up into the room here."

No one knew how much of what Henriette said Fujino understood. He heard about the mule all right, for once he tried to question her about his own mule, but she would only say, "No, it's Finn's mule," and then she'd carefully tell him that she hadn't seen anything of his since winter began.

In a week or so Henriette moved her cot into Fujino's room. "It's warmer in there and I can help him if he needs anything in the night," she said. From below they could hear her talking. Or if they couldn't they knew she was busy writing, putting everything down in the little notebook that she made.

———

And Finn too now, as Ellen had been doing from the beginning, began moving in Irish circles, gliding over the smooth surfaces of memory, going back, much as he said he would never do. He stood in the frame of the window looking into the eyes of the snow-covered mule and saw himself reflected there twice, in perfect unison. Since childhood Finn had had the habit of talking to his mirror image, so why not into the mule's eyes? "Well, when are you going to make something of yourself?" he might ask, looking into pub mirrors or into the dirty glass above washbasins in lavatories.

Now if he turned sideways his image in the eyes of the mule turned sideways as well. He saw himself as two small marchers who had timed their turns so perfectly that even the most demanding drill sergeant would not be able to find fault. It had been that way in school if he remembered correctly. Boys lined up on the playground as if they were soldiers. He remembered cold knees more than anything else. It had been so long since he'd let himself slide into Ireland this way. No good living in the past was his motto. Still, if he turned in the room now he knew he would find Ellen standing, swaying in front of another window, and if he asked her something it would take a moment for her to respond and he would be able to see in the tightening of the muscles on her face the stages of her awakening. It was like being alone in the house, except for the cries of the man upstairs.

Whenever Finn thought of Fujino he thought of Kaneda and knew he was responsible. Hadn't it been he, after all, who'd asked the young man to stay? He could remember telling him how happy Kaneda would be with the extra gold. And wasn't it time to wonder about the nature of the accident? Accident—it was suicide, however unlikely. Still, if Finn knew anything about the Japanese it was that there was a connection between them and suicide. He had read it or heard it somewhere. He even knew the word, *harakiri,* or something nearly like it. Finn remembered that there had been a boy in school who'd taken his own life and left a note saying he was not a coward. He had leapt off a cliff and onto the rocks below because of the taunting of other boys, Finn among them. Still, that boy was a boy who demanded taunting. They had all done pensum. Finn and some of the others took flowers to the boy's mother and had them scattered back in their faces for their trouble. They had gone to the funeral as a group and stood in school rows behind the teacher priests. Finn remembered praying for the boy's soul. He prayed hard, his every muscle tight and straining, though he didn't think it would do much good. He knew that a boy was not supposed to take his own life and so it would be very hard going no matter why he had done it. He had prayed, therefore, not so much for the boy as for his own part in the boy's fall. He hadn't a lot of guilt, but he had had some. He had been what might be called a medium taunter, the only hard evidence against him being a time he'd knelt down behind the lad and let another boy push him over. Finn could still remember the feeling of the boy's buttocks and legs rolling over his back. The boy had fallen and cracked his head on the hard dirt and Finn had stood up and offered the boy his hand, which he immediately pulled away when the lad reached for it. On the day of the funeral and for weeks after, Finn had dreamed that he knelt at the edge of the jagged cliff and let the boy be pushed over him onto the sharp rocks below. He had dreamed of extending his long arm toward the boy. Off the cliff his arm would go, fluttering like a scarf in the boy's crushed face. They had been terrible dreams and he ran to confession with them and with his part in the taunting as well.

"He was an odd boy and you may know that God does not hold you to blame," the priest had said.

"Father, forgive me for I have sinned."

"Do three Hail Marys and feel yourself cleansed."

"In my dreams he fell across my back and onto the rocks below."

"He was a strange boy. . . ."

Three times he'd gone and on the third he left the confessional feeling the weight of the boy's death falling from him. Later the priest invited him to tea and that night he slept soundly and saw the dead boy smiling and running on the playground, kicking a football with speed and precision past Finn and past the others.

Finn had not thought of the dead boy in years, but now with Fujino the memory of him came back. He knew Fujino would not die. It had been a fortnight, or nearly that, and if he were going to die he'd have done so by now. Pensum. That strange schoolboy word. The memory of it made him realize how his language and his life had changed since leaving Ireland. Hadn't he cleansed himself of it yet? Couldn't he be sure of himself even now, after all these years? He was like a fighter between rounds, he was, taking a moment of reflection in the eyes of a dead mule.

Finn looked up and noticed that it was snowing lightly again. He could hear the mumbling above, and when he looked at Ellen he found her looking back at him. He was hungry, bloody hungry, but the fire had nearly died away. He would build it up again and Ellen would prepare a meal. Phil must be nearly home by now. He could make the trip in winter as fast as most of them could in summer, him being an Eskimo and all.

———

The mule's head was clear to them for only a few hours each day. It was like a sundial, letting them gauge the hours of daylight, letting them know that the shadow they saw quickly passing down over its eyes was the shadow of night. The sun came through the windows briefly, like the dull back of a rolling whale, and then was gone. Finn slept more hours each day than he ever had, and Henriette sat rocking on the stiff hind legs of the straight-backed chair, drawing the shades if the sun shone in, remembering the way sickrooms were supposed to be and keeping everything quiet and dark. Her eyes reddened and from that she got the feeling of satisfaction that she believed belonged to nurses. When she came downstairs for meals, she ate quickly and talked to the others about the condition of the patient, about the amount he was eating and drinking, about the general state of his skin. She told them everything except what he said. That was in writing, and the act of transcribing it made further discussion seem an impossibility.

Henriette wore heavy clothes around the house; she wore her sealskin jacket with her heaviest dress underneath. She seemed always to be cold, but when Ellen or even Finn tried to talk her down the stairs to be for a moment next to the bigger fire she resisted.

"I've got my place and my job to do," she said once. She climbed the stairs with a smoking tray of food and closed the bleeding door behind her, leaving Finn and Ellen alone again.

Finn said, "Daylight's gone. I had thought to go out."

"It's not too far to the Gold Belt that you couldn't get there and back without freezing."

"It mightn't be a bad idea," he said vaguely, already searching for his greatcoat. "I've been staring through this window so long that I feel like a painting and it my frame."

Ellen, casting her eyes toward the ceiling, said, "Bring back some beer. It might revive the young man's spirits." Finn was fitted into his outside clothes but hadn't yet started toward the window.

"Wouldn't you consider coming along?" he asked. "I've seen proper women in the place before. Think of it as a change of scenery."

It was a matter of form, his asking. Ellen had been inside Irish pubs as a girl and could remember the smell of stale talk and ale. She remembered rubber faces turned on their stools to look, to see who'd come in, and she could recall the voice of the owner as he called to her father, "Lem, it's your girl come to fetch you home."

Had she come full circle then? Finn stood with his hand out, waiting. He too realized that she might go with him. His standing there reminded Ellen of herself waiting for her father to make up his mind. Even if he took an hour, once she'd let him know she was there she could not speak again, and looking at Finn, she knew that he too would wait for her without speaking.

"You don't think I'd be hindering the fun of it?"

Finn smiled broadly and moved toward her. "Not in the least," he said. "It's something we both need. We could make a night of it, really we could."

He took Ellen's heavy coat off its hook and held it open for her now like the cape of a matador. Ellen walked to the window and looked out at the dark. "Time seems to mean nothing," she said. She stepped into her coat and selected one of the skin-and-fur caps that they'd collected over the past few weeks. They could hear Henriette talking quietly in the room above them. One of the things Ellen had noticed about her bath was how clearly sound traveled. She didn't like that. She wanted silence from the occupants of the rooms. She wanted the effect of privacy.

Finn opened the window and they backed out, stepping quickly onto the crusted snow. Stars were dim and dusty and the nearby tents were dirty next to the white snow. They stopped for a moment and looked through the front window of the bath. This was the mule's view. They saw the empty room and the clean table and the red glow from the stove. It didn't seem nearly as cold as they'd expected it would. Though the path between the tents and bath had filled with snow, they found it well packed and easy to walk across. Only occasionally did one of them step through the top crust. Mostly the snow held them, let them step on its crisp top without breaking.

The Gold Belt was not the only saloon in Nome, but it was

the largest and it was the only one that had the frame of a
building built up around it. The tent flap opened precisely where
the door would be. The room was smoky and full, but they
found a corner table and sat down. It was dark. There were
dozens of girls wearing long trousers and wool shirts whereas
before they'd all dressed as ballerinas. There was music and
loud talking and they were forced to wait for a long while before
being served. Neither of them spoke. They looked around the
room, so different from the one in which they'd spent the last
days. Even Ellen felt a certain release, a certain sense of celebration. More people were arriving; no one was going home.
The owner spotted Finn and waved. Business was booming,
though it was not yet four o'clock in the afternoon.

———

At selected spots around the Gold Belt iron-bellied stoves burnt
heat into the room, and at each stove a wire mesh fence kept
people away, kept them from locking their cold hands to the
metal. Snow from the boots of customers melted into the sawdust and dirtied it so that every few days the owner laid the
floor again, fresh sawdust covering the old. At the end of winter
it would be higher than the floor of the city and customers
would have to step up to get inside.

For Ellen and Finn the room was in half light, the ceiling as
black as a starless sky. It gave them the feeling of limitlessness.
At the center of each table a kerosene lamp glowed as far as
the faces of the customers, round circles of light extending only
to the table's edge, making it difficult to see those who walked
near. A waitress appeared out of the darkness and took their
order. A whiskey for Finn, tea for Ellen. Music drifted across
the room, soft military marches. There were soldiers in the bar,
the luminous stripes that ran down their pant legs visible in the

dark, vertical shafts of light swinging across the room like clock pendulums.

"A whiskey and a tea," said the waitress, suddenly beside them again. Finn placed heavy coins in her hand.

"It's more like a country carnival than a pub," said Ellen. "It reminds me of a circus or a traveling show."

"The man does have a flair for the grand spectacle," Finn told her. "Look what he's done."

He pointed to one of the waitresses passing their table. The waitress and most of the others had round red circles of rouge painted onto their cheeks, large red lipstick kisses on their mouths. And each girl had a gray wool shirt tucked neatly into canvas trousers. When the waitresses were not tending to customers they often picked partners and danced between the tables. Familiar faces from the bath and the beach strike appeared around Finn and Ellen as they sat sipping their drinks.

It was a surprise to Finn to discover that many of the creek mines had shut down late, caught by quick winter, and now some of the men had nowhere to go and refused to leave places like the Gold Belt and the New York Kitchen even at closing time. At the edges of the room in which they drank, a few men were rolled into blankets, asleep on the dirty sawdust floor.

Ellen pushed her teacup about the small table. "Men turn out this way or that depending on what's inside them," she said. "That same group would be lying flat on the lower streets of Belfast. Those that turn out well here would turn out well elsewhere."

"Such talk," said Finn. "No credit given to a bit of luck? None to a twist of fate?"

Before Ellen could answer, John Hummel, whom she'd not seen since the day before Fujino's accident, came into their circle of light, still wearing his canvas necktie with its twelve-hundred-dollar sign. A new lively tune began and Hummel stretched his necktie into a dancing partner and whirled with it two or three times around them. It was a waltz and the dips and stops that it afforded him pleased some in the crowd and encouraged him to continue. He held his left arm out stiffly and pressed the canvas sack to his chest, making it the back and shoulders of his dancing partner. He glided and turned, dipping nearly to the floor. The heavy coins in the necktie clanged together in clumsy time to the music. He smiled broadly at Ellen and Finn, letting small liquid whips of spittle escape from the corners of his mouth and arc to the floor. Hummel danced until the music ceased, then he let the sack bounce dully on his chest and come to rest once again as a dead weight, one that he might dance with, but one that might carry him to the bottom of the river as well.

He scooted onto a chair, letting his elbows rest on the back of it, wiping his mouth on his sleeve before speaking.

"Hello, Ellen, how's your bath?" he said.

Though until now Ellen had had sympathy for the man and his condition, she detected the note of menace in his voice and answered guardedly: "Hello, Mr. Hummel . . ."

"Have you forgiven the community for jumping your claim then?" Finn asked, half smiling at the man. "The last I saw of you, you'd have liked to shoot us all."

Hummel knew what the result of his work had been. Every day since the incident he'd scurried through the blinding snow to hide behind the rump of Finn's dead mule and peer through the windows of the bath. He had seen them standing, heard them talk. He'd moved back from view when Phil left and to-night had followed the two of them as they tried not to crack the frozen top of the paths that the winter had made.

"Forgiven," he said, "but not forgotten. Everyone is rich on my discovery." He wanted to ask after the condition of the Japanese, but knew he could not. He turned his attention to Ellen.

"I would have been by before now, miss, but I've noticed that your place is closed."

"We've a sick man there, and the winter has been more than we'd counted on. Even our door is frozen shut."

"Well, I want to be the first customer again, after you re-open."

Hummel stood and saluted, then marched once more around their table, his stick shouldered again like a gun. Finn and Ellen looked toward the bar as he marched that way. They watched him duck through the heavy flaps of the tent and into the darkness. The Gold Belt was still crowded and many of the girls and customers were dancing. A few moments after Hummel left a fight broke out and one of the men cracked his head on the corner of the bar and was carried away. He bled into the sawdust from a wound in the back of his head. There was not much blood, but Finn saw Hummel in it, smiling at him from his wounded mouth. With the beginning of another tune the girl who'd been waiting on them extended her hand to Finn. He looked at her briefly then recognized the invitation and stood quickly. He waited to see if he could detect disapproval on the face of Ellen before he began roughly whirling her across the floor.

———

Mounds of earth were covered with snow and dotted the flat area of the Eskimo village like insect bites. The lean-tos had been dismantled pelt by pelt, the materials placed inside the storage sheds, away from the water's edge. The reverend's house still loomed, its large front window reflecting the sun, but otherwise only Nanoon's cold coming-of-age hut could be seen.

During the daylight hours the men and women of the village walked again on the paths between their underground houses and out onto the ice of Norton Sound, where they cut holes and pulled fish out of the freezing water. During the daylight hours Phil's women wore their golden snowflakes on the outsides of their jackets, dangling down their fronts heavily. The reverend wore his too, not hanging from his neck, but pinned to the outside of his greatcoat just over his heart so that sometimes when he walked from his house toward the village the sun caught it and the villagers knew who was coming.

This was a village of crazes, and soon Phil's golden snowflakes had been seen and handled by everyone. Phil had brought back not only the product but the method of the snowflakes, and the reverend decided that he would send all the children scurrying, when winter broke, into the streams and rivulets for nuggets. A snowflake for everyone, he promised them, for though it was a village of crazes, none would be content unless all possessed. There were too many examples to number, but going back just a year, each member of the village had collected a pink parasol, a soft-lead pencil, and a sketch pad.

And now the golden snowflakes. The children lived in anticipation, asking questions. They wanted to know if the shapes of their snowflakes would be something they could choose and if all the snowflakes would be of equal size. Phil told them what they got would represent purely the shape of chance, but they were not satisfied with his answer and within a week there had been a revival of the popularity of the pencils and pads. Each would draw the snowflake of his choice according to the web of his imagination. Then in spring, as the golden snowflakes were made, they would be compared to the drawings and given to the person who most truly had imagined what the first and then the second and then the third snowflake would be like. The members of the Eskimo village believed that no two imaginations were alike. Thus, rather than saying, "I am first; the first snowflake is mine," they decided upon the shapes of their snowflakes and then waited for them to come true.

Darkness falls, whatever the activities of the day have been. The villagers crawled into their huts, into their underearth homes, through the tunnels they had made. The walls of the

houses were truly made of ice, and of dirt and wood and pieces
of cloth. Inside there was tar blackness and lamps that lightened
it slightly and chimneys that projected upward and air vents
that came in from the sides. The floors of the underground
rooms were covered first with skins and then with small dried
pieces of fur from rabbit or beaver or fox. Game was not plen-
tiful in this area but the robes lasted years and during the
summer were stored carefully away. The Eskimos tried to sleep
only as much in winter as they did during the summer, or only
a little more. During the long hours before sleep, when it was
dark and early on the outside earth, the families sat and talked,
told each other stories, or made love. There was an unsureness
as to the parentage of the children, so as a precaution everyone
was mother or father to each. Stories were told of the old days
and the old were revered for their storytelling.

Each night the reverend reentered his house and started his
fires and sat with tea in one of the warm chairs in front of his
window. At sunrise and at sunset he saw the Eskimos fading in
and out. At night he saw the area in front of his window take
on the appearance, once again, of a wasteland. This was the
time he used for writing long letters and for preparing his next
day's lessons. Several times he had written to Ellen, but of
course he had no easy way of sending his letters, and as much
as they were letters to Ellen they were letters to himself. He did
not believe in loneliness, with his memories and his God and
his busy schedule as teacher.

With the quick descent of darkness the window in front of
the reverend became a mirror, and it was his habit to look at
himself in it for an hour each night and in a loud voice to
practice sermons as he remembered them being given in seminary. He was not a preacher really, but he liked what he saw in
the window. He was a happy man but did not suppose he was
responsible for that happiness or for the happiness of the village. On some nights he sat in his chair, forgetting to eat, just

staring at his poor face in the reflected darkness. He liked the sound of his voice and it would occasionally stir him to stand and descend the ladder. By this time his stomach was usually growling and he could not imagine how he had ignored it for so long.

———

The village and Nome and the camp on Topcock Creek form a triangle across the permafrost. At the third point, up on the edge of Topcock Creek, Kaneda still waits, leaning asleep over the fire that he does not let die. He has stopped mining but has hunted, piling each new pelt, no matter what the size, close around him on the floor of the tent. He has built fires around his camp, on four sides, and he feeds them with moss, for he believes this will keep the wolves away. Though he is older, he looks so much like Phil that even he will be surprised when they meet. He is sure that Fujino is very late. If nothing has happened to the boy it is unforgivable. The gold that he has been able to take out by himself is not a quarter of the amount that Fujino has, and if he is forced to work alone he will not be able to make that much again. He is not strong and cannot work more than nine or ten hours a day.

Kaneda has continued telling his stories though there is no one around to listen. In order to pass the time he decided to start at the beginning, to remind himself of all he has read and learned about the history of the country he loves. He talks in a loud voice and shakes his finger in the air when making an interesting or important point.

"It is always best to begin at the beginning," he says. "Though Japan has existed forever, we began taking notice of ourselves only three thousand years before Jesus. That was during the Jomon period and we know of it only because some of its pottery has survived."

His goal is to tell himself everything he has ever known about Japan, from the beginning of time to the arrival of Commodore Perry, whom he himself saw. Fujino will be sorry when he finds out what he has missed. Kaneda knows not only the events of history but many of the stories behind the events. He has read journals and diaries and looked through the libraries of Tokyo for the notes that generals used to send each other. He would be able to teach Fujino as much as he could learn in the best universities if only the young man were there to listen. But in fact not hearing it will be a part of Fujino's punishment for being so late. When he comes back he will have lost all that Kaneda has already told. That will be lost to him forever. Kaneda takes a deep breath and sighs. "We don't know very much about the Jomon," he says, "but we do know this. . . ."

———

Finn secured the window, the cold tin handle of it sticking briefly to his skin. He saw the dead mule and thought how strange it was that he could get used to such a sight so quickly, that he no longer noticed the frozen corpse much. Ellen placed a large copper pot upon the stove. The smell of freshly cut boards was renewed to them and the room seemed much too hot.

Henriette appeared from the bath and stood staring. "You've let the heat out," she said. "The room's got cold again."

"We thought you'd be upstairs," said Ellen.

"He's worse. As soon as you left he got worse. I had to bring him down all by myself. He stopped talking and began to shiver. I thought you'd never get back."

Finn and Ellen moved quickly across the room to Henriette. They pushed her back and peered into the steaming bathroom.

It was difficult to see through the mist and hot air, but as they walked into it Fujino appeared to them, sitting naked up to his neck in the hot water of the bath.

"I had to drag him," said Henriette. "He's bleeding from the other end."

Fujino's mouth had hardened into the surprising shape of a zero. His lips had turned the color of his gums. His hands floated in the water next to his knees, and from deep down blood the color of ink floated to the top of the tub.

"He's hemorrhaging," Finn whispered.

"He's stopped talking," said Henriette. "The last thing he said was that he was an interpreter. I brought him down here as soon as I saw the blood."

This was the first time either Ellen or Finn had seen Fujino outside of bed since his accident. He had lost far more weight than they'd expected and there were long scratches along his arms and thighs where he'd drawn his sharp fingernails.

"Is there no one in this town who can help?" said Ellen. "I thought he was getting better." She turned to Henriette. "You gave us the impression that the man was improving."

"I'm the only one who ever took any interest in him," Henriette said quietly.

"You took an interest in pretending to be a nurse," Finn told her. "Why didn't you tell us the condition he was in?"

Like Fujino's Henriette's mouth formed a little circle. Tears climbed to her eyes, bringing Finn's arm quickly around her and making him say he was sorry. "We are only surprised to find him so," he said. "We really thought he was getting better."

Ellen carried three stiff chairs from the main room and placed them around the wooden bathtub. "We should keep the water hot," she said, "the perspiration out of his eyes."

Henriette calmed down and brought already prepared water and poured it gently over Fujino's face. The excess flowed over the sides of the tub and through the loose floorboards. The room quieted as the lapping of the water in the tub subsided. Fujino still held that surprised look. Finn asked him several times if he could hear them, but he got no response. Henriette had her paper handy in case he said anything, but she didn't think he would. Through the open door of the room, through the window of the bath, Ellen could see the shadowy form of Finn's mule, its dead eyes shining.

"A vigil," she said, looking at herself and at the other two. "Is there nothing else a human being can do?"

Ellen let her hand fall over the edge of the tub occasionally, and if the water grew too cool she nodded and Henriette got up and poured more in. "Waiting for death," she thought and she could picture, through the steam, through the depthless zero of Fujino's mouth, the pursed white lips of her own dying grandmother. Ellen's grandmother had fallen coming downstairs and had been carried back up again. "I'm going down," she'd shouted, but the place for the injured was in bed so she was carried back up by her loving son and placed in the bed she'd come from. After that the house was quiet. None of the children were allowed to laugh, nor were they allowed to speak.

"Don't say whatever comes into your head," her father had warned. "Speak only if it's well worth saying."

Ellen remembered that the air of that house had seemed as hot and heavy to her as her old grandmother's breath, as the bath did now. She sat in the kitchen for hours trying to think of something she knew that was worth saying, that could be said out loud without bringing on a scolding. She eliminated first those things personal: a lesson she had learned, the torments of a school chum. And by these eliminations she discovered she could talk of nothing else for these were her only subjects. She sat for hours waiting to be admitted to the upstairs room. She felt so foolish, a girl of her age with no other subjects but those. Still, as quickly as she thought of something to say she was forced to discard it. She could speak of nothing. Her father had ordered her to be quiet or if she couldn't be quiet to be sure of the value of what she had to say, and so she discovered that nothing she could think of was of any value at all. Everything was better left unsaid. Everything except the one sentence, the one question she had been permitted to utter over and over again. "How is grandmother?" She said it ten times every day and always it passed as the real concern of a child.

"As well as can be expected, Ellen dear," said her father. "She is very old."

Each time she asked he answered slowly and looked at her or touched her on the chin or shoulder, and each time he believed, with all his heart, that she cared.

How is grandmother? How is grandmother? Of all the subjects of the world was this the only allowable utterance? She cleaned the corners of her small mind but found only this. Again, How is grandmother?

Ellen stood in the hallway when the other members of her family were upstairs and watched the old clock's pendulum sweep across her mirrored face. She remembered wanting so much to smash it. Before her grandmother came to live with them this space had contained a coat rack and she was able to stand behind the coats buried in the smell of her father. He would see her feet and would throw his arms around the coats as if he didn't know she was there, and she would be his bundle, to be carried, squealing, over his shoulder and through the house. And now only the clock, its pendulum moving like a heartbeat inside the dustless case, defined the corner.

Ellen's father stood behind her imagining worry in the child's glass face. "You'd better see her now," he said, so she climbed the stairs with him, moving as he did, letting all her weight fall on her left foot and then her right. Slowly.

Inside the room were heavy quilts and heavy curtains. Her father left, feeling that this was a time for the child and her grandmother, a time of communion.

The child walked on cat's feet across the floor and peered at the bird's head that was her grandmother. The skin hung from her neck and face so loosely. The bed covers were nearly flat over the wasting body. Her grandmother was a tall woman and the rod-thin line of her body extended, even now, all the way from the top to the foot of the bed, and as she stood there a hand came at her from the side of the covers, snapping. She stood back slowly out of its reach and watched the hand pecking at the air, blind until the eyes of the grandmother opened to it.

"Come here."

Ellen moved forward and bent low. The fingers clasped the front of her dress like clothespins. The sharp point of her grandmother's nose was smooth and waxy, the eyes were small and dry. Ellen said quietly, "How is grandmother?" but there was no answer and in a moment her father came and took her out again. She felt her father's heavy hands guide her toward her room as if she were a stranger there. She felt him squeeze her shoulder and felt him leaning over her in the dark, waiting for her to fall asleep.

"Sleep now, Ellen, don't be afraid," he said. He stroked her head and pushed the hair back out of her eyes. He waited and she felt herself lowering, getting further from him. "How is grandmother?" she heard herself say.

In the morning her grandmother was dead and the curtains and windows of her room were opened. Ellen could see the fields behind the house and the sun, and she was hungry. She bounded down the stairs and into the kitchen. She saw the heavy arms of her father across his knees and she saw the tears in his eyes.

"Father?" she said.

He took her on his lap surrounding her and said, "She is gone. My mother is gone," and Ellen felt his tears and tried to get away. It was the first time she'd seen her father cry. He who was able to go into pubs and who smoked a pipe. He had said "my mother," and Ellen thought, How silly, *her* mother was standing in the kitchen, nobody really cared about the grand-mother. They were all pretending. It was important pretending while she was alive, but why continue? It was supposed to be over now. All those days of asking how is she were supposed to be over now and it wasn't fair.

Ellen felt disgusted looking at her father, and for the very first time. And what she did next everyone supposed was due to grief. She got away from her father and without hesitation smashed the face of that grandfather's clock. She did it with her grandmother's cane and heard her father and mother rush into the hall and expected to be beaten for it. She waited, stiff-ening, even pushing the cane in her father's direction, but all he did was pick her up and hold her. She tried to wiggle but he held her tight until she was quiet. And all she could hear was her father's heartbeat, sounding from deep within his chest.

———

When Fujino died Henriette pushed the other two out of the bath and would not let them return until she'd dried him off and had him into clean clothes. Finn went again into the night to find out what was to be done with the remains in this city. There had been deaths before yet there was no doctor. People like John Hummel were allowed to leak blood over everyone and grin about the fact that there was no professional man nearby to heal them. Finn felt now, for the first time, that he was in a wilderness. The dim oil lamps of the bath died before he was a dozen feet away and there were no stars or lights from the dirty tent sides, which, like the flat white sides of ghosts, he kept bumping into. He headed toward the Gold Belt, but even after all this time he couldn't find it alone, totally unguided by any light.

The man is dead, thought Finn. He's been dying the whole

time and I did nothing but stand by watching. This time there
was nobody to blame but himself. He could have asked someone
other than Fujino for help at the beach strike; there had been
others around. Finn supposed he viewed suicide less tragically
than he did accidents. The man took his own life, after all, and
who is to say that he should have been saved from it? Still,
though the evidence was clear, it seemed impossible that Fujino
had wanted to die. Even that last evening he had talked about
Kaneda and how he'd be glad to get back and how he hoped
that the old man had not worried. It had been wrong of Finn
to talk Fujino into staying in Nome for so long. He should have
let the man go. He should have drunk with him and then sent
him packing, back to Kaneda, back to Topcock Creek.

Finn stopped and looked around him. The paths turned in
six directions and he had no idea which might lead him to help.
A man had died and the first thing he'd done was run into the
night, getting himself lost. This was the second time in his life
that he'd felt touched with blame. Someone had died and he
had not been unconnected. When Finn noticed that it had again
started to snow, he continued walking, no longer choosing the
path he would take, but merely turning on impulse. The snow
was tiny and hard-hitting, yet when he closed his eyes he could
somehow take comfort from it. He felt it encasing his eyebrows,
he felt the increasing weight of it settle and freeze on the hood
of his heavy jacket.

But Finn soon regained a sense of where he was. He had
worked his way out of the canvas labyrinth and now found himself on the path that led up the hill behind the city and directly
to the door of Dr. Kingman. He remembered the short man and
even at this distance could see the yellow glow of the crystal
chandelier. He knew immediately that he would knock and ask
his question of whoever answered. The light from the chandelier
did not seem brighter as he got nearer to the house, and in
every window it was now possible for him to see the tinier glow

of other, smaller lamps. When he stepped onto the porch the boards took his weight without comment. He swung two pieces of brass together three times, then waited and knocked again. In a moment a thin strip of wood slid from the middle of the door and someone peered out at him.

"It's late."

"There has been a death. I must ask someone . . ."

There were two doors, an outer one and an inner one, spaced three feet apart. Finn stood for a few seconds more, until the voice told him to come in, then he pulled back the first big door and walked into an entryway. He was told to close the door behind him. Now the eyes were looking at him through the next door.

"Who are you?"

"Finn Wallace," said Finn, pushing the hood off his head. "There has been a death." He decided to say no more. Though he had pushed his hood off so that they could get a better look at him, he did not want to give the impression that he'd come with his hat in his hands.

Presently the second door opened and the small man, Dr. Kingman himself, stood in front of him. He held a wine glass in his hand and had a small pistol stuck in his back pocket.

"You aren't with our group," Dr. Kingman said flatly, holding the door open and watching Finn closely.

"I am independent," said Finn.

"You're an Irishman, aren't you? I've seen you before. You're connected with the public bath."

"A man has died, Dr. Kingman. A Japanese named Fujino. He is in Ellen's bath even now."

"Yes?"

"Well, the truth is I've been looking for someone who can tell me what is to be done with the remains. There is no doctor. There are no facilities."

"Who told you there was no doctor? We have a doctor. He stays out at the mine site, but he might have come."

Finn felt that the man was going to say, "Why didn't you come to me earlier? If I'd only known," but instead he turned on his heels and walked away from Finn and into the room that held the chandelier.

Dr. Kingman poured more red wine into his own glass then filled another to the top for Finn. There was a large fire burning at the hearth and there were two heavy chairs in front of it. The light from the chandelier and the fire cast the room in unlikely brightness. Dr. Kingman motioned to Finn. "Sit down. I'm curious why you came to me with your problem."

"I was looking for someone to help me with the remains."

"But why me?"

"Yours was the first light I saw. I got a bit lost down below and when I saw your light it seemed the most expedient place to stop."

"Expedient? You came to me because it was expedient?"

"A man has died, Dr. Kingman."

"Ever since the freeze people have been knocking on my door for some favor or other, but this is the first time anyone has done so because it was expedient."

Finn drank the wine and put the glass lightly on the small table next to his chair. This man was playing with him. Perhaps he didn't believe there'd been a death; perhaps he thought Finn was there out of a desire to get close to him in some way. Finn thought of the look locked on the poor face of Fujino. That round circle of a mouth, those peaked eyebrows. Fujino hadn't seen death closing in on him until the last moments and he'd been taken aback, that was clear. He'd been taken completely by surprise and now Finn was being surprised by this pompous man. He stood and said, "I've business to attend to. Thank you for the glass of red."

"But you've barely told me why you came. Isn't there anything else?"

Such comfort, thought Finn. He felt like picking the little bugger up and pushing him into the fire. He was embarrassed to have been so intimidated by the man earlier. He walked slowly toward the door, trying to give his own face the surprised look that Fujino's had.

"Good evening," he said over his shoulder.

"Put your friend on ice," said Dr. Kingman. "There is nothing else to be done before the thaw."

Finn opened and closed one door then opened and closed the other and was outside again. The storm was heavier than it had been when he'd entered the house, but from here he knew his way back to the bath well enough. It seemed colder to him now than when he'd ventured out and the snow that hit his face and clung to his eyebrows began, strangely, to feel hot. Finn walked, rubbing the backs of his furry gloves across his forehead as he went. Put him on ice, Kingman had said, and in truth it seemed like the best idea. Poor Fujino. Finn would have to go and tell Kaneda. It was his fault, as much or more than the fault of the others, and he'd have to be the one to tell the old man. He remembered going to the home of his dead school friend to have his flowers thrown back in his face. He worried about Kaneda, hoping that the old man had enough to eat and that he'd been able to keep warm. Fujino had come to town to trade in their gold and to get supplies. Of course the old man had sent him for supplies *before* the cold weather set in. So he was up there with nothing and likely frozen with that same look upon him! Finn ran now and was among the tents very quickly. The old man! He would do pensum for the death of Fujino by saving the old man. If only he wasn't too late. If only he could find the campsite, get there without freezing himself. Finn rounded the corner nearest the bath building. There was an oil lamp burning in the window of the room where Henriette had for so long taken care of the dying Japanese. He pulled on the door handle twice before remembering that it wouldn't open, before stepping around the corner of the building.

Ellen and Henriette had their faces pressed to the cold glass of the window and were crying. Quickly he took a step toward them and stopped. *Freezing the body was the only thing they could do....* Ellen and Henriette had thought of it too. Fujino was wearing a heavy gray coat, a fur hood pulled up warm around his surprised face. Perhaps he thought he was going back to Kaneda, even in death, going back to fulfill his promise to the old man. Before bringing him outside Henriette had closed his eyes. His mouth was open, but for sight he relied completely on the eyes of the frozen mule he rode.

———

No one knew what to say. Henriette took it the hardest, and retired, when Finn got back, to the upper room, where she had for so long nursed Fujino. She sat in her stiff-backed chair facing the bed, or she wrote for a while in the journal she'd been keeping. She wrote "the end" but continued to cry with abandonment. Tears dropped from her eyes, and her shoulders and back shook as if from violent laughter. He was dead and could be seen below, riding the awful mule she had so recently described to him. A dead mule and rider, seen through the swirls of snow from the sickroom window, the nurse standing, defeated. It was too horrible. She had been sure he would pull through and from his sitting-up position look past the others and toward her, and stretch out his hand and say, "It was you, wasn't it? who took care of me? who saved me?" Such a vision of victory. She would glide to him and let him take her hand. She had decided long ago that she would allow herself only a moment of such intimacy. After that she would withdraw, return to being the Henriette that he had known before his illness. She would not let him thank her again, and she would not, even for a moment, let him fall in love with her.

Henriette remembered the times when Fujino had been com-

pletely asleep and she had lifted his covers to tuck them back
in around his legs, under the thin mattress. She'd let her eyes
fall upon every part of his wrinkled body then and she had
touched him. It was too awful, but once and with a dull pencil
she had written her name long across the length of his thigh.
She had been surprised at how little hair his body had
when she'd laid her arm, soft, against his sallow stomach. He
had been asleep, dying, and she had used his body as a curiosity. Sometimes she imagined that she was looking at the body
of a very old man, of Kaneda, or even her own father. "He is
Japanese," she said to herself. "He came from Japan." She
remembered the Chinese she'd seen in Seattle, but he was nothing like them. They were to be suspicious of and scurried in
groups. He and Kaneda were quiet and wore regular clothes,
and though they spoke to each other oddly, they were always
careful to explain what they were saying to the others.

Henriette's crying subsided now, though she tried desperately
to maintain it. What a fool she had been. She'd treated him
like one of the stuffed rag dolls of her childhood. She looked
down at herself and at the dress that she for so long had imagined to be the uniform of a nurse. She knew that if she looked
out the window she would see the hollow-mouthed patient, riding, leaning forward on the mule, his hands tucked into his
jacket pockets like some trick rider. The mule's eyes were
opened and she knew, if she looked, she would see them staring,
trying to lead that blind one back to her.

Henriette silently and slowly began unbuttoning the front of
her dress. She let it slip from around her shoulders but caught
it before it fell to the ground. She took off the rest of her
clothing then walked to the window, looking straight ahead. She
hung the dress from tacks, draping it over the window like a
curtain. She hung her stockings and underwear, and she placed
her shoes on the window sill, using them as weights to hold the
curtain down, to keep it from moving with the breeze that came

slightly sifting between the boards. Though her own body was pale, as she looked down at it she knew that she was in good health, would outlive everyone.

When Henriette got in the bed and pulled the heavy covers up to her chin, she could feel her body settling into the contours that had been formed by the dying Fujino, and she let herself lie as he had. Did the bed still contain some of the warmth of his body? She wanted to continue crying, but she knew that was impossible. She wanted to stay awake and in mourning all night long, to know that the others were asleep and that only she was conscious and remembered, but that was impossible as well. She felt sleep moving in. Like the tide she felt it washing over her, and she let it pull her gently. Though she'd failed as a nurse, she wanted to be successful at grief. Could sleep come so easily to one who mourned? How could she let herself find peace when her failure stood hard as granite and staring at the building where she slept? These questions died like candles and she was dreamless and did not toss or turn. Later she would look at herself in the mirror and call herself heartless.

4

Just as the land stretched back from the sea-less shore the snow piled up, the wind blew it into drifts, and the drifts into mountains. The freeze reclaimed that top four or five feet that the summer had softened. In the Eskimo village the reverend felt the cold. Though it was his fourth winter, and though he had thought for weeks about all he would need to stock up on to be comfortable, there were certain things he had forgotten. He had enough firewood, and enough food, but he had neglected reading material. Stories. Those he had he had reread many times. He loved the sound of the words as they came off the page and he especially loved reading aloud, but he wanted to be unaware of what the story would bring him, of what would happen. Sometimes he had the urge to tear final pages from the books and replace them with endings of his own. He was a willful man and could be a willful storyteller, one whom the listener would know could handle himself, come what may.

The reverend often thought of writing down stories. He told them frequently enough, when he preached to the village people. And, though he would never have admitted it to his superiors, there were many times when he got carried away. More than once, indeed nearly always, he took what he remembered to be the point of his sermon and added to it. He made up characters that the Bible never knew and his characters always worked well for him. Of course his teachings were always Christian, but the characters, and the way they saw the light, with those he had taken liberties.

Anyway, for today the reverend didn't need to worry about stories. Today he was having a party. He tried to have at least two parties each winter, so soon his house would fill up warmly with all the members of the village. If he climbed to his balcony he could probably see them now, emerging from their underground homes as if by magic. It always amazed him to be looking out at the vast expanse of whiteness and to suddenly see people appear. They came out of the ground like spring vegetables and moved about. It was a hard life, being an Eskimo, and he had nothing but admiration. Summer homes, winter homes. Fishing, hunting. My, how he admired them sometimes.

The reverend prepared what he could for the party, according to the stock of his shelves. He baked cookies and made punch, using an old family recipe. He knew that the children liked to climb up and down the rough ladder to his loft, so as a precaution against splinters he had wrapped each of the rungs with old pelts, no longer of any use as clothing.

At the first knock on the door the reverend slipped into a light coat with the cherished golden snowflake on its breast. He adjusted his clothing and opened the door. Everyone in the village was there. They had come as a family, all at one time. They did not want the heat to escape from the room as it would if the reverend had to keep opening and closing his door.

"Hello," they said, walking in single file. They had arranged themselves short to tall. The children disappeared up the fur-covered ladder and the main room was left to the adults. Immediately, as the door was closed, those who had not yet completed their snowflake drawings pulled off their coats, exposing sketch pads and pencils pressed to their bodies. They sat and wet the ends of their pencils, then stared hard, as if looking into the paper for ideas. The others took off their outer clothing and stood waiting to sense the temperature of the room. It was a treat to dress lightly in a heated house. They moved to the punch bowl, tapping tin cups against it like prisoners.

A child hung by her knees from the balcony railing.

Phil's women, displaying their snowflakes proudly, stood back to back in the center of the room, waiting to be admired.

Phil himself sought out the reverend, wanting to continue a conversation that they'd had briefly the day before. They were talking about suicide, about its suddenness and its conse-quences. Phil retold the story of Fujino, how he had seemed so normal, so full of anticipation. "It was the very eve of his return to Topcock Creek and he seemed happy to be going."

"The human mind works mysteriously," the reverend told him.

"Are Japanese Christians?"

"I suppose if there are any there are only a few."

"I don't know whether he lived or died."

The reverend had never been comfortable in private confer-ence with his parishioners. He preferred the distance of the pulpit for serious talk.

"Oh, he probably lived," he said weakly.

"But if he died the gates of heaven are closed to him. Whether he is a Christian or not."

"Well . . ." said the reverend. He looked at Phil and realized that this man, a village leader, a hunter, was asking him for guidance. These were the toughest times.

Phil asked, "Thou shalt not commit murder means suicide too, doesn't it?"

"Oh, I guess so. . . ." The reverend leaned down and dipped some punch out of the metal basin. He handed it to Phil and took another cup for himself. Out of respect for the fact that he was giving them a party, the other men and women sat or stood quietly, listening, waiting for him to more fully answer Phil's question. By now the story of Fujino was well known, and had been passed with precision around the village. No one knew what Japan was, but they understood that the man looked like one of them and that he'd tried to take his own life. Many of them thought it must have been a matter of illness, or of no food. He died so that others could eat, something along those lines. But he was a young man and certainly must have been able to hunt. It was puzzling.

The reverend stood stooped over the punch bowl for a few seconds, thinking. When he straightened up again he laid his thin hands on Phil's shoulders and gazed around the room at the others.

"Andrew the Suicidal," he said, pausing, waiting for the words to show themselves on Phil's face.

"Andrew the Suicidal lived and marched, for a while, with Jesus Christ himself. He was not a hunter, and he carried from the day he was born an intense dislike for himself." The reverend was confident now, and in his mind's eye could picture Andrew moping around the outskirts of the band of Jesus' followers.

"He was not an easy man to like, and for that reason Jesus spent more time with him than with many of the others. Some were jealous of their relationship, for to Andrew, you see, Jesus was more than a savior. He was an object of intense desire."

Several of the Eskimo women looked to their neighbors to translate the words of the reverend, and several others dipped their cups again into the delicious punch. Phil, the direct recipient of the reverend's words, remembered for the first time in years his boyhood fling with the leader of another group.

"Of course Jesus was celibate," continued the reverend, "and though he recognized the soft eyes that Andrew cast upon him, he would promise him only that they would be together in the kingdom of heaven, and would rejoice.

" 'Rejoice, rejoice, rejoice,' Andrew said to him once. 'All you ever talk about is rejoice. What about me? What about now? If you won't have me I'll kill myself. I'll cut out my heart.'

"Well, each time that Andrew was reduced to such threats, Jesus would take him in his arms and, talking lowly, walk with him around the inside of the circle of followers, until Andrew was calm again. And after he was down and quiet the others would breathe a sigh of relief. 'Jesus,' they would say. 'How do you put up with it? I'd go out of my head.'

"Three times Andrew built up enough nerve and enough guilt to go to Jesus and say, 'I'll cut out my heart,' and on the third time he did it. He waited until the last of the late-sleeping disciples had slipped between his blankets, then he marched to the place where Jesus slept and, baring his chest, stuck a knife into it to the hilt.

" 'Ah, ah,' he said, 'Jesus, Jesus!' for the sharp pain was surprising to him. And the savior was on his feet in an instant, and Andrew fell where Jesus had lain and clutching the still warm blanket to his bloody breast he said, 'At last I have known the warmth of your bed,' and he died.

"Well, Jesus cried, and though Andrew had never endeared himself to the other followers, Jesus' tears led them to mourn Andrew with wails and tears of their own, and the following day Jesus gathered them together, and while some stacked rocks for the tomb of Andrew, he told the others that though suicide was murder and that both were wrong, Andrew was forgiven and waited for them even now beside His father's throne.

"Well, as you know, Judas was there, and this was more than Judas could take. Rules were rules, he thought, and so he asked, 'On what grounds?' for he had always hated Andrew and more than once had succumbed to the impulse to strike him.

"Jesus looked at Judas for a long moment before answering, and then he said, 'On the grounds that it was not suicide at all. It was an accident of fate.' And with that he gave Judas such a low and mournful stare that it made Judas cringe and it was as if to say, 'Do not, Judas, deny forgiveness for accidents of fate.' "

The reverend stopped for a moment and looked at Phil and

the others. Should he be going on like this? Clearly they believed him. As he stood in front of them, only the noises of the
children could be heard. He had been talking for a long time,
and while he had done so the Eskimos had been slipping their
cups quietly over the side of the metal bowl and scooping up
more punch.

He took a breath and continued. "Anyway. If Andrew can be
forgiven on the very bed of Jesus, surely your friend Fujino will
have no trouble. Consider it an accident of fate."

After the reverend's little speech the party fell to normal
rhythms. Eskimo women fed their children, men drank until the
tin bottom of the reverend's bucket was scraped loudly by the
edges of their cups. When the punch was gone they pushed
the furniture out of the way and let an old man begin a drum
dance using a new drum that he'd made especially for the occasion. Though the drum was simple, a flat skin with no echo
chamber, the old man got three distinct sounds from the instru-
ment, and once he'd established the rhythm he began chanting
a story of his own, one about a seal waiting in the freezing
depths of the bay, waiting to feed the starving Eskimo people.

Eventually everyone danced. They depicted the quiet waiting,
the patient, breathless waiting of the Eskimo hunters. They became the sea under the ice and the seal gliding toward an air
hole. It was a familiar dance, and with punch and time each
Eskimo felt the need to hunt seal, right now, on the icy bay in
front of their village. This kind of hunting was called feather
hunting, and while the women left the reverend's house in search
of feathers, the men went for their harpoons, and the reverend
was left with the children alone. His winter parties often ended
as abruptly as this. He took some food and his tin punch cup
and, climbing the ladder, looked at the scattering people through
his beloved window. The side of Nanoon's cold hut shone in the
sun for him. Like the smooth shoulder of a hunched bird it
stood, its feathers perfect for hunting so snatched here and
there by the searching women. He imagined the girl wrapped

in her furs and waiting. Could she feel her feathers lightly lifted? Did she know the hunt was on?

The idea of the taste of fresh seal was on everyone's mind, and in a few moments the Eskimo men popped from the earth again, harpoons pricked against the sky. All the hunters wore white boots, invisible against the land, so that as they walked toward the ice they appeared to be legless and floating, cruising above the earth. At the edge of the sea they broke into groups, fanning away from the shore and out onto the ice. They searched for holes the size of apples, the breathing holes of seals. They walked far out and when they stopped they bent and peered into the ice and remained still.

Phil found a hole and bent and scooped the snow and loose ice out of the way until he could see clearly the short dark tunnel that led to the water below. Carefully and quietly he placed an owl feather where the snow had been then slowly held his harpoon high, ready to plunge it downward. Today there would be only one seal. No one knew which air hole the seal would choose, yet all about the bay harpoons were cocked high above the heads of hunters. A seal, lungs cramped and heavy, would come to breathe and a feather would move and the chosen hunter would cast his harpoon so precisely that the feather would fold around its tip and disappear into the body of the animal. When the seal was dead the others, perched like eagles above their own air holes, would come running, would begin pulling the line hand over hand until the lean body of the seal slid from the broken ice like a baby from a shattered womb. Later, on the shore, when the hot meat of the seal warmed and colored the lips of the Eskimos, someone would dig the broken feather from the flesh and hand it, red now, to the hunter. And it would serve as a decoration for a drum or for the wall of his summer home, his lean-to.

The reverend watched from his window. The children had stopped playing and stood around his soft loft as quiet and still

as those on the ice. From this distance the bodies of the men
and women, curved like boomerangs over the air holes, looked
to be dark shadows laid upon the ice. They waited. One seal
would be enough for everyone. Even the reverend, after four
years here, understood the anticipation, had acquired a taste
for the hot red meat. He liked to let it please his fingers and
he was beginning to understand touch as the first stage of taste.
The reverend waited with the children, looking out at the white
earth and the dark shadows.

When the hunters, frozen apart for so long on the canvas of
his window, finally came together, only the reverend made a
sound. He betrayed his newness to the village by a slight intake
of breath. It was impossible for him to withhold it. It was a
miracle, like watching the figures in a painting only to have
them begin to move about. When the hunters came together
black spots remained in the reverend's eyes. The hunters ran,
even now were pulling the dead seal from the sea, yet they
remained where they had been, dark shadows painted on his
very eyeballs. The reverend blinked and waited, knowing that
the spots would fade from their fixed positions, melt into the
whiteness again or trail across his window and back into the
bodies of the real men. He thought of the dead body of Andrew
the Suicidal. He looked with the children and saw the long slim
seal, born of the earth's cracked shell. He waited as the Eskimos
did, he watched with a calculating eye, wondering how large it
was, anxious to warm the tips of his fingers in its neat flesh.

Finn, off to see the old man, carried money in his pockets and
pulled supplies behind him on a sled. He'd found a map among
Fujino's possessions and would follow it, if necessary, throughout the rest of winter. It was not snowing on the day he left,

yet the cloud cover was a shade grayer than the earth. Finn followed the map or saw the round mouth and the pinched eyes of Fujino in front of him. Pensum. Penance. Repentance. He'd be a different man after this. He'd be stronger because of it. After this, though he was forty-five, he'd try to begin again. Finn had read Fujino's shopping list and filled it, and when he found Kaneda he would explain. He would say he was sorry and would prove it by working for the old man and by taking none of the gold for himself. He'd brought Fujino's whiskey for he knew the old man would want it, but he'd have none of that himself either. He had potatoes and fish and salt. The old man might not be happy to see him at first, but Finn would make him glad. He would explain what had happened to Fujino, making the old man's memory of Fujino good and letting the old man take stories of Fujino's bravery home with him to Japan.

Before leaving Nome, Finn bought a dog. He'd been told by a man that the dog was of a breed that could walk through high snow drifts and that it would easily pull a sled as small as the one Finn showed him. The dog was gray like the sky and had almond eyes. And he was silent. Even under the most pressing circumstances, the man told Finn, the dog would make no sound. Finn called the dog Mute. They had been traveling long days slowly, but though the dog was good at walking through high snow he was not a puller. Each time Finn harnessed him to the sled he sat back, not understanding what to do. The dog leapt, gray like a wolf, through the surrounding snow, but Finn pulled.

They were able to move during daylight hours, but when the earth blackened they sat by a low fire, hollowed into a snow-bank, or buried under furs. Finn cooked over the fires he built, and though the orange flames gave little heat, he had regained the sense that it was not as cold as it ought to be. Finn saw the darkness around him as the expanding depths of the mouth of Fujino, and he was often sure that he saw, beyond the fire, the golden eyes of his dead mule as it kept its blind rider close to

the man who would explain, who would tell Kaneda how it had
been. Death was all around him. Finn had been responsible for
Fujino, for that child in Ireland, and if he found Kaneda too
late ... He pursed his lips and bore his responsibility quietly.
He leaned against the dog. "Father forgive me for I have
sinned," he mumbled, and there was no echo in the night.

————

"It's scandalous," Ellen said. "People are getting used to the
winter. They'll be coming past here soon to stare at him."

Henriette stood at the window looking back at Ellen and out
toward the sea. She too was ashamed. It had been her idea to
place Fujino on the mule but at the time Ellen had quickly
agreed for it hadn't seemed right to lay him on the snowing
ground. And now he was frozen. When they came to their senses
they dug a shallow grave in a bank of snow but it was too late.
He couldn't be moved. He was locked as if one with the hairy
body of the mule. Even his clothes, the way the trouser legs
wrapped themselves around the poor man's thin ankles, were
now fixed. And both the mule and the man had turned the color
of lead. Henriette had seen statues like him in the parks of San
Francisco, of military men riding with swords high.

"We'll need a man's help. Or we'll tip the mule and bury
them both," she said.

Ellen, sitting by the fire far from the window, knitted. She'd
not stand staring as if there was nothing to be done. They'd
received an invitation from the reverend and from Phil. Would
they be interested in experiencing Christmas in the Eskimo village? If so, there were sixteen children in the village and could
they bring a little something for each? The very smallest of gifts
would suffice, the reverend wrote, but something would be necessary.

Ellen read and reread the reverend's letter. On the day of its arrival she remembered the wool she'd brought all the way from home. There'd been no chance to use it until now, but at Christmastime children got stockings. As a girl she'd found them tacked to the mantel above the fireplace quite early on Christmas mornings. Always two pairs, one from her mother and one from her grandmother. It had never been a surprise. And if there was time she might have a sweater as well, and from her father a coin tucked deeply into the toe of each stocking. She wore the stockings, one pair and then the other, and she threw the coins into the air and had them come down into her hands.

There was a Christmas game that she played with her father, who would always be dressed and friendly on that day. He'd swing Ellen high into the top of the main room then let her go just as she threw the coins, and he'd catch her just as she was supposed to catch them. She'd shriek and the coins would roll and she'd chase them, sometimes out of the living room, under chairs and under the big clock in the hallway, the one that ticked the seconds of her grandmother's life away. And after her father had three times thrown her and after she was exhausted and nearly in tears from laughing and running, her grandmother and her mother would come disapproving from the kitchen and one would announce the goose and the other the pudding, as though the goose and the pudding were guests in their house for the day. Her grandmother, looking stern and evil, would always speak more clearly than her mother. She'd look with her rooster eyes at the father and the child, then she'd sweep her arm and head forward and in her most cultured voice, acting like a butler, she'd say, "Ladies and gentlemen, the goose," and Ellen and the others would walk quietly and with dignity into the next room to dinner. It was her grandmother's only joke, the only time Ellen had ever been able to see in the eyes of the old lady any spark of good humor.

As Ellen knitted she thought of her mother knitting stockings for her; she thought of her grandmother sitting with stiff collars pinned at the neck by cameos. The wool was gray and the stockings were all the same size. Those that were finished were washed for shrinkage in one of the bathtubs and hung around the front room of the bath like fish carcasses. Ellen tried to string the line as close to the heater as she could, and on the floor around their chairs now water drops left dark circles. Henriette, sitting again, moved her chair this way and that, each knee damp and the material of her dress sticking slightly to her skin. She too would give gifts, knotted necklaces, ready to wear with the golden snowflakes. She looked toward the ceiling and thought of the dripping stockings as long and slender teats coming from the dark underbelly of a cow somebody had forgotten to milk. She laughed. She had been depressed too long. It was nearly time for them to meet Phil, nearly Christmas.

———

Kaneda was almost out of food. He had not taken precautions and by the time he realized that Fujino was indeed late, his food supply had dwindled too rapidly to get him through the winter. He still had tea and bags of ground meal, but his lack of other food had forced him to begin a fast. It was not a complete fast, of course, for he would eat some of the meal and drink tea each morning, but though he knew it to be spiritually weak, it nourished his anger with Fujino and allowed him to continue his history. He was not happy with the telling of stories when there were no listeners. In general he had allowed only a day or two for each century since Jomon, and he caught himself skipping many of the smaller details. He spent almost no time on personalities, and sometimes he let certain geographical areas go unmentioned for as long as five hundred years. Now he was in the middle of the sixteenth century when things were really beginning to happen in Japan. He had just finished all of the gruesome stories of the feudal wars and was anxious to get on to unification. Unification! For the first time the entire nation was at peace with itself and under one leader. Fujino knew little of this time in history so it would be too bad for him, for under no circumstances would Kaneda repeat it.

"Hideyoshi," Kaneda said in a low monotone. He paused, remembering statues he had seen of the great hero Hideyoshi in armor or Hideyoshi reading. A portrait of the great man was on one side of the new paper money, and a likeness of him had been etched on several of the country's coins.

"Hideyoshi was our first modern hero and the man who first unified Japan." There was music in the telling of stories. He could hear it in his voice. "Hideyoshi defeated both the small and the great armies and instigated change. Under his rule Japan had her first land registration, her first census, and the sword hunt that left most of the wandering samurai without the instruments of their trade."

It was hard to continue in the formal monotone of a storyteller. He knew the time of Hideyoshi so well there was no use telling himself. When he tried to picture the small face of the great general, he had no trouble. It was for someone else that he wanted to do the telling, to make the thing come alive.

Kaneda heard the approach of Finn at sunset and for a few moments confused those noises with the internal sounds of sixteenth-century Japan. They were like the sounds made by a cart being pushed from behind by a man. He imagined Hideyoshi riding, and himself a tradesman trying with all his strength to get his cart and his wares off the road in time.

Outside, Finn saw the water wheel first and remembered Fujino trying to explain to him how it worked. He stood before the closed shelter that the two men had built. He'd rehearsed a hundred times what he would say, yet he hesitated now, afraid to push the hide door back, afraid to find Kaneda wearing

Fujino's mouth, his body frozen into those same angles. He unloaded the sled, moving boxes up close to the entrance, hoping that the old man would come out, would greet him. The dog pushed his nose under the flap, smelling the fire, and Finn saw an orange tongue of flame. He was alive then!

Kaneda moved slightly to one side, picking up a knife and thinking "wolf." Finn pushed the dog out of the way and when he threw back the curtain Kaneda's knife was inches from his face. Finn looked forward out of his thick hood and for a moment saw the flames dancing in front of the face of Fujino, highlighting the pink flesh of the inside of his mouth. Kaneda held his thrust. Finn pushed the hood back away from his face.

"Mr. Kaneda?"

"You are not a wolf."

"Do you remember me? I'm Finn. From Nome."

Finn turned and pulled the closest box of supplies into the small room. Already, in the moments he'd been in camp, the sky had turned toward another night. Finn took the knife from Kaneda and slit the side of the box. He pulled out a bottle of whiskey and several small packages of salt salmon. He sat next to the old man and waited.

"Where's Fujino?" the old man asked. "What are you doing here?"

Finn held out the bottle. "Fujino's dead," he said quietly.

Kaneda unwrapped a little of the salt salmon and looked at it. He had, after all, been fasting only because there was not food. He put a little of the fish to his lips and sucked on it. "Sending you won't get him off the hook," he said. "He is late, very late."

Finn reached inside his coat and handed Kaneda the package of money. "This is what he got for your gold. And the raw gold is his share for the work he did on the beach."

Kaneda counted the money. "Why did he not come himself? Fujino is not so big a coward. Is he so big a coward?"

"Harakiri," said Finn.

Kaneda closed his fist around the whiskey bottle. The word came to him late for he had expected English, expected not to understand.

"Harakiri?" This time the voice was his own. Four distinct syllables. He let the word slice the air. *"Fujino? Harakiri?"* The old man stood and stupidly saw himself as the sixteenth-century peasant again. He looked at the knife stuck in the side of the box that Finn brought and pictured the soft hairless abdomen of Fujino and the knife moving through it. He saw a wound open cleanly, robust intestines bursting forth like Christmas gifts.

"Fujino? Harakiri?"

Finn put his arm on the old man's shoulder. "It's my fault," he said. "I talked him into staying."

There were noises inside the old man's head. He heard drums and horns. The mute dog entered and sat quietly next to Finn.

"Seppuku," the old man said. *"Harakiri."* The dog cocked his head, listening.

"I'm sorry," said Finn.

The old man reached down and pulled the knife from the side of the box. He felt the pressure starting way down in his bowels, moving up. He thought he was going to be sick. He swayed, nearly falling. In his hand the knife moved, swinging easily, and the dog, recognizing a game, took it in his mouth and sat with it between his paws. It was a sharp knife, one that Kaneda honed each day, and on the blade now were drops of blood. The dog, surprised, cleaned the blood off the knife and began sniffing around the room for more. He could taste it in his mouth but didn't recognize it as his own. He thrust his muzzle deep into the open side of the box and began to pull on the sharp tail of another of the frozen salted salmon.

Though Finn and the old man could speak to each other, they couldn't understand. Finn knew Kaneda had no English, but he'd assumed that it wouldn't be a big problem. Sign language, certain words, drawings; these were the tools they would use. And Finn, at the old man's insistence, abandoned early his decision to give up whiskey. He'd been there only a few hours and already a bottle was gone and another was opened and on the ground between them. The small room was hot. Kaneda was in no danger of freezing, and though he was very low on food he had managed well with his meal and his tea.

Finn leaned forward, pressing his face close to the old man's. The fire reflected yellow off his beard and eyes.

"It was my fault," he said. "Do you understand the meaning of the word 'fault'?"

"Harakiri is an old and honorable method. The samurai, the *ronin,* used it quite often. But Fujino . . ."

"He did it with mercury," Finn said slowly. He took a piece of the paper he had been drawing on and drew a picture of a bottle and wrote mercury on its label.

"Whiskey," Kaneda said, pushing the bottle toward him.

"No, mercury. Like the planet." Finn drew the sun and placed circles around it at various distances.

"This one," he said. "The circle closest to the sun. The smallest . . ."

Kaneda looked at the paper then shook his head. He didn't understand.

"It was not at all uncommon during the phase of history that we are now studying for a *ronin* to commit *harakiri,"* he said. "Things were pretty bleak then. In fact it used to be the custom of *ronin* to stand at the gates of the homes of rich merchants and threaten to disembowel themselves if the merchants did not offer money and food. Very disgraceful to see the decline of such an honorable group."

Finn listened hard to the sounds that were coming from Kaneda's mouth. Nothing. He understood nothing.

"Fujino. Fujino. Fujino." The old man repeated the name

evenly, in the same monotone he used when telling stories. "He died knowing nothing of our heritage. Knowing nothing!"

"Suicide," said Finn, taken away by the grief that he heard in the old man's voice. "All my fault."

The two men talked, each unsatisfied with the sounds he heard coming from the other.

"Penance," said Finn. "Do you know what that is? I am here to take his place."

Finn held the bottle high, trying to show the old man the strength of his pledge. "I will work for you while the gold lasts. I will consider my duty finished when you return to Japan. Until then I will act as Fujino did. I am here to take the place of Fujino." He sat heavy with the weight of such a promise.

"Fujino," the old man said, shaking his head. "I wish you were able to tell me the circumstances surrounding his death. I never thought Fujino would do that."

"Mercury," said Finn. "Mer-cu-ry." He pointed at the drawings of the bottle and the solar system.

"Certainly. Help yourself," said the old man. And then, "You know, Fujino was going to be my son-in-law. He was going to marry my daughter." He looked at his watch. "It is midnight. That means in Tokyo it is late and my daughter is standing at our gate waiting for the postman. Do you know, was Fujino able to post a letter when he arrived in Nome? Did he write to my daughter?"

"It's bloody cold," said Finn, "and dark. What kind of land is this for men to be living in?"

The old man began to cry. "Of course not. He would not have dared to write her without my permission. And he would not have dared ask me."

"Here, here. Wait on that," said Finn, trying to reach across the fire. "That'll do no good. Those tears'll freeze on your face." He picked up the whiskey bottle and stuck the neck of it underneath the old man's nose. "Wouldn't a spot of this help? I'm sure it would." He nudged the old man with the bottle, trying to get him to look up.

"I should have given him permission. I should have volunteered it. He was a good boy whom I did not appreciate."

The old man took the whiskey bottle and poured a little of the liquor into the tin cup that he held in his lap. He drank, then poured more and offered it to Finn.

"You are from Ireland," he said. "You probably know nothing about the history of Japan."

Finn heard, miraculously, the word "Ireland" as it cleared the cave of the old man's gibberish.

"Ireland?" he said. "I'm Irish."

"I should have told Fujino these stories. I, in my selfishness, started without him as a punishment for him being late. But I was slowing down. I wanted him to hear especially about Hideyoshi. About his invasion of Korea and all the strange things he did that are not easy to find in any of the history books." The old man wiped his eyes and looked up. "Would you be interested in hearing?"

"Ireland," said Finn. "What was that you were saying about Ireland?"

The old man adjusted himself under his blankets and furs. He put another log on the fire and poured whiskey into two cups. Finn watched carefully, sensing that something might happen. When the old man felt quite comfortable he closed his eyes and waited for a long time. Finn thought he was asleep, and at the sight of him, tiredness from the week of long travel swept over him. The mute dog was asleep behind Finn and provided a comfortable backrest. He closed his eyes and had the sense that he was pushing the sled, looking for the proper trail markings, trying to find the old man. His feet slipped through the crust of snow once and he jerked awake, and then fell immediately into a deep sleep. The old man tracing the story of Hideyoshi in his mind came to what he thought would be an interesting starting place. He said, "Hideyoshi," three times, testing the evenness of his monotone. He kept his eyes closed, waited a moment longer, then began:

"Hideyoshi was the ruler of all Japan but felt that if he wanted to stay in power for long he would have to do something about unemployment. For years his army had been busy defeating the armies of all the local barons, and now, in the late 1580s, he had tens of thousands of soldiers sitting around the castle towns with nothing to do. His advisors thought the situation to be critical. . . ."

The old man stopped for a moment. He felt he had gotten off to a good beginning. He didn't want to make any mistakes or say anything that would be confusing. One could not be too careful. When talking to a foreigner rhythm was everything.

———

Large branches cracked and fell upon the Snake, ice heavy. The army, on the far side, used the river as an extension of its camp, laying it with straw and wood chips, then bedding down their dogs. The raft that was used in summer for transportation protruded from the ice now, at angles. It was tied to the nearest tree by a rope that had crystallized and that was supported by icicles growing from it and rooting themselves in the ground.

The army had been nearly invisible in Nome, was nearly so now. The tents and buildings blinked dim light out at the winter or an occasional command shot pistol-clear off toward the frozen sea, but the soldiers and the officers stayed inside. They were surveyors and would sleep or play cards until their equipment could once again be pushed into the spring-soft soil. They had no fence and expected no visitors. A single man, on guard duty, stood inside a closed house on the river, leaning over a charcoal fire.

Phil, in the village these few weeks, was rested and had come to the river early this day so that he would be standing on the ice when Ellen and Henriette arrived. It would be hard for them coming even this far, so he'd brought a dog sled ready with blankets and furs. He let his dogs stand close to the army dogs, each group looking at the other, none barking, the leaders quietly rolling their lips back away from their teeth.

Phil had a pair of heavy metal blades with him, ice skates that he now strapped to the bottoms of his hide boots. They belonged to the reverend, who'd shown him how to use them and who, as a child, had been able to move backward as well as forward across the ice. He and Phil had spent several secret hours out on the frozen shallows of Norton Sound, and Phil, supposing that Ellen and Henriette might be late, had the skates today, knowing that he could practice the length of the river without worrying that the members of the village would see him and then would not rest until their feet too slid smoothly across the land.

Phil sat on the rump of the lead dog, tightening the straps with his bare hands. From here he could see the trail that the women would use. He pushed his hands back into his gloves and slid, still kneeling, away from the dog, his arms trailing next to the skates across the ice. He stood and, clasping his hands behind him, began to move in the manner the reverend had taught him. He kept his ankles stiff and circled down toward the sound once then back up the river. Behind him he left two small grooves in the ice. The air that pushed around Phil's hood and into his face made his mustache freeze, and the hairs in his nose too, froze when he inhaled and thawed when he exhaled again. The army dogs and the dogs of his sled forgot each other and followed Phil with their heads.

The river, as it moved back from the bay, grew smaller, turned a corner and then turned back again so that it looked like two rivers, a stretch of white land between them. The Snake, that source of all the gold, unchanging for as long as Phil could remember, had changed the territory. Phil wondered whether it was good or bad. Men here had lust for gold as they should have for a woman. Still, there was no denying what the gold could buy. It was hard for him to understand how one metal could be worth more than any other. The steel of these skates, for example, was a tribute to what men could do to improve upon what they took from the land. This steel was harder than anything, and it was smooth and sharp whereas the gold was soft and cumbersome and heavy to carry around. Of course the golden snowflakes were beautiful, but the men in Nome cared nothing for them. It was money they were after, and Phil knew that with gold in hand money was easy, but it seemed a strange choice of metals. He had no idea who had started the rumor that gold was valuable, but that it had begun as a rumor he had no doubt. And like many rumors it had long outlasted anyone who could remember its origins and had become a truth. As with invention and discovery, white men looked at the concept from the front and then from the back and then forgot that what they were seeing was a single concept, one idea.

Rumor. Truth. Invention. Discovery. Phil used the four words as cues for pushing first his left leg, then his right. He was far up the river now and turned so that he might not miss Ellen and Henriette. The dogs were craning their necks to see him, sniffing the air for clues. Phil coasted. The problem of skating would be in building up one's ankles and keeping one's rhythm. Rumor. Truth. Invention. Discovery. He saw the two women standing on the Nome side of the river, looking with the dogs. He waved. A few of the soldiers stuck their heads out of their tents and watched him skate by.

"Hello," Phil shouted, gliding, letting the skates dig him to a stop next to the women.

He turned toward the dogs and yelled something in Eskimo and the lead dog stood, nipped at the others until they too were up and stretching.

"My," said Ellen.

Henriette held a package containing the stockings and necklaces that they had made, and Ellen carried her carpet bag, the one she'd brought with her from Ireland, the one her father'd given her the day she left.

"Where's Finn?" asked Phil.

"He's gone to tell Mr. Kaneda about Fujino's death, to offer his services."

"He died then."

"He bled to death," said Ellen. "Finn feels we didn't do right by him."

Phil stood with the lead dog, walking bent over and talking in its ear until they were well past the army tents, then he went to the rear of the sled and alternately walked behind it or stood on the back runners. His ankles were sore from skating and the skates hung like the snowflakes around his neck. Ellen and Henriette were tucked into the sled, completely covered by pelts, rubbing their hands together silently.

———

Waiting in the village the reverend wrung his hands. He stood at his window looking up along the coast toward the Snake, then struggled into his outdoor clothes and paced the frozen beach. All of the Eskimos waited under the earth. The reverend thought of himself as an apparition alone in the utter wilderness. He paced like a worried head of state, wondering if they would come, if his letter had ever reached them. He'd spent many of his last days preparing his Christmas sermon and cleaning his house. He'd boiled buckets of water and washed his window and done his laundry.

Behind the village the reverend and the children decorated a tree. Phil's wife and sisters lent their snowflakes for the top of it and the men of the village dyed strips of white fur red with the blood of a seal they had caught. The reverend, following an old custom of his own, made popcorn and taught those who were interested how to string it and drape it around the tree. It would be a fine Christmas. He had dusted his carol books and practiced playing the village piano, which spent every winter in his house. He was in the spirit, looking forward to seeing the women from Nome, to waiting with the children for Christmas morning.

When he saw the sled, the reverend's heart sank. Phil was there but he could see no one tucked under the folded pelts, he could see no one else walking. The reverend strode, trying not to slip, over to the sled shed to help Phil unharness the dogs. Ellen and Henriette pushed the robes away and stood when he had his back turned to them.

"Hello, hello," they said, lifting their parcels to him.

"Oh, hello, well ..." he said turning. "I didn't think you'd come. Hiding in the sled, were you?"

"Popped up like prairie dogs," said Henriette.

The reverend grinned and took their bags and lifted the sled robes and peeked under. "Finn?" he said.

"Do you think we had him hidden under us?" asked Ellen. "He went to the Japanese camp. Explaining the tragedy."

"Suicide," said the reverend. "I heard from Phil."

The reverend was so happy to see Ellen, to see Henriette, that he could not adjust his face to the subject of suicide. "We prayed for the young man," he said, grinning. "Phil and I."

Ellen said, "Finn's Catholic and would confess that he had some hand in it if there was a priest about. He finds strength in that kind of thing."

"The Lord works in mysterious ways," said the reverend. "If

Finn were here I would tell him so. Was the young man a Christian?"

"We talked gold," said Ellen. "He was with us during the beach strike and we talked of nothing else. Finn asked him to stay on when he came to town for supplies. That is why Finn feels responsible. He taught us how to mine the stuff."

The reverend nodded and told the women he'd be honored if they would stay with him again. He walked between them, linking an arm in each of theirs, telling them not to slip, guiding them. When they got to his house he said he hoped they'd be pleased and opened the door and pushed them through. Phil was with them and hung the ice skates on their proper hook.

"The whole village has disappeared," said Henriette.

"If you look hard you can see us," said Phil. "We've gone mostly underground. It's easier that way in the wintertime, and much warmer."

The reverend had a fire in the wood stove and had hung the walls with anything that reminded him of Christmas. Behind the stove were two red stockings, one marked "Ellen" and the other "Henriette." Next to them was a small box marked "Finn."

"It's lovely," said Ellen. "Like having Christmas at home."

"Any port in a storm," said Henriette.

The reverend pushed the door shut and hung layers of everyone's clothes on all the spare hooks. He'd made Christmas cookies and reaching into his small kitchen brought some out, laying two in each hand. In the center of the room his tin punch bowl was full again, steam rising from it warmly. He handed everyone a cup.

"Cheers," said the reverend, holding his cup high.

"Cheers," said Henriette.

"To the health of hard-headed Finn on his journey," said Ellen.

"To Fujino," said Phil.

"May God have mercy on his soul," said the reverend.

The punch in their cups cooled as they drank it. "Christmas comes but once a year," said the reverend, getting everyone another drink.

They drank and talked and made preparations for Christmas. It was the twenty-third, the reverend told them. Did they realize how close that was to Christmas? Two days. My, how time flies. He would give his service at midnight on the twenty-fourth and then while the children slept they would ready the gifts. And they would have Christmas dinner on Christmas day, at two in the afternoon.

After more punch, Phil went home to rest and to talk to his family. The reverend and the two women went up the loft ladder to sit in the big chairs looking out at the empty village.

"It seems like no one lives there now and no one ever did," said Ellen. "You must feel lonely during these long winters."

"The view sometimes makes me feel that way. And, of course, I am alone. But as for activities, my days are as full as your brimming cup of punch."

The reverend sat smiling. He'd pulled a hard-backed chair from his kitchen in anticipation of the three of them sitting here this way. He wanted them to take pride in the winter view as he did, so he had placed the big easy chairs close to the window. They watched Phil walking across the whiteness. He stood by his sister's hut a moment, then turned toward them, raised his hand, and sank into the earth.

"Like a captain gone down with his ship," said the reverend.

"Like a prairie dog," said Henriette. "I know what you mean."

The reverend carried the remaining punch up the fur-runged ladder and placed it on the floor between them.

"If it's not finished while it's hot, ladies," he said, "it is very weak in spirit."

He filled the cups, squeezing the dents out of the tin as he did so. He handed the punch to the women, his thumbnail stained.

Ellen said, "By way of gifts, reverend, we've knitted stockings and made them necklaces. A gift should be useful as well as desired." She reached into the bag at her side and carefully unwrapped one of the long packages. "I've knitted a size that, though it might be large for some, will be too small for no one." She handed the stockings to him, pointing out that the bulge in the toe was Henriette's necklace.

The reverend was beside himself. "Oh, ladies," he said, "I meant only a trifle, a piece of candy, a balloon." He held the long stockings up to the window then pulled the necklace out of the toe and placed it around his neck. "You really shouldn't have." He stuck a hand deep down the throat of each stocking and pinched them into puppet faces, snapping his fingers together for mouths.

"It was the best of times; it was the worst of times," his left hand said.

"I only thought they must have a hard time of it keeping their feet warm," said Ellen.

The reverend let the mouths of the puppets yawn open until they turned to stockings again. "It's a wonderful gift," he said. "And that every child will have the same thing couldn't be better. It will avoid capriciousness. The many will not cast aside their gifts for the toys of a few."

The reverend stuffed the necklace back into the toe of the stocking and refolded them into their Christmas wrapping.

" 'It was the best of times; it was the worst of times,' " said Ellen. "My father read me that book across the open fire, with the flames warming our own cold house. Your having said it takes me back. Do you remember what comes next? Do you remember the next line?"

The reverend held the lightly folded Christmas gift in his hands and sat back. Ellen was looking out into the whiteness and Henriette had pulled the sleeve of her sweater around her hand, making a puppet.

" 'It was the best of times; it was the worst of times,' " he said. " 'Good and evil were rampant in the world and drew, like magnets, the willy-nilly hearts of men.' "

Ellen nodded into the blank window, trying to remember the way it had been.

The reverend stopped himself, quickly sticking his lower lip into his mouth and biting on it.

"Willy-nilly?" said Henriette. She laughed once and then held up her own wool-skinned hand. "You are engaged in the game willy-nilly, and cannot be mere lookers-on," she said.

———

Quiet so the old man could sleep, Finn watched the gray light through a space between two pieces of hide. The dog was warm and curled around his back like a chair; the old man was wide-mouthed and snoring. He had prayed and his prayer had cleared the air of ghosts, gape-mouthed Fujino gone, riding his mule, slump-shouldered. Finn, exhausted but unable to sleep, thought about his life and laughed at himself for not being able to live it easily. Ah confession, where has it failed me? he thought. His guilt hung heavy whether he confessed or not. Father, forgive me for I have sinned. Sometimes he dreams of priests leaning forward, peering at him through the confessional wall.

"Finn? What? Is that you again?"

"Yes, father."

"Bloody hell! You send 'em out into the world and ninety percent of 'em are back within the month. Guilty the lot!"

Light, cold like shafts of ice, made Finn close the hide curtain once more. Things would be different now. The old man's prayer had changed everything. His was a prayer with force, a prayer with power. Finn had floated on the old man's monotone for hours, the taste of salt salmon bracing him. As soon as he heard the beginning buzzes of the voice he knew what it was, that the old man was calling forth the following spirit of Fujino, bringing it right into the dark room with them. In a half dream Fujino had floated in clear liquid, a fetus like the one Finn had once seen bobbing in its small glass sea in a country sideshow in Ireland. It had been a restful sound, the old man's voice. It contained a sense of familiarity reminiscent of the priests when Latin licked Finn's childhood.

Finn, warm now and wound into the memory of the old man's prayer, dreams a meaning into the Japanese language. Kaneda snores with the wide mouth of Fujino. Dark, dank odor like the den of a bear, but a good home for the dog. Finn pushes the dog a little with his elbow. Look at him, sleeping every minute. "Hello, Mute, mute dog, wake up." He takes a piece of salt salmon and chews on it. He gently takes a broad fish tail from between the jaws of the sleeping dog and holds it up in front of him. Broad tail, slack-jawed dog. A weapon such as this is what Fujino should have used, frozen sharp as it is. Would it have cut his belly as it did the water? Finn sets the tail back in the dog's mouth and the mouth closes upon it softly. What dreams does a dog have? Of food? Of mounting or being mounted? No, those are men's dreams. Dogs dream of rabbits skimming across spring fields.

Finn looks again at the old man, envies him sleeping deeply, proof of his innocence. If men get rich in Alaska this one will. Already his head is pillowed on lumps of money. Gold weighs the tent flaps down and reflects yellow off his skin. He looks like Phil, this old man. Long-lost brother, maybe. Alaska was once a part of Asia, he'd heard that said. . . . Alas, the land was broken and drifted apart, like family members, like marriages. Maybe the alphabet is the key to the way things are. Asia, Alaska, America, that fits too. And Finn, failure, Fujino. No, I'm too tired for this. The old man has prayed me away from all my guilt. If Fujino's dead it's Fujino's fault, not Finn's. I've my pensum to do and then I'll be free. I'll work for the old man

and I'll take what share he gives me. I only hope to God he'll
be fair. I wonder, were he and Fujino fifty-fifty? Finn leans
heavy against the dog. What's this—contentment?—I feel? He
stretches, feels the short beard of his face. Chuck the guilt.
Chuck the whole bloody raft of it. I'll try marriage then. There's
Ellen. There's Henriette. But enough, I should have been to
sleep hours ago. Enough of this. Do other men spend such time
thinking of themselves? Are there those who think only of others? Are the priests like that? Have I been unfair with them?
So many possibilities.

Finn near sleep tosses about. I've my family's name to think
of; there'll be no compromise. There's Ellen. There's Henriette.
There's Phil's sister all tucked away in her virgin hut. A movement from the dog and Finn slips down further, droopy-eyed.
This is silly, a man of my age. He chases thoughts here and
there, missing each and every one. He casts about in the black
back of his mind a bit, then gives up. Lord, Lord, what a week.
Let it go. The warm tide of sleep washes him. Dark room, Finn
dogged, old man sawing away like a lumberjack. Outside cold
cold night. When will it ever stop? Sleep. Sleep. Not a fit night
for man nor beast, would you say? Cold. Cold. Must be thirty
degrees below zero.

———

The reverend was nervous and said, "Did you ever notice, in
the village, the absence of a church? Services, during the winter,
are held right here, in my house. People sit wherever they want
to. I walk among them and talk, or sit and play the piano."

"Do yourself the favor of relaxing, reverend," said Ellen.
"To be sure the services are held in your house. What did you
suppose we thought the candles to be for?"

"It is so cold. On the eve of Christ's birth you wouldn't have
thought it possible."

"On this night nineteen hundred years ago the three wise men were following the star to Bethlehem," said Ellen. "I once played the bearer of gold in a school play."

"Three kings," said Henriette, "wise or not."

Last-minute details: the house turned to chapel, dozens of long candles burning bright, the reverend's clean scrubbed head protruding from a boiled shirt, Ellen the calming influence, Henriette bright-eyed, struck by singing, no help at all. They sat, the dark window in front of them thick with night and sprayed by gusts of snow lifted to it and then laid like gifts onto its outer sill. 'Twas the night before Christmas and all through the house . . . They told each other stories.

Ellen said, "In Ireland we had services, eleven to midnight. It was grand. Eleven to midnight for a small girl was an hour so rarely seen. And at the church we had our own pew, and I my spot in it, next to my grandmother, who hissed and pinched at me the entire time, saying, 'Don't fidget.' I'd not be surprised if my legs were black and blue still."

They talked and laughed. The packages were labeled, the loft floor laid with stocking pyramids, each pair folded like two tongues inside. They sighed and stood, snapped to their feet by the knock-knocking of the parishioners, lined up at the door.

"Oh, come in, welcome," said the reverend. "Christmas comes but once a year. Come in. Come in."

Short to tall they came. This was not a time for levity. The children climbed the ladder and sat, still as Ellen's memory, legs dangling, waiting. The adults, too, were ushered to their usual places. They said hello to each other in whispers. "Hello there, how are you this evening? Merry Christmas. Merry Christmas."

After a moment's settling Henriette at the piano struck a chord and the reverend raised his hands. Quiet. Quiet. "Thank you for coming," he whispered. He cleared his throat and began.

"Everything boils down to this," he said, "if it hadn't been for His birth nothing else would matter." The reverend paused a moment. "Well, well, well," he said, smiling at everyone. "Merry Christmas."

This will never do. The reverend had the strong urge to end it right there, to sit down and let them know that it was over. Everybody knows about Christmas, what was he going to say that they didn't know already? His prepared sermon drifted from him casually. If he didn't lunge now he wouldn't be able to retrieve it.

People began to shift in their seats a little. If only he didn't have guests. Quickly he began to speak. "Uh . . . at the time of any birth, whether it be that of a savior or of a child of God like one of us, the people crowd around to see if it is a boy or a girl, to see how the mother is getting along, to help if they can, or just to celebrate the arrival of a new human being. And that is what happened in Bethlehem. Manger . . . Manger . . . We hear a lot about Him being born in a manger, but Judea was a country of mild climates, and to be born in a manger was no great hardship. There were people around. Others were staying in the stable too, and people strolled in the cool evening air. There was a general sense of excitement. 'Hey, a baby is being born in that manger over there,' someone said, and the people poured in. A thing like that doesn't happen every day."

Was this the right beginning? What he had planned on saying seemed dull to him now. This is a time of celebration, praise the Lord, Christ is born, who wants to listen to a sermon?

The reverend looked at Ellen, who looked at him. Henriette shifted in her chair then leaned heavily on the rumbling low notes of the piano.

"No," said the reverend, "on that night there was no thunder or lightning. There was only Mary and the baby, and Joseph. . . . " The pressure was off for a moment and the reverend got his idea. He looked at the ground and said, "Joseph . . . When a baby is born, who ever thinks of the father?

"Joseph was a quiet man. He walked around with his hands

in his pockets much of the time and he, though no one knew it, was a kind of philosopher. He thought about the nature of the universe and the differences between people. Think of it. Mary was exhausted and asleep, the baby at her side. All of the strangers, the excitement over, went back to whatever they were doing, and Joseph was left alone, late at night, wandering around the streets with nowhere to go. He was tired but he wasn't sleepy, and a single question played upon his mind: What is it that makes a good father?"

The reverend looked at the faces of the people and knew he had them. They were interested, even Ellen and Henriette, and the familiar translations had started, people whispering into the ears of their neighbors. In his mind's eye he gave himself the part of Joseph and furnished Bethlehem with dark doorways and drunks, an occasional lowered veil.

"What is it that makes a good father?" he said. "Joseph was not the first nor would he be the last to ask himself that question. He wandered up one dusty street and down another thinking about it. He was a father, sort of, and that made this no moot philosophical point. What is it that makes a good father? He decided he would ask the next three people he met."

During the whole beginning of his sermon the reverend had stayed in one place, but he began to move now, first shifting from one foot to the other, then walking across the room in front of his parishioners. He took his hands out of his pockets and clasped them behind his back.

"The first person Joseph approached was a woman, but he decided to ask her anyway.

" 'Excuse me,' he said, 'but what is it that makes a good father?'

"The woman lowered her veil and smiled with black teeth. 'Thirty pieces of silver,' she said.

"Thirty pieces of silver," the reverend said to the group again. "Well, Joseph thanked her, and though he did not understand the answer, he knew to be patient. He knew from past

experience that time might well provide him with the understanding he lacked now.

"After that, finding other people was no easy matter, for the
streets were dusty and the hour was late. Of course there were
drunks, but Joseph preferred not to ask one of them.

"He turned corner after corner, met only by darkness. He
would teach the baby his ways, and the baby would make him
proud. People would say, 'Joseph of Nazareth's son went further
than he did.' Joseph's son . . . Does it take a real father to be
a good one?

"A blind man with snapping fingers sat on a rug in the
middle of the dark street. 'Ho,' he said, hearing Joseph's heavy
footsteps.

" 'Ho,' said Joseph. 'What is it that makes a good father?'

" 'I am blind,' said the blind man. 'And I live here in the
middle of the street. Are you talking to me?'

" 'Yes,' said Joseph. 'What is it that makes a good father?'

" 'Not all men are fathers, but all men are sons. Ask me how
to be a good son.'

" '*I* am a father,' said Joseph. 'I know how to be a good son,
what I need to know is how to be a good father.'

" 'Being a good son is being a good father,' said the blind
man. 'Don't ask silly questions.'

"Joseph moved away quickly. Strange answers, he thought.
Being a good son is being a good father? Thirty pieces of silver?
That's what you get for asking such a question at night.

"Joseph looked into the sky and saw the star that the three
wise men were following, but he didn't think much of it. He
was beginning to get sleepy and he still had one more person
to ask. It was bad luck to suspend these things before they were
finished. A veiled woman, a blind man, who would be next?
People were getting scarce. He'd even ask a drunk if he had
to."

The reverend took a moment and quietly walked the floor in

front of them all. This was a pretty good sermon. The candles flickered off the round faces of the Eskimos, off the faces of the long-nosed women. People were listening. . . .

"A woman came up behind Joseph," said the reverend, "and Joseph thought, 'Oh no, thirty pieces of silver will do for one answer, but not for two.'

"The woman pulled hard on his sleeve. 'Did you upset that blind man back there?' she asked.

" 'Upset him? I only asked him what it is that makes a good father.'

" 'Who put you up to this?'

" 'Why, no one. My wife just had a baby and . . . '

" 'He went blind trying to be a good father and you have to come along and rub salt in his wounds. His daughters lurk in the doorways around him, his sons are dead soldiers and you have to ask him how to be a good father! Of all questions!'

" 'I'm sorry,' said Joseph. 'I didn't know.'

" 'You didn't know,' said the woman evenly. 'That's what they all say. You want to know what it is that makes a good father? I'll tell you what makes a good father. Go blind!'

"The woman fairly screamed at him, then turned on her heels and marched off. 'Go blind!' she had said, and her words had hit Joseph in the eyes, dimming them. Go blind. Suddenly the light from the star seemed too bright for him and he feared that, yes, he might go blind even then. What kind of answers were these? Thirty pieces of silver. Being a good son is being a good father. Go blind. Had he asked all members of the same family? He wanted good advice. He had taken the walk to clear his head and to ask some sound advice from those he met, from those who knew better. Never tell a lie, that would have been the kind of answer he expected. Or be firm and strict but kind and fair. He'd heard someone say that before, or he'd seen it written down. But this . . .

"Joseph threw up his hands and turned back toward the

manger. He was sleepy. He'd learn to be a good father day by day. He guessed he already knew how, but he had wanted a piece of advice, a saying to live by. When he got back it was nearly daylight. Mary and the baby were asleep in the dry hay, and the cattle, of course, were lowing, chewing their cuds. Joseph yawned and stretched. He found a spot a little way off and lay down. He closed his eyes. What is it that makes a good father? he thought. Ask a silly question . . . Still, he wanted to be involved in raising this boy, and already he felt secondary. Mary was more interested in the baby than she was in him. Too tired to think now, he decided to worry about it later. He'd make himself known to the boy. What is it that makes a good father? He'd gotten three answers, and nineteen hundred years later the question still confuses us."

The reverend looked at his parishioners. They were still involved. A few of them were writing down the question and the answers and many others were still quickly translating the problem into Eskimo and putting it to their neighbors. He nodded toward Henriette at the piano, so she played and began to sing in a clear, high voice, and after a chorus alone Ellen and the reverend and the Eskimos joined her. "Joy to the world," they sang loudly, until the children understood that the sermon was over and got up and ran to the window looking seaward.

"Good sermon, reverend," said Ellen, stepping forward. "A story I've never heard before."

"Oh well . . ."

After the service there was a light snack, but nobody wanted to eat much. It was important to have an empty stomach on the day before a Christmas meal. Everyone seemed anxious to get home and to sleep as quickly as they could. As the Eskimos left, each took one of the candles and the reverend's house got darker and darker.

"I guess I won't light the lamps," he said. "It is late and we must be up early with the gifts."

The reverend, round with pleasure after his sermon, pointed toward the two sleeping areas, then stepped into his small kitchen, discreetly allowing the two women the freedom of changing their clothes alone.

———

"Nightgowns over clothing, clothing out from under nightgowns," said Ellen. "Like this."

Ghostlike, heads covered, the women undressed in their small tents. The Christmas packages were in a stack by the door, ready to be taken out into the later darkness. Candle wax froze warm in its run down the sides of the remaining candles, some burning faster than others. "Candles made from seals!" Henriette exclaimed when she'd first heard about them. And she could only imagine circus animals balancing flames on their noses.

Ellen went businesslike to bed, thinking how little sleep she would get before they'd take the packages out to that frozen tree. This was Christmas Eve. Other Christmas Eves stacked behind her like fence posts. She reached up and felt the skin across her face, looser than she remembered it. She locked her fingers at the base of her throat and prayed. Lord have mercy on poor Mr. Fujino. He died a terrible death and lived a good life. Lord keep Finn Wallace safe from himself and from his Catholic ways. Bless the reverend, who loves you, and bless Henriette, who is like a child. Ellen stopped, seeing herself kneeling at the side of her own child bed, large-bodied parents swaying above. God bless mother and father. I wonder do they live? Is father still stone-faced at his pub rail? Mother in her kitchen? And is grandmother's clock still smashed? Christmas Eve, oh how she longed to be home. Amen. She rolled to one side, ashamed. Who could have guessed the path my life would take? She heard her father's voice: "You'll be wishing for home with a passion far greater than the one which makes you want to leave. Mark my words."

The reverend, ready for bed in the kitchen, saw the other room turn dark. He thought of himself as Joseph, saw himself waiting as Joseph might have, outside the manger, ready to tiptoe in, careful not to wake.

The reverend tiptoed in quietly, past the woman in his bed. He was as tired as Joseph and he wanted to be as quiet. Still, the sleeping figures drew him. He wanted to look into their faces, to pull the blankets warm around their necks. He stood for a long time, then touched the pelt-runged loft ladder and stepped, fur-footed, higher into the room. He looked, as before, straight forward through the darkness. The ladder was sound-less so the reverend stepped higher, once, twice. Blankets dark as night wrapped the sleeping figure in the loft, a shadow etched on the dull light of the window. He remembered Ellen bound in her summer cocoon and wanted to see her again. How dif-ferent she looked now. He thought of Mary, bone-tired from childbirth.

The sleeping figure turned on its side, then sat up, eyes wide, facing the reverend.

"What?"

Oh my God, Henriette! Joseph sped from the manger. The reverend's red face was hidden by the dark.

"I'm sorry. I wanted to see if you were all right." Whispered.

"What?"

"Shh."

Henriette, sleep falling from her like fish scales, misunder-stands. "It's not time yet? It's not morning?"

"No. Be quiet. Don't speak so loudly."

"Oh."

"I wanted to see if you were all right. I'm sorry."

Nothing more to say. Wait until she lies down again, then back away. Make her lie down. Oh God, make her lie back down.

Henriette sat farther up, holding the bedclothes to her neck. She could see him now, a little, dark head stiffly balanced there. Must be terrified. Room's quiet, nothing could wake Ellen, she knew.

"I'm sorry," the reverend said again. And then, "Morning comes early. You'd better sleep."

Henriette pushed her hand slowly into the darkness, letting it meet the cool flesh of the reverend's cheek. Her fingers were on the side of his neck, rubbing. "It's cold in the house," she said. She pulled him, nearly weightless, from the ladder, settling him on the loft floor beside her. Sweet Mary and Joseph . . .

"Thank you for your concern," she said, whisper of whispers, laying the words in his ear like gifts.

The reverend felt his head spinning. "I am very, very lonely," he said evenly. And then he peered at her dark face and added, "At times."

Henriette moved near him, pushing her breast to his head like a pillow. "I wonder if there is a colder spot on earth," she said, pulling her blankets around them both.

The reverend couldn't speak. She, warming him, took the shaking of his limbs for cold and put him down on her mattress, arms around his shoulders lightly.

"There, there," she said. The reverend's mouth wetted the outside of her nightshirt, mound of breast pushing his lips against his teeth.

"There, there," she said, nursing him.

Oh sweet Jesus, thought the reverend. Mother of God. Was he freed from the confines of his body? He could feel nothing of his arms and legs.

"There, there."

God, he felt sorry for Joseph, hands pushed into pockets, walking the lonely streets. Utter freedom. Glory be to God, did the man have a life of his own? Joseph, Joseph, Joseph. The reverend wet Henriette's shirt with his mouth and eyes giving her a second skin, soft as the breath of God. He closed his eyes

vice tight, dams bursting throughout his body. Still the image
of Joseph clung. "Go blind," he told himself. "Go blind."

"There, there," said Henriette.

———

Finn and Kaneda ate a large meal and sat, in the aftermath,
full-bellied, the dog between them cleaning himself like a cat.
Kaneda counted his money. There was more than he expected
there would be. There was the right amount of coin, but there
was pure gold too. This man had brought pure gold all the way
back from town, where he was supposed to have exchanged it.

"Gold," he said, pointing at the delicate webbing.

"That's right," Finn answered, head nodding vigorously.
"From the beach placer. It's Fujino's share."

"Fujino?"

"Share," said Finn. "It's his share."

The two men spent much of their time discovering ways to
communicate. They used single words and drawings. They
pointed to objects. Kaneda looked at the dog and said, *"Inu,"*
until Finn did the same, the dog's eyes darting from one man
to the other.

Time passed slowly. They went outside in the gray daylight
for a while. They sang to each other. Finn cut blocks of ice from
the stream bed and brought them into the room. He had a sharp
knife and carved figures from the blocks. As he finished them
he looked at Kaneda, asking him with his eyes to guess what
the figure might be. He carved Fujino, head and shoulders protruding from the bath, mouth a gaping zero, then he let it melt
away without explanation.

After the first few days Finn was careful not to mention Fujino by name. When it was dark and they had nothing to do,
Kaneda would again begin to pray. He found his posture each

night, then spoke to Finn a moment, then began to chant. Finn listened as if he understood, and each night, after only a few minutes, he'd begin to hear it as if it were Latin, and was impressed with the power of it. It took him back. As Kaneda prayed for Fujino, Finn swirled through the streets of London-derry, in and out of memories. He followed himself as a boy and as a young man. The tone of Kaneda's voice brought him to it. . . . The priests and how they entered his life. His teachers had nearly all been priests, as many of his classmates were now, his own brother, his cousin. "Have you thought of a life of the cloth?" they'd say, but only to the best students, only to those who exhibited themselves properly. It had been a joke among the lower classes, among seamstresses and tailors and shoeshine boys. Have you thought of a life of the cloth? Oh how they'd laughed, holding up pieces of material and smiling through them.

Finn thought of crook-necked priests turned away from him, visible through the dim slats of the confessional. He had always tried to disguise his voice.

"I've had impure thoughts again, father."

"What's that? Speak up son, it's hard to hear."

"In my mind I have traveled a dangerous path."

"And what path might that be?"

"The curve of thigh, the bend of knee."

"Lust, my boy?"

"Yes, father."

"And who was it? Toward whom were these thoughts di-rected?"

"Toward the girls I pass in the street. Toward the women friends of my mother. Toward those whom I happen to see in rooms. Toward my sister and the nuns of her school. Toward a woman that my mind has shown me, no one I have ever known, but someone who is with me always."

"Toward your own sister and toward nuns?"

"Yes, father."

"Shame on you young man. Shame."

Had it ever happened? It made Finn smile now. He'd left the confessional like a crab, jacket pulled high over his head, priest peering out. "Who's that? What boy walks like that?" Perhaps not. Perhaps it's a story from a mix of memories, bits of a dozen confessions remembered as one. Finn thought of priests confessing to priests, of nuns confessing . . . "I'm in love with one of the priests, father." Bur-headed confessor perks up. "Which one is it? It's not me, is it? Which one?"

Finn laughed inwardly and came back to Kaneda, who was still chanting, still nailing the soul of Fujino to the walls. He could hear bits of familiar prayers in the old man's speech. The church, it's like flypaper; did he ever think he was away from it? Foolish man. You can't escape. *You* are what ties you to it. *You* are the temple and the source of it all. Finn turned and cracked the hide door. Black night froze them in once more, its cold breath touching his face, but in a moment quiet hit the room like an explosion. The prayer was over. Wide-eyed Kaneda, tired, looked at Finn, waiting for a glass of whiskey. Finn poured. It had become his job at the end of prayer to tend to thirsts. "Cheers," he said. "Cheers," said Kaneda, his first new word.

Kaneda drank the liquor down, worn throat dying for it. He had been hurrying again, taking shortcuts because the listener was a foreigner. There were gaping holes in his history, Fujino would be appalled at what he was leaving out. Still, the gist of it was there. And the order was correct, and the style. It's only the speed that he'd worried about. He covered fifty years tonight. Just enough to finish the seventeenth century.

———

The stockings were laid at the base of the frozen tree before any of the children were awake. The night before, the reverend had told the women not to worry about oversleeping. "One of the things about me," he said, "I can get up whenever I want to. I just repeat the time to myself before I sleep, and sure enough, that's the time I wake up."

They had laid the packages on a blanket, hoping they'd be free of ice and easy for the children to pick up. The dark morning air hit their lungs like knives. They worked quickly, silent as foxes, then scurried back to the reverend's house for a cup of the coffee brought to him from Nome. A gift from Ellen and Henriette.

Christmas had made Ellen expansive. She'd slept well and had the reactions of the children to look forward to. She supposed it wouldn't be a bad life, living here. Ellen sang to herself, hands warmed over the stove. The reverend and Henriette stood behind her, not looking at each other. Henriette leaned toward him, occasionally letting her hand touch his, but the reverend stood straight, trying to think of other things, humming along with Ellen, giving her cause to turn and look at him.

"As much as Henriette is a singer you are not," she said, smiling. "But don't let it worry you. Christmas gives us hope."

They sat in the candled room, in three chairs equally spaced and facing each other. Still hours to daylight, Christmas morning. Henriette looked at the reverend and remembered the feeling she'd had when Fujino first took sick. She could be of some use to this man, help him, be the one he relied upon, the one that gave him strength. His mouth upon her breast had warmed her over, made her remember what it was like not to be alone. She would not be a nurse to him, but she could perform a service as valuable. She got up and went to the kitchen for more coffee.

Gray light brought Phil first, then others, carrying parts of the Christmas meal, building fires, reheating, slicing slabs of seal. The children had their stockings and wore them like slippers, warm-footed, throughout the house. They hung the necklaces around their necks, or tied them to the tops of the stockings and let them trail behind. Everyone brought their drawings and set them around the room for everyone else to admire. They would ask Ellen and Henriette to make comments on each, not as drawings, but as snowflakes. Not as paper, but as gold.

The reverend gave his gifts to Ellen and Henriette. "My mother was French and taken with jewelry," he said. "I have no more use for it."

In each of the packages a pair of earrings, Henriette's long and silver, Ellen's neat and round. "I know there's not much chance to wear them here," he said, "but my mother would have liked to see them used."

Ellen thanked him, holding the jewelry in her warm hands. Henriette hooked the earrings to her ears and ran to see herself in the small cracked mirror of the kitchen. She felt like spinning around, and swung her head to make the earrings move. "I'll wear them rain or shine," she said. "I'll never take them off."

Phil gave each woman small bone carvings that he had done. "They are made from the tusks of a walrus and will give good luck," he said. "Always remember, however, to leave them home when you go walrus hunting."

The reverend held up Finn's gift and shook it. "I do wish that he had come," he said. "It's just a piece of old wood given to me by a teacher, but I think it would give him confidence, keeping his faith strong, whatever his persuasion might be. These things should be passed on."

"I have been home too long and am growing fat," said Phil. "I will take it to him. Topcock Creek. I know where that is."

Phil took the small package from the reverend and tucked it into his pocket. Henriette wanted to ask if he would take it today, but Christmas dinner, red feathers riding on top of it like flags of distress, was carried in on a wooden platform and placed across two chairs.

"Ladies and gentlemen, the goose," said Ellen quietly, standing behind the others.

People pressed to the edges of the table, child fingers poking out from between them. Seal in all its forms, and salmon. There were steam-heavy potatoes and more meat, and more meat.

"Ladies and gentlemen," the reverend said, getting ready for his prayer.

"The goose," whispered Ellen, again.

"When Joseph awoke the next morning tired and hungry and confused over the three answers he had gotten, three kings were poking their heads in the door.

" 'This couldn't be the place,' said one, but Joseph was on his feet and walking toward them before they had a chance to leave.

" 'Being a good son is being a good father,' he said. 'Here's the baby. What makes you think this isn't the place?'

"That was Christmas Day," said the reverend, "and when the three kings saw the baby they said: 'There are not three kings here, but four,' a comment that pleased Joseph quite a lot.

"Anyway, this is Christmas dinner, in celebration of all that. While we eat we should remember it, but not to the point of forgetting to enjoy the food. Amen."

The reverend picked up a piece of fresh seal and slid it into his mouth. He brought forks and knives for Ellen and Henriette, but everyone else used their hands.

"Ah seal," they said. "Your liver is gone but you are still here. Ah seal," they said, "your heart is gone but you are still here. Ah seal, your body is gone but you are still here." These were the prayers of the Eskimos; low voices, talking to the food between bites. "Ah seal, ah seal . . ."

———

Phil put strips of the meat in a hide bag and hung the bag next to his body, next to Finn's boxed gift. He talked to his family, gesturing in the direction of Topcock Creek, then strode toward the door, slipping the ice skates under his jacket as he went. Another course, same as the first, had been brought in. People ate, and the reverend looked at Ellen. "To think," he said, "we have done this with just two seals and with no bread at all."

Phil closed the door on them, stepping warm-footed onto the trampled ground. He pulled the hood around his head and marched off. The Snake was a smooth path; he'd leave the dogs and be there faster. He got to the beach and could see the shining window of the reverend's house behind him. He walked with his head down, feeling the weight of the seal in his stomach, pretending not to notice the cold.

Inside the house the seal diminished. The reverend walked about the room talking to his parishioners, always knowing exactly where Henriette was standing. Ellen, upstairs, saw Phil go, watched his dark shape move across the window of the loft. He'd find Finn, bring him back safely. Finn, a man with a will like the tides as they flow under the ice, a pubman, a talker. Her father fell forward in her mind when she thought of Finn. She loved her father with all her heart but she'd not end up with one like him. Had she come to the furthest ends of the earth only to find Finn smiling like a neighbor, welcoming her from the ship? No, Finn, father had me years and years and that's enough. I'll not be passed from hand to hand.

Ellen turned away from the window, a smile on her face, a laugh for herself. Here's me talking as if he wanted me and turning him down. I am as a sister to the man and that's as it should be. Still, it's uncanny how he resembles father in his resolutions and his defeats. Father's Christmas speeches were nothing like the reverend's. More like something Finn would say. Yet Finn and father would come to blows if they were forced to spend ten minutes together. Politics and religion. Each would bloody his hands on the head of the other.

From the loft railing Ellen watched the reverend making his

rounds. If his mother was French then his father must have been English. Here is a tender man, a gentle, harmless man. Him being a man of religion would be enough to hold her father at bay for a while at least. But religion would be his only weapon and he doesn't know how to use it.

Father'd have him sitting quietly in the corner of the parlor among darned stockings and women's talk. It'd be no match, after all. Ellen shook her head as if to get the thought away. And who I spend my life with will be my own business, she said, punching her voice back into her memory. Never mind who I choose and I'll not be bringing him home to boot, thank you very much. You've seen the last of me.

She turned and started down the ladder, backing into the voices of the Christmas party. Her father, bull-headed even about leaving her thoughts, stood in the parlor one hand each on the throat of Finn and of the reverend. She could see his thumbnails digging into their flesh, she could see them wriggling, trying to get away. "These two? Are these what you've brought back after such a long cast?" Finn and the reverend hung like trophies from her father's arms. Ellen turned to the room where the Eskimo women were full and joking. She took up a piece of meat quickly, like a change of subject.

———

Phil, at the river now, locked the skates to his feet the way the reverend had shown him, the way he'd done before. Sharp knives on his shoes, he always expected the skates to disappear into the ice when he stood up. Like a ship's keel, the skates would keep him up, letting him lean, but not letting him fall over.

Phil circled down toward the sound once, testing the strength of the leather straps that bound the skates to him. He could feel the soreness returning. The bay stretched vast in front of him, white-gray ice touching light-gray sky, nothing protruding. He had the gift sack tied around his neck and his hands clasped behind his back. He made a wide arc, watching his skate line in the ice, then started up the river toward Topcock Creek. Gray narrow path, trees frozen in tangled positions at the sides, logs rotting but hard as granite, sticking like cannons out of the bank. Thank the gods there was no wind.

A small part of Phil's face touched the weather, the hinge of his jaw was locked tight by the cold, cheeks were like leather. Left, right, he thought, keep your ankles stiff. Words to skate by. Rumor, truth, invention, discovery. Was his life better now or better before the gold was found? Nome has scarred the land like a wound the body. Who would want such a city? Left, right. The muscles in Phil's thighs were very tight, but he was making good time, moving quickly. The sound that the skates made on the ice was like that of a knife on the bone of a seal, the tusk of a walrus. He imagined his whole person as etching some picture on the face of the river, a message for the gods to see. Or for God, for these were the reverend's skates and would carry his message.

Rumor, truth, invention, discovery. Phil slid up the river to the beat of his heart. Left. Right. If he looked back now the bay would be gone. The path behind him would look like the path in front. On both sides of the river trees were scarce. Just grass and tundra moss and dead trunks all frozen and silent. Only the sound of the skates. Knife on bone. He passed a pile of shallow gold pans and a miner's shack. Deserted. The gold pans were stacked like coins on the river bank, like pie plates, and soon other claims began appearing along the sides of the river. All were deserted and all had their shallow pans stacked at the water's edge, the river their poker table. Left, right. Was this what would happen to his people? The Eskimos, forever scurrying around the edges of the game ...

A man with a rifle stood near a larger claim, watching. No

surprise on his face, only staring, gloved finger moving from
stock to trigger just in case. Rumor. Truth. What does he think
he is seeing? Why is he outside? Who does he expect? Larger
claim placers projected into the river. Company man perhaps,
hired for a share to do the guarding. Phil kept his hands behind
his back to show he meant no harm. Just skating by. Invention.
Discovery. Phil quickens his pace a little until he is around a
corner where the man's eyes can't follow. There are a few more
poker-chip sites, and then nothing again. From here on into the
foothills the river coils, easing back to its source. Topcock Creek
is at its tail, but its mouth bites gently down on the edge of the
bay. The Snake, aptly named, slithers down from the hills.

The Christmas dinner was no longer heavy in Phil's stomach,
and the sun was down, and everything was dark. He stopped
the pumping motion of his legs and glided to the side of the
river. He looked around to see if anyone was watching. Silence.
With his knife Phil cut blocks of ice from the river and formed
a small igloo at the side of the bank. He made no doorway, but
stepped over the low walls of the igloo, carrying a block of ice
with him, and sat down before lowering the block until it covered the hole he'd entered through. It was dark and warmer
than on the outside. Phil took off his long sealskin coat and put
it between himself and the ground. His legs still seemed to be
pumping and he believed it would be difficult to sleep well. All
night long he would dream of skating. Phil lay down on the
clothing, wrapping himself in it. From the gift bag he took slices
of seal. Tomorrow he would start early and arrive at Topcock
Creek before resting again. Ah seal, he said, chewing slowly.

———

Birds, nocturnal snowy owls, swoop the silent highways, follow
the river fifty feet above it, game eyes cocked darkly, white

bodies invisible because it is night. Topcock Creek is their territory. All of their brethren have gone south, yet these two fly from Finn to Phil. They sometimes move like birds of the sea, coasting inches above the land, raising and lowering with the terrain. The swivel-headed owls fly, wing tips touching, wide human eyes looking down, heads sometimes turned to look at each other, faces blank, eyes inches apart, registering nothing. Finn and Kaneda saw them lift themselves into the air at dusk. Phil sleeps under them and they view his igloo suspiciously, something new, smooth-topped lodging for lemmings.

Phil awakes when the two owls land on his igloo but he doesn't make a sound. He can feel their weight and a sense of tension holds him just as their talons hold the ice. The owls listen. They stand facing each other at opposite sides of the top block, the one Phil had lowered in over himself. They are identical, white-feathered chests puffed, like the two sides of Nanoon's hut. They are three feet tall but not nearly as heavy as they were before winter. Phil feels their presence and knows they are hunters. What could it be this late in winter? Is it a bear or a wolf? He is afraid and he is afraid that they can smell his fear. Not a bear or a wolf, what is he thinking? Bears and wolves don't need silence. They would rummage, push against the ice. Phil has never seen an owl so late in winter and for a moment he can't consider them. What could it be? He imagines his fingers and lists on them all those he can think of who hunt creatures under the ice.

The igloo is filled with the smell of Christmas dinner and suddenly Phil knows that it is a man. Strips of seal. The odor is so strong that he feels he must move closer to his air hole to breathe. The air hole! Phil knows that if he reaches for the ice a harpoon will come into him and he will die, red-feathered. He thinks, If this hunter has exactly my skills I will die, for I know nothing about being a seal. His body aches. He has not moved since waking. Phil, swaying on his heels at the breathing hole of a seal, can wait for hours, harpoon cocked. How long can he wait as the hunted?

The two owls feel their talons melt deeply into the ice. They cannot grasp ice without waiting, for it is too hard for them to push into. The eyes of one watch the eyes of the other. No thoughts.

Phil, after hours, begins to feel for the first time that he will not die. Not hunters, perhaps. Sentries. He imagines that if he pushes the top block away he will see the reverend's three wise men looking in and saying, "This can't be the place." His discomfort eases though he has not moved a muscle. He had forgotten the smell of the seal strips; indeed, it is as though he can breathe without using his lungs, as if he is floating in the swollen belly of the earth like a baby, birth bound. After hours of no sleep he feels rested. The reverend's skates still dig into his back but he has forgotten them. The reverend's wooden gift for Finn lies dead in its box, in the sack next to him.

As the darkness begins to fade the word comes to him out of nowhere. Owls. He sees them stiff as statues, standing above him. Owls. Phil, fearless now, moves about his small room. He kicks lightly at the top block and then pulls the skates out from behind him. His space is filled with shadows. Phil eats the last of the Christmas seal. He gets ready to continue his journey.

In the cold daylight the owls shake themselves. Their talons are secure enough to lift the heaviest of game. They feel betrayed by nature, hungry and tired of searching the ice-bleak land. Their broad wings beat the air slowly and the top block cracks loose from the igloo. Phil watches it go up and thinks of himself as a seal again. View of the outside world as the ice melts. When the owls have cleared the ground one of them releases the block and the weight of it lowers the other in the sky. They move off toward Topcock Creek, tired and slender as salmon.

Phil stands up, the skates already tied to his feet. The sides of the igloo come to his knees and he can see the owls in the distance, like scars on the belly of the sky, one above the other. When he steps back on the river Phil feels the soreness in his muscles as he did the day before. The sound of the skates seems wrong to him and he regains his rhythm by saying his words. Owls, he thinks. He would have been embarrassed had his family known that he'd first thought of wolves or bears.

At their camp on Topcock Creek Finn and Kaneda are still sleeping, another sack of salt salmon opened between them. The dog sits awake, seeing the light through the tent flap and wishing to go outside. He cannot whine or growl. When the owl-carried ice hits the ground near them the two men open their eyes and the dog stands. Morning.

The block of ice lands flat, its talon marks facing up like some Stone Age calling card. The two men put on heavy coats and go out and stand around it. The dog sniffs and then raises its leg and fills the talon holes with steaming urine. Blank-faced Finn and the old man kick at the dog. The urine melts the talon marks deeper into the ice, making Kaneda think, for a moment, that it is a message written in Japanese.

The two men look skyward but do not see the owls. Nor do they ask themselves questions. It is winter and they have only a few moments outside.

The owls follow the river south now, ravenous for warmer weather, nearly starved. Phil, ice skating into the mountains, sees them, so unusual, snowy owls flying in the daylight. They glide past like shadows, their images touching the ice on either side of him. Skating. This could easily catch on in the village; he would have to watch it for there was not nearly enough metal for everyone. Rumor. Truth. It is very important to keep proper rhythm. Makes the whole thing much easier and faster. Invention. Discovery. Phil thinks of the reverend skating backward around his childhood pond, and he abstractedly wonders which

of the two women the reverend will marry. He is no longer
worried about Finn. Finn is alive, at least, the owls have eased
his mind about that. Phil turns around and begins to skate
backward. He brings his hands around to his front and says his
words, trying not to break his rhythm. He can still see the owls
dotting the distance, heading south as fast as they can, surprised
at themselves for staying around so long. He would make it a
point to tell his children about the owls. He would make it a point
to tell the reverend.

No speed in skating backward, Phil turns around again and
begins to bear down. He will get there today, the trick is in the
rhythm, not in the muscles. Long strides, get as much out of
each as you can. Phil locks his hands behind him again. He has
gotten a very late start. Left. Right. Keep your mind on the
skating. Rumor. Truth. Invention. Discovery. Think speed.

5

Slow, cumbersome, the days after Christmas trailed into the new year. It was a new century, and Ellen stood in the reverend's house pulling a leaf from the calendar. She enjoyed seeing the date appear ... *nineteen hundred. Nineteen hundred years!* She paced the house like a curator, watching the pendulum of the reverend's attention swing from her, but her mind was on the river. She wanted news of Finn. Was he all right? Had Phil found him? The reverend came up beside her now, looking as she did, out through the window, over the expanse of bay. He said, "The second breath of winter," and drew his finger across the freezing glass.

The reverend, for the first time since they'd known him, seemed generally angry. When Henriette spoke she sounded weak and silly to him, making him want to shout. He played hymns on the piano throughout the short days, or walked the room red-faced, or stood still in the kitchen. Henriette sought his eyes constantly. Her fingers sprang to his hand in passing but he ignored her. Nevertheless, she told herself, he needs me. I am needed.

On the final night, the last before their return to Nome, the reverend, grim-lipped, entered Henriette's bed once again. It was incredible. God, how he hated himself. He could think of nothing to say, so he bit his lip and pushed into her, seeing himself as one dealing out punishment. Henriette, for her part, quickly unfolded for him, wrapping herself around him like gift paper, her fingers a bow in the center of his back. The wife of a minister, she said to herself, who could have imagined it?

When the reverend finished he lay heavy on her, head turned toward the winter window, eyes tightly shut, waiting for the weight of it all to rush in on him. What have I done? Henriette held him gently. Their breathing was synchronized, fooled into a common rhythm, so Henriette was fooled too, thinking that their heaving and sighing together meant they were both of the same impulse. The reverend waited for the guilt like a child waiting to be struck. He pictured the veil lifting again and Henriette saying, *"Thirty pieces of silver,"* the whore, and he, Joseph, understood that what he was doing was getting even. He saw himself bursting into the manger, all wine-headed and shouting, "What do I care what it is that makes a good father? That's not my baby! Whose is it? Whose?"

Henriette peered through the dark, trying to look at the reverend. Was he sleeping?

"Darling?" she said, in a whisper. The reverend's face was prune tight.

"Are you sleeping?"

That such a thing could happen twice. Oh, dear God, let it be a dream.

Henriette, very slowly, slipped out from under her sleeping man. She faced the window now, he the edge of the loft. I am needed, she told herself. Henriette Raymond. The Reverend and Mrs. Raymond. Henriette realized that she did not know the reverend's first name and thought of that as somehow appropriate. She would call him "reverend" like she'd heard the wives of other reverends do. *"Good morning, reverend. The reverend will see you now. Supper's ready, reverend, when you are."* Such a strange turn of events. She had so much to think about.

The reverend stood and was two steps down the ladder before

Henriette noticed he was gone. She sat up facing him as she'd done on that first night, and momentarily he got the feeling that it was not too late, that as yet nothing had happened, that if he stayed his hand nothing would take place.

"Reverend . . ."

"It is very late. We must sleep."

"Ellen and I are supposed to go back tomorrow."

"Yes, you must rest for your trip."

"It wouldn't look right if I remained. People would get the wrong idea."

"Yes, you must go back. It is late. We will talk in the morning."

The reverend backed down the ladder, the look on his face hidden by the darkness. He's right, of course, thought Henriette. For me to stay here is out of the question. Marriage comes before housekeeping. The reverend stood in the dark at the bottom of the ladder. Again he had the feeling that he was about to go up. To go to his bed would be so easy now, why had it not been before?

The reverend walked away from his bed and toward the sleeping figure of Ellen. This was what he'd wanted in the first place. Only to cast a glance, to look upon the sleeping face of Ellen. The light in the lower part of the house was better than in the loft so he could see her clearly, slack flesh hanging low. She is not a beautiful woman but she is a woman of strength. To Ellen, Henriette was "the girl," younger, more delicate. Look at her; even in sleep she has bearing. He remembered the sense of tension he and Ellen had shared the first time she'd come to the village. Anything was possible then. And even this trip had she not waited for his attentions? Had he not pulled himself up the ladder expecting to find Ellen there? A mistake, switched sleeping positions deciding his destiny. The reverend went quickly to bed and pulled the blankets up over his head. He could feel the presence of the women on either side of him and it was morning before his thoughts were awash with sleep.

Invention, discovery. As quickly as that Phil slid off the Snake and up the little spur that was Topcock Creek. He spotted the snow-bound hut and the frozen water wheel and he heard the low incantations of the foreign language. It was dark but for once the sky was clear. He knew they expected no one. He stood on his skates at the edge of the creek and cupped his hands to his mouth.

"*Finn.*"

Inside the hut Finn and the dog sat listening again. Would the old man never stop praying? Finn had thought he'd not be able to forgive himself for the death of Fujino, but he was all right now and if he ever got back to Ireland he'd tell them what the word "prayer" really meant. Guilt. Maybe this time he'd be rid of it.

"*Finn.*"

This time Finn heard his name and it was like ice on the back of his neck. "Fujino?" Kaneda stopped in midsentence and listened with him. They peered into the corners of the room. The dog perked his ears. It had been Finn's name, and it had been a whisper.

"Finn. Hello."

Finn and Kaneda were both on their feet and pulling on their warm jackets.

"Hello."

When they came out through the hide flap they saw the man standing tall on the river and they stopped. Kaneda had his hands around his sharp knife again.

"It's Phil," said Phil. "I've come with Christmas gifts. I've come to see how you've been."

Finn ran down to the creek and put his arms around Phil. To Kaneda they looked like two bears dancing in the moonlight.

"Phil. Phil." Finn was absolutely overjoyed.

"I'm glad to see you too," said Phil. "Are you all right?"

"Me and this fellow here can't speak to each other."

Phil looked past Finn at the old man and raised his arm in greeting.

Kaneda walked up to the two men and extended his gloved hand. *"Hajimemashite,"* he said.

Though Phil spoke no Japanese, he immediately understood the sense of the greeting and answered Kaneda formally, in Eskimo. He could see the old man's face now and he was surprised.

"You look like I did twenty years ago," said Kaneda. "I was taller then, too."

It was cold so Finn turned and took a step in the direction of the hut, expecting the others to follow, but they stayed where they were, standing in the dim moonlight, staring at each other. It was embarrassing. They glanced as lovers might. Phil bent to unbuckle the frozen skates and then stood down, level with the old man.

"Who are you?" Kaneda asked slowly. "Have you come to take the place of Fujino?"

"I am Phil," said Phil, "but I don't know what you're saying."

Finn stood looking from one man to the other. Where before he'd only been confused by one, now he could understand neither. Why was Phil speaking Eskimo? "Can you understand him then?" he asked, looking at Phil. "Do you speak the same language?"

The two men kept staring at each other and speaking in their languages and Finn kept waiting. "Bloody hell," he said finally. Then, taking each man's arm, he pulled them toward the warmth of the shelter.

Once inside, Phil let his heavy coat and pack drop to the floor and hurried to the fire. He sat next to the sleeping dog.

"This man has come to take the place of Fujino," Kaneda

told Finn. "Look at him. He looks like me and is young enough to be my son. I don't know how, but he has come to take Fujino's place."

Finn reached into a box and pulled out an unopened bottle of whiskey.

"Phil," he said, setting the bottle in front of the fire, "drink up and speak English. That's what I have such a thirst for."

"Ellen and Henriette are in the village. They came to spend Christmas with us. Yesterday was Christmas and the reverend sent me with a gift for you."

"Christmas," said Finn. "I'd no idea it was so near."

"*Ku-ri-su-ma-su?*" said Kaneda, looking at both of them. "In Japan that is the name of a day of celebration."

Phil pulled the small box from his bag and held it out to Finn.

"This is the gift he sent you."

Finn was watching Kaneda, who sat brightly, the look and the word "Christmas" still with him. He took the box from Phil and swung it over into the lap of the old man.

"Merry Christmas," he said. "This is for you."

"Ah ha!" said Kaneda. "He is here to take the place of Fujino and he brings me a gift to prove it." He took the package in both hands and stretching it out bowed toward Phil, touching his forehead to the ribbon. "I am receiving this gift," he said. "Thank you very much." He sat up straight again and put the package behind him, out of sight.

Phil took the bottle and let some of the whiskey roll into his mouth. He said, "The women and the reverend are worried that you are hurt. They were not even sure that you were able to find this camp."

"I found it all right," said Finn, "though it wasn't so easy. I told the old man here about the death of the other and he has been praying for him ever since. Every night after we eat he prays. That's all he ever does."

"I am surprised to find that he looks like my father," said Phil. "The resemblance is shocking."

Finn and Phil sat for a long while talking in detail of Henriette and Ellen, and Kaneda sat bright-eyed watching them, his fingers touching the package behind him. *If I had had a son he would look less like me than this man does,* he thought. *Fujino could have been my son but I lost him.* Kaneda quietly decided to try to take Phil back to Japan with him. Perhaps his daughter would like him as well as she had Fujino. He would give Phil land in the center of Tokyo and he would have a beautiful wife to bear his children and a father-in-law who would willingly retire from the active running of the household. Money, power within the family. What man could refuse it?

Kaneda took his package and moved silently away from the talking men. It would not be rude to open the gift in Phil's presence, he decided, since there was no other room for him to retreat into. He faced the wall of the hut and pulled at the ribbon, wondering what it might be. He held the ribbon away from the package and unfolded the heavy paper. What he found was a good sturdy box containing a shiny piece of old wood. He held them, one in each hand. Two good gifts, a box and a piece of wood. Kaneda was a carpenter and marveled at the exceedingly good workmanship of the box. Its joints were perfect, put together to stay together. He himself could not have made a box to equal it. If the box were to break it would do so somewhere along the flat of it, not at the corner or the joint. An exceedingly good box. And so that the box may complete its function, this piece of wood. It is old and shiny. It shows what the box came from and how a carpenter must never forget that the beauty and perfection of his work must always equal the beauty and perfection of the material from which it came.

Kaneda held the two pieces, his heart in his throat. *I am a carpenter and should never have come for gold. I have neglected my trade and my family and have caused the death of* my daughter's future husband. He looked back over his shoulder at Phil. He has awakened me, he thought. He mirrors my face and reminds me of the perfection of my profession. He turned toward the two men and held the gifts high above his head, his eyes tearing.

"*Arigato Gozaimashita!*" he said.

"What is it?" asked Finn. "What is the gift the reverend sent?"

"A box and a piece of wood!" said Kaneda. "Now I understand what a fool I have been!"

Kaneda slept with his new gift. He could tell that Finn and the new man wanted to talk, so for this night he decided not to mention history. There is a time and a place for everything. Rather, he curled up with the gift and with his thoughts of Japan and his house and his daughter and his wife. Even if he were to return soon he would have *some* gold to show for his trouble—indeed, more than most men found. He would talk to the new man, to Phil, and see what struck him as a good time to leave. And if Phil agreed to go he would not act toward him as he had toward Fujino. He would say everything right out, not waiting for Phil to ask. First thing tomorrow he'd show him a photograph of his daughter. And he would show him photographs of his house and land. No one could refuse him. He would call Phil Taro, the name he had once reserved for the son he never had. And if Phil, if Taro, made the box, they would go into business and their reputations as master carpenters would spread throughout Japan. He turned toward the wall and closed his eyes, waiting for sleep. It was a crazy thing to think about, he knew, but it gave him something to hold on to.

In the morning Finn's mute dog stretched and blinked at the sleeping men. He pushed at the hide entrance and walked out onto the snow. Finn and Phil had stayed up late and Phil was very tired, so today they would breakfast later than usual. Even

Kaneda stayed rolled in his blankets for a longer period than was his custom. The dog peed on the talon-marked block of ice, then stood over the warming steam. The cold sunlight brightened the shadowless ground. The dog ran by himself, padding the icy earth and playing, sometimes lying in one spot for a while and then standing quickly and drinking from his thawed form.

Among dogs what is noticed as a weakness is any kind of frailty of limb. What is noticed as a strength is silence. A quiet dog, one that does not bark or growl, does not work well on teams. When Phil arrived the night before he noticed the dog and was glad he'd decided to leave his own dogs behind. The silence of this one would have forced those of his sled to try to draw a noise from its throat. They would have attacked when their howls were not answered, seeking to draw sound with blood. This dog would have died, but so would several of his, they howling like wolves, this one silently.

Phil stood in the hide doorway looking at the dog. The others were still asleep behind him. All during the night he had had the feeling that he was skating, his body pushing outward from its sides. He had made the trip in two days. It would have taken him six if walking, three had he brought the sled. There was an axe inside the tent and a sled with harness nearby. Phil held his hand out silently toward the dog. He buckled the slight harness around the dog's heavy chest and then slid, his ankles still hurting, out and away from the tent toward the scrub timber to the north. The dog pulled easily, head down to the task, mouth closed. It would not be difficult to cut firewood on a day such as this. He would have several hours before the cold would touch him. It was far too late to do anything about the condition of the shelter in which they lived, but the snow had sealed it tightly, so at least they would be able to keep warm.

After only a few moments of sledding, Phil stopped the dog near some snow-heavy trees. He slapped the flat of the axe against the trees and heard the sound of snow falling to the ground, like laundry on rocks. He cut trees for an hour, then branched them and piled them as high as he could on the slender sled. He wove some of the thinner branches around the outer ones to keep them from falling off. The land was clear between here and the camp, so with a long piece of rope Phil tied the remaining loose branches together, then tied them to the back of the sled. He turned the dog and swatted him toward home. There was not room on the sled for him as well.

The dog pulled the mass of firewood down the easy slope toward the campsite, running slowly sometimes, in order to keep the front of the sled from bumping his legs. The ground was so hard that even the back branches could not snag. This was the kind of work the dog could do. Though the sled was heavy he knew the distance and could follow the scent that he and Phil had left when heading out. The dog had no thoughts, but there was a sense of not having worked in a long while. The smell of the timber and the feel of the sled seemed a part of his body.

Phil walked in the runner marks, turning his ankles in ways that the skates had not. It had been several years since he'd been to this branch of the Snake. Not since long before the gold was found, not since before the first missionaries had smiled their way into his life. The site where the village now sat had only been a meeting place before the missionaries. His father took the family there several times each year for dancing, but they had never lived there. Even now it seemed to him like something temporary. And if his memory served him correctly, they, his family with his father at the head, had spent some time near this spot, for he could remember the roll of the land.

It had been a long time since Phil had thought of his father. It must have been the face of the old Japanese that brought the memory back. His father had died in an accident, falling through the ice while trying to red-feather a seal. That was the only time in anyone's memory that the winter ice had broken under a man. Under a single man, not under three or four. Phil had been standing not far off and saw his father plunge his harpoon downward and then saw him follow it through the ice as if he'd been a part of it. By the time Phil and the others got near, the broken ice had already formed a thin new skin. Still, the harpoon had been anchored well and the seal was there like a parting gift from his father to the family. Phil remembered breaking the ice again and pouring a bit of the seal blood in so that his father would know the taste of his last catch.

When Phil came into view of the camp the dog came out to meet him. The sled had been unloaded by the others, the wood placed near the hut. For a long while now Phil had heard the sharp bark of an axe and knew that someone was cutting the wood he'd sent. As he got closer he saw that it was the old man who was cutting the wood, and doing a very neat job of it. Seldom did it take him more than two strokes to get through the tough thickness of the dying tree. Even the branches had been chopped through and piled neatly.

Finn called to Phil when he saw him standing on the ridge. The dog was at Phil's side now and looking around for another sled to pull. Finn was on the frozen surface of Topcock Creek with the ice skates laced tightly to his shoes. He had fallen once or twice just in the time that Phil had been watching. He stood now and slid clumsily across the ice, gripping the sides of the locked water wheel to keep himself up. He looked at Phil and waved and then pushed off again, clasping his hands in a determined manner. Left. Right, feet upward, back down. The sound of Finn's falling was a dull one to Phil's ears. Quite the opposite of the sharp crack of the old man's axe.

———

Reentering Nome was easy and uneventful. The town was still frozen in its tent swirl, the half-done skeletons of buildings still stood. It was a disappointment, coming back. Both of the women had hoped for a real town, somehow sprung from the loins of the one they'd left. One of Phil's friends silently left them at the first sight of Nome, turning to hurry back to the village. He handed them their bags then stepped away quickly, as if what lay before them held some danger for him. Both Ellen and Henriette knew that nothing had changed, that they would soon be standing before the same windows once again, staring out. But Ellen decided during their return that there were two things she must do: bury Fujino and reopen the bath. The city was full of dirt, frozen to the skin of the men who lived there. Sickness and death had made them close the bath early and now they would reopen it by removing that which had been sick and died, by burying poor Fujino, come what may.

For a long while as they walked toward the edge of it, the town shimmered before them, seeming closer than it really was, a mirage. The tents rose like mounds of dirty snow and neither of the women spoke. It was twilight but they could hear no voices, could see no others walking as they were, across the outside world. At the entrance to one of the first tents, though, the snow had been melted away and the brown earth had re-appeared. It was a clean tent and as they walked around it they discovered that it was entirely circled by cleanliness, that for a meter out from any wall there was earth, and that salt had been laid to prevent refreezing.

"Here's a tent that's been cared for," said Ellen. "There's even a path."

They circled the tent once and then started around again, feeling the crunch of the rock salt beneath their feet, but hear-ing the sound of gravel on a summer road. It was a pleasure; it made them want to open their jackets and smile. They circled the tent three times, one behind the other, like children march-ing. It made them laugh to think what they were doing. The warm stovepipe pushed straight out the top of the tent like the central pinning of a carousel, and they moved like riders, Ellen following Henriette, joining in, but hesitantly, always on the lookout for someone watching.

As they circled, surely for the last time, the flap was pulled back and a man ducked out to see what web they were winding. He was in shirt sleeves, as if as long as he stayed here, on his path, in his tent, the weather could not touch him. He wore slippers and waited for them to cease their marching and look up.

"An unexpected pleasure," said John Hummel, forcing their eyes to him. "I have fresh coffee." He held the tent flap wide, introducing the odor of coffee to the air around them. It was cold and they had had a long trip, and Ellen could do nothing but follow Henriette through the low-slung entrance of the man's home.

"Though I sense it was an accident, I cannot say how happy I am that you have come," said Hummel, sucking at his teeth as other men might a pipe.

"Mr. Hummel . . ." said Ellen. The neatness of his tent overwhelmed her. Though it was of standard size it seemed much larger. There was a tarpaulin covering the ground and a thick carpet over that and a real bed and a high burning stove and two oil lamps. The large tin can that the man had used to relieve his bleeding gums now stood full of long stalks of candy in the center of a finely made wooden table. He smiled, showing a normal mouth, but then began sucking on his teeth again, a habit lingering after the cause had gone.

"I have recovered," he said quietly. "There is a doctor in town now. It was simple, once he told me what to do."

"Mr. Hummel," said Ellen, "you have a beautiful place. It has the appearance of a real home."

As quickly as she realized that his gums were mended, Ellen began repairing her impression of Hummel. His clothes were clean but whether they had always been so she could not say, for while he bled she had seen him only as bleeding. He had seemed to her like a man turned inside out. That he could be cured and that he could lead an orderly life as well seemed nothing short of a miracle.

Hummel busied himself with cups from the cupboard and with sugar. He talked over his shoulder about how long the winter had been and how much longer it might last. He'd taken a job with Dr. Kingman, who had gold, he said, but no good way of accounting for it. And he had taken the job at a high enough salary to allow him to leave Alaska, when he finally did, with more money than all but the most successful miners would have. Ellen had taught him the importance of good business, he told her. Her bath was a potential gold mine.

Hummel used his clean mouth for talking. Ellen and Henriette sat in comfortable chairs near the stove, hands across the black mouths of coffee cups. He had looked for them, he said. He'd gone to the bath daily, hoping to find it open. During his meetings with Dr. Kingman he'd been told of Finn's visit and of the horrible death that the Japanese had suffered, and he'd wanted to pay his respects.

"Indeed, though the man has died, he lingers with us yet," said Ellen. "If you've been to the bath I'm sure you know that."

"I know he *was* there," said Hummel. "He's gone now. Dr. Kingman ordered me to have him removed."

"Ordered you?"

"He assumed that it was your wish. After Finn visited him and after I mentioned what was standing outside your bath, we all got to thinking. There'd been several inquiries and we thought it best to tuck away the evidence, so to speak."

"He's gone?" asked Henriette.

"It was impossible to separate him from the mule. They are merely buried in the deep snow toward the north of the town. In spring the job will have to be done once again."

"I was not aware that Finn had visited your Dr. Kingman," said Ellen. She felt strangely upset knowing that this man had disposed of Fujino so. It was a personal matter, not one for the whole town to be getting their hands into.

"I thank you for what you've done," she said slowly. "You may tell Dr. Kingman that, come spring, I will take responsibility for making sure he gets a Christian burial."

"It might be a larger problem than that," said Hummel. "By spring there'll be land set aside for use as a cemetery. But did you ever think there might be someone else's hand in the matter? Some men have mentioned murder and wonder if this man's death shouldn't be investigated in some way, even if he was Oriental. Besides, he isn't the first hidden in the snow waiting for his burial place, you know."

The long stalks of candy stood like budless flowers on the table between them. *"He isn't the first hidden in the snow waiting for burial."* It seemed a heartless thing to say, even if it were true. It made Ellen picture poor frozen men hidden like nuggets here and there around the landscape. When the snow melted they'd emerge like excavated ruins. Of course it's no worse than sitting atop that mule like an old soldier. She didn't know why it should upset her so. And what's this talk of murder? Nonsense, the lot of it.

"We must be getting home," she said, standing and speaking to Henriette. "Mr. Hummel, you have a well-kept place and we thank you for the coffee."

"And for getting rid of Fujino and that mule," said Henriette. "I was dreading going home because of it."

Hummel smiled for a moment then sucked his teeth and said he'd be around for a bath as soon as they reopened. He also said he would spread the word among the employees of Dr. Kingman and that there wasn't a man among them who didn't need a bath right now. The two women stood on the salt-worn path and looked back at John Hummel. He'd gone from outcast to company man merely by corking his bleeding mouth. Ellen remembered him marching the beach, down at the tide's edge, pointing his stick, like a rifle, at them all. He'd tried to claim the entire beach as his own. He had been angry and laughed at by everyone. How could a man who could not keep the blood in his veins be so neat? Keep such a clean house? Look at him smiling, white teeth and pink gums like the rest of us, a company man standing in front of his candy. Ellen remembered how her father had hated company men, those who bought up the small farms and linked them together on the map like sausages. They had come to her bath and taken the dead man and buried him in the snow with his mule still under him. If it was such a Christian thing to do why did she feel like calling them a bunch of bloody body snatchers? Was it because they laid no caring hands on him? No more feeling for Fujino than for the dumb mule?

Ellen and Henriette walked the swirl of tents toward the bath, leaving Hummel standing on his clean path like a woman in the doorway of a cottage. They were thinking different thoughts. Henriette smiled at the image of the clean, mule-free path. Fujino was gone and none too soon for her. It was always better to look toward the future. It was nice, what Dr. Kingman and Mr. Hummel had done for them. There's little enough of helping others around here.

The bags they carried were heavy in their hands as they circled. They passed the Gold Belt, its tent inside, a wooden frame without. From here they knew the way, could even see the top of the bath suspended oddly, as if hanging from the gray sky. It was the only building finished during the rush on the beach. Indeed, the town would have been better off without its Mr. Hummel, thought Ellen. It would have been a complete town. If not for his beach gold, people would be living in buildings and able to carry on normal lives. Yet it was not Hummel's fault. He believed the beach strike had been his alone. No, it was the fault of them all, and of the bloody golden snowflakes as well. Men chased after those things like children after real ones. It was the way they appeared so magically in the frypans, all finely webbed and beautiful. Ellen wanted them as much as anyone else ... for the things they could buy.

The door to the bath had been locked by winter, the window sealed as well. Henriette pushed on the window, chipped away at the ice that held it, and pushed again. Ellen stood back looking at the spot where the mule had been. They had done a neat job, Hummel and his friends. The mule had been locked in place for so long that they'd not even tried to dig him up. Rather they'd sawed, as close to the ground and as evenly as they could, through the skin and through the meat and bone, just above the mule's ankles.

Ellen removed her glove and bent and felt the smooth surface of the top of one of the remaining mule's hooves. So smooth you might think it had been sanded to free it of its rough spots, she thought. She imagined that a table top would fit on the mule's legs without the slightest wobble. She could hear the tapping of Henriette as she tried to reopen the window, and at that instant she felt the tip of her finger freeze to the top of the mule's hoof. She pulled back gently but could not free herself.

"Henriette," she said, "come help."

Henriette tapped and peered at her work, but did not answer, so Ellen sighed and then very quickly snatched her finger away and pushed her hand back into her glove. There was no pain. Her finger, frozen from the knuckle, had not yet begun to thaw. But on the top of the mule's hoof a round piece of thick skin curled halfway over itself and then froze into the shape of a little wood chip. Ellen tried to push it off with the tip of her boot. She imagined those men sawing through the mule's legs, then carrying it off toward the north of the city. They'd made no distinction between the mule and the man, she was sure of it. She wondered, would they have sawed through Fujino's legs if he'd stood on solid ground? She could remember the look on Fujino's face so well, but with the spring thaw she was sure that look would soften, his jaw would slacken and fall and his head would loll on the muddy ground. And here in front of the bath, would the four mule hooves soften and begin to bleed? Would the smooth finish turn liquid and warm around Ellen's poor piece of skin?

Ellen had hoped to find Finn tending the store when she got back, but she knew he wasn't there when she saw no smoke curling upward. She wanted nothing to do with Finn, but she wanted him safe just the same. She wanted nothing to do with him because the women in her family had always married men like him. After all, they had a country full of them so there was little choice. But he was all right enough in his own way and it would ease her mind to know that he was warm.

Ellen held one hand tightly in the other. Her hand had warmed now and it surprised her that such a little wound could hurt so much. And she was cold. They'd been five minutes standing here, Henriette tapping at the icy window.

"How much longer will it be, Henriette?" she asked suddenly. "Do you think we'll have to break it?"

Strips of silver ice struck the ground around Henriette but again she did not answer. Surely she'd heard. She worked slowly, never losing patience. Whatever else she might be, the girl was meticulous. Slow, careful, considerate. Surely the reverend was now more interested in Henriette than he had been in her. He was a timid man, and though she liked the daydream of the two of them she knew it wouldn't be a good match. And she'd not take a man because she was worried about time, about growing old. Others had done that; indeed, she believed her own mother had. Think of your age, Ellen, had been her mother's advice. When you meet a man, think of your age before deciding to what degree you can abide him. Not her. What she liked about

Finn and what she liked about the reverend, if she could find those qualities tied up in the same bag of skin she might consider it. Not to say that she was any great catch herself, all big-boned and proud. She knew she was not a favorite with the men but what did it matter?

"There," said Henriette, "no thanks to the help you've given me."

She pushed the window wide and then stood back for Ellen to climb in first. "I'm sorry," said Ellen, "I was taken with my own thoughts."

Henriette was in the room behind her and had closed the window. "Never mind," she said. "Out there the one who works is the one who stays warm."

The room seemed dustless in the twilight and was as cold as ice. Ellen hurried about lighting lamps, and Henriette pushed several large sticks of wood and some moss into the frozen stove. In the bathroom the two tubs glistened, their insides coated a half inch and all shiny and slippery. Ellen set a lamp in the bottom of each and stood watching for a second as the texture changed, as the sides lost their frost and began to slide toward the bottom. Henriette was already upstairs; Ellen could hear her footsteps, pacing the floor. Whatever Hummel had said, he was right about one thing. They would reopen the bath. Tomorrow, no later. They'd burn the winter out of this new building and out of the town as well. They'd clean everybody, money or no.

Ellen pulled the lanterns from the tubs. The wooden floorboards were soft with the dripping water. Her finger throbbed in her glove. In the main room the chickens looked about like stored puppets. They were, of course, dead. It couldn't be helped. The one nearest Ellen sat stupidly upon the marble egg and upon two or three of her own.

———

By the time Phil had been at the strike site for a week they had enough firewood to last them for more than a month. The dog stood or slept by Phil now, still silent. The old man and Finn, staying outside when Phil did, learned to skate, but at dusk they all went back inside, rubbing their sore muscles and warming themselves by the fire. When the old man spoke, Phil answered him in Eskimo. It had quickly become a pattern, and just as quickly Kaneda fell into his old habits, spending hours each night retelling the history of Japan, starting again at the beginning so that Phil wouldn't be confused, so that there would be no gaps for him, just as if he understood.

"He's praying again," said Finn.

"Not praying," said Phil. "He's telling us a story. If he were an Eskimo he'd be telling us a story."

During the time that the old man spoke each night, neither Finn nor Phil interrupted him, Finn because he believed it was a prayer, Phil because he did not want to be impolite. The old man leaned toward Phil, speaking only to him, and when he finished he set a bottle of whiskey on the ground between them and then pointed to it as though it had been there all along and he was surprised they had not touched it.

"When we get to Japan, Taro, I will show you how to drink sake. You won't believe the sweetness of it."

Finn took the bottle and poured three tin cups half full. He set one in front of each man and then looked back down at the fire.

"You too, Finn," said Kaneda. "If you come to Japan you won't believe the sweetness of sake either."

When the whiskey was gone from all three cups, Kaneda refilled them, this time all the way to the top.

"This old man has started a kind of drinking contest," Phil told Finn. "He looks so much like my father that I cannot act normally in front of him."

Now, very quickly, Kaneda drank all the whiskey and sat back smiling. And once he'd moved to fill the cups again, Finn had managed to get himself out of the contest by taking the job of pourer. He didn't feel like drinking. He had introduced these two and now he felt like getting out of the way. He knew they could not understand each other, but they talked on anyway and he had had enough. It was beginning to appear to Finn as though a common language was a luxury in the world. Look at them. One speaking Japanese, the other Eskimo, both happily passing the time. There were people in the world who were meant to run across each other, he was sure of it.

"I have something I have been meaning to show you," Kaneda told Phil. "It is an old and formal photograph but you will be able to see her features from it nevertheless."

He reached back into his bedroll and pulled out a paper wallet containing a few thin bills, a few cardboard photographs.

"This is my daughter. Her name is Kimie and I want you to meet her. I wouldn't show Fujino this photograph, so I must volunteer it to you. Maybe he'll be able to see it through your eyes."

Phil took the photograph in both hands and leaned closer to the fire. It showed a grim-faced young woman in a dark and formal gown, standing in front of a shrine. Her hair was pulled back from her face and fixed in solid-looking waves.

Finn, peering around Phil's shoulder, saw a lean-bodied woman on the dark paper. Kaneda had never shown him these photographs. He wondered if the woman was his wife.

Kaneda waited until the two men stopped looking at the photograph, then he took it back and handed Phil another, showing a house of plain wood on a very narrow and curving street.

"This will be your home. I will live in it with you until I die and then it will be yours. It is in the very center of a certain part of Tokyo and cannot be said to be substandard in any way. I am a carpenter and have done everything myself."

Finn and Phil looked at the house. Finn glanced back at Kaneda and smiled, but Phil looked at every corner of the pho-

tograph, studying the walls and the support posts and the curving street in front of it. The gate was open, and through it he
could see a stone path through a garden and then another door
that he assumed led to the living quarters.

"Thank you," he finally said to Kaneda. "You are a very
lucky man."

"Oh, you have so much to learn," said the old man. "First
the language. It will be much easier to teach you things after
you have mastered that. Japanese history and carpentry and
then how to play Go or perhaps the Shakuhachi. From my
daughter you will learn tea and be in the presence of flowers.
She is even proficient in dance, which is not such a common
thing as it used to be."

Phil nodded and held his cup high. "Here's to your woman
and your house," he said. "Though you look like an Eskimo,
your life is quite different."

The two men turned their attention once again to the whiskey, swaying in the lapping shadows of the flames. Finn poured
and watched as they gulped, each speaking his own language,
but full of goodwill, reunited, like father and son. The old man,
loose-jawed now, was the first to slip away from the steady flow
of the booze. He lifted an edge of the hide floor and poured
the remaining contents of his cup out onto the frozen earth
below. Then he leered back at Phil as if he had finished first
and waited impatiently for Finn to pour again. Phil, for his part,
drank everything but remained himself, sitting round-shoul-
dered, hunched forward as if he were considering what to say
next. He looked into the fire and remembered that it was not
his father that sat across from him. Finn poured a small amount
of whiskey into each cup again then held the bottle up so that
the two men could see that it was empty.

"It's gone," he said, "and very quickly too."

The old man finished the last sip of his whiskey, held the cup
high in the air and hit it with the bent knuckle of his other
hand.

"In Japan our sake is as clear as creek water," he said. "If I were to fill my cup with sake it would appear empty, as it does now."

The old man shouted but his voice was dulled by the soft walls of the shelter. "In the fall, when Fujino was here, we would get drunk and walk over the creek and up into the hills. Fujino in his young body would often run ahead leaping into the air like an animal. He was in excellent physical condition, not like any of us."

Finn reached behind him and brought out another stiff piece of moss to lay on the fire, darkening the room while the flame burnt through.

"You may know a lot," Kaneda said, looking at Phil, "but you don't know what it is like to grow old. Nor do you know what it is like to be Japanese. Growing old is indescribable; to be Japanese is to live your life as the brass tip of a walking stick. The weight of the rest of the stick and of the walker are constantly upon you. It is something that severely limits freedom."

Phil held the last sip of his whiskey in his mouth, letting it wash between the wide spaces of his teeth. His father had not been a drinker. Nor had he been a talker. He could remember long evenings like this spent under the earth but he could not remember his father's voice. And, if he tried to recapture what his father looked like, he saw only the face of Kaneda instead. After they got to know each other he would ask the old man if he'd like to visit the village. Everyone would comment on how he looked like Phil's father. His wife would remember, so would his sisters. His children would be told, "This is what grandfather looked like." Ah, but if he said that, they would ask if this was grandfather and Phil would say no, not grandfather, only what grandfather looked like, grandfather's face, grandfather's body.

Phil watched the flames poke through their moss lid. The faces of the other men were highlighted quickly by the fire, washed as if by a snake's tongue. The old man had stopped speaking and closed his eyes, probably thinking of his home and daughter. The fire's shadow danced about the hair on Finn's thick wrists. Finn and he had become friends, he supposed. People who came in search of gold were generally very friendly. Still, he questioned their intelligence in coming here to look for it. Why not stay home? Surely if there was not gold in their country there must be something of value. Of the five foreigners he knew, Phil liked the reverend best. He was a good storyteller. He had energy for his stories, and though he might tell the same one a dozen times he always changed it. Phil suspected that the old man, that Kaneda, was a good storyteller too, and even though the style of his storytelling was nothing like the reverend's, even though he couldn't understand, Phil enjoyed the stories. It was like listening to music. It was like it had been years ago, listening to his father's father and to the other old men telling wild hunting stories. It would be interesting sometime to discover what the old man spoke of. He would not be surprised if they too turned out to be stories of a good hunt.

Phil reminded himself that it would be necessary for him to begin telling stories himself soon. He should have started long ago but he didn't seem to have the knack. He remembered his experience with the two owls and thought that that would make a good story. He was pleased that he had had the presence of mind to pick up all the owl feathers he'd found stuck to the ice of the Snake. White feathers, exactly the kind used for sealing. The owls had presented him with dozens of them in return for the block of ice they took. He could use the feathers as proof, bringing them out in the middle of the story to add weight to what he was saying. Still, the reverend would never do that. No really good storyteller would. It was like wearing a costume or drawing a picture. It was a crutch, was really much like saying that the story or the teller was not good enough on its own. No good storyteller needs a feather to lean upon.

The old man was asleep and the whiskey soaked Phil's

thoughts until he too smoothed out his bedroll and turned toward the wall of the tent. That left Finn. It was an unusual experience for him to be awake and sober while others lay in drunken sleep. What an evening. Three men, three languages. It didn't seem to matter to either of the other two that there was no communication. Kaneda, praying or not, could go on this way forever, Finn was sure. And Phil, hardly more than a sentence to Finn and he shifts to his own language. Eskimo. Japanese. Maybe it was the drink that let them enjoy their isolation so, and if it was Finn would be sure to join them next time. He'd see what he could remember of Gaelic and add that spice to the pot. My God, and now they're asleep without so much as a goodnight. Is it the booze or the terrible weather? Each desires more than anything to talk and so he talks to himself and pretends that the other is listening. Finn spoke out loud a moment in the sleeping room. Not much satisfaction. If it's booze that makes them sleepy I should have matched them cup for cup for I'm wide awake now. Damn, it was irritating. Each talking to his own like that. No sir, an Irishman would never do it. In an Irishman there's love for the other, not just for the self. What in God's name would be the purpose of a pub if all were like these two? A room full of people, warm and cozy, all speaking bloody different languages. Finn had to laugh at the thought of it. Maybe it was just as well after all, for look how well they got on. No, not so. Sociability is a man's responsibility. Customs. Politeness.

Finn pushed at his bedroll and lay down, staring wide-eyed at the darkness. The fire was nearly gone; only a few orange stars remained in the gray ash. Each man should stay with his own then, that's the answer to it. The Irish with the Irish or with those close to them. Here he was, starved for the sound of English, and Phil spoke Eskimo to a man who didn't understand it.

Finn reached over and took another bottle of whiskey in his

dark hands. Sleep is liquid. He pulled on the bottle, letting his tongue act the cork. Even drunkenness takes time. While Finn waited he played a game with himself. He began listing all the things he and Phil might have said to each other had they had a conversation.

———

The pale path in front of the bath was peopled with bathers waiting. A hot bath when the winter had been so long, what better way to make time pass? For a week it was more popular than the saloon. Ellen was forced to set a temporary soaking limit of fifteen minutes and to charge double should a customer require extra water. Clean men walked the streets, back to their dirty tents, the hair they had washed forming frost caps, making them all look old. Ellen worked the front room, Henriette the back, and they both carried snow and ice in buckets and watched it settle over their slow fires. They collected money in a cigar box and kept supplies in the empty chicken coops behind the counter. Towels. Soap. They gave the bathers what was needed to get clean, Henriette washing the towels after closing, hanging them above the tubs to dry.

Henriette went to the Gold Belt and gave the owner a card allowing free baths to the winners of the bar's continuing contest. Nearly every man in Nome had tried to balance himself on the Gold Belt's scale swing, to equal his body weight with those sacks of sand. There had been a few winners, perhaps one in twenty, but the contest had been good for business. The owner, in return for the gift, bought each of his employees a bath and arranged for them all to come at one time, early in the morning after the bar had closed. He turned toward Henriette and asked about Finn.

"Finn?" she said. "Fine. We tried like you did at the beach

but we didn't make much. Since then, for one reason or another, the bath's been closed."

"Yes," he said. "There's not a man in town who hasn't seen the sculpture that closed you. Some thought you'd gone into the mortuary business as a sideline."

The owner grinned at Henriette from behind his mahogany bar. As always he held large cloths under his hands, continually turning them, shining the spot where he stood.

"That was the result of an accident," said Henriette.

A mock chandelier pushed light over the edges of tin cans so that one customer could see another in the bar. Henriette had never liked this man, though Finn thought he was all right. She compared every man now to the reverend. Had she never met the reverend she would never have known what it was like to hold a man as a man holds a woman, of that she was sure. Henriette liked to remember how the day after their first night together he'd been deeply embarrassed, busying himself with Ellen, talking to her and doing little favors. He spent hours making breakfast and then said he wasn't hungry and left the two women to eat alone. Henriette had seen him from the loft window, standing waist deep in one of the Eskimo tunnels, looking down into the earth. It was such a strange sight, seeing a man whose body from the middle down seemed stuck in the frozen ground. He'd looked like the trunk of a tree. And when he finally came back home he spoke to neither of them. He went to his desk and composed a little note and then sat at the piano playing until Phil's friend came to take them home. He was such a funny man. Afraid to say a word to her, forced to write everything down. *"Will you do me the honor of becoming my wife?"* That is what the note had said. No greeting, no signature, no date. Just the one sentence, printed and dark, as if he'd pressed very hard on each letter with his pen. Still, he'd used the best paper, and Henriette carried the note, tied through a loop, on a string around her neck. She hadn't told Ellen; she hadn't told anybody.

"Accident or no accident," said the bar's owner, "it was a shocking sight even for such a rough town as this and I'm glad to see something was done about it."

Henriette stood still in front of him. The bastard. He'd never talk this way to Finn or Ellen. She was trying to think of what to say in reply when the flap was pushed back and John Hummel came in, neat as a pin, in his heavy coat but still carrying that sack of money around his neck.

"A drink for myself and one for the lady," he said, looking straight at the bartender. He pulled at the tips of the fingers of his gloves, then set them on the bar, his light hands on top of them. He smiled and Henriette peeked quickly at his gums for any sign of what had been. Though they were as clean and pink as those of a baby, he still had that sucking habit, as if he too could not quite believe that the scurvy was gone. He alternately smiled and sucked, giving the appearance that he was trying, abstractedly, to dislodge a particle of food from between his teeth.

"I was on my way to the bath," he said. "If you're going back we can walk that way together."

The owner placed two glasses of sherry in front of them and received proper payment from Hummel. He worked his way down the bar turning his rags under his hand as he went. It was his policy never to listen to the conversations of customers.

Under her heavy coat Henriette wore her thin sealskin jacket so Hummel ran the back of his hand along its fur and let the sherry run slightly along the seam of his lips.

"I'm going to build a house," he said, "right where my tent is now. I'm going to build a tall house and buy the best furniture for every room."

"Your tent is in such good order that it seems like a house now," said Henriette. "You're a man who doesn't need a woman to keep things straight."

"I can't stand a mess," said Hummel, sucking grimly at the side of his upper lip. "Never could."

Hummel took his hands off Henriette and began to tell her about Idaho, his home state. He'd lived without a father and said he tried to keep his tent as clean as his mother had kept their house. Alaska had taken him by surprise, the harshness of it, the terrible difficulty of everyday life. Now he was all right, but when he first arrived he began to bleed from the mouth almost immediately. He was forced to stay in Nome where he could get occasional fruit from the ships, and because of it he hadn't been able to stake a claim and had no chance for the big money that everyone always spoke of. Big money. Now he knew better. He'd make big money as Dr. Kingman's accountant and be able to stay clean and warm and dry while he did it.

"You seemed like you wanted to kill us," said Henriette. "We were all afraid you'd try something."

"The beach belongs to me," he said. "I still believe that, but I no longer think looking for gold is important. I was angry for a long time, but I'm not anymore."

Hummel smiled and, to prove his goodwill, bought more sherry and made Henriette touch glasses with him.

"Here's to the business end of it," he said. "You and Ellen and Dr. Kingman and the saloon owners. Now that I'm an accountant I know how much the average miner makes."

Hummel and Henriette touched glasses twice more, then ducked through the flap and into the twilight. Hummel took Henriette's arm and pointed off into the gray sky toward the second floor of the bath, toward the room she had used so well for nursing. No one ever talked much while walking here, for the winter moved into open mouths and clung to wet tongues. Hummel tried to walk beside Henriette on the narrow path, but soon gave up and took a step in front of her. His head, as she watched it, bobbed in and out of the collar of his coat.

Inside the bath Ellen had finished pouring and was ushering another bather into the back room. The fires in both rooms

were down a little and as they came in Henriette hurried to
restoke them, nodding while she did so at each waiting customer
and telling Hummel to have a seat.

"It takes two to run a bath," Ellen said.

"I've brought Mr. Hummel. He says he's going to bathe
himself every day."

Ellen ignored Hummel, took the money of two clean miners,
and walked with them toward the door. Ellen had fixed the door
the day of their arrival back in Nome. It was either that or ask
their customers to come and go through the window.

<hr>

The reverend was in a blue mood, sitting at his loft window,
rereading something from his small collection of fiction. *Mc-
Teague* again, the horror and greed of another gold rush. It
was Sunday and the reverend had finished another hollow sermon. Had they always been as bored by what he said as they
were today? He hadn't been involved. He'd given only cheap
truisms, an hour of the kind of rote Christian rhetoric he'd
hated as a child and promised never to stoop to himself. He'd
read from the Bible and heard in his tone the same boredom
that he saw on their faces. Boredom and anger. Once he had
told them never to come out of a sense of duty.

The pages of the reverend's book were loose in their binding
and slipped out of it into his hands. He needn't put them back
in order if he chose not to. That was what he liked so much
about storytelling. And he knew *McTeague* so well that he felt
free to reorder the story in his imagination. He could change
parts of it here and there and still be true to its essence. Many
variations were possible in the world of *McTeague,* just as many
were possible in his own world or in God's. Christianity frees
the imagination. If he could teach just one lesson that would be

the one he would choose. Christianity frees the imagination. He
had proven it so many times in his sermons. He was a magician,
not a liar, even if today he had failed. Someday he would discover in the fabric of his Christianity an eleventh commandment, another golden rule. Thou shalt exercise thy imagination.
Thou shalt carry thyself to the limits of what it is possible to
think, bending thy language and thought fearlessly. Blessed are
those who imagine for they shall view the world through the
eyes of God. Oh what a sermon that would be. So why hadn't
he given it today?

The reverend made notes on the edges of the loose pages of
his book. There is no difference between the truth and what
one imagines the truth to be. When you search for God, search
for Him in your imagination. It was stunning. If missionaries
were of any use at all this was the lesson they needed to teach.
The reverend imagined all the questions that might arise from
such a sermon, all the bad uses men might put it to. What a
joke, here he was in his misery, rediscovering the essence of his
religion. He had always known it but had never before considered it so clearly. Yet it must have been common knowledge at
the time of Christ. So much a part of thought that no man
feared that it might be lost. So much a part of thought that
God himself had failed to command it. It would have been foolish, like saying, Thou shalt breathe. The imagination is bound-
less. Imagine and let imagine. Let this commandment be your
guide.

The reverend considered his body and knew he had let it
limit the imagination of Henriette. Being with her had not been
an act of love but an act of violence. It was the first time in his
life he had so severely broken God's law. And he had broken it
again with the note he had written: *"Will you do me the honor
of becoming my wife?"* How could he have been a party to such
lies? It made him sad. For days he'd told himself that when she
returned he would tell her the truth. Thank God he was past

such sober-faced frankness now. The truth was as volatile as quicksilver. He'd relived his moments with her countless times and each time the experience was altered. He remembered the violence but he did not relive that part of it. And, as a matter of fact, each time, in his memory, the act became less violent, became, even, more lovely.

The reverend rose and padded down the ladder on the soft rungs. There were papers scattered about the house where earlier people had sat listening to his listless sermon. He would never be a bore again. God help him. He still held his book and walked with it into the kitchen. It was always a little cooler here than in the loft, until he kindled the fire. The reverend was hungry and in no hurry to return to the world of *McTeague*. He had thought, once or twice, of reading to his parishioners from this book. He might read just a little each week until they'd heard the whole thing. He could use it as the beginning of his sermon on the imagination, a springboard into a whole series of such sermons. The reverend poured oatmeal into a pan and looked out the small kitchen window at the nearby trees. Henriette beamed at him from the branches. He had been right to make her go away, for when she returned it would give their life together some sense of formality. They would not speak of the night in the loft yet each would continue to imagine it. The reverend brushed the vision of her from his eyes and looked into his steaming breakfast. He would carry his food and book and climb the ladder softly, just as he had that night. He could imagine Henriette waiting there, asleep and then sitting up and then pulling him to her. She always held him by the back of the neck, lifted him off the ladder like a flag lifted high off its pole by the wind. Her soft skin. How he fluttered around it.

The steam from the bowl covered the reverend's spectacles and swirled around the loft ladder as he climbed. No matter how soft his foot she would awaken. The reverend peered across the loft floor, finding her obscured a little, but nestled on the gentle boards. Henriette, diminutive of her father, who wanted four sons all trailing in his footsteps down the dusty ruts of his farm. Henriette, swallowed whole by this salmon preacher who turned her in his mind to suit himself. The steam from the oatmeal thinned. The reverend began reading again, eating between sentences, at the ends of paragraphs. The pages of the book were ever so loose in his hands. It did not matter what order he read them in, for as yet he was only testing, seeing if he could read, could leave the proper intervals between the words. This was not the Bible, was never meant to be. Only *McTeague.* Fiction. A proper springboard into his sermon on the imagination.

6

ome awoke from winter long before the season ended. Construction started again, and for a few hours each day hammer shots cracked the thinnest ice, workers pooling their talents, everyone doing one job and then another. When someone posted a plea for a town meeting Ellen offered the use of the bath. She turned the tubs on their tops and brought in benches and baked bread. Everyone contributed something, tea or cookies or bowls full of hard-boiled eggs. Ellen expected one hundred people and got fifty more. Many hadn't seen each other since the beach strike and were embarrassed into a light kind of laughter. It was a time of low talking and gentle movement. Many spoke of the dead man, and of the mule he'd rode so coldly in front of the very room where they now met. They sat toe to toe on the stairs, or on the floor, backs against the wall.

Ellen waited an hour before finally knocking for quiet on the top of her counter with the rounder end of the marble egg. Though no one was in charge of the meeting, John Hummel spoke first, offering his services as town secretary. He said he'd be honored to record what was said at the first town meeting. Ten minutes later Dr. Kingman was elected mayor.

"This town will be a good one," Dr. Kingman said. "One that avoids the problems other frontier towns have had. If we work together we can raise all the public buildings by the end of winter. And then we can start on private homes. We will do them by lottery so that though the length of time a man has to wait may be unlucky, it won't be unfair."

Hummel had devised a shorthand and bent seriously over his journal, taking down every word. Henriette sat next to him fingering her necklace and the reverend's note, and Ellen sat across the room holding her marble egg. Someone nominated the assayer as tax collector and it was agreed that he'd be able to levy taxes best, on the prospectors at least, at the time he weighed their gold. The tax revenue would be used for public buildings and for paying the construction crews. Everyone agreed on everything. They talked about what the town needed: a hospital, a newspaper, a bank. Did they need a sheriff? Did they need a jail? Did they have the power to make their own laws and punish those who broke them? The mayor ordered the town recorder to write to the United States government for answers to their questions. At the next meeting they would nominate and elect the other town officials.

"I'll put nomination lists on the wall of my pub," said the owner of the Gold Belt, and when he said it Ellen raised her hand.

"In that case perhaps we've voted for mayor too quickly," she said. "There should be nominations and a proper election for that office as well."

Some of the prospectors protested, but Dr. Kingman insisted that she was right and it was decided that, yes, that too was only fair. They should elect the mayor too, only after nominations.

When the meeting ended nobody wanted to leave. It was warm and friendly in the bath, and the walls were made of wood rather than canvas. John Hummel immediately began transcribing his notes, shorthand to long, writing in a clear and beautiful script. The minutes would be posted on the walls of the bath for anyone who hadn't attended the meeting. Henriette found some tacks and sat ready to help post them when he'd finished. She appreciated anyone who could write clearly. All of the others had taken to socializing again. There was a group standing around Dr. Kingman, and another large one in the other room, helping the owner of the Gold Belt turn the bathtubs upright again. Tonight would be the night that all his employees took the baths he had bought for them.

Even though his election had been put off for a while, Dr. Kingman would be elected mayor. Everyone in the room thought so. He was the logical choice. Still, it was hard to congregate around a man who volunteered so little. He stood in the center of a group of talkers, the shortest among them, but the man everyone spoke to. He hadn't been the first to arrive in Nome, but he was the first to strike it rich, and that made him important. He'd started just like any of them and now wore European clothing and was refined in speech. Ellen stood near him and listened to the others telling him what they thought he wanted to hear. They didn't know him and she didn't know him either, for he had a bath of his own. He's no dummy, our Dr. Kingman, she thought. Still, he hired Hummel and he had the mule cut down. Ellen moved along her counter and in among Dr. Kingman's group. Someone said they doubted there'd be any opposition at all, that it was obvious who was the best man for the job, but Dr. Kingman remained silent. Ellen stood a few feet away, waiting to catch his eye. Finally Kingman said, "Striking it rich is not necessarily the sign of a responsible man. Why should it be the sign of a good mayor?"

"The mayor must be someone who is willing not to go to the fields once the spring comes," said Ellen. "That's why being rich is a good qualification."

"Then any of the town's businessmen . . ." he said.

"Yes," said Ellen, "but any of a very small number of people. Everyone else is gold hungry."

Dr. Kingman and a few of the others looked at Ellen. There was always a woman or two around who was willing to speak her mind and this one was nearly the only one who was not working in one of the tent saloons.

Ellen took a deep breath. "I've been meaning to ask about the mention of murder," she said. "Our friend Mr. Fujino's death was sponsored by his own hand, no one else's."

The men standing near her looked about. Hummel, still hunched over his notes with Henriette, stood.

"Investigation is the proper path," he said from across the room. "If he'd been a white man we'd all be worried about it."

Ellen heard Hummel but was still looking at Dr. Kingman, who simply shrugged. "Hummel took care of all that," he said. "Who'd want to kill him? Why ask me?"

"It was you who ordered him removed, was it not? Do you know we've got the poor mule's feet stuck like the stumps of saplings in the ground out there? What made you take it upon yourself?"

"I was trying to do a favor," he said. "One of your men asked me to help."

It was the remaining mule's feet that really bothered Ellen, though she knew they were fast in the ground and would have been very difficult to dig up. She had an image of the evil uses those feet might be put to. She saw them strapped to the legs of a man and making false tracks. Still, it was not Dr. Kingman's fault. It was Hummel who'd seen fit to use the saw.

Ellen moved off a little toward the door and opened it. "Anyway, we've got a bath to run," she said. "The meeting's over." She walked back to where Dr. Kingman was tucking his light hands into his gloves. He wore a fur cap that fit down over his ears and strapped around his chin. His coat was long and stainless.

"We'll be wanting to give a Christian burial with the spring thaw," she said.

"He's not the first waiting under the snow," said Dr. King-man. "Burial is a rite of spring around here."

Finn had told Ellen once that Dr. Kingman was a man who carried weight in his words. Influence. Now she remembered Hummel saying nearly the same thing.

"You'll be sure to show us the spot where he's buried?"

"I'll have Hummel draw a map. I wasn't there myself, so I don't know the exact location."

Dr. Kingman answered Ellen's questions as if he recognized no complaint in them. When he left he went through the door by himself, not waiting for the few men who'd been standing back waiting for him. Here was a man who'd been so successful he'd had to alter his ideas of success. For him anything was possible. Ellen followed him out a few feet with buckets for the gathering of snow. It was hard work drawing baths, and there'd be no rest now until the early morning.

"Goodnight," said Dr. Kingman, speaking back out of the pitch darkness.

When Ellen returned, Henriette and Hummel were standing next to the wall nearest the door, carefully tacking his neat notes to the dried boards. "Oriental," she heard Hummel say. "If you ask me someone slipped him something."

The bathers were sitting on the regular benches, the women wearing greatcoats, looking nothing like they did when they worked the bar. It seemed to them a kind of punishment, to have to wait so long for a bath. Henriette started the fire under the burners and placed some of the waiting water in the tubs. Ellen said, "Goodnight, Mr. Hummel. You'll have to try your theories elsewhere; we've got work to do," and Henriette walked him to the door.

The minutes of their meeting were as neat as anything Ellen had ever seen printed by hand. John Hummel was a man of strange talents.

———

"Late winter always seems warm to me," said Phil. "Perhaps it has something to do with the longer hours of daylight."

"Perhaps it has something to do with the longer pulls on the whiskey bottle," said Finn. "This old man is teaching you to drink all over again."

Phil splashed the sleep from his eyes at the side of the ice-torn creek. Finn, squat beside him, spoke from deep inside his fur-lined hood. Five nights in a row now Phil and Kaneda had emptied one of the fifths of whiskey, slipping with each sip into their own drunken languages, into Eskimo and Japanese.

"I am not a drinker," said Phil. "We are not drinkers."

"Nor am I, it appears, judging from the last few nights," said Finn. "And if you're not why do you carry on so?"

"I am his guest and must follow his lead. What would you have me do?"

"This old man drinks a dozen times more than he did when it was just he and I. He is doing it because he thinks it pleases you."

Phil, rebuttoning his jacket, watched the water of the creek turn still again. He felt a little better, though his head still ached. It was true, he could not keep this up very much longer. His real father would not have been so demanding. The whiskey bothered his stomach even in the hours furthest from the end of drinking, and he could tell from the pale cast of the old man's eyes that he also was tired. Neither of them spoke during the day, but at the end of dinner the old man began, and after a few minutes, when he had at last achieved the strange tone he was after, his hand would flutter off toward the whiskey box and, clutching weakly at its neck, he would bring forth another bottle. It was as if that hand worked independently, mindlessly, like Finn's dog after a stick. And it was Finn's job to pour. Phil thought that was where the cycle might be broken.

"If only you would not pour," he said as they pinned the hide flap tight from the inside. "If you did not pour it is my feeling that he would say nothing. But for him to leave the bottle where it stands is impossible."

The old man lay gape-mouthed and snoring, his waxen face reminding Finn of Fujino in death. Phil stepped over him and sat back down on his unrolled bedding. The flesh on his face was still cold from washing, and felt to him like a mask frozen in its lines. How long had they talked last night? It was not unpleasant to listen to the old man without understanding the words, the meaning. Phil would like to become a storyteller himself and had the perfect story of the owls to practice with. Phil could remember that his father had not become a story-teller until he had become a grandfather. With the warming of his face Phil felt sleepy. "There is nothing for us to do today," he said to Finn, and turned toward the wall to rest.

Finn lay with his hands behind his head listening to the two men sleeping. Perhaps it was time for him to be getting back to his other obligations. Kaneda wanted Phil, not him. And as for the death of Fujino, Kaneda was over that now, so what would be the use of staying around and trying to help? He was needed in Nome. He was a man of the city and was foolish to try to make something else of himself. What was becoming of the bath without him? Certainly they'd still be in need of help.

Phil's deep breathing merged with that of the old man. The room stank of dirty men and dog. Stubs of jerky were lying about, and in the corner the dog had placed bits of his own stash; bones and fish heads floated in his bowl of water. Men living with animals, at home in the company of such a dog, warm in their dirt-stiff shirts and growling at each other in their private languages. Enough. Finn was a sociable man and pre-ferred to be growled at in a language he understood. Ellen and Henriette would know what he meant. My God, when they'd stayed together they'd treated each other civilly, even through the tragedy of Fujino's death. There were boundaries and considerations to be made toward one another and he and Ellen and Henriette had known it.

Finn was disgusted with himself. He and his vows, his guilts, his obligations. He remembered coming here on his sled and with that awful dog. He remembered what he'd thought and what he'd told himself he had to do. It was his fault, in a way, the death of Fujino, but what was to be done about it now? His sacrifice was unwanted so the best thing to do would be to redeem his life where he'd left it off. He would find out if his future was at the bath and if it wasn't he'd look elsewhere for it. If not in Alaska then back in the United States or all the way back, even, to Ireland. Finn was a great one for making pledges but a poor one for following through. He could see his pledges built up behind him, leading all the way back to his school days, nay, even further. Finn the promiser always promising. Still, what was there for him but to keep going? Take another breath and start again. That was something about being a Catholic. Go to confession, get it out of your system and start again. Make a clean breast of things, put it all behind you and start afresh, that's the Irish thing to do. And who had a better handle on that than Finn? He'd learned how to start with the best of them. He could talk and charm. And he could always, always, pick himself up again.

So that's what Finn would do. Tomorrow, or no, the day after, he'd head off again toward Nome, though he didn't look forward to another long winter trek. Tonight he'd try not pouring and see how the men did sober. Would they be able to carry on so? The lion and the tiger growling at each other from opposing cages. He liked these two men; he should not forget that. He liked them but was not one of them, and the best thing for all would be for him to try to get back to his own. No soul could rest if not Fujino's, soothed and wooed by prayer as it was. Finn only hoped that someone would pray for him half so fervently. It was electric, whether you knew the language or not.

Well then, it was settled. Tomorrow, or no, the day after, he'd start out again for Nome. It always made him feel better to have made a decision. And no talk of going for supplies. He'd tell them that it was time for him to be getting back and they'd not question it. Tonight he would try not pouring. He remembered a trick or two in that direction from the old days in the pubs of his hometown. It would be easy with these two paying attention to nothing more than to what they were saying in their secret languages. And then he'd be on his way. Phil would give him directions and he'd make an easier journey of it than he'd done in the coming. For now he'd sleep on it. He pictured the room with all three of them and the dog asleep and with the sun beaming in through the cracks. The air was dank and putrid. In the spring he'd sleep out under stars once more.

Finn was very impatient to see Ellen and Henriette. It would be fun coming in the window and seeing the looks on their faces. There would be fresh air in the bath. A fresh start. He felt like he'd been to confession.

———

John Hummel stuck to Henriette, appearing each day with those flower stalks of candy from his old spittoon, or with long, evenly printed poems, copied from a book. Henriette compared the way he wrote with the reverend's single sentence as it hung from the twine around her neck. She listened to his talk about working as an accountant, about the long rows of small numbers that he kept in the neat ledgers of the mine.

"Showing him the way I could write helped me get the job," he told her. "It was half the battle. A good part of accounting is penmanship, you know."

Hummel laid his hands upon Henriette's wrists, a guide.

"Give me something you've written lately and just from the way it looks I'll be able to tell you what you're doing wrong."

Henriette brought him the only thing she'd written since coming to Alaska, the death diary of Fujino.

"I've never let anyone see this," she said. "You can look at the letters, but you mustn't read what it says. You'll have to promise."

"Certainly," said Hummel, already into the second sentence. Henriette's hand was impossible. The letters stood high or leaned back or ran forward across the page. "My stomach is hard and small," he read.

"You have to learn to be consistent," he told Henriette. "You have to choose the style in which you'd like to write and then keep your mind on it. Never let your mood take you from that. Always be consistent. 'My life was planned, do you understand? I knew whom I would marry and I knew the house where I would live. It is terrible to have to tell you this.' "

"You're reading!" said Henriette, snatching the book back and standing and tucking it into her sweater. "You promised you wouldn't."

"Not reading," said Hummel, "only a word or two, to get the idea."

Henriette held the book to her middle, but in a moment leaned back toward Hummel once again. He apologized and, taking Henriette's elbow, guided her back down onto the bench beside him. He held her hand in his, laying it upon his lap, upon the practice paper that he had there. "Your best letter is the one that stands straight," he told her. He pulled her toward him slightly, she looking at the paper, he at her fluttering eye. He smiled and sucked, then took another long candy stalk from his jacket and tucked it down into her sweater, next to the diary.

"I am an organized person," he said. "I am a good printer. I am an excellent cook."

Henriette let her hand be pulled from the page and held. She could feel his dry breath on her. What did he want? Why did he come to visit each day? Though she had not answered the reverend's note, Henriette had been thinking of herself as engaged; she had no second thoughts about it. But now her hand was encased in the dry hands of Hummel. She could see him smiling at her out of the corner of her eye. It was the most amazing thing, the way his mouth had cleared up like that. She'd never have let him hold her hand previously.

"Why do you come to visit me?" she asked quickly. "What do you want?"

Hummel, embarrassed by the question, looked at the wall.

"Never mind," said Henriette.

"For the moment what I want is to make you dinner," he said, letting go of her hand and closing his notebook. "I said I was a good cook and I'd like to prove it to you. If you're sure that Ellen will let you have the evening off. I've noticed that evenings are often the busiest time around here."

"Ellen and I don't have days off," said Henriette. Then she added, "But I'm sure she'll let me go."

Hummel stood and looked at his pocket watch. "Seven o'clock, then," he said. "And don't eat anything until then. I've a surprise in store for you."

Hummel left, opening and closing the big front door quickly and walking lightly over the path in front of the bath. Henriette could see him through the window. He walked with his shoulders straight, his head down. Henriette saw, once, the sucking motion that he made and she saw him spit on the snow just before he stepped out of sight. Seven o'clock for dinner. She fingered the reverend's note and wondered what Mr. Hummel would prepare for her. He couldn't cook anything very special on that wood stove of his. In the Eskimo village the reverend had cooked fish, mostly fish, but she knew that Mr. Hummel would be making something different. He planned to build a house on that very spot, the spot where his tent now stood. He talked of rising with Dr. Kingman's mining company, and everything he said made her believe that he'd stay in Alaska forever, would consider this place his permanent home.

When Ellen came down from upstairs Henriette told her of the invitation and received a rude reply.

"Leaving one woman to run a bath's no way to fulfill your responsibilities." Ellen spoke and then turned away. "The business is starting to go so well," she said. "This is not the time to be taking a vacation, either of us."

"A woman has the right to accept an invitation," said Henriette. "Especially if it's the first in the whole time she's been here."

Ellen stopped and looked at her friend. "That man is up to no good," she said. "I can feel it and you'd be able to as well if he'd not cleaned up his mouth as a disguise."

She spoke harshly, pushing the day's receipts from one box to another. "What this town needs is a bank," she said. "You've got no choice but to trust that assayer. And he'll be the tax collector too, and I don't like it."

Henriette was angry and pulled hard on the twine around her neck until the reverend's note came off in her hands. She tucked it quickly between the pages of Fujino's diary. One chance to have a pleasant evening and Ellen has to act this way.

"It wouldn't hurt either of us to put aside an evening for fun once in a while. I've been invited and I'm going. And another time I'll be happy to work the bath alone while you go off somewhere."

Ellen closed the money boxes carefully and swished in her skirts back up the stairs without speaking. She closed the door to her room quietly and stood at her window looking down at the holes in the snow and at the black tops of the mule's dead feet. This was the room where Fujino had stayed. It was the last room finished, so even now the walls were slightly sticky with sap, not completely dried. Still, the room had its own stove and was warm and homey. This was where Ellen spent her own free time, what little of it she had.

Henriette, hurt and angry, worked hard for several hours more, cleaning all around the bathtubs, and taking the last of the lonely chicken feathers from the empty coops. Before she left the bath she took warm water up the stairs and washed next to the stove in her room, trying to make noise enough for Ellen to hear from across the hall. Henriette wore a wool dress and the sealskin jacket under her greatcoat. She stroked her hair one hundred times with the brush Finn had given her then touched each cheek with scent. Would the reverend mind, as much as Ellen, her having dinner with a friend? She thought of Ellen's angry face, her large jaw all tight and muscular. It's her lack of invitations that makes her mope so. It's jealousy, not the rigors of working the bath, that has jammed her sense of a person's freedom.

Henriette removed the twine, already lightened by the loss of the reverend's note, and walked quickly down the stairs and out along the dirt-black paths, using landmarks instead of memory to guide her to Hummel. It was perfectly all right for an engaged woman to have dinner with a friend, and Mr. Hummel had gone out of his way to be her friend. She looked back and tried to see the look on Ellen's face as it glowed from the little window on the second floor. Ellen would be thunderstruck if she knew about the reverend. And though Henriette had no trouble understanding it herself, there would be no way she would be able to explain.

———

John Hummel was hungry for he'd saved himself, hadn't eaten since morning. Ptarmigan, frozen in bunches around his tent, feathered and cleaned before freezing, was to be his main course. Then potatoes, cooked deep under coals, and wine and a salad made of fruit, every bite of which meant to brighten the pinkness of his gums, lining his teeth into even brighter rows.

It was past seven so he poured the wine and sat in idleness, warm in his good clothes, waiting for Henriette to arrive. He was on the right track now, he felt it, he saw it in the way he kept the room around him. On a peg to the right of the entrance Hummel hung his canvas sack. He still had some of the money left but he kept it in Dr. Kingman's safe now. And he made that much on his new job nearly every month. Already he'd saved money enough to start building the kind of house he wanted, and if he was lucky in the construction lottery he'd be able to begin with the coming thaw, with spring. He'd be able to plant vegetables and walk on the softened earth. The town would be underway, and the news of gold would bring even more people; perhaps twice or three times the number that were here now would come during the warmer months. There was no way he could lose. The newcomers would buoy him up in their scramble to get in under. He'd stick with Dr. Kingman, and he would do fine.

Hummel heard Henriette on his frozen path so he swept his tent flap back and smiled into the darkness. Henriette circled the tent once and surprised him by coming up on the left.

"Hello and good evening," she said. "I like the feeling of your path beneath my feet."

"I'm so glad you've come," said Hummel. "The possibility that you would not was beginning to enter my head."

Hummel secured the flap from the inside by sewing it shut with a large cord. He had candles burning all around the room and music coming from a large gramophone, borrowed from Dr. Kingman for the evening. Henriette had seen gramophones in San Francisco but had never been in the same room with one. It was so strange, wound up and with its thick disk whirling around like some dinner dish on the finger of a juggler.

Hummel took Henriette's heavy coat and placed it on a peg next to one of his own. He had wine glasses sitting one on each side of his shiny candy container, and he picked them up, handing one to Henriette. He took a small amount of the wine in his mouth, satisfying himself with its taste, and Henriette saw, for a moment, the old Hummel, all red-lipped and smirking.

"Dinner can be served any time we are ready for it," he said. "The surprise I told you about is called ptarmigan, it's a local bird and has a wonderful flavor. And there are other things: potatoes to remind you that I am from Idaho, and fruit that only Dr. Kingman had the foresight to freeze before winter."

Henriette looked around him at the stove. "We're not having fish?" she asked. "It's been nothing but fish for weeks and weeks."

Hummel had pushed his long bed against the wall and made it up to look like a sofa. He'd put candles at either end, and the remainder of the bottle of wine was on the table next to the candy.

"For the time being this must serve as my dinner table," he said. "But when I finish my home there'll be a whole room for only that purpose. I plan on taking part of my design from what you and Ellen have done at that bath of yours."

"I don't know what I'd have done without my room," said Henriette. "It's the only place in the whole country that I have to myself. For those times when I want to be alone."

"I'll be building three bedrooms," said Hummel, "though I suppose I'll be living here alone."

Hummel had the wine bottle wrapped in the snow-white folds of a clean undershirt. He'd borrowed special wine glasses from the owner of the Gold Belt, but had his own silverware, given to him by his mother as he was leaving Idaho. He refilled both glasses, smiling at Henriette through the candlelight.

"If you haven't eaten since I saw you this morning you must be starving," he said. "Relax, finish your wine. I'll get dinner."

Hummel made the tent seem larger as he slid away from her and began moving about the stove. He had a talent for using space well. She could smell the slightly burnt skin of the ptarmigan as it floated to her through the wine.

"Do you like cheese?" Hummel asked, looking at her. "They make the best cheese in Switzerland. It will last for years. Dr. Kingman gave me some."

He came back for a moment with a plate of cheese. He refilled the glasses and offered a toast.

"Here's to a time when we'll be able to live like human beings in this cold country, all year round."

Henriette touched glasses with him again then nibbled at the edges of a piece of dry cheese.

"Cheese is something I haven't had much chance to taste," she said. "We used to make it at home but it was a different kind, a different color."

"This cheese goes particularly well with the bird we are about to eat. Light or dark?"

"Pardon?"

"Light or dark meat? We've got plenty of each so don't be shy."

"I'd like the drumsticks. Do ptarmigan have drumsticks?"

Henriette was having fun. The wine was soothing her, making her forget the argument with Ellen and the hard work of carrying buckets of snow all day long. Hummel was a nice man, a man pleasant to talk to in the same way that the reverend was, though both were very different from others that had entered her life. Had she finally broken the pattern of loud farmboys drinking boot liquor and thinking dirty thoughts all the time? The reverend, Mr. Hummel, gentle men who busied themselves with gentle things and who treated a woman right, that's the kind of man she liked. She wondered if she'd tell the reverend about the others before they got married. She didn't think it would make any difference to him what she'd done before. One thing though, she ought to tell Mr. Hummel about the reverend.

It wouldn't be fair to let him go on too long if he was interested in more than just her friendship.

"Just one more second," said Hummel, unlacing the tent and reaching out for another bottle of cold wine. He had everything on serving plates and had the plates that they would eat from warming in hot water in a bucket near the stove. He wiped them dry and placed one at each setting. The steam rose around Henriette's eyes like the wine to her brain. He placed a potato on each plate and then sat down on a small chair across the table from her.

"This is the first time I've been able to cook for anyone since I've been here," he said. "Thank you for coming."

He lifted a tiny drumstick and three or four other pieces of ptarmigan off the serving plate and across the center of the table to Henriette. He produced a small container of sauce and told her that it would enhance the flavor, make her savor each bite. "The trick to the flavor of a meat is in slow cooking," he said.

Henriette chewed and nodded at him. She'd grown up on a farm and could remember great meals, though they were uncommon. "We used to do the same thing with beef," she told him.

They ate, Hummel proudly looking up from his plate every few seconds. The candlelight showed pale and warm on Henriette's forehead, reminding Hummel of his mother. "I told you about my mother," he said. "She sent the silverware along with me. The candelabrum too. She loaded me down with all the necessities. I complained quite a lot at the time but I'm beginning to be glad she made me bring it all. She was against me coming here for a long while. But as far as I was concerned it was now or never. Getting away from home, I mean."

"I never knew my mother," said Henriette.

"I'm going to bring her up here as soon as I get the house built. She'd never be able to understand my living in a place like this." Hummel spread his arms out, taking in the entire tent. The shadows of his arms stood like clubs along both walls. He reached across the table and poured more wine.

"She was always afraid of raising me wrong. I mean alone and all. She tried to replace those things that a father could teach with a touch of class. Those are her words and that's the reason for the accessories."

"Did you know your father?"

Hummel waved the question away and continued with his own thoughts. "You'd never believe the worst of it. I've got bedspreads and a place setting for twelve. I've got needles and thread and material for making clothes."

"Where do you keep everything?" asked Henriette. "Your tent seems so spacious."

"Along the walls of my office. In Dr. Kingman's house. I've got boxes stacked four high."

"You never knew your father and I never knew my mother," said Henriette.

"Before I got that office everything was here. I told her when I left that it was too much. I told her all the other prospectors would laugh at me, but she wouldn't listen."

Henriette laughed and told Hummel how much she liked the meal.

"When I get her up here you'll be the first one she meets. And then Ellen. She'll like you two. She'll like the fact that I've become a bookkeeper too. When I was a child people asked me what I wanted to be and she always had me say that I wanted to be a supervisor. In a way it's come true, I suppose. Funny how things turn out."

They finished their meal and the second bottle of wine, so Hummel reached across the table to pick up the dishes. The breeze pushed the candle flames, and shadows fluttered across the canvas. He put everything in a waiting tub of warm water and returned with more wine.

"My mother was very good to me," he said. "I hope I didn't give you the idea that she was not."

Hummel turned the table back parallel to the bed and, sitting down next to Henriette, started the new bottle of wine.

"I've got one last surprise," he said. "I've baked a pie. I spent the afternoon at Dr. Kingman's and I baked a pie in his slick new oven. If you'd like a piece now it'll still be warm."

Henriette showed her delight at this last and greatest of surprises, and Hummel got busy again putting pie to plates and slipping them onto the dark table. When Hummel returned he linked his right arm with Henriette's left and they ate in unison, like a crab with two mouths. Apple pie, the fruit of Hummel's healing. The forks worked like pinchers, snipping long slices of apple and bringing them to their churning mouths.

"Dr. Kingman gave me the apples," said Hummel. "In case you'd like to know. He thought of everything before the freeze and stored them in his wide basement. You asked me if I ever knew my father and I must say that I sometimes see him in Dr. Kingman. Though, of course, he's not nearly old enough. Besides, my mother's told me quite a lot about my father and the description doesn't match at all."

Henriette washed the last of the pie from her mouth with the last of the wine. She felt snug and satisfied, the food heavy around her middle, making the diary tight and uncomfortable in the taut waistband of her skirt. Hummel still held her arm and gazed at the long clean table in front of them.

"Everything has been so lovely," she said. "It is the nicest evening I've had in years."

Hummel reached down to the ground and brought a waiting plate of cheese up to the table. He slid it toward Henriette and then very gently laid his head on her shoulder.

"Oh, no thank you, I couldn't," said Henriette. "I'm stuffed. Right up to here."

She held her free hand parallel to the ground and raised it to her eyebrows but Hummel wasn't looking. His breathing was regular and audible in the gray-dark room.

"The reverend, the missionary at the Eskimo village, is a

friend of mine," said Henriette. "I've been there twice to visit him."

Hummel didn't speak but sent his own left hand, like a scout, across his lap and around Henriette's waist.

"He's a very good man," she said. "He's a lot like you, very gentle and interesting to listen to. Perhaps one time we could go together, for a visit."

Hummel turned his head and attached his lips softly to the side of Henriette's neck. His tongue touched her skin and then his own clean teeth and gums. He began sucking, first gently then not, and soon he could taste, very slightly, the tinge of blood that had come through Henriette's skin, like the emergence of a wound through gauze. It was a taste he knew and it lodged between his teeth, making itself at home on the tip of his tongue.

Henriette, spinning with the wine, bent her head toward the pressure on her neck.

"I like a gentle man," she said. "Everything is so confusing."

Hummel laid Henriette along the thin bed and draped himself over her. The wine buzzed in their lips like a bee seeking pollen. The tent swirled as through space though it held its pattern, part of the town's tail, whipping in wider and wider circles along the edge of the peninsula. Twice, how could it be happening twice? Henriette felt skin next to her own, clothing opening. She thought of the reverend alone in his loft; she could see him sleeping against the lids of her wine-shut eyes. She could feel the diary outlined against her stomach, still stuck in the skirtband, though the skirt itself was now up around her shoulders, and she imagined the reverend's simple note pressed like a flower at its center.

Henriette held Hummel to her in his silent movement. She could hear her own voice pushing sharp sounds out into the wide room, and she heard Hummel say, "It was me, it was my mercury mounting in his mouth."

Hummel rolled and heaved, making Henriette reach out into the room with her hand for balance, and she brought it to rest atop the table. She felt the Swiss cheese, cold like the skin of a corpse, and as she touched it, all movement stopped and the room became dead quiet once again.

Hummel lay heavy on her and she opened her eyes and saw through his hair the stub-wicked candles flicker, shadows grown shorter on the wall. She pushed three fingers through the silly holes of the cheese and brought her hand up in front of her face. Three fingers emerged through the cheese and stood like naked sisters on the floor of a barren room. Beyond them she could see the three last stalks of Hummel's candy, large in the candlelight like sister shadows, and beyond that the scar-shut weave of the canvas flap, making her think of the tent as a belly and of herself as not yet born, and of Hummel as her twin brother, locked like a Siamese inside her. He began to move again, making her see the reverend rolling in his sleep. In her mouth she had the sweet sense of her own blood, given back to her on the tip of Hummel's tongue, and she mistook it for a remnant of the meal, a last bit of pie gone liquid. She brought her hand to her mouth and began to nibble a bit at the edges of the cheese. "It was me," Hummel said again, excited, and the sound of his voice made her wrap her arms around him one more time.

7

Periods of daylight grew perceptibly longer. The cold sun lay high in the sky, and on the tundra dead tree trunks still drove icicles down into the snow, but the days were longer. On Topcock Creek Finn got directions from Phil and told the old man in every language he could think of that he was leaving.

"Nome," he said, pointing off in the direction Phil had shown him.

The old man nodded and repeated the word tiredly as though this were another of Finn's English lessons. "I'll never learn," he said. "That's why I brought Fujino. I don't understand English."

The night before, when the old man started his prayer again and when Phil, like a dutiful son, sat in rigid reception mumbling through his teeth in Eskimo, Finn had refused to pour. The old man reached at his regular time through the water-weakened sides of the whiskey box, but when he set the bottle between them, Finn simply removed it from view. He took the tin cups as well, and then sat looking from man to man as they spoke. No one mentioned the whiskey. Neither the old man nor Phil dragged a hand across the fur floor in search of the cups; neither of them cast an eye toward Finn or changed the quality of his monotone in the slightest.

"I'm going back to Nome," Finn said now, one last time. He took the old man by both shoulders and shook him gently.

"Good-bye," said the old man. "Thank you for keeping me company. Thank you for telling me of Fujino's *harakiri.*"

Finn shook hands with Phil and ducked quickly out of the terrible tent. He had given Phil the mute dog, but the dog pushed through the flap and ran with him, down along the edge of the river a ways, until he realized that this was no firewood run.

Finn carried a light pack with food and a change of clothes. He didn't need the sled or the dog. He would follow Phil's landmarks, expecting to see the river to the northwest of him at all times. He would follow it to the coast and then turn south and take a familiar path into the city. Four days. Five at the most. He'd learned from Phil how to build a shelter of ice and he'd received from the old man the unopened bottle of whiskey that was saved the night before. It was exhilarating, this being away again, heading toward Nome and the warmth of the bath and his friends. Finn took large steps. He could feel his toes, warm in the cage of his boots, and he pulled the strings of his jacket until only his eyes looked out into the cold world. His destiny had led him in so many circles. Maybe this time things would be different. He would see how he felt when he got to Nome. It was time to return to his own kind but for now it was the walking that demanded his attention. Phil had told him to time his steps with his breathing, for that was the only way of telling if he was getting tired. Finn did so now, discovering that he was good for two steps per breath and being satisfied.

Back at the camp on Topcock Creek, both Phil and the old man were awake inside the tent. They felt fine and sober and would spend the day in one more search for small bits of firewood. The old man again took out the photograph of his daughter and thrust it into Phil's hands. He had written her name and age on the back and waited until Phil saw what he'd written and repeated it. They nodded to each other and the old man thought what a fine time they would have together in Tokyo. He was still amazed at how much Phil resembled him. And if Phil and his daughter married he was sure that his grandson would have as great a likeness.

The dog was ready and the two men pushed off toward a place where they believed they would be able to find wood. They carried axes and ran behind the sled, taking turns leaping on and off the runners. When they arrived at the area the old man was panting and sat on the sled to rest while Phil began cutting. The high, clipped sound of the axe shot far down the river and into Finn's ears. The old man was satisfied and felt at home. He liked Phil so much better than Finn, better even than Fujino. He stood and offered to take the axe for a while and was surprised when Phil stood back to give him room.

"Now that Finn is gone I will tell the best story of all," he said. "It was easily Finn's favorite but I didn't want to repeat it while he was here."

The old man began chopping and then stopped and leaned heavily on the handle of the axe.

"Tonight I will tell the story of Hideyoshi," he said. "It is exciting and humorous. You are in for a great surprise." He stood back lost for a moment in his decision as to just how he would begin the story. He would tell it better to his future son-in-law than he had to Finn. He got the idea for a new rhythm for the story from the sound that he heard snapping at the air around him. Phil had begun chopping again. What a good boy. He had seen in a moment that it was not right to let an old man work.

———

Ellen stood outside, at the city's center, and shook her head. Did the town not know what a monopoly was? Assayer, tax collector; rich man, mayor. It was too much for the fragile honesty of these men. Still, she could imagine a wide town before her, the tents gone, a city laid out in its finery like a section of Seattle. Her bath would still be second to none, could stand next to anything these builders might put up. It was strong and attractive. And it was a money maker as well.

Ellen gauged the speed of the coming spring by the amount of time she could spend standing in one place and by the look of the ground under her feet once she moved. As she stepped aside there was moisture and she could see it now turning hard again. Wouldn't it be nice to be able to spin in loose clothing on the sand once more, to watch the heavy ships pushing the salt sea into a froth? In the spring she would be kinder. She would buy fresh foods and give them to her friends. She'd buy clothing for Henriette though she was still angry with her, and she'd buy a fine cherrywood pipe for Finn. And she would conjure correctly the desires and needs of the reverend and of Phil and of Mr. Kaneda if she ever saw him again. As for Fujino, he would have a headstone. She had boxes of money, was making more each day. What could be more honorable than keeping people clean?

And Ellen would find time for herself, come spring. More than wanting a husband she wanted to be a mother, and if she was not such a fine catch for the way she looked she was certainly no bad bargain. She had a business and an ordered mind and she was strong. She'd been a fool to expect a man to come along who was exactly the man she supposed he should be. Let the man alone, let him be himself, within limits. Still, she'd not have a drinker, no pubman who'd cast his hat for the home hook every night at midnight or later, leaving her to the care of the house. She'd not have a drinker or a politician; otherwise he could follow his natural impulses and she'd love him for it. A man with the fine side of her father would do nicely. A lovely man who would wrap his children in his greatcoat and hoist them high. It is enough to give a child wings, that kind of attention. And a man who would need his time alone, who would sit by the fire with the wrath of God for whoever might inter-rupt him. Ellen would tiptoe around, she swore she would. Oh, she laughed at the image, herself all big-boned and tiptoe-ing around the house. And he would have a soft hand for her and a word or two to set on the floor of her bedtime ear, all private like there were only the two of them scratching the sur-face of the earth. Was that too much to ask? For a man like that?

The cold came through her greatcoat as if to say that it was, that she ought to settle for the first man who'd have her. Had there ever been a longer winter to make the promise of spring seem so great? Ellen didn't know. She was a daydreamer so could survive the winter well. And would she take a daydreamer for a husband then? She could see the two of them, bodies back to back yet worlds apart.

But for now, still winter, it was time to get back to the bath. She'd let Henriette work alone from the earliest part of the morning as punishment. It was back-breaking work, lugging those liquid buckets about. Maybe after today there'd be no more asking for an evening off to go running to the tent of that bleeder.

It was impossible for Ellen to enter her bath without noticing the round-topped mule's feet. Weren't they more hideous than the entire frozen mule, rider and all? And each time she saw them she thought of Hummel, and each time she thought of him she found him sitting in some corner of the bath's front room, tying his eyes to the moving figure of Henriette or talking to Ellen if she stood still for it.

Today he was perched atop the counter, examining in his hot palm the marble egg given her by Finn.

"Unhand my egg and get off the counter," she said. "There are chairs all about you if you'd care to look."

Hummel slid to his feet but held the egg up in the air be-tween them.

"How much do you want for it?" he asked. "It's a silly thing but I'll take it off your hands."

"We sell baths, no longer eggs," she said. "Besides, it's not something you can sink your teeth into."

Ellen took the egg and placed it back where it belonged, rolling about the floor of one of the empty chicken coops. She could hear Henriette in the back and could tell from the sound that there were no customers.

"I believe you're next, Mr. Hummel, if you've come for a bath."

Henriette came out when she heard Ellen's voice. "The baths are clean and the last of the morning crowd is gone," she said. She took Ellen's hand and shook it. "Did you know, Ellen, that Mr. Hummel plans to bring his mother to live with him? As soon as he gets his house built."

Ellen looked from Hummel to Henriette. No doubt he'll be needing a wife for his mother to browbeat, she thought.

"Did he feed you as properly as he claimed he would?" she asked.

"Ptarmigan," said Henriette. "It was fowl where I expected fish."

Ellen put her arm around Henriette. "Lord knows we've had enough of fish this winter," she said. "It would be a pleasure for anyone to have a taste of something else."

This was the time of day when there was a chance for one of them to rest before the afternoon rush began. People cleaned themselves in the morning or just before supper, or just before bed. One of them always stayed downstairs, but the other took a real nap, stretched out on a bed above. Hummel's habit was to come every other day, when it was Henriette's turn to tend the bath.

"Go ahead on up," Ellen said to Henriette. "You didn't get your proper sleep last night and I've a mind to stay down anyway."

Henriette nodded and turned toward the stairs without looking at Hummel. "I thought you'd stay down today," he said, but Henriette didn't answer. She merely motioned with her free hand, trailing a sweater behind her in the other.

Hummel walked to the bottom of the stairs and put his hand on the railing, his foot on the lower step.

"Feel free to sit upon the steps, Mr. Hummel," said Ellen. "Walking on them, however, is reserved for the employees."

"We had such a good time last night. I came here today especially to talk to her."

"Well," said Ellen, "what's another day in winter? If you want me out of the way Henriette will be running the shop alone this time tomorrow, I can guarantee you."

Hummel lowered himself foot and head, then turned back toward Ellen as she stood behind the counter.

"It was you who told everyone about my beach strike," he said evenly. "You're the one I should have blamed."

"It was the assayer, not I," she said. "The man you've all appointed tax collector. And you were not so ill treated as you think. It was no real strike and it was municipal property. Consider yourself lucky to have found it first."

Hummel wiped his sweaty palms on the top of a stack of bath towels and then looked up quickly to see if Ellen had seen him do it. He picked up his heavy coat and stepped toward the door.

"I'll draw you a map to your murdered man's grave soon. To the snow mound where we've dumped him."

Ellen stared up from her counter but said simply, "Suicide."

With the soft closing of the door Ellen was left alone once again. While Hummel had hovered about her she'd pretended to count the morning's receipts three times and still had little idea how much they'd taken in. She tried to think of what it was she needed to supply herself with and where she might be able to get her hands on it. She needed soap, that was one thing, but there'd be no soap until the ice broke and the ships could come into the bay once again. She turned around and

looked at the barren shelves and empty chicken coops behind
her. Next winter, if she lived so long, she'd triple her stock and
stay up nights, if she had to, to keep them alive.

Ellen saw her marble egg and took it out of the coop and
held it between her hands. If the egg ever disappeared she'd
know whose door to pound on for it. She felt the need to hide
the egg even now, but its shape made finding a hiding place
difficult. The egg was made to lie snugly under a chicken, not
to roll around the floor of an empty coop. She put it in the
cigar box that held her money, then took it out again. She
walked to her coat and pushed the egg deep into the fur-lined
pocket. This way when she wore the coat she'd have something
to rest her hand upon. The bottom of her pocket held the egg
perfectly. With her hand on it she felt like a mother, protective
and waiting. And she felt it would not do to let the egg grow
cold again.

———

On impulse and not long after Finn left, Phil took the runners
off the sled and made a pair of ice skates for Kaneda. They
were longer than the reverend's but Phil tried them himself and
was satisfied with the way they worked. He made platforms out
of wood and strapped the skates to the old man's feet, using
strips of hide. Later he drew a map of the camp and showed
Kaneda the river path to the Eskimo village, and the old man
understood.

"We are going to take a trip to your place," he said. "We
can leave everything but the gold. It will be our vacation before
the work of the coming spring."

That night the storytelling went well and they slept without
whiskey, both of them excited about the next morning's departure. Phil had made special covers for the mute dog's paws so

that he would be able to run on the ice, and he strung the remaining golden snowflakes together so that they fit over the old man's shoulders and hung down his back and chest like armor. The dog sat all night licking at his feet but getting none of his usual pleasure from it. In the morning, dressed in his skates and gold the old man did figure eights on the familiar front ice and, seeing his chest glimmer, pulled a stick from the bank and made samurai passes through the air.

"Like this and like this!" he yelled, his long skates pointing like swords in the direction he chose.

Phil was afraid the old man would tire on the journey so he pulled a long rope from the shelter and tied an end to each of their waists. They looked like flatland mountain climbers. They would make good time if they left immediately, for the hours of daylight were far greater now than at the time of Phil's arrival. Phil thought briefly that they might even see Finn, trudging along the shore path, looking toward the river.

"Come, Taro," cried Kaneda, and he gave a slight pull on his end of the rope, forcing Phil to leave the shore before he had secured all of the gold pans in their poker-chip chimneys the way he'd seen them stacked at other abandoned sites. They coasted away from Topcock Creek, the old man in front, his armor looking to Phil like a gold woven net thrown over the shoulders of a fisherman. They turned onto the Snake and then skated side by side. The tips of the old man's skates were curled slightly and they were longer so he worked less, pushing off once for every two of Phil's steps. Their faces were covered and the fur collars of their jackets were packed hard around their eyes.

Phil could feel the pressure again, around his ankles and against the sides of his feet. He looked toward the old man but could see nothing of the discomfort he must feel. The old man skated as Phil's father might have. He was old but his body was taut, every tuned muscle involved with the skating.

When he got home Phil would tell his children the story of the owls. He went over it in his mind, deciding which rhythms to use, deciding his pace and tone. He would take his style from the old man or from the reverend and he would tell the story in both Eskimo and English so that the reverend could hear it and make helpful suggestions. Now he practiced telling the story according to the rhythms of the skating. He pulled out a rope's length in front of Kaneda, then was held back and remembered that in storytelling a common rhythm must be maintained, that it is not good to be continually speeding up and slowing down. At this lesson from the old man's steadiness, Phil thought of a way to relieve him of part of the hard work of skating. He turned slightly and grabbed the rope and pulled it hard so that the old man slipped past him, grinning with his eyes. Now the old man was a rope's length in front of Phil and they could skate at different speeds until Phil passed him and was in a position to pull him forward again. Back and forth they went, the tundra trees flipping past silently, the wide Snake twisting beneath their skates.

The old man could feel, more than the soreness of the skates, the weight of the golden snowflakes that hung from him, backside and front. Phil had tied the gold in such a way that there was no chance of any of it breaking and falling soft and unnoticed on the quiet ice, so he wasn't worried about that. Still, the old man would not have objected if the gold hung from Phil's shoulders rather than from his own. Had he been skating with Fujino he would have ordered him to carry it. But with Phil it was different. Though he was like a son he was not like a son. He was an equal and would never allow himself to be subjugated in the way that Japanese sons-in-law were supposed to be.

Phil was older and it had crossed Kaneda's mind that all these random thoughts about his daughter were pure madness. His daughter might find Phil less desirable than she had found young Fujino. He suspected that he might also have a difficult time explaining why he had returned to Japan with this man who did not speak their language and why he had allowed the young man of his daughter's clear choice to so spiritually decline that he had chosen *seppuku* over continued life. It was so unlike Fujino that the old man feared they might not believe him. And, though his daughter was beautiful, he worried that Phil might find her shyness unbecoming. He might want her to be more visibly strong like the two women they'd arrived with, the two women from Nome. And there were so few foreigners in Japan that Phil might find himself lonely and might find the task of learning Japanese as difficult as Kaneda found the study of English. These little problems were something he was not facing. He'd been so overjoyed at the discovery of this man who fit his plans so well that he had failed to look at the obstacles.

Phil was a rope's length ahead again and pulled hard, and Kaneda felt the surge of speed and bent his knees slightly so that when he shot past Phil he saw only the blurred side of Phil's coat. It was thrilling, being pulled forward with such a rush. He could see the curled fronts of the sled runners out ahead of him and he could see, way out ahead, the brown speck of dog, trotting. And, though the gold was heavy, it kept him warm. He had no sense of winter except as pinpoints of ice, shafts of it stabbing him directly in the eyes.

The river turned, and when the two men skated together the rope between them swung to the ice and touched pieces of debris that the wind had set in their way. There was no sound other than the sound of the skates, and no place did the ice show a weakening, any of the bluing that preceded its thaw.

In an hour the skaters had moved on the ice so that Phil was always in the lead and the old man always being pulled. It was the weight of the gold and the spreading soreness in his legs and ankles. Much of the time he squatted down, letting the tail of his snowflake armor nearly touch the ice. He could sit that way for a very long time and from there could see clearly the true nature of the ice they passed over. He let his skates fall into and widen the grooves made by Phil's thinner blades.

The ice Kaneda saw was cloudy, with grains running as the water had, toward the sea. It appeared to him that the water had merely stopped in its pitch and roll, frozen in its churn, and he thought that it would have been proper for men to have stopped as well. Ice is slippery because it demands no movement and winter should be a time of no movement for men. Happily the old man touched with his glove the gold webbing that lay over his heart. It was soft and heavy and not subject to the laws that governed the river and men. Suddenly he got the idea that gold would not freeze at any temperature and thus had become so valuable. It was constant, and though it came in many forms it remained persistent and persuasive. Like the flaw in a man's character, it is sometimes hidden but always reappears.

The old man stood and skated forward until the rope once again draped itself on the cool ground. He could see his shadow in the smoky ice and could see the dull yellow of his jacket, like a cloud-dimmed view of the sun. Birds passed overhead, disturbing him. He saw Phil straighten with the slackening of the rope, so he immediately returned to his crouched position, making Phil work once more. It was his gold but half of what he had would be Phil's. If he must carry it Phil must pull. He wondered for a moment what Phil's home would be like. Certainly nothing like Japan, but he was sure, if it was a town of any size, they would have a historian. He wanted to meet the man, to exchange views. He wanted to see what he could see, to learn what he could, in the time he had left, about other parts of the world.

———

Henriette had missed her monthlies before, but this time she was widely suspicious. She'd lost track of time, letting one day flow to the next like merging beads of quicksilver, but now, as she stood before the window of her room, she was sure. She cupped her hands together just below her navel and perceived the skin tightening. It was three weeks since she'd been with Hummel, five since her engagement to the reverend.

Soon after the night with Hummel, Henriette told him that she could not see him again, but he came now, the silent serenader just below her window. He stood long hours in the cold, his head turned upward in the moonlight, or when she worked and when Ellen was at rest he stood silently in the corners of the bath, his features hanging heavy off his bones.

"I can't see you and I'm sorry if I led you on," she had said, but he wouldn't answer, would only look about, furtive, sorrowful.

And now her monthlies missed. Henriette knew she could confide in the reverend, tell him the baby was his and that he would never doubt it. Or she could tell John Hummel. Both men wanted her and to tell the truth there were ways in which she would not be unsatisfied with either. With Hummel she'd be rich and warm, living in his imagined house, and with the reverend she was sure to be needed, would be able to help in his work. She was afraid of Hummel's mother, but was afraid of everyday life in the village as well. Maybe she'd get tired of it, want to leave, and be forced by the reverend to stay, or worse, force him to leave and then lose him. In the village too much would be expected of her. In Nome nothing would.

Henriette saw Hummel moving along the paths below so she stood back from the window. She could hear him standing in the snow. She turned the lanterns low and began dressing in the orange light of the slow stove. It didn't seem as though her skirt was any tighter than it had been, so perhaps this pregnancy was too soon imagined. Perhaps it was time, not her skin, that stretched so thin and long. Each night took the time of two to pass, and at that rate wouldn't it be another week before her period was even due? Ah, if that were only the case she'd still have two men to choose from and it would be pleasant, in a way, to be sought after. In the end she'd probably choose the reverend, who'd asked her first and in writing. There was something about the weakness of that note. Not what it said exactly, but the way it looked. Now that she'd seen Hummel's hand she could compare. Hummel's life had been ordered by his mother but the reverend needed somebody. One look at his note would tell you that.

Henriette sighed and went down the stairs to the main room and saw Ellen alone, throwing her marble egg high into the air and catching it. She wore a pair of canvas trousers and was lifting her leg and throwing the egg up from under it. It was a schoolgirl's game, and each time, when the egg was in midair, she'd clap her hands lightly and count, one O'Leary, two O'Leary, like jumping rope but with only herself and the marble egg.

Henriette stood quietly and watched. She'd never before thought of Ellen as a girl. And she was good at it. She sometimes let the egg go from behind her back yet caught it deftly in front of her without really looking. And from wherever she happened to throw the egg it always came down in the same place. Ellen merely placed a hand against her stomach and waited, nearly casual, for the egg to fall into it. Then she flipped it to the other hand and released it again, higher into the air, higher and higher. Of course there were no customers and Henriette hoped that Hummel would remain outside, that no one would come in to destroy Ellen's mood. It was strange to watch the marble egg lift closer to the dusty ceiling each time. It rose heavy end first and then turned slowly and descended that way as well. As it reached its apex it stopped in the air before turning and Henriette could see the shafts of brown marble laid through the white, like a child softly growing. The pattern ran from the base to the top and Henriette thought, each time, that it would surely come apart in Ellen's hands, that this time when she caught it she would have two pieces of egg, equal and heavy and good for nothing. Yet always the egg rose and fell without incident. It rose slowly, as if a bubble in a liquid room, and always as an accompaniment to Ellen's song: One O'Leary, two O'Leary, three O'Leary, four. . . .

Henriette thought of the egg in her body as floating and turning as Ellen's egg did. Perhaps it too rose heavy end first around its half child. She couldn't imagine that it too had a fault, that it was cracked or would break. Its shell was made of sterner stuff. Yet as Ellen continued her game Henriette remembered the expanding skin of her belly and began hoping that Ellen would miss, that the marble would fracture on the hardwood floor and that she would be able to hold the flesh of her abdomen, loose again, in both of her hands. She knew, suddenly, that if the marble egg broke she'd be safe. She knew it. Yet Ellen kept skillfully at her game, fast and sure. Henriette imagined Ellen dancing along the dusty roads of Ireland, this egg of hers always reaching a bit higher into the sky. It is the nature of lonely children that they have patience and she knew that Ellen would never miss.

Henriette got up off the step and ran into the room toward Ellen. She pushed Ellen forward and the egg fell onto the floor. Ellen scraped her palm on the counter top and turned with wild surprise toward Henriette, who knelt on the floor and felt hot tears on the backs of her hands. Of course the egg had not broken. It hit with marble hardness and, making a little indentation, stood, not even rolling its egg wobble across the floor.

"Here!" said Ellen, and then more softly, "Here, here, you'll be the death of me running in like that. What's come over you?"

Henriette lifted the egg and handed it back to Ellen. It was at this time that John Hummel opened the heavy door and stood smiling at them from the entrance. He truly was healed, you could tell from the pink tightness of his gums. And it was not hard to tell from the cast of his glance that he still had his eye on Ellen's egg.

The reverend saw them first. It was late and he was walking the beach again, alternately thinking of Henriette and dreading the sermon he would have to give the next morning. It was getting so that he liked the village better the way it was now, with everyone underground, everything out of sight. Occasionally he'd see one of the village people step from the earth, but generally when he looked to where the spring lean-tos would be there was nothing.

The reverend saw them first, and when he did he recognized Phil by the flash of his skates in the dull, low-lying sun, by the sound of them still distant on the ice. Phil was pulling a sled and it looked as if a person rode it. Out to sea the setting sun laid a path of wet light across the ice and outlined the travelers for him.

The reverend moved quickly up the beach and across the snow to the entrance to Phil's home. He lifted the hide flap and called into the earth. "It's Phil. Phil is coming," then he stood back and waited, looking toward the beach again. He hoped Phil would not be bringing bad news about Finn. He hoped that was not Finn lying bent and wounded on the sled behind him. But it was a man, he could see that clearly now, and the man appeared to be hurt. He was surrounded on the sled by a clutter of objects, clothing and nets that hung from him like bandages.

From his kneeling position behind Phil, Kaneda began rubbing his eyes. In front of him and around him there had been nothing but ice and snow and the rolling lowlands. They were skating nearly into the sun so he had been keeping his eyes closed. Now though, on the bank ahead and to his right, he saw the dark shapes of people. They appeared to multiply each time he looked, until, squinting and rubbing his eyes, he saw forty or fifty of them, all quiet, some with their arms raised in greeting. He saw Phil straighten and begin to slow down. Perhaps they would rest here for the night, though there was still an hour of daylight and it was unlike Phil to want to stop so early.

When they got to within seventy meters of the shore it was clear to everyone that Phil had brought a visitor. The man was not riding on a sled as the reverend had thought, the man *was* the sled. He was being pulled by Phil and therefore must be injured, but most of the people who waited looked at Phil's feet. Many shook their heads and looked again.

When they got closer to the beach Phil turned somewhat sideways and took the tight waist rope in his hands. Yes, they were going to stop here. Kaneda knew that Phil was about to pull him forward, but he had been sitting for so long that he found it difficult to stand. It was exhilarating being pulled forward in such a way but he was afraid that this time he might fall. All of the people were very close now. Phil pulled and he jerked forward and was able to stand at the last moment and heard a gasp from the crowd. They too seemed afraid he might fall.

The old man stood shakily before them. He counted one white man but all the rest looked Japanese. All of the adults stood with heads downcast, but the children were wide-mouthed looking at him. He had always liked children and had always sensed that they liked him. Phil pulled back the hood of his jacket and a few of the people came close to him. The old man was very glad to see that Phil was known here. It felt good to be standing and it would feel much better once he got the sled runners off his feet. He reached out to touch the nearest child, but as he did so all the children turned silently and ran from him. They fanned out across the snow and then, much to his surprise, stopped and disappeared into the ground.

Phil took off his skates and handed them to the reverend. Then he bent and helped the old man unstrap the runners. It was a very good feeling. People in the crowd had their hoods off and followed the skates as they changed hands. The old man undid the lacing around his neck and pushed his own hood away from his face. The crowd shifted their glance to him, and quickly three women stepped forward to get a closer look. They held him by the arms and looked at Phil and spoke. Though the old man did not understand what they were saying, he was pleased with the reception he got.

Phil assured everyone that the resemblance between Kaneda and his father was a coincidence. Those who fall through the ice do not return unless they do so immediately. Still, he enjoyed the surprise on everyone's face and he told them that he too had reacted in much the same way.

The villagers came forward and began shaking Kaneda's hand. They formed a circle around him and led him gently up off the shore. Phil's wife shaded the old man's eyes and frowned at the fact that the word "coincidence" had escaped her husband's lips. Of course she did not think that Phil's father had returned, but this was no coincidence. Her husband had been spending too much time with white men. Coincidence. She suspected that even the reverend would have to laugh at such a thought.

After they'd progressed a few meters up the beach the old man looked at her and spoke, but she did not understand him. Everyone stopped and was quiet and waited for him to speak again, but when he did so they still did not understand. The language he used was familiar but not understandable. And it was not the language of another group of Eskimos, for though there were many dialects they didn't know there were none they could not recognize. They looked at Phil and he told them

"Japan" and some of them remembered the name and looked toward the reverend, who nodded as if he too had definitely heard the word before.

The general movement of the group was toward the reverend's house. It was important for the old man to get warm and for them to have a better look at him. The reverend and Phil moved on ahead to build up the fires and make room. The central group surrounded the old man, standing near him in case he might fall. Behind them the children reappeared. They ran around the silent sides of Nanoon's hut frowning, and fell in with the others.

Inside the reverend's house the reverend and Phil exchanged words. The reverend hung his skates in their usual place, then asked about Finn and was told who the old man was. He went quickly around the room picking up objects from the floor. It was Saturday and he had not had a chance to do his cleaning. On Sunday, for the services, his house was always very neat, but he didn't clean again until Saturday night. And now all these people were coming. He scooped papers and books into his arms and threw them up onto the hidden floor of the loft. The door opened and the old man was ushered in and for a moment the reverend had the image of garlands being laid before him.

"Do you speak English?" the reverend asked.

"I do not speak English," said the old man.

Phil told the reverend and the others about Fujino and how the two Japanese and Ellen and Henriette had all come to the country together. He impressed them with the fact that it took half a year to make the trip from Japan and said that he and the old man had talked of how surprising it was that they should look alike.

"Surprising, maybe, but no coincidence," said Phil's wife.

The children, who had been standing at the back of the room, stepped forward, each holding a large piece of sketch paper. They began to circle the old man, shifting their glance from him to the golden webbing that he still wore. After they had circled him several times the children stood their drawings on the furniture and against the walls around the room, and this time, when the old man reached out, they allowed him to touch them on the tops of their heads. The gold was heavy and he wanted to take it off, so Phil stepped forward to help him cut it away. There were sixteen drawings and the old man had snowflakes in excess of three dozen. He shook his shoulders until a woman came up behind him and began rubbing the sore spots away. Each child stood behind the drawing that was his own.

The old man, in the center of the room, at the center of the circle of people, stood doing calisthenics. After the gold was off him he removed his coat and stretched his arms high over his head and bent forward and down until he had touched his toes. He did deep knee bends and rolled his hips and torso from side to side, breathing deeply as he did so.

"Though Taro here did all the work, my body is in pain from crouching in one position for such a long time," he said. Then he laughed once. "Taro made me carry all the gold so I made him do all the pulling."

The Eskimos listened again as hard as they could, but could not catch what he was saying. The old man had hoped they would smile, but when they did not he put on a serious face again and began to circle the room, looking carefully at each nervous child, at each drawing. The children stood like dog owners. When the old man had circled the room twice he began around again carrying one of his golden snowflakes. When he'd gone less than halfway around the group he carefully placed the snowflake in front of the drawing that equaled it. The size and all of the webbed lines matched perfectly. Each time he circled the room he carried only one snowflake. Occasionally he found no drawing that matched the snowflake he carried, but in the end each drawing was matched to the finest of its lines, to the last of its detail.

When the old man finished, the children picked up their

snowflakes, looked at him through them, and showed no surprise. Phil took those remaining and laid them in a pile on the
old man's coat. Someone thought of hunger and went out and
came back with dried fish. Now that the ritual of greeting was
over the people of the village began to question Phil about what
he had been doing while he was away. There had been a death
in the village while he'd been gone and they told him about
that. Only Phil's wife stayed with Kaneda. She continued to rub
at the sore muscles of his back and shoulders. She helped him
walk about the room, spied on by the children like spider prey.

———

There was a new notice board in the exact center of Nome and
Finn leaned against it with all his weight. He could see the top
floor of the bath and the frames of a dozen new buildings. Frost
clung to his snowbeard. He could hear the hammers ring and
he read about the organization of the town, about the public
construction crew and the drawing of lots. There had been a
town meeting and there would be another one in three days.
There would be an election. Finn lifted the pencil that hung in
front of him and wrote his name second on the list of mayoral
candidates, under that of Dr. Kingman. He laughed and picked
up his pack again. Now there was organization, a notice board
in the center of town.

It had taken Finn a week to walk to Nome but he felt in good
shape from it. There'd been no distractions inside the evening
ice houses that he'd built, so he had had a chance to rest.
During that time he had not spoken or sung or whistled, and
now, as he approached the bath house, he felt really tired for
the first time. He took a wrong turn once and then corrected it
and came around from the right. He saw that the window was
closed and clean and that the door was working again. One man

entered and another left as Finn stood there watching. The building seemed strong and beautiful. He walked very close to it, then stood in the dead center of the four mule hooves, pushing his bearded face to the glass and peering in.

Henriette and Ellen were dressed in long white skirts and sloshed about, doing their work. Three customers lined the waiting bench and one walked briskly from the back room, rubbing his wet hair with a towel. Finn could see the line of empty chicken coops to his right, behind the counter where Ellen stood, and when he looked at the three customers again he recognized one of them as John Hummel. Finn stood staring for a full minute before jumping back and passing his hand through the air where the mule and Fujino should have stood. He remembered the strong zero of Fujino's mouth, how it was dark to look into, how it was the startled look of death taking him by surprise.

Finn went to the edge of the building and peeked around it as if perhaps he'd come to the wrong window. He came back and saw the dark snow holes and bent over to look at the black tops of the mule hooves. When he stood again Ellen and Henriette were there, both of them looking out at him as the three of them, weeks before, had looked out at Fujino. He could hear them dimly calling his name: Finn . . . Finn . . . Henriette jumped and Ellen had a tear for him too. She was happy with the sight of him as no one had ever been with Fujino.

Henriette and Ellen saw Finn laugh, his mouth moving wide through his beard. They stepped to the heavy door and opened it. "Finn! Finn!" said Henriette. She kissed his cheek and turned to Ellen as though presenting him to her as a gift.

"You're safe and I thought you'd be frozen solid," said Ellen, smiling.

They closed the door and wove a pattern around each other, all of them talking at once. Ellen took a sign from behind the counter and placed it on a hook outside the door: CLOSED. "We'll have a feast right now," she said, "just the three of us." She turned to the customers, assuring them that their dirt would come off as well the next day as this and then held the door for them.

"Of course," said John Hummel. He took Henriette's elbow and turned her toward him and told her that he'd be going, that he'd see her later, as if his leaving was his own idea. "Your Finn's come back of his own accord," he whispered to her. "Welcome him back, you'd both better welcome him back."

Ellen closed the door firmly behind him. Henriette held Finn's arm tightly, laying her head on his shoulder.

"Ah, it's good to be back among my own kind," said Finn. "To speak English again, that's the ticket."

"Did Phil find you?" asked Henriette. "We were in the village when he went off looking."

"He found me and he and Mr. Kaneda hit it off so well that there was no further use for me. They're up there still, jabbering at each other in their own tongues."

"And how did he take the news of young Fujino?"

"He donated over an hour each night to long prayers for the young man's soul. I could feel Fujino's presence though I didn't understand a word."

Finn sat up on the edge of the counter and looked down at the women. "But nothing's happened up there that's not bleakness and bitter cold," he said. "Tell me about yourselves. The bath seems busy. There has been some organization since I've been gone. I noticed the sign board in the center of town."

"We had a town meeting right here," said Henriette, "and there's going to be an election; you must have seen the notice."

"I not only saw it, I signed my name atop the list for mayor. We can't let this Kingman have the town for his signature alone."

Ellen, who had been lifting food from shelf to counter, stopped and gave Finn the longest of her looks. She wiped her hands down the front of her apron.

"It's a good idea," she said. "The man not only expects to win, but expects no one to run against him."

Ellen forgot the occasion of Finn's return and left the food where it stood. She went up the stairs to her room and returned with a sketch pad given her by one of Phil's children as a Christmas gift. Henriette still held Finn's arm, moving toward and away from him like a dancing partner.

"If you weren't joking we've no time to lose," said Ellen. "The election is in three days."

Finn said that indeed he hadn't been joking but that he'd had a long walk and was dirty and hungry and tired, so Henriette released him and went into the bath to pour water from stove to tub, and Ellen went back to work on the meal.

"You can bathe and we can eat," she said, "but after that if you'd like to sleep for a while Henriette and I will make your posters. I haven't seen a one for our friend Kingman."

Finn remembered Ellen. He had forgotten what it was like to be surrounded by her but he remembered now. So he was going to run for mayor. He didn't like Kingman but in truth he'd signed the list only because the idea had occurred to him as he stood there, only because of an impulse. Now he was in a campaign and he hadn't been back in the town thirty minutes. He went into the bath when it was ready and sat in the burning water and closed his eyes. For weeks he'd listened to men speaking in languages he did not understand. Then he'd left them and been by himself, silent as he walked over the earth or sat inside the ice tombs Phil had shown him how to build. Each night they had been identical, and in the bath now, with his eyes closed, he could picture himself still housed in ice. For a week he'd let his thoughts go random. He'd not thought about Fujino or the state of his life, or where he ought to be at forty-five years of age. For a week Finn had been in a state of grace and cooling, and now he was running for mayor. It made him want to laugh. He could hear Ellen and Henriette like two winter animals outside his ice shelter, planning his campaign. Three days. All they could do would be to put up signs and talk to people who came to the bath.

Finn the politician stayed in the water a long while, imagining that he was smoking a long cigar. When he came out the table was set and the women were seated. Around the wall sketch paper had been laid or tacked and on each piece Ellen or Henriette had written his name. They told him that after dinner they'd go out and place the signs in the bars, scatter them about town, tack them to the sides of tents.

"You must think of something to say at the town meeting," said Ellen. "That will be your job. Henriette and I will do the rest. And you must go to the Gold Belt and talk to those who are interested in the election. Tell them what you'll do if elected. Tell them your platform, the kind of town you'd like to have."

Ellen smiled across the steaming food as she talked to him. He tried to remember how long he'd been gone but could not. He looked at Henriette and saw her, head hung, picking at her food. A strong woman and a weaker one. Between them he wondered which he would choose. Neither probably, nor would they have him if he did. They were all here because they'd been thrown together and he could think of no better reason. He was running for mayor because he'd seen the list, and was there any higher motive? Things happen because they do, that was what he'd discovered during his time alone, and it made him proud to have discovered it at last. He would resist the urge to mourn the years he'd lived not knowing it.

Finn looked across the table. There sat his friends speaking to him in English, but it didn't seem so important to him now. He had, after all, been just as at home listening to the others, to the tones of Eskimo and Japanese. It is the sound of the human voice that is important, not what it might be saying. No, out at Topcock Creek he'd not been upset by the languages they'd used. He knew that now. Finn listened and nodded at what Ellen told him was the proper way to conduct himself as a candidate. He would do it too, exactly as she said. And he would work on his speech. He laughed to himself and finished his meal. If he only knew enough of it, he thought, he'd be sure to give all his campaign speeches in Gaelic.

———

Ellen lowered the price of the bath and asked the bathers to vote for Finn. She sent Henriette with tacks and sketch paper, out into the streets, and for one whole day Finn stayed in his room upstairs, pacing, thinking up things to say and practicing his speech. Ellen had been involved in a real election once before and remembered now how it had been. She should get others, one or two in each part of the town, to visit their neighbors and to tell them just exactly why Finn was the man for the job. But it was too late for that. Only three days and no one to tell and not a single reason that made Finn out to be a better man than anyone else. No, in a case like this everything depended upon the speech that she could hear Finn practicing upstairs. She couldn't really understand what he was saying, but the sound of it was political and made a good impression on those who bathed below. And the election preparations had given her the opportunity to tell Hummel that he must not come around at all. He came once again the morning after Finn arrived and blinked at the campaign posters around him. He didn't wait for Henriette, but stepped back out the door and disappeared up the path toward Dr. Kingman's house right away. And now he followed Henriette around the streets asking her if she wanted him to take what she was doing as a personal insult.

"You're working for one man and I'm working for the other," he said.

He took her arm and turned her toward him and asked her

what he was supposed to tell Dr. Kingman, and Henriette thought and then said that she didn't know why he had to tell him anything. Hummel hung behind her for a while longer then shuffled off toward his tent. He could write better than any of them and would make up a few signs of his own.

Henriette posted the signs slowly, tacking all around the edges. When she finished she stood back a few feet, then took out a pencil and wrote her name neatly in the lower left corner. "Henriette." It was by her authority that this sign was posted. She liked her name and liked the way it looked sitting soft and neat at the bottom of the sign. She was the only Henriette she had ever known.

Henriette believed she could feel the band of her skirt tightening around her middle so she'd taken Fujino's diary out and hidden it in her room. She was going to have a baby, she had no doubt. She was going to have a girl, and if she did she would give it a name like one of these: Bertha, Martha, or Agatha. If it was a boy she'd name him Henry and make him clothes and take him with her wherever she might go. Henriette decided not to marry or if she did to marry someone she as yet did not know, or maybe, perhaps, the reverend. She wished he lived in Nome and had a good job. Or no, the job was all right, but she wished he lived in Nome. She wanted the baby to be able to see the town grow and to be a student in its first school. She didn't know for sure, but she suspected that hers would be the first new baby since the strike. Little Bertha, Martha, Agatha, or Henry.

The first person Henriette would tell, once the baby began to show, would be Ellen. She was afraid of that, though she was not ashamed. In a way it was better not to know the exact father, for then she could not be forced to have an exact husband. Still, she hoped the father was the reverend so that must mean she liked him best. If the child was Hummel's it would cause all kinds of problems, though she didn't expect to be able to see the father in the newborn's face. . . . Unless the gums bled.

Henriette tacked her signs and held her belly. The baby would be born in winter but part of the time she grew with it the weather would be warm. She could see signs of the end of winter in the ground, in the longer hours of daylight. If Finn was elected mayor she'd ask him for a job working for the city. She needed time to be with the little one, and even now, though she made money working for Ellen, the work was too hard and she was afraid the baby would feel the strain.

Henriette tacked up the last of the thin posters and walked about the town looking at her work. FINN FOR MAYOR. Ellen had written each one as neatly as she could. Behind the lettering she had tried to draw a silhouette of Finn, but it was unrecognizable. Spring was coming. As Henriette worked her way back to the bath she saw a group of men standing in front of one of her posters.

"The one who hangs around the bath house," one of them said. "He came here with politics in mind."

8

The problem of the golden snowflakes had been solved by a miracle. The reverend told the children they would form snowflakes in the spring but they had all been surprised by the coming of this stranger who wore the snowflakes as a tree wears Christmas ornaments. Whereas a few days before the villagers had remained in their underground homes, now they walked in perfect patterns across the snow. They wore their snowflakes like sheriffs' badges or like necklaces that hung all the way to their belts, riding softly on their hard middles.

As the children walked across their roofs the men of the village began bringing lean-to poles out of the storage sheds that stood at the edge of the forest. They placed the poles along the ground and set thin rolls of hide and canvas next to them. From the reverend's window the material looked like the solid foundations of buildings. The reverend had invited Kaneda to stay with him, but the old man did not want to be away from Phil. That first day as Phil lowered himself into the ground the old man had tried to follow. It was Phil's wife who'd met him before he could get inside and escorted him, stringing her arm through his, all the way back to the reverend's house. Now he sat in the soft chair next to the reverend, watching small figures fishing way out on the ice. The fishermen were using the snowy owl feathers that Phil had brought out the evening before, when he'd made his first attempt at storytelling. He had held the pure white feathers in his hands to give the story power. So it was important that the hunt be successful today to give his story credibility. But it was a difficult time of the year. The men spaced themselves far apart on the ice in order to avoid falling through.

"This is called red feathering," said the reverend. "If you like we can walk out onto the ice to get a look at it first hand."

"Do they never stand straight?" asked Kaneda. "Whenever they walk on the ice they remain bent. It looks uncomfortable and is certainly bad for the posture."

The figures had locked themselves into their hunting positions, legs straight, bodies bent at the waists, eyes peering at the white feathers on the ice, arms cocked skyward with harpoons. "If we are lucky we will soon see one of them pulling a seal straight from the water," said the reverend. "When I watch from here I always imagine that they are rescuing someone from drowning. It is in the way they hold the seal, the way they prop it up between them, like a friend who has had too much to drink."

The reverend had been watching Phil and as he spoke the old man leaned forward and pointed. "Look! They are drawing a man from the ice."

"Yes," said the reverend, following Kaneda's finger. "It looks as though it will be a good day. It is very early to have made a kill."

The old man looked at the reverend and then looked quickly back at the ice. The hunters had laid the seal down and had backed off quickly to avoid breaking through.

"A seal," said the old man.

"It must be very difficult for you," said the reverend. "After having lost Mr. Fujino, I mean."

"They are hunting seal, now I understand."

Another seal and then another slid from the quick ice in front of them, and the reverend and the old man grew quiet. Each felt a sense of goodwill toward the other. The chairs were soft and they had tea in a huge pot between them. They watched the children watching the hunters. The old man thought of his daughter, of how she should be here to see her future husband in action, and the reverend thought of Henriette and when he might see her again.

When the reverend looked at Kaneda he too could see Phil's father's face. It had been his first winter in the village when Phil's father fell through the ice. He had been sitting where he was now, in front of his new window, and he had rushed out of the house without a coat. Before he reached the bay he found himself freezing and was forced to turn back, to return for his jackets. He'd dressed and gone out again only to find the village, every member, standing on the ice staring at a small hole filming over.

Phil and his sisters and his wife, he didn't really know them then, slid up to the opening on their bellies and let their heads fall into the water and turn at the necks this way and that, searching. When after minutes they emerged, their faces were frozen and wide-eyed with grief. Water did not drip off them, for their features were incased within a fine ice shell. None of the other members of the village moved to their aid so the reverend held back as well. Phil's father's harpoon line was taut and still attached to its base. Phil and his sisters and his wife picked it up in their cold hands and, leaning away from the hole, began to pull it in, hand over hand. It took time because all of the line had fed itself into the sea and the sea in this spot was deep. Still nobody helped and still the grief frozen to their faces did not break. Cracks ran across the ice but the people were spread wide and no others fell through. Finally after all of the line was retrieved the dark head of a large seal appeared at the hole and they leaned against it with all of their weight and using all of their strength made it slide dead out of the water and across the ice to stop at their feet. Nanoon, just a child then, knelt and dug at the tip of the harpoon until it was freed and then from the wound she took the red feather and handed it to a sister. Phil cut the seal from neck to tail and the carcass opened to all of them easily, like the unbuttoning of a jacket. And then they ate. Not just the family of the man who had died, but everyone ate, the entire village. The reverend stepped forward with his Bible, his heart in his throat. He was going to say something, but when he looked at the family all he could see was ice masks facing him, all red around the mouths. He could see eyes where hot tears had melted the ice and tears where they ran down the outside of the ice masks and froze again around covered noses and mouths. He ate and, flushed with embarrassment, slid his Bible under his shirt, out of sight.

But on the ice in front of them now the hunt was a success. Each time someone pulled in a seal the old man applauded and sat forward and turned toward the reverend. There were six or seven big seals whereas on a good day the village was lucky to have three. The old man wished that the reverend would make some move to go out, for he wanted a closer view. He rubbed his hands together, and when a seal that appeared to be larger than any of the others was caught he stood up and pressed his face against the glass. When he turned around again the reverend was smiling at him and handing him his coat.

Outside the old man ran toward the beach, leaving the reverend to walk behind. He had never seen fishing like this. He saw as he approached that the big seal and all the others were being pushed on their bellies toward the shore. The hunting was over and Phil, in the center of the group, held the remaining owl feathers high above his head and walked along the line of children triumphantly, making each of them admit that his story must have been true. It had been the best single day's catch in anyone's memory.

By the time the old man arrived the hunters and the others were in high, festival spirits. The old man ran his bare hand along the soft wet fur of the big seal and Phil commenced to telling the entire village the story of the snowy owls once again. While he talked a seal was slit and the liver brought to him as a trophy. Each of the successful hunters retrieved red feathers, and then everyone bent over the opened seal to eat. Phil, behind them, continued telling his story. Everyone in the village ate and listened. Phil's wife took the old man a fine piece of meat and he knelt with the others.

Only the children seemed uninterested in the story and the food. They'd heard it all the night before and had eaten just before coming down to watch the hunt. They stood at the back of the group near the reverend. They rubbed their jacket sleeves over the fronts of their golden snowflakes but soon edged away. The reverend alone saw them go. He had seen it coming since the moment Phil and the old man came back. The children wore their golden snowflakes with pride, but they were headed in a different direction now, in a quiet line toward the storage houses. By the end of the day all of the sleds of the village would be dismantled for ice skates.

———

Finn picked up a few supporters and talked about the town in a few bars. The owner of the Gold Belt let him place his signs on the inside, but did not say no when John Hummel asked to place Dr. Kingman's alongside them. Hummel had neat advertisements for his candidate, but he had taken to posting slim innuendos as well. *"Has Nome Known Murder?"* and *"Is Killing Orientals O.K.?,"* written in large letters on the bottom of the town's new notice board.

On the day of the second town meeting, on the day of the

election, Ellen could find no one who was not going. She asked
them on their way into the bath and on their way out again.
She said that this was an election in which there was nothing
really wrong with either man but that too much power in the
hands of one was dangerous. Everyone seemed to agree with
her. She'd tried to get the site of the election changed but had
failed. Her bath and Dr. Kingman's house were the only wooden
buildings large enough. Besides, everyone wanted to look inside
that house, to stand beneath the shining chandelier.

Both Ellen and Henriette believed they noticed a change in
Finn since his return. He smiled at them out of his wide beard
and talked more softly than he had before. In the evenings when
they sat beside the warm stove he would sometimes tell them
how it was to be alone for so long, how it was being isolated
within his own language as he'd been.

"The evenings stretched out," he said. "And when I would
ask a question or make a comment they would turn their heads
to me and answer differently, in other languages. And both of
them were as satisfied as they might have been had we all
understood everything perfectly. There were times when we
laughed, when I myself forgot that none of us could understand
the other and rolled back on my bedding in the utter hilarity
of it all, in the utter hilarity of what had been said."

But Finn was not satisfied with the response he got from his
two women friends whenever he mentioned his time at the creek.
This was a philosophical point he was trying to make and yet
it was received with silence or with momentary nods, until one
or the other of them would make a comment that brought their
talk back to the subject of the election once again.

"Reality there was triple what it is when a single language
is used, does that not mean anything to you?"

But no, they would not answer or let themselves get involved
in anything but talk of the matter at hand, and so Finn soon
gave up. There'd been a breakthrough in his life when he'd sat

by himself inside those ice tombs of his on that cold ground, but the nature of his breakthrough, of his discovery, meant that he'd not successfully be able to tell anyone about it. And in a way it was a pity for he had ideas now that would revolutionize the lives of those who thought them. He had plans for testing his theory the first time he found a priest who knew not a word of English. He'd go to confession though he hadn't gone in years, and it would be no mere ritual. He'd pour his heart out to the man, make his tongue lick the very walls of whatever he knew that was sayable, and the priest would listen, not understanding a word. And then, what was most important, Finn would receive absolution, heeding the priest's words, doing exactly as he was told, listening with ears wide, letting the words of the foreign language run together on his brain like hot wax.

Ah, there were as many realities as there were languages, he was sure. And wasn't that a revolutionary idea? There were as many as there were people and perhaps people ought to speak different languages, that's the crux of it. Nobody understanding the slightest word of another, that would be the world for him. It was strange that he should come to this now, after having done so badly at the creek. It would not do to suggest that such a world would be easy. No, it would be difficult, impossible maybe, and that would be the beauty of it. But it would give our lives direction, and what's more, it would give our lives charm. People would set about learning the languages of those they loved as an act of faith. They'd never be able to learn enough to really understand the language, but perhaps a few words, the basic grammar, maybe to the point of knowing a dozen or so verbs, a little about the syntax. Theories, speculation, comments upon the nature of the world: these would be reserved for one's private language and therefore there would be no limitations. New sounds would be attached to the expanding world within your head. Not a bad theory.

Finn was half listening to the political advice being given

him by Ellen. She was telling him that he had a good chance,
really he did, but that everything depended upon that speech,
and she was right, he knew. There were many people in the
town who were naturally against Dr. Kingman for his having
struck it when they did not. And Finn would like to be mayor
of Nome, helping to change the swirl of tents into a mass of
buildings. He liked the layout of the town as it was now, twisted
from its center outward. He might propose that the buildings
be constructed in precisely that manner. He knew he would lose
the election if, no matter how casually, he mentioned his theory
about language, about the privacy of it all. Still, it was beautiful
and true. Nothing could be more revolutionary than to live in
such a world. It would be a testament, absolutely, to his new
belief that only what is unthinkable is unreal.

Finn was pulled back to ordinary life by Henriette.

"Think of it, Finn," she was saying. "You all dressed up and
sitting solid as a tree trunk behind your own oak desk.... The
mayor. Can you imagine that?"

———

The crystal chandelier was bright and the path leading down
from Dr. Kingman's house was lined with oil lanterns showing
the way. It was election day and all the bars were shut, laced
from the top and tied at the bottom in bows. All the week before
the meeting people had been talking about the weather breaking, and now many of them moved along without hooded jackets, cool with only wool bands tied about their ears. There was
still an inch of ice curving the shore, but a thin film of water,
pushed into practice waves by the warmer wind, rode cold upon
it. On the election path the frozen land gave way, in places
turning brown, the earth balding through its snow wig, showing
its age.

Inside the house Dr. Kingman and his wife had covered all the good furniture with sheets and brought in benches. The living room under the chandelier was twice as large as the main room of Ellen's bath, and in the front with its back to the fireplace stood a small podium, and on a stand next to it a glass container with ice water, a tame version of the outside world. At another table Hummel sat with stacks of yellowing paper and his pens and ink. He wore a loose grin and spoke to himself under his breath, mumbling murder more frequently now but still getting no response.

Ellen and Finn and Henriette sat toward the front, together on a bench, warming their hands by sitting upon them, placing them under their thighs. Finn had been away from them all the day, pacing the floor of his room, practicing his speech and thinking, and Ellen, never tiring, had told each bather of the dangers of monopoly government, the safety to be found in diverse rule. "Let Finn be mayor," she'd said. "Diversify. The other man already has a job. He is the richest man and the richest man should never be mayor."

Though Ellen was the constant campaigner Henriette was the tiredest of the three. She'd been the street canvasser, the one who'd relied on slogans, walking up to people and saying, "Vote Finn, Finn for mayor." She'd kept the collar of her sealskin jacket turned tightly around her neck as she spoke, for she could feel the swelling of her pregnancy even in that part of her body. The jacket also was now too tight; it pressed against her skin and left a mark that faded slowly, even in the heat of the bath.

Henriette worked for Finn's election because she liked Finn, not because she cared. She hoped Finn would win but if he did not it would not matter to anyone in a week. She had been thinking a lot lately of men, of the first few who'd poked around inside her, thrashing about like hungry sharks. Now that she was with child she thanked God that the father was not one of them. She knew who the father was and she was proud. The reverend coming to her like a serious owl in the night. He was a light-boned man and rode her like a feather. And unlike Hummel, who locked himself to her peach skin like some hungry fruit bat, the reverend seemed to wash over her like warm bath water.

Because her rounding body pressed so firmly against her clothing, Henriette now carried Fujino's diary in her hands, like a Bible. She kept the reverend's broken note still pressed inside it. She liked to take the note out and read it whenever she saw Hummel's perfect script hanging from the notice board or tacked to the walls of the city. And somehow it did not seem odd to her that Hummel was a neat man. To Henriette, Hummel's body was like a room where all the dirt had been swept under the carpet. And neat or not it was as if he were in balance with his own nature only when he was in ill health. The boundaries of his body, his very skin, seemed an artificial limitation.

Henriette looked up and saw Hummel staring at her from his corner writing desk, so she took the reverend's note out again and read it, holding it up between them like a cross. She saw him severely scratching at his pad and she knew that he was writing down a mean message, lies about the fate of Fujino, a habit he'd gotten into of late. The room was full and had grown quiet and then noisy again. Everyone was expecting an early beginning. What was keeping them?

Dr. Kingman's wife rose and rapped lightly with a gavel on the top of the table. Since her husband was a candidate it did not seem right that he be master of ceremonies as well. Hummel dipped the tip of one of his pens into an ink bottle and held it sharply in his hand, not letting it drip. There were people sitting along all the benches, lined along all the walls and floors. Finn tipped his head back and looked at the long tear-shaped shadows that were cast across the faces and below the eyes of his fellow citizens. He remembered the lonely day of the chande-

lier's arrival. He remembered standing on the porch of this
house and watching the workers lift it to where it hung now,
ready to drop and stick him sharply to the floor. It was the
chandelier that had first set him against Dr. Kingman. He had
not known it at the time but he supposed that to look up among
its tears and facets was to look, absolutely, along the corridors
of another world, one to which he couldn't belong.

"First we have the election for mayor," said Mrs. Kingman,
"then the mayor will run the rest of the meeting and do what
he thinks best for the smooth organization of our town."

The people in the room settled themselves like concert goers
and Mrs. Kingman looked toward her husband and stood back
as he got up to give his speech. The bright lights dimmed
considerably as he began to talk.

Finn did not listen. He could feel Ellen, tense and political
to his right, and Henriette, listless and pretending to listen on
his other side. He was aware that people considered Ellen the
smarter of the two. Or, more correctly, that they thought Ellen
intelligent and Henriette not. Henriette flickered in and out of
intelligence like a faulty electric light. But she didn't busy herself as much as the rest of them with the petals of her memory,
so she lived her days well. He could tell that, like himself, she
was not really listening to what the man said. Ellen, though,
was taking notes.

Oh, if Finn only knew enough Gaelic he would give his speech
in it as a lesson on what it had been like living at Topcock
Creek. What a joke that would be. Gaelic! He was sure of the
reaction he'd get from his two women. From Henriette there'd
be the same countenance that she now directed toward Kingman. But by Ellen he would be abandoned. In Nome everyone
tried to speak the same language and expected that language
in return. It was little enough to ask of him and he would
comply. He would speak to them in English and would ask that
they elect him mayor. He had practiced his speech many times

though he'd refused when Ellen asked him to say it once in front of her. He wanted it to be a surprise.

Finn looked at Ellen's notes and for a moment heard what Dr. Kingman was saying. He heard the words "kindly consider what all this would mean ..." and he thought of an aging Dr. Kingman walking along the boardwalks of a squarely built town nodding and tipping his hat. His house, though old, would still be the most prominent in the town. Once his plans were established he would pass the mantle of mayor on to someone else and would return his full energies to his business. When he spoke everyone would understand that he really did have the best interests of the town at heart.

When the speech was over everyone applauded and Mrs. Kingman stood and said Finn's name. Finn took a glass of water and looked at the audience through it. His vision was as blurred as he hoped his speech would be. He took a long drink.

"If I had written my speech out longhand I would roll the paper into a telescope and look at you all more clearly," he said, and a few people around the room laughed, surprising him.

"I have been pacing about my room speaking to the walls about the mayorship and through many attempts I have rather telescoped in on what I believe the future of Nome to be."

Finn stopped again and saw that they were all taking him seriously. He sought the eyes of Henriette and found comfort in the knowledge that she, at least, was not paying any real attention to what he was saying. She sat comfortably listening only to the sounds he was making, and from then on he spoke directly to her.

"We will build our buildings and make our laws no matter who the first mayor is so it might as well be me. You all heard Dr. Kingman say what he would do just now and I'm telling you that if you choose me above him I will do the same things. If I had spoken first then it would be Dr. Kingman who'd be standing here now copying my programs. So, rather than re-peating everything so that you can hear what it sounds like coming from my mouth and using my voice, I'd like to say, ditto. I will do everything he will do and with equal energy."

It crossed Finn's mind that he could sit down now if he wished, for he had explained himself clearly. Yet only a moment had passed and all but Henriette looked at him quizzically. He decided that as long as Henriette was not listening he would continue, for he was speaking for her. If she once cocked her head in that questioning way he would stop, but not until. It was the music of his voice that was guiding her daydreams, so it was for her that he must continue singing.

"Of course it is easy to say ditto and I would not say it if Dr. Kingman's programs were not sound. Those things which he spoke of would be good for our town, would be good for any town." Finn could tell that the tone and speed of his voice were not satisfying Henriette. Though she was still not listening, she might begin to soon if he didn't give a better accompaniment to her thoughts. A change of pace, a lullaby.

"Back at home, I might say, back in Ireland where I come from, there are those who believe in the politics of chance. They don't care who's in charge or which party might be speaking, and I've seen what can happen when a people are like that."

Finn looked quickly at Henriette and found her safely back out of his control once again.

"Let me tell you about a man I knew, Hugo Reily, who had connections everywhere, was disattached from none. He was a man of my own village and he spent a year of weekends riding in his carriage from farm to farm so that on election day he would be able to collect each vote as a man collects the fruits of his field labor."

Finn had succeeded now on two fronts. Henriette was not listening and neither, in a way, was he. For Henriette he could not say, but he was thinking of a day Hugo Reily had come to their farm, hat in hand, how he had roughed Finn's hair while talking into the eyes of his father. Though Finn's father and his elder brothers and perhaps even Reily himself had believed that the words were what got the votes, Finn had understood that it was the roughing of the hair.

"He was a wardman in our area for seventy-five years and during that time he did not miss a funeral or a wedding or a single night at the pub that was known as a political center. Hugo Reily, I can see him now, and I wonder as I'm standing here if he's not still making his rounds, for indeed when I left that country it was he that saw me off, it was he who reached up to my tall head and ran his fingers through my hair. It might have been my own hand he knew the terrain there so well.

"It was a coach that I was taking into the town of London-derry, and as I looked for the last time among the members of my family, there he was, third from the shortest, and as the coachman got the horses moving it was Hugo Reily who began to sing. Oh he was the consummate politician! He had a grand voice and he did not stop when the coach was out of sight or even when the rest of the family had gone on home. Indeed, I know because miles away when we had occasion to stop for a man who stood at the side of the road, I thought I heard his voice coming thin and sharp along the road behind us.

"Do you understand what I'm saying?" he asked the quiet room. "Regardless of which of us you elect you'll have your programs for the development of our city, so it is not very important who you choose. But beyond that my able opponent is in business for himself and I'll be in business only for you. This town will become my family and I'll treat your children like Hugo Reily treated me. If I am elected mayor I will rough their hair. And if any of you decide to leave I'll be at the dock and I'll sing to you so that you can stand at the ship's rail and listen and I won't stop singing even when you are gone, even when your ship's smoke no longer darkens the horizon."

Finn looked down and was disappointed to see the moon eyes of Henriette upon him. Only a moment before he was sure that she'd not been listening but now he knew she was. The whole room was quiet. He had everyone's attention so he sat down quickly to the rising applause.

9

As near as anyone could figure, spring broke during Finn's speech. In the morning, at first light, the townspeople crowded the beach, looking out along the waterway that filled a huge crack in the sea of ice. It was like looking down a long blue road. And by the end of the day there were other roads cracking off into the solid ice halves. There was a general giddiness among the people, a tendency to run about in shirt sleeves, to run about underdressed.

Henriette spent the morning bent at the waist, her head lodged between her knees. She had eaten nothing and therefore had little to give other than a retching sound, a hollow imitation of the soft ice tearing through the middle of the bay. She tried to be sick gently so as not to give the baby discomfort. During the meeting the night before Henriette had thought of the baby as a boy, as a small copy of the reverend, floating, like a marble egg, inside her, and she did not want him to be sick too. Luckily she was alone in the bath. Finn and Ellen had gone with the rest of the town, down to watch the sea parting. It was like a miracle and she knew that the reverend would rejoice as the expanding crack passed the village. She saw him clasping his hands together and standing on his toes; she pictured the entire village engaged in a dance along the still-hard sand. It was a painful moment for her. Her jaw was tight and saliva ran slowly from the corners of her mouth.

Finn lost the election. He was defeated three to one. Ellen stood with him on the upper part of the beach and talked quietly about his speech.

"I maintain you had a chance," she said. "It was that 'ditto' that lost it for you. It isn't done. One political speaker does not follow another and say 'ditto.' "

Finn smiled and tried to hold her hand. "I got fifty-three votes. Not counting the three of us, fifty people in this town weren't stopped by my speech. Fifty people would have me over that other fellow."

In truth Ellen had enjoyed the speech and was not upset now. There'd been an old politician in her village as well and at his death it was her own father who'd vied for the position. But why hadn't the fool told the story and then presented a genuine platform to the people? Maybe he would not have won but he would have collected more votes, more than just the fifty-three.

"Look at the way the ice breaks," said Finn, turning her attention back to him. "In a week the ground will soften and the prospectors will go back to their gold fields. Won't it be easy running the bath when there's no thawing to do first?"

Ellen looked at him then saw herself working the difficult bath for innumerable seasons ahead. She had not been there a year yet she was very tired. When spring comes can winter be far behind?

"I'll tell you something, Finn," she said, letting the election skip behind her. "In a week, in two, when the ground softens enough, we are going to have a proper funeral for Mr. Fujino. We'll ask the reverend to preside and we'll commit that poor man to his maker."

She looked at Finn as if daring him to disagree. It surprised him that she should mention Fujino now. Except for Hummel's constant hounding Finn hadn't thought of Fujino since leaving

Topcock Creek. If the reverend came, perhaps there would be word of Phil and the old man, but Finn did not look forward to seeing the frozen zero of Fujino's mouth again. It seemed impossible that the dead man could still be alive to all of them. No matter whose fault it had been, the man was now dead and should have been buried long ago. "A Christian burial though he was not a Christian?" asked Finn.

"A Christian burial to get the man out of sight," said Ellen. "Do you suppose he will stay hidden once the snow has gone? Do you suppose it's not our duty?" Ellen fairly shouted, then reached over and twisted Finn's arm. "Respect," she said. "That's what is lacking." The word echoed in her head as she said it and she pictured herself carrying endless buckets of water.

———

As soon as the village children had their skates cut and tied the ice became too soft to support them. The sleds lay like amputees along the path from the storehouse, and deep practice grooves zoned the ice in front of the village. It was too abrupt an end for the popularity of skating, and the children had a difficult time bringing their enthusiasm back to the golden snowflakes. They wore them on all occasions, but with the discovery of skating the snowflakes had become commonplace, followed the course of sketch pads and parasols in their lives.

The reverend and Phil and Kaneda had been giving lessons. Each was popular with the children and each enjoyed the chance to do some free skating. When all were finally forced to hang up their skates they went back to their snowflakes without speaking. Many trips were made back and forth past the broken sleds until finally the abandoned runners were stuck in the softening ground beside them, like steel totem poles.

The reverend was making preparations for school. It was his habit to begin longer lessons the morning after the children moved back above ground, and he intended, this year, to be more organized in his planning. He would ask the old man to visit the class and perhaps teach them something about Japan. As for himself, he would teach his weak subjects well and would read aloud to them from the books he loved, from *McTeague* and from others.

The reverend and the old man sat in the soft loft chairs and watched as the lean-to poles were driven through the thin snow. In a few days the summer village would stretch before them and a few days after that parties of other Eskimos would come, like bears, out of the low hills, lean and hungry after hibernation. In other years this was a time when the reverend felt the beginning touches of homesickness, a time when he sometimes considered going home. This year, though, the old man sat next to him and talked continuously. He rarely looked at the reverend but his voice sawed through the quiet room like a prayer. He made the reverend remember his schooling, the times he had studied Latin, the peacefulness of not understanding. It was a pleasant sensation. He sat there easily, making believe that his large chair was a rocker, that he was being sung to sleep.

When Finn arrived in the village he found construction well under way. He had been sent to announce the burial of Fujino and to ask the reverend to come to Nome to say a few words. The snow had already melted down around the mule and rider and the two women were forced to take snow from other parts of the city, and to heap it wet about the remains.

Finn made the short trip in less than half a day. It felt fine to be out of Nome again. In the few days since the election Ellen and Henriette had treated him gently, telling him that he had done well to get as many votes as he had. And indeed there was a moment after his speech when he'd thought he would win. Since the election he'd been called in twice for visits with

Dr. Kingman. He was asked his opinion on certain subjects, and each time Hummel had been there scribbling silently, his scratch pad balanced on his bony knees.

Finn did not expect to find Phil and Kaneda in the village, and when he did he embraced them, turning them in the snow until only dirt remained under their feet. They broke into their three languages like strangers. Finn turned to Kaneda. "We are going to bury Fujino," he said. "You must all come to Nome."

"Yes, I have never forgotten," said the old man. "I have been wondering again about the nature of his death."

"Fujino," said Finn again, looking at both men.

The reverend approached the trio from the direction of his house, walking on the spotted earth, avoiding stepping on the patches of snow, thinking of his mother.

"Finn!" he said.

The three unlocked arms, allowing the reverend to come into their circle, and together they turned the thawed earth to mud. "Winter is over and everyone is safe," said the reverend. "Thank the Lord."

"Can you come to help with the burial of Fujino?" Finn asked. "You've heard talk of his tragic death. Now it is time to bury him."

"If he had only come to me with his problems I would have understood," said Kaneda.

Late on the afternoon of Finn's arrival the villagers stretched the canvas hides across their lean-to poles while the children collected snow, rolled it into balls, and threw it far out onto the liquid surface of the bay. In an hour the view from the reverend's window changed. The reverend and Finn sat toasting springtime, toasting the village and the women they knew.

The reverend said, "I can see that winter has weathered the lines of your face. Was it hard on the women as well?"

Finn looked at him through his wine glass, laughing. "On

Ellen it was," he said. "And both of them have put their shoulders into the carrying of bath water a few more times than they should have. Ellen's the strongest but somehow it shows on her and does not on our Henriette."

"Henriette's all right?"

"All right and untouchable," said Finn. "She turns her thoughts inward a bit more than she used to but it's a habit that'll protect her complexion."

Finn ran his fingers over the loosening skin below his own eyes. The top of his beard came very high up his face, giving him the feeling that his eyes were deeper than before, his sockets more sunken.

"You are an interesting man for one so religious," he told the reverend. "I might have come to you if you'd been handy. Over the death of Fujino, I mean. I had a very stormy session over that."

The reverend had been thinking of what he might say at Fujino's funeral. He'd never been very good at that particular service. He couldn't muster the resonance of voice, the massive seriousness.

"Oh well," he said.

"I've always been quick to grab at guilt," said Finn, "but this time there was no stopping me. I was eaten away with it. I had gone a little 'round the bend."

He told the reverend about the old man's prayers and the reverend said that there had been evidence of that ever since the old man had been in the village.

"Yet he does not seem unhappy," said the reverend.

"Not unhappy, not guilty," said Finn. "And the sheer power of his prayer knocked all my guilt away. I find it hard even to think about Fujino anymore."

They sat quietly a moment and saw the old man walking among the lean-tos below them. He examined the way the lean-tos were built, climbing to the top of one and sitting with his heels bouncing against the door.

"With him at Fujino's funeral you'll have your work cut out for you," said Finn.

The reverend nodded and stood. "I'm sure he'll want to say something," he said. "I never knew the man, don't know what he was like, what kind of service might make him happy."

They started down the ladder to join the village for a feast. They would leave for Nome in the morning, and since it was no longer freezing Phil was taking his entire family. It had been a long winter for the Eskimos, so there were others going as well. Word spread among the villagers that there would be a special outing. Tomorrow those who felt like it would be going to Nome.

Finn and the reverend walked under the pale sky, following the scent of seal. The reemergence of the neat rows of lean-tos had taken only the morning and now, in silence, the entire population of the village surrounded the still-standing coming-of-age hut of Nanoon. For weeks the hut had sat silent, its feathers graying, some of them plucked for fishing but most still stuck to its mud sides. Finn remembered shouting through it and hearing nothing for his trouble. Surely she'd not survived. He remembered seeing her fragile face as they'd dressed her that day. She was so young. He imagined a few sprouts of pubic hair, like spring vegetables, like the lovely tops of dark carrots, breaking the smooth surface of her skin. To each his own, he thought, but customs such as this one are barbaric.

When everyone was ready and the long seals were propped like sentinels at each side of the sewn-up door, Phil stepped forward. The sight of the dreary feathers made him want to turn and tell the owl story once more, but instead he drew his sharp knife up the side of the hut as smoothly as through any seal fat. Like a painful cesarean, thought Finn, but no sound came from the dark hole, no arms or legs kicking angrily out at the new world.

"Nanoon," said Phil. "Wake up. Winter's gone and you're a woman."

The light from the wound in her wall came hard into Nanoon's head. She pushed her eyes shut but it spread through her anyway, looking into all her corners, pushing her limbs out like flowers opening. Phil slit the wall further and found her far back among her blankets and pelts, frozen bits of all her winter meals still standing like sculptures around her. They took her arms and lifted her to the light like a captured mole, her nose sensing the seal, her knees still dug in under her chin. "Stand up," said Phil. "It's all over." With her arms Nanoon held her sisters and the entire crowd watched as her long legs inched toward the ground. Finn's heart flew to her as his guilt had flown to Fujino. She'd looked young before but now her face was furrowed, her color gone, her hair, like wisps of winter, making her look old. Finn stepped past the reverend and helped hold her, put his big hands under her arms while Phil pulled at her legs, massaged her muscles downward. She was a woman now, would soon be married, gone to Port Clarence or off toward the north.

When Nanoon's eyes opened Finn found himself their focus and freeing his hand pushed the crumbs from his beard and stood straight. The sun setting behind them was still strong, so the others moved in to darken the ground around her, letting their shadows shade her eyes. Lord, thought Finn, how can one so young look so old? Phil, beside him, bathed her face with seal oil, laid some salt slabs on her tongue. "She's a woman now," he told Finn. "If you look at her long she'll mistake your meaning."

When Nanoon was standing by herself, Phil pulled Finn back and the others too moved away, allowed her space to step in. She rubbed the wrinkles out of her face and pushed the hair from her eyes. "It's true, she's a woman," said the reverend, shaking his head. "It was only a year ago that she was among my students." Finn saw the look of old age fall from her like snake's skin, saw her former face return. She put one leg forward and then another, and by the time she could walk in small circles most of the villagers had turned their attention to the standing seals. Phil dug the dry heart of the smallest seal from its flat chest and breaking it into pieces gave half to Nanoon to eat. He found Finn and handed him the other half, and Finn was gone again, caught off balance, gouged once more by guilt and head over heels in love.

———

Though the ground was still hard the snow was nearly gone, and Ellen and Henriette had to carry bath buckets of it from as far as one hundred meters away. They dumped the wet snow on the dirty mule mound and waited for Finn and the reverend. They had not seen the dead man that they covered and they would not, they hoped, until the time came for burial. They'd hired a man to dig the deep grave next to the mound they protected, and though they did not know how far under the snow he sat, they were taking no chances. They worked continuously, carrying their buckets on the ends of long poles balanced across their shoulders. When they passed each other they did not speak. The weather was getting warmer. She with the empty buckets moved more easily than she with the full.

When the evening came the snow held, the temperature moved it to ice and let the women go back to the bath and sit around the stove, their heavy arms hanging. They had closed the bath until after the funeral for it was impossible to carry buckets for both purposes. Ellen wondered if the others would be surprised to know that she was thinking of leaving. She had made a business of the bath and could sell it. Of course she would not return to Ireland but she had seen the greenery of Washington state and would not mind an easier life. What surprised her, as the idea grew, was that she had not entertained it at all until the moment Finn lost the election. If he had won she would have stayed, she knew. If he had won, Nome would have grown in wider directions than it would now, and yet she believed that in almost every way Dr. Kingman would do a better job. Dr. Kingman moved for laws and civil codes. He was asking people to zone land, to section its use. He was organizing construction so that all would be finished before heavy winter came again. He was setting high penalties for claim jumping and low ones for street brawls as well. Ellen agreed with all and knew that Finn would have done none of it. Think of the way he'd laid his proposals before the community. Ditto. Dr. Kingman talks of laws and sectioning the land and Finn says ditto. Yet he was Irish and had made the lovely figure of Hugo Reily dance for the people. His ditto would have taken five years where Dr. Kingman was taking one. And now she was thinking of leaving. If Finn had won they would have moved forward ever so slowly, but with endless possibilities. Now the town's fate was sealed, and because it was, living in the deadening cold and with back-breaking work was no longer worth it. No, Nome would have had to remain a frontier for her to put up with all of that. Now that it wasn't she would leave.

Henriette stood to go for more firewood, startling Ellen. What a place it is where everyone sits through the winter staring, lost in some memory or sorry to God that she ever came. It is the end of winter. If spring is here can winter be far behind? Ellen was numbed by her decision, and as she watched the girl coming back in she stood. She would sell the bath and move away, let the others do what they might. As surely as the direction of the town was locked, so was hers away from it.

Ellen looked at her heavy red hands and told them there would be a few more buckets, only a few. She saw the thin-skinned end of her wounded finger and thought, If I leave them something let it be this, a bit of dead skin grafted to the top of a mule's foot. If she had left her family, she could leave this group whom she loved only with that part of her that was not consumed with daydreaming, with scenes from her unknown future and past. If Finn had won the election she would have stayed. She looked at Henriette, her nose all poked into her small drab diary again. Ellen would tell her grandchildren that she had been responsible for the very first building in Nome, Alaska. That she had been a frontier woman. Thank God for small defeats.

———

On clear days Nome smoked gray on the horizon, otherwise the Eskimo children had no real proof that it was there. Today they would find out. There would be no school because their teacher was going to Nome, and because many of them were going as well. Everyone dressed in finery for the occasion. Four years earlier when the reverend first walked into the village he wore a thick gray suit with wide lapels, and was the cause of one of the village's earliest crazes. The heads of families made formal requests, and by the beginning of his first winter the reverend had successfully ordered boxes of the gray flannel material complete with pattern paper. And now they all had suits. Everyone. In some cases the suits of growing children were passed down to others, but by the morning of their departure no one went without. It was formal dress for a formal occasion. The reverend hadn't had his own suit on in nearly three years, and as they marched out of the village even Finn had shed his winter clothes. It was still cold and the group walked quickly. They wore hide shirts and in place of neckties each wore a golden snowflake.

Only Phil took his entire family. His children walked in front, and behind him his sisters and his wife and Nanoon too. Nanoon still had not spoken, would not, they thought, until winter was really gone. But she'd fixed her gaze on Finn and stared at him constantly, aware of where he walked, sensing the strength of his own sentiment toward her. The excitement of the villagers was mixed with the knowledge that they were going to a funeral. They made Mr. Kaneda walk in the very center of the group. They were going to see the city, yes, but first they were escorting this man to the funeral of someone he loved. And as a gift to the old man the village had reserved the best gray suit for the corpse, the one that had been Phil's father's and had not been worn since his death. From Phil himself Fujino would receive the first of the golden snowflakes, the one that he had taken from the converted frypan the moment after Fujino had shown them how it was done.

Each member of the entourage had his own reasons for wanting to go to Nome. Only the old man was a little nervous. He did not know how he would react when he saw the poor body of Fujino. Certainly he would not look the same after so long, after slicing his abdomen open and letting the wind whistle through it. When the funeral ended Kaneda would talk to Phil about plans to leave for Japan. His idea was that they would work the strike until just before the freeze and then ride out on one of the last ships. He had an image of the sea icing in just behind them, and another of Phil arriving in Tokyo and needing to rely on him just as a son should rely on a father, just as he relied on Phil now. But though the old man thought of leaving he had not forgotten Fujino, nor had he forgotten that he was a carpenter. If he could find lumber his parting gift to the dead boy would be a fine handmade coffin. He could carve "Fujino" in deep Chinese characters on the coffin cover and he would not be satisfied until each joint fit together perfectly and was waterproof. He would see if it was not possible to take a photograph of the coffin, something that he could give to his daughter by way of explanation.

When the Eskimo group entered the tent city they walked less quietly, heads turning like Phil's owls. They could see the wooden frames of new buildings, and Phil pointed out the bath to them, telling them that it was Ellen's and that it was he who had helped to build it.

"Very little progress," said the old man.

"They've messed up the building of their lean-tos," said Phil's wife. "No easy way to get in and out."

When they got closer in, they walked on the gravel path at Hummel's tent and he pinned back the flap and came out to watch them. He'd painted his name in high letters on the canvas now, just under his message of murder. He held his hand over the front of his mouth, sucking noisily on his teeth. "Henriette and Ellen are waiting for you, Finn," he said. "Which one is the reverend?"

The reverend, wearing his original gray suit, raised his hand but Hummel did not address him, so he lowered it again, feeling the weight of the snowflake rise and fall. When they moved on into the city he looked back and saw Hummel again, resetting path stones where their feet had dislodged them.

The bath was empty so the gray-suited visitors hung about the hot stove in the center of the room. On the floor, as if Kaneda's need had been expected, there were lumber and tools, so the old man, without a word, began fitting the pieces together, making the coffin. The others rubbed their hands together over the heat.

The reverend sat to the side, flipping through the pages of his Bible, looking for something appropriate. This man had been dead for months, was not a Christian, had taken his own life. He looked at a passage or two and then let his eyes lift to the bath door, wondering if the next person to enter would be Henriette. He did not want to officiate at this funeral. He hoped that he would be able to read a prayer and then let the old man or Finn relate something personal about the dead man. There was nothing he could say. Maybe the twenty-third psalm or something like that. Tried and true. The door opened and Henriette walked in followed by Ellen carrying buckets.

"Ah, hello, you've made it, thank the Lord," said Ellen. The gray-dressed people turned to face her like a choir. The old man put down his tools and bowed.

"And you've dressed," she said. "If you'll give us a moment we'll be ready as well."

The two women passed through the room but stopped when they got to the reverend at the rear. Henriette let her hands fall to her stomach and Ellen stretched hers out toward him.

"Once he's buried I believe I'll give it up," she said quietly. "Maybe you could help me decide where to go."

The reverend smiled absently, looking past her at Henriette. "How are you?" he asked.

He stretched his hand out to her and she took it and shook it. She was carrying the log of Fujino under her arm and held it out to him.

"These are all the words he uttered, what he said before he died. I wrote it all down." She opened the book and took out the reverend's note before letting him have it. She turned and followed Ellen up the stairs.

The visitors sat at distances around the room, waiting and watching the old man work on the coffin. The lumber had been cut to correct lengths so he busied himself notching the ends in order not to have to use nails. He worked steadily with a knife or with the smallest saw he could find. Once or twice he turned and motioned to Phil, and when Phil finally joined him he spoke softly, explaining what he did as he did it.

"The notches must be made just so," he said. "Thus at the first sign of moisture they will expand, making the box water-proof."

Across the room the reverend held both black books in front of him, looked from one to the other for clues. In the Bible he wandered over familiar passages absently. He'd been tempted to bring *McTeague* and to read from it but now he had this other, this thin diary written in Henriette's faint hand. He opened it to the first page. "Medical Record," it said, and then,

"Mr. Fujino's disease." After that for three pages Henriette had listed all the things she'd done for the man to make him comfortable, to try to cure him. The reverend read page after page, his eyes adjusting to her strange scribble. At times when the dying boy was quiet Henriette simply wrote down what she had been thinking. Here's what she said about men. "They are rough creatures, always kneading your flesh. They are all the same, that's what I've learned. Even him, if he could get up, would let his hands wander out toward me."

The reverend stopped reading and reddened. This was written before he'd been with her yet he had proven her right. She had accepted him calmly, opened her blankets to him and had not been surprised by his actions. He'd only hoped for a moment of silence, a chance to watch a woman sleeping, to hear her breathing regularly. And as he climbed the ladder he'd expected Ellen, it had been Ellen who'd first fired his imagination, toward whom he'd first directed his dreams. The reverend had trouble bringing his mind back to the death of Fujino. He could hear the old man working softly on the coffin a few feet away. Kaneda had begun carving Fujino's name in the coffin lid and had captured the attention of everyone else in the room with the shape and beauty of the characters. The reverend stayed alone, holding one in each hand, the thick book and the thin.

———

Workmen finished the grave and stood back among the others. Though they dug not three meters from the mound of snow, they did not dig into it, were not curious as to how the winter had moved a mule and rider.

When the procession arrived each looked up at the mound then down into the grave. After a moment Henriette and Ellen stepped forward and held their knotted blankets high. The old man and Finn and Phil opened the newly made coffin, lifted out the folded gray flannel suit and golden snowflake, and stepped around behind the curtain to dig. The reverend took a step forward and stood holding each black book tightly in front of him. He would have to say something soon. He stared into the crowd as if looking for the right words.

For Phil and Finn it was a difficult matter scraping the melting snow away from the body that lay beneath it. They used their hands and the old man helped by using a small flat piece of wood that he'd slipped into his pocket when he finished making the coffin. The coupled figures lay on their sides, flat along the ground, Fujino's left shoulder and the mule's left flank riding the softening earth.

The first parts exposed were the footless back legs of the mule. Phil grabbed them and pulled as he might have the roots of a fallen tree, the handles of a plow, but there was little movement. There was no longer any evidence that feet had once graced the rounded stumps. The legs in his hands were stiff and fixed a certain distance apart. Like the handles of a dog sled they felt secure and he knew that he could put his weight against them and they would not break. The others continued to bare the brown body. Finn recognized the mule as his own by the markings on its flank, and by the tattered brown blanket that he had draped across the mule as protection against the coming cold.

Two men from the crowd stepped forward and took the ends of the blanket from Ellen and Henriette, for their arms were tired and they had lowered it considerably. And when they stepped back into the crowd they saw for the first time how many people there were. There were more people waiting for the beginning of this funeral than had attended the town meeting or had voted for mayor. People fanned out, were peering from distances, trying to view the separation of the mule and man. Ellen and Henriette stood looking down. The reverend still held his two books tightly. There were noises coming from behind the blanket but the crowd was quiet. It was as if a single prospector, far from the nearest settlement, patiently separated bedrock from a vein of pure gold. The sound of snow coming off a dead mule.

Fujino appeared to the men first as a deformity of the creature he rode. His buttocks moved grotesquely away from the natural contour of the mule's body. As he appeared to them out of the snow Finn thought of a camel's hump, or of a hunchback scooting through the streets of a damp city. When the entire body was exposed to them the men stepped back. Fujino was riding loosely on the mule now, not frozen to its back as they had expected but all hunched up like a rider heading into a sandstorm, his hands pulled up to his chin, his great zero of a mouth showing dull surprise at the changing weather, at the sudden turning. The eyes of the three men struck Fujino's poor face carefully. It had weathered, was cured like leather, looked as old as time. All of the muscles in his body were flexed and tight and it seemed as if he were trying desperately to stay on the mule, to keep from falling off and being left alone on the deadened earth.

Yet, strange as it was, the old man seemed the only one of the three taken off guard by the sight of Fujino. Though the dead boy was bleak-skinned and closed to the world, the old man easily recognized him as Fujino. It seemed strange to him that the young man should look so grotesque while the mule looked so natural, so much the way a mule ought to look. The old man began to cry. His tears moved slowly to his eyes and then fell away quickly like water breaking finally away from the winter ice. He felt that if he let himself he could melt, that he could become his tears and wash into the spring-soft soil at his feet.

The dead wrinkles of Fujino's face so drew the men that it

was not until Finn stepped forward with the gray suit that they saw that Fujino too, like the mule, had no feet. At first they thought that his feet had withered, rolled like the dead heads of flowers up along his legs, but no, they were simply gone, cut off like the mule's and taken. Phil peered quickly into the clumps of snow they had removed, searching. Finn and the old man looked back toward the people and saw Hummel holding a sign high above him, its slogan blurred by the sun. The crowd swayed together like a thawing field of wheat.

"Give me the suit," said Phil. He stuck his hands under the cold armpits of the dead man and was surprised by how easily he came loose. The faint hint of human flesh still rode the mule; bits of gray mule hair still clung to the insides of Fujino's thighs.

Fujino was heavy and cold. Phil set him, face up, on the ground next to the mule, then motioned for Finn to push on the dead man's knees. He had ridden high on the mule and would have to be straightened out if they expected to be able to close the coffin lid. Finn and Phil lent their weight to his straightening, and the old man stood back of them, ready to drape the golden snowflakes around his partner's neck, but capable of little else. His eyes were fixed on the stubbed ends of the dead man's legs. They were like the mule's, like axe handles waiting for the attachment of blades. When he looked at Fujino's legs he thought of fresh blond wood, the kind he had seen protruding from barrels at the tent where men bought provisions. He thought of the wide mouth of *harakiri*, its dried opening hidden somewhere under the boy's clothing.

At first when the two men tried to straighten Fujino's body they were unsuccessful. Then quickly and with a snap that perked the ears of the city, the body gave a little, cracked. Finn took the gray trousers and slipped them onto the angled legs. He pulled at the arms of the corpse and held them apart, like huge springs, until Phil was able to get the jacket on. Then Finn leaned over the corpse and looked into the bottomless mouth and believed he felt the lazy warmth of living human breath around his eyes and on the bridge of his nose.

It had been a long time since Finn had thought of Fujino as a man. The name no longer conjured up the smooth speaking boy but rather this piece of petrified wood, this changeless winter mold, this park statue. He reached out and tried to close the dead man's mouth, but though the legs and arms were thicker, it was this mouth that would stay, that would not vary from its depthlessness, its initial expression of shock and surprise. And for Finn it was only this circle, empty and deep as space, that remained human. Looking now into its blackness, Finn remembered himself coming back down to Nome, camping in the unlimited darkness of his hand-built igloos. It was then that he'd captured his proper view of the world, and he saw it again now in this circle of a dead man's mouth.

"Lift him up," said the old man. "I will place the snowflake around his neck and we will bury him."

Finn and Phil buttoned the front of the gray jacket over the dead man's chest, over the shirt that covered his invisible *hara-kiri*. His hands were still bunched in front of him and the old man pushed the golden snowflake between them so that it looked as if Fujino held it on either side, was trying with all his strength to break it in half. They lifted him by his shoulders and footless legs and placed him in the coffin and placed the lid over it before anyone from the crowd moved up to look. The two men who held the blanket lowered it when they heard the light tapping of nails.

———

"Dearly beloved," said the reverend in a voice that cracked across the crowd. He stood looking gravely down at the box sitting crooked on the dirt before him. He held both black books and could feel himself growing red. He was never fully prepared when he began a sermon but this was too much. And yet no one seemed to have noticed his mistake. They still remained as quiet as the dead man, still moved on their feet like wheat, as if the wind pushed them. And this, if he was any judge of numbers, was his largest crowd. From his position on the slight incline at the edge of the grave he could see the town but could see no one walking the twisted streets. Everyone was here, close by, staring up at him.

"When thinking about this eulogy," he said, "I had two books to go by and both were about the life of the deceased. This," he held up the Bible and shook it, "is the story of all our lives, and this other one was written by the deceased's nurse and contains his dying words."

The reverend found Henriette in her long dark dress standing among the Eskimos, looking at him. Her hands were clasped in front of her and she leaned forward against them strangely, as if they belonged to someone else who stood behind.

"As I read this second book I was struck by the fact that I could not understand much that the dead man found so important to say during the last moments of his life." The reverend opened the thin volume and read at random.

"*Kimie . . . Kimie . . . Gomennasai. Boku no yakusoku . . .*"

The old man looked up, peering at the reverend as if he'd been struck. From where he stood he could see only the edge of the coffin, but he had heard the voice of Fujino calling to his daughter. He should have taken her photograph back from Phil. It should be inside the coffin riding on the boy's dead chest. With that photograph as his guide he would have been able to work his way back to Japan, to find her, to float about her and protect her when the news of his death arrived.

"Who knows," asked the reverend, "what those strange sounds might mean?" He looked at Henriette again, at the way her hands protected her stomach. It always amazed him, the things he was able to think of during these pauses in his sermons. He sensed that the audience stood there as much to feel the earth beneath their feet, as much to feel the warm wind coming off the recently liquid sea, as to hear him. He saw cumulus clouds being pushed about above him and he sighed and raised his hands to the sky.

"Isn't it a beautiful day?" he asked. "Only the tedium of winter can give us a day such as this."

He saw people twist their necks skyward, like sunflowers.

The sun ran through the clouds a moment, lighting up all their faces and letting the reverend see, momentarily, the scrawny face of Hummel, the man whose pebble walkway they had stood on when entering the city. Though the others looked skyward, this man looked, from where he stood, directly at Henriette, directly at the reverend past her.

"Behind you I see the frames of buildings," said the reverend. "Look at them. The reason we see them so easily from this distance is that one story is built upon another and another is built upon that, and so on until we have a structure that will house our needs and keep us warm when winter comes once again." It was always at this point, when he was just a few moments into what he was saying, that the reverend had misgivings about his calling, that he believed he should have done something else with his life. He knew it was only a matter of time before other preachers arrived in Nome. And with other preachers would come the hampering of his tongue. His place was in the village and after this he would go back there and would not come out again. Perhaps he was having trouble getting started because he had heard that there were preachers in Nome already and he feared that someone from the crowd would step forward and scream, "No! That is not the way it is at all, this man is a phony, an imposter!" He looked once more from Henriette to the coffin that lay in the hole in front of him.

"What do you suppose would happen if we did not stop with

the second or third floor of those buildings back there? What would happen if we built our houses higher and higher without regard to our needs? There was a people once who were so ambitious that they thought they would build a tower all the way up to the heavens and one at a time climb it and stare straight into the eyes of God. Remember? Oh they were a strong and wonderful lot. They understood each other and used their voices as tools, like hammers.''

The reverend stopped again and looked around him. Now that he had started how was he going to tie this in with the poor dead Japanese? He could tell by looking that the old man had not understood a word of what he said. Among the faces of the crowd only Finn's looked at him brightly, as if he were anxious to determine what the point might be, what lesson might be lodged between the teeth of it. He held the Bible and the diary high in the cool air above his head.

''This city was called Babel and the people believed that they could do anything. After they built their tower to such a height that it shifted and leaned dangerously with each breath of wind, God got angry and had them open their mouths to that wind and from then on they could not speak to each other again. Can you imagine it? Each in his mind had a language that was clear and full, one that allowed him to think and sing, but when he turned to his neighbor he sounded foreign, like the Japanese I just read sounded to all of us. Each to himself must have seemed light and clever, but to the others was dull as molasses, thick-tongued as taffy, un-understandable and alone.''

''Praise the Lord!'' said a voice from the field and the reverend searched the faces before him. Were there other missionaries listening in? Shaking their heads in disgust?

''Babbling brook, babbling idiot, stop your babbling, et cetera, et cetera. Such expressions as these are the legacies of that people. With phrases such as these we remember them. How many times have you stood in a merchant's tent and heard such

sounds coming from the mouths of the men and women standing next to you? When the people of Babel understood that
they could no longer understand they left their tower and town,
giving up their tower and their climb toward God. Across the
globe they went, not stopping until they were away from all
those they knew, not stopping until each was alone in a wilderness of his own. They moved, some to the larger plains, others
to dense woods or mountains, and there they built cities where
everyone spoke the language of the founder, and for centuries
they stayed that way and did not try to remember or to communicate with those others who had left Babel as they had."

The reverend felt that this time he was not making it. He was
not turning the corner that was necessary if he was going to
include the dead man in his ramblings, in this babbling of his
own.

"It strikes me," he said, "that we are descendants of those
who left that city and that we are those whom God has chosen
to finish it. We have come back, arrived from all parts of the
world and built this new Babel and have learned our lesson
well." He pointed again at the building frames. "Our towers
are squat and flat-topped. Rather than looking to the sky and
trying to build our way up to it, we look to the ground and dig
our way down. We search not for His eyes, but for His golden
veins."

The reverend heard himself laugh. "This young man is dead
and has spoken his dying words in the language of his ancestors.
Most of us are taken now with English, making English the
language that will once again tie us together, make us one and
understandable. This young man took his life and even from
the grave has preserved the language that was brought to him
out of the streets of Babel."

The reverend opened the book and read again. " 'Kimie . . .
Kimie . . . Boku no yakusoku . . . ' Perhaps he is telling us that
the world was small, became large, and now is getting small

again. This man's death signifies for us here the death of one
of the languages given us by God. When all but one language
is finally gone, perhaps we will once again try to reach God by
mechanical means and perhaps we will once again be banished
into unknown tongues.''

The reverend turned to the grave and pushed some dirt in
upon the coffin with his hand. He was deeply worried about
what he had said and knew that before him in the audience
there were those who might question him on it later. It was
bewildering. For the first time he'd failed to understand the
point he was making himself. Only Finn nodded enthusiasti-
cally, from among the number below.

''We return this man to the earth from which he came,'' he
said quietly. ''Those of you wishing to share in the covering
may now come forward.''

Fujino was buried and people walked back toward the town in
groups of three and four. Phil and the other Eskimos surrounded the old man, peering into his face to see what they
could see. They spoke in their languages, telling him again parts
of the story of Phil's father's death, of how the village felt the
same pain he was feeling now and how they covered their faces
with ice so that their tears would come into a world of their
own. The old man asked Phil about the photograph of his
daughter in a quiet voice, and Phil nodded slowly and patted
him on the shoulder.

Finn and Ellen and Henriette waited for the long moments
it took the reverend to step down off the grave mound and walk
toward them. Finn shaded his eyes and looked at the building
frames, stunned at the closeness of the reverend's thoughts to
his own. He felt the presence of God now in his theory about

language and communication, and he clasped the reverend on the shoulder like a brother, feeling he had verified it, feeling he had given him a sign. If there was beauty in all men speaking one tongue then there was as much in all men speaking differently, that was the point. He'd learned that coming down from Topcock Creek. He laughed. They had been like the small blisters on the rump of his dead mule, those igloos of his, yet he'd been born of them as surely as he had from the warmer bump of his mother's middle. Forty-five years old. Forty-six. He knew now that he'd spend his days here, adding what he could to the general confusion, watching everyone fix his sights on unity and doing what he could to prevent it. That everyone should have the kind of experience he'd had with the old man and Phil, that would be his goal. Finn looked around to see Nanoon among those surrounding the old man. She was the one for him, for as far as he knew she didn't speak English and hadn't she had the same experience with her coming of age? He put his arms around the reverend's shoulder and called him a man of God.

Ellen took the Bible and the diary out of the reverend's hands and handed the one back to Henriette. "It was as if winter would have stayed upon us forever had we not buried him," she said.

Ellen pushed Finn forward, making him walk quickly with her, up a few paces, so that the reverend and Henriette were left alone. She held the flesh on the back of Finn's arm between thumb and finger, pinching it tightly if he tried to turn or resume the conversation. She guided him between building frames and around several tents toward the bath. From here and there they could see the gray bay before them and were surprised by its jerky movement, by its choppy waves rising.

"And now those bulbous clouds will cushion us all spring, I suppose," said Finn. "It will be all too short a time before winter sets in."

Ellen looked at him and heard the matter-of-factness in his

voice, saw as he did the brevity of this warm respite. Finn had turned a corner, could no longer see back around the bend, she could tell that by looking at him.

"Finn, you won't be surprised, I hope, to hear that one winter is enough for me. I'll be leaving while I can slide out smoothly, before there's ice bobbing in the bay again."

Finn pulled the soft flesh around his eyes into a squint and peered at her.

"If you've a mind to try to talk me out of it you'd best save your breath," she said. "You'll be losing a critic but gaining a bath."

The two of them walked down upon the softening sand of the beach. Everything was as it had been when winter surprised them all. It looked as if the beach strike was still alive, and indeed they saw prospectors peeking over the mounds of earth, wondering if the ground would move again, if the sea in its fresh churning had salted the sand once more. They walked into Finn's tent and looked at the frozen bed from which they'd pulled the dying Fujino. Food lay edible and forgotten on the floor. The mercury frypan poked its curious hose into the ruffled blankets. Everything showed a softer edge.

"I'm not giving you the bath," Ellen said. "You can send me half the profits every half year for my trouble."

"Half the profits for a prescribed period," said Finn. "Every year's too much to ask."

Finn and Ellen stayed in the shambles of his tent, talking hard business for an hour, until evening came. Fool's gold winked at them from the dirty upturned sand at their feet. When they left it was dark and grimly cold, but they saw others and could hear surf sounds coming from the senile sea. Ellen held a shawl close around her neck and touched the back of Finn's shoulder on the blind path. She kept her eyes closed and could imagine once more the stony fields of Ireland coming up to meet her feet. She could see the dim lights of her house above the knoll and knew that to go inside would mean looking into the face of her father, avoiding the rooster hands of her grandmother, seeing her own face sliced thin by the passing pendulum of time. Even the wind was Ireland at her back. Even the sea was tall grass blown flat. One hand on Finn, she walked near the house and saw through the window the scene: her grandmother and herself at different stages, her father, and the knitting circle of talking women, tongues clicking, voices soft as wool. Ellen stumbled on the rough road, letting her hand slip from the ridges of Finn's jacket. She opened her eyes and touched the ground, nearly falling. She would carry them all, like luggage, when she left: Finn and the reverend and Henriette too. Finn turned to help her, so she brushed the dirt from her hands and thanked him, this time taking a firm hold of the sleeve of his coat. Clouds parted and she now saw constellations pointing toward home. She laughed and asked Finn if he thought he might ever go back. And as she stepped to the rhythm of his answer she knew very clearly that like the rest of them it was only convention that kept her from seeing into the future, that kept her from predicting the rest of her life.

One of the gray-suited Eskimos weighed his golden snowflake at the assayer's office, sold it, and bought several large packages of goods. He toured with the others through the narrow paths but was at once aware of a lightness around his neck and turned to take the goods back and to retrieve the snowflake. The rest of them watched him go. Though spring had broken it was only late afternoon and already dark. The Eskimos stood across from the Gold Belt, their snowflakes still visible, but dim. After a few moments they broke into small groups and separated. Phil and the old man moved out of the darkness and into the saloon.

Only Nanoon stood where she'd been, watching the others leave her. She saw them rushing away, darting through alleys and into narrow passageways like tourists.

———

John Hummel sat in his spotless tent, the twelve-hundred-dollar canvas sack wound tightly around his neck. Before him on the neat dirt floor Fujino's feet bled darkly, thin red lines overflowing the ankles. He had been ready for anything but nothing had happened and he had not been ready for that. The feet appeared to him to be in excellent shape. Around him nothing was out of place. There was a setting for two at the table. There was no ice in the harbor now so he could expect his mother any time. Everything was packed and ready for her to take back.

John Hummel reached down and removed his own heavy shoes. They were warm and thick and had lasted him easily through the winter. He sucked hard on both his lips and spit into his hand, but there was still no trace of red; the disease was completely gone. He looked across the room at the shoe-laced entrance and could see a single remaining candy stalk growing like a long, thin finger from his old spittoon.

John Hummel had written a note, which swung from a single piece of twine, turning slightly before him in the breezeless room. He had taken his time with his note, giving it his finest hand. It was addressed to his mother and was an inventory of exactly what he had placed inside which box. Hummel picked up Fujino's feet and held them gingerly, trying not to touch the lines of blood. He slid them slowly into the warm pockets of his shoes then placed them out in the middle of the room and stood barefooted upon the edge of the couch he'd been sitting on. He attached the canvas bag to a hook that was looped up over the stovepipe that stretched across the ceiling of the tent. He had tested it several times, was sure it would hold. He decided to use the couch as a starting place because he did not want a chair directly under him, or worse, tipped over by his swinging legs and messing up the room. He had arranged things so that his note, his inventory, swung not too far from him. With luck he would be able to read it; it would appear large and clear to his bulging eyes, his fine lettering his last vision.

John Hummel did not want to wait long after things were ready. He had hoped to figure a way to use the canvas sack so that the twelve-hundred-dollar sign would be visible and right side up, but he'd had to settle for it this way; the metal hook connected the bottom of the sack, upside down. When he stepped off the couch he tried to do so lightly, for he knew that to jump would lessen the strength of the stovepipe and that he might fall. He stepped off, looking toward his note, and was aware of the flapping of his arms and the sharp kicking of his feet as he rode across the small room for the first time. He did not know whether his eyes were open or not but he was aware of the sensation of looking directly into bright sunlight. And there was noise, a continuous single and disorganized blare that was of a pitch and intensity equal to the brightness of the light. And there was pain. There was a burning at an exact spot at the back of his neck, the point where the pursed mouth of the canvas bag sucked at his skin.

John Hummel's mind pitched. Thoughts, like people evacuating a burning building, ran wildly about. He lost most of them but others came clear to him before disappearing, screaming into the sun. He was aware of the swinging and slowing of his body and concentrated on the quick opening of his eyes, on getting one look at the perfection of his lettering. When finally he was able to open them he was aware of the familiar taste of blood and was looking up into men's faces. He could not see them clearly but he could hear them as if they spoke from within his own head. They were fishermen and he was a fish and the blood he tasted was at the spot where they had removed the hook from his mouth. They seemed pleased with the size of him, with the fight he had given them and with the clean landing. After they removed the hook they walked forward, away from him, to cast their lines once again onto a cloudy sea. They fished like cowboys, and from his place in the dirty bottom of the boat he could see them swinging ropes over their heads, throwing them out as far as they could, using no bait at all. John Hummel felt his body stiffen and shudder. He heard the noises that he made thumping against the boat's wet bottom.

John Hummel's body slowed as his mind did. He hung with his long back to the inventory, his eyes opened but attached somewhere else. His muscles were slack and his feet stretched down, toes pointing, directly over the tops of his foot-filled shoes. The conversation of the fishermen was no longer audible to him. He had not expected to grow in death, but he did and his long toes now entered the shoes and dipped themselves into the thawing blood of Fujino. The slight swaying of his body pushed at the edges of the shoes, and both of them, at the same instant, fell over and spilled their stored blood onto his clean floor. His toes hung red and drying, like the thick pens of a sloppy printer. He had lost the image of the fishing boat entirely now and opened his dead eyes to the tent. He swung around so that he faced his inventory, though he could not see it, and drops of blood from both his toes fell to the ground, punctuating the room.

———

When Finn entered the Gold Belt the huge balance scale, the one he'd used to win his hapless mule and odd equipment, stood on the makeshift stage at the side of the room. There were sacks on one side, so Finn sat on the shiny chair opposite them and looked about the bar. There were Eskimos everywhere, dotted among the prospectors. The owner poured beer from his barrel, busying himself with gazing at the gray-suited ones, with frowning at the fact that they stood in his bar so unself-consciously.

Finn sat on the scale for fun, but as soon as he did so people stopped and smiled at him, and Phil and the old man tried to turn the crank at the back, wanted to lift him as high as they could, to bring him above the rest of them one last time. Eskimos moved like gray night through the place. They untied the canvas by pulling at the end lines and rolled the entire wall evenly off the ground. Behind him Finn could hear the two languages of Phil and Kaneda gently knocking against each other once again. The customers and the women in wool shirts stood about. From the open side of the tent the dark earth peered in, but the audience leaned away from it, watching Finn. Winter was over. The wind that blew in through the side of the tent was bearable. Night was returning a portion of itself to the day.

Phil stood behind Finn on the low stage and turned the crank until Finn and the sacks were lifted high. They moved off the stage evenly, the needle not swaying even as much as it had the previous fall. Finn was aware of Eskimo voices and could hear a light cheering from the room. Slowly at first he spun out over the city, then back through the quieting bar. Now night swept across the long mirror, replacing the silver with black, and he could see dimly the moon faces of the customers turned up toward him: moon-faced Phil and Kaneda.

The chain links that held Finn stretched out across the city, pushing him to the windows of the bath, letting him recognize the blue bodies of Henriette and the reverend entwined. And it was as if the sacks that weighed him, in their turn, tapped gently upon the glass, for the next time he looked they were standing facing him, Henriette holding her belly, the reverend unsure, long legs dancing yet worried, keeping his eye out for missionaries. And once Finn thought he saw the sewed-up scar of Hummel's tent, gravel circling it like a rocky beach the continent, canvas walls rising like cliffs. Through his matted beard Finn felt his lips purse while watching, felt saliva escape and roll across his forest chin.

The people in the bar had been involved with the duration of Finn's spinning, so when they finally stopped him he came down dizzy. He stepped off the chair, then leaned against a table looking down at Phil and the old man. He excused himself and walked outside. Nanoon was there waiting for him, covered in shadows. She held an arm up to him and then, still rubbing the wrinkles from her eyes, followed as he hurried past her toward the bath.

Finn wanted to find out whether or not the mule's feet were still stuck in the mud outside the window. He remembered Fujino's feet too, gone at the burial, and he wanted to see if they were now somehow embedded in the earth next to the mule's. He thought of them as plant bulbs wrapped in the earth and ready to sprout again in spring, ready to grow anew the man and mule, turn and turn about.

Above Finn clouds descended upon the city like pillars, but between them the stars drew him and were clear. The name would remain the same, Ellen's Bath, for the sign was made and the letters were deep and even. He was in front of the bath now and peering down at the place where the mule had stood. He could see the tops of the hooves in the dim light from the window, so he bent over them and kicked dirt across them and reached down to pat the soil solid. He'd heard that from the arm of a starfish the whole animal will grow, from the smallest part of an arm, so why could it not be so with mules? He would water the land in front of the window until the next winter froze it all. And if he did not mention it to anyone it would not stretch the seams of his sanity any further out beyond his already loose control. Finn looked up at the light that came from Henriette's window. He pictured the reverend's gray jacket hanging from the nail on the wall, the golden snowflake casting its spider shadow across the floor. Quietly he thought he could hear the firm slapping of human flesh, coming from the window like slow applause.

Finn went into the bath and settled Nanoon on a bench, like a waiting bather. From the window he could see the patch of ground he had patted smooth. He turned and looked at the empty chicken coops, cleaned and closed tightly. The clasp that held the door of the one nearest him turned in his hand and he felt the soft wood of the floorboards. He would get more chickens and when the winter came he would stay close to them, breathing warm air across their feathers. Finn walked into the back and poured water into the waiting tubs. He removed his clothes and looked at his snow-white body in the shaving mirror. His dark arms and face were like rude strangers. He climbed onto the edge of the tub, hooking his heels on it and letting his toes touch the top of the water. It was as cold as the wind outside, had perhaps been brought in by Ellen just before she climbed the stairs to bed. Finn balanced there, his face turning around the room. He could feel the delicate threads of the web he'd woven break, swing like lines of cotton candy in the air. He slid into the water and watched his body tighten under it, felt his skin adjusting, closing its doors. He was more at home in this water than in the air. Though the coldness of it jarred him, the lines of the room were jerked into vivid clarity, his thoughts no longer rovers. Sitting there he could not stir up wild philosophies but could imagine only Phil's father falling through the ice, jarred awake by his own cold death. Finn knew in the clarity of this cold room that the sea would one day take him too, he too would break through the ice or slap against the rough whitecaps, skimming the surface before making his slow descent. It was in his name.

Finn moved in the water, watching his legs part like long fish leaving. It wasn't hard to sit here now; he could no longer feel the rough bath boards against his toes. The only sound was the lapping of the waves against his chest, the shore. He bent his head and looked up at the magic ceiling. He watched the weight of Ellen as she walked silently back and forth, glancing sideways at the open carpet bag on her bed. Now that she had decided to leave she would take the first ship south. She stood with hands on hips, sandwiching the hard floorboards between Finn and herself. Earlier in the evening she had stepped into her traveling clothes, fastening her blouse at the neck with the hard cameo of her grandmother. She'd pulled her hair into weaving strands and woven a bun for the back of her head. This was the way she looked her best, dressed and groomed and standing tall. She had broad shoulders and large hands. She would not live in Ireland or stitch sweaters to ticking time, yet she was who she was. She decided to button her high shoes and step out and walk darkly along the sand streets one more time. She worked the wire button hook well though she was out of practice. She looked at her round face in the glass and tucked a fold of skin down under the steadfast cameo.

Finn watched the pattern of her walking on the lucky floorboards as he dried his watered skin. But the clarity of the bath left him as he stepped from it. The warm rubbing of the heavy towel moved the blood inside him and built stories onto the bath, higher and higher into the air. And perhaps he would build a staircase winding up the outside, perhaps a ladder so that he could cling to its sides and wave to the grim-faced city below. He imagined that he would enlist Phil and that only the two of them would work on it, or no, Phil and he and the old man would make three, tapping and shouting at each other in their personal grammars. Finn rubbed his thighs and laughed. He tied his towel tightly about his waist and walked out into the warmer main room of the bath where Nanoon sat, speechless, waiting for him to end this old life of his and start again

with her. He saw Ellen on the stairs all finely dressed and pointing, her hair turned into its bun so well, her clothes and the
buttons on her shoes and her heartbreaking cameo. Finn turned
in his towel to face her. He followed the long line of her finger
streaming toward his towel and he understood in the flare of
her nostrils his continuing failure to understand.

Finn was warm and dry and wild-looking in the quiet room.
Without taking his soft eyes from her he reached to his waist
and let his towel fall away, and her accusing finger turned, her
hand unmoving until he stepped up the stairs and took it. Finn,
a man of revelations, revealed again. He walked by her side
from the stairway to the door and opened it for her and waited
while she passed on through. He stood at the window, the empty
city in front of him, and watched as Ellen walked by and saw
her bun bobbing in the night. Her face was before him as he
searched the floor for the towel again. His hand struck the egg
he had given her, so he held it at arm's length. He could see
her in it. Her face was made of marble and would last forever.

A NOTE ON THE TYPE

This book was set in Bodoni Book, named after Giambattista Bodoni (1740–1813), son of a printer of Piedmont. After gaining experience and fame as superintendent of the Press of the Propaganda in Rome, Bodoni in 1768 became the head of the ducal printing house at Parma, which he soon made the foremost of its kind in Europe. His *Manuale Tipografico,* completed by his widow in 1818, contains 279 pages of type specimens, including alphabets of about thirty languages. His editions of Greek, Latin, Italian, and French classics are celebrated for their typography. In type designing he was an innovator, making his new faces rounder, wider, and lighter, with greater openness and delicacy, and with sharper contrast between the thick and thin lines.

Composed by Creative Graphics, Inc.,
Allentown, Pennsylvania

Printed and bound by R. R. Donnelley & Sons,
Harrisonburg, Virginia

Designed by Julie Duquet